HAND OF GOD

A JASON TRAPP THRILLER

JACK SLATER

Artwork by Onur Aksoy at One Graphica.

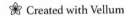

Created with Vellum

1

It wasn't yet 7 a.m., and the air in the cell was already thick with heat and fetid from the emissions of dozens of grown men packed into a space designed to fit a class of schoolchildren.

The door had been replaced with a set of thick iron gates, set into the rebar-reinforced concrete walls that were the primary reason the old school had been chosen for its new purpose. The place had been built by the Soviets, back when Mother Russia was in a generous mood with her Middle Eastern client states. Those days were long gone, and yet the building remained, as did all these former foot soldiers of the fallen Islamic caliphate.

The man sat cross-legged against the back wall of the cell, his orange overalls tied around his waist to reveal a naked torso on which swathes of pale pink scar tissue were more prevalent than unmarked skin. Wounds like his were not so unusual in that place. Those prisoners who needed them were not allowed crutches—to prevent their use as weapons—so they either limped or dragged themselves around, when they found the space to move at all.

In a space filled with such men, the only cause for interest was the faint line of empty concrete that was left around him. It was barely a foot wide, but a careful observer would have noted that those were the only square inches of unadorned concrete to be seen anywhere in the cell. Everywhere else men sat, squatted, or lay curled on the bare floor, taking turns sleeping.

He said nothing. But others did.

"Please," a prisoner begged nobody in particular as he clung to the iron gate. "Please, I cannot be in this place any longer. You have to let me leave. I need to get out of here!"

He beat his head against the iron bars over and over and over, until dark streaks of blood appeared on the rusted metal and thick chunks of hair tore free of his scalp. No one stopped him. They had seen this before, the previous day, and the one before that. He was not the first who had been driven mad by their prolonged, inhumane detention, or even the scenes of unrestrained horror that had preceded their capture—often inflicted by their own hands.

He was unlikely to be the last.

Before he was able to knock himself insensible, a masked guard wearing tan fatigues appeared on the other side of the door. The man drew a baton from his belt, reached through the bars and beat the prisoner around the head before jabbing him away from the entranceway, all the while unleashing a relentless stream of curses and epithets.

"All of you, get back," he called when he was finally done. "Stand ten feet away from the door."

The man with the scarred torso crossed his arms. This was a break in the pattern. Very little happened in the prison before eight in the morning, which was breakfast. Every single day, it arrived at the same time, and had done so week after week, month after month, and year after year. Only then did the ordinary business of the prison begin.

Except today.

The guard stepped toward the door, revealing several more masked men behind him. This was no surprise. The Syrian Democratic Forces fighters who guarded this place knew better than to travel alone. They were not formally trained to perform the role that had been thrust upon them, and certainly had not been five years before. Many of them had been farmers, office workers, or cashiers at grocery stores when the war came to their doorstep. They had learned hard lessons, for which the price was paid in blood and pain.

So now they worked in packs. They had learned to be vicious, to strike their charges before the prisoners could fight back. It was the only way to survive. And it made every day in this place a living hell.

"Back!" the guard repeated, dragging his baton against the bars to generate a harsh rattling sound, a reminder of the damage that he could inflict. The prisoners behind the iron gate stared at him warily, not yet retreating. In truth, there was precious little space for them to back into.

The man by the wall continued watching. He locked eyes with another prisoner, an individual named Omar who stood a full foot taller than most others in the cell. His head was shaved, as were most of those imprisoned in this place—a defense against lice and parasites, the guards claimed. The prisoners knew better. Stripping away their hair and beards was just another way to dehumanize the soldiers of Allah's fallen caliphate.

He nodded, just a slight incline of the head, and Omar blinked in recognition. "Do as he says," Omar roared as he maneuvered himself toward the front of the packed crowd of prisoners. His jumpsuit was also tied around his waist, and it revealed a powerful, broad chest, if one that was somewhat sunken after years of sub-standard and insufficient rations.

Still, if there was anyone in this place willing to challenge him, they were yet to show their face.

The prisoners nearest the gate responded by backing away sullenly. The guard opposite them studied them, called his colleagues closer for support, then placed his key into the lock and twisted it. The mechanism protested before it finally clicked open—a recognition of the fact that this door was rarely unlocked. Food and supplies were passed through a metal grate cut halfway down. Waste travelled in the opposite direction.

The guard with the key pushed the door open. It swung inward to prevent prisoners from being able to force it open through the application of sheer mass. That had happened once before, in the early days.

"Keep back," the guard called as he retreated. On either side of the open doorway, an armed guard positioned himself with an outstretched pistol. Another guard held tightly to each man's belt, ready to hoist them away from danger in an instant.

The crowd of prisoners twitched, tumbling forward a couple of steps like a wave cresting on a choppy sea. They quieted as Omar stretched his hands out wide. The guards by the open gate flinched but did not open fire.

The first guard turned away from the door and spoke to somebody that the man by the wall could not see. His words were barely audible. "Bring them in."

Two more prisoners appeared, pushed by masked SDF fighters. Each had a black hood pulled over his head, as well as hands and ankles that were chained to a thick leather belt looped around their waist. They wore orange coveralls which hung loose on shrunken frames.

The guards unlocked the new additions, pulled the hoods away from eyes that blinked as they readjusted to the harsh overhead light, then pushed them inside the cell. The taller of the two men stumbled, only remaining upright because Omar caught him.

"You'd better make space," the first guard called as they departed. "There are more where they came from."

The man by the wall had no doubt that what he said was true. Although he had only seen the four walls of this packed cell for almost as many years, he heard the plaintive cries of despair that echoed down the prison's corridors from the many others as cramped and confined as this one every hour of every day.

Occasionally a message from the outside world was transmitted through a game of telephone as prisoners were moved from cell to cell. The last anyone had heard was that they had been forgotten—both the prisoners and those who guarded them.

It was no secret that the jails were full to bursting. The guards shuffled troublemakers—or their victims—around with no discernible purpose other than to quench the flashpoint that had emerged that day.

The shorter of the two new prisoners shrank away from the motley crowd in front of him—as well as from the individual who'd entered alongside him. The man by the wall noted this fact.

Omar extended his hand. "You need not fear. You're welcome here, brother. We have little, but what we have, we share."

The smaller prisoner looked nervously back, as if distrusting what he was being told as the words of some false prophet. Slowly, he extricated himself from grasp of the iron gate and shuffled toward the crowd, favoring his left leg. He cut a wide berth around the man who'd entered alongside him.

He said nothing as he disappeared into the crowd, anxiously pushing his way as far back as physically possible.

"You too, brother," Omar said to the prisoner he'd caught a few moments before. "We are all equal here. What's your name?"

The taller of the two men was—unusually—about Omar's height. He carried himself like a street fighter, although that was not unusual in this place. The two towered over the rest of the crowd.

"Ghazi," he said. "Why do you ask?"

Omar frowned. "You don't think it important to know a friend's name?"

"Is that what we are?" Ghazi asked, his stance widening confidently. "Friends?"

"Why not?" Omar asked, raising his palms peacefully. "None of us want any trouble here. We are a peaceful community."

Ghazi snorted. "You're sheep."

Omar's gaze glanced toward the man by the wall, if only for a fraction of a second. Seeing no command there, he turned back. He kept his tone reasonable, which was why he was so trusted. "How so?"

"You've given up," Ghazi said. "All of you. You're weak. Feeble. Unworthy of paradise."

"And what would you suggest?" Omar said, gesturing at the iron gate that was still stained with the moaning madman's blood. "Can you break us out with your bare hands? I will be the first alongside you if you can. But many have tried, and all failed."

"I suggest you need a leader," came the reply. Ghazi stepped forward, forcing Omar to retreat a pace back.

"And that leader is you?" Omar asked.

Ghazi turned away from him. He addressed the crowd of prisoners directly. "Is this all you want?" He sneered. "To be locked in here like pigs, sweating in your own filth until you sicken and die? Don't you think you deserve more? Why do you follow this man? He's leading you to disaster."

"They don't follow me," Omar said evenly.

"Then who?" Ghazi said, his hands forming into fists. "Point him out to me so that I can challenge him. We will leave the outcome to Allah's judgment. Is there a fairer way than that? Or was I right after all—have you all simply given up?"

The man by the wall watched as an uneasy tension ran through the crowd. He knew many of these men, had commanded some of them in a previous life, and fought side by side with others. They were proud individuals who had left comfortable lives behind to take up arms for a cause in which they believed.

It would not be easy for them to swallow their pride and take such insults without responding. Worse still, the addition of such a poison could so easily sour everything he was building. It could not be allowed to continue. Not with so much at stake.

With his mind made up, he rose from his seated position and smoothed his jumpsuit around his waist. A trickle of sweat dislodged by the movement ran across a lump of knotted scar tissue, and he wiped it away, grimacing from the pain. He glanced up at the cameras that were screwed into the walls and the ceiling and made sure he moved in their blind spots—like the one he'd just been sitting in. After so many years, he knew them intimately.

"Enough," he called loudly.

A pathway opened as the prisoners shifted to provide a direct line of sight between him and the newcomer. "Omar has already explained to you that we are a peaceful community. You will stop this nonsense at once."

Ghazi's forehead wrinkled. "You," he said, pointing at the man with the scarred torso. "I know you. Why?"

"You don't know me," the man replied in a firm tone. "I advise you to find somewhere comfortable to rest. You will share in our prayers and our food."

"Or what?" Ghazi said, a disbelieving grin stretching his face into a sneer. "Are you going to stand in my way, cripple?"

The man said nothing. His eyes clouded over as he opened the question up to Allah's judgment.

"I asked you what you were going to do about it," Ghazi repeated.

Spreading his hands, the man said, "Brother, I implore you to think about what you're making me do. We do not need to travel this path. But that is up to you."

Ghazi's face wrinkled with disbelief. "Why talk in riddles? Perhaps it's time for somebody to teach you a lesson about power."

"Or I you," the man sighed sadly. His chin sank slowly to his chest. There were a few moments of silence in the cell, except for the howls of broken men that drifted down the prison's hallways. It was as if everybody was waiting for somebody else to make the next move.

Finally, the man pinched his thumb and forefinger together and slashed them across his throat.

He turned away, unwilling to confront the consequences of his failure, but then caught himself. It was important to watch. To remember that he must do better.

Ghazi didn't react quickly enough. He seemed puzzled by the entire affair. A giggle began to bubble from his throat before his head whipped to one side as prisoners began to rush around the room, climbing on top of each other's shoulders in order to block the cameras.

"What's happening?" he demanded, a tightness in his voice betraying his sudden fear.

Nobody spoke. The man watched as a practiced ballet unfolded in front of him. It had been a long time since his power had last been challenged. But the mechanics of enforcing it unfolded as though their mechanisms were frequently oiled.

A small circle formed around Ghazi. He turned three hundred and sixty degrees, twisting around and around as he searched for a threat. His chest was rising and falling with ragged intensity now, spit flying from his lips as the air was forced from his lungs. His eyes bulged as his head snapped from side to side. He staggered to a halt, staring wildly at the man who had set all this off.

"I remember," he said before lurching toward him. "I remember who—"

It was the last thing he ever said.

Omar emerged from the crowd like a ship from the winter fog. The big enforcer wasn't as strong as he had once been, but he was powerful enough. He wrapped one of his strong arms around Ghazi's throat and squeezed, kicking the back of the man's knees so that he staggered and fell.

The interloper wriggled as Omar applied pressure to his neck and throat, tightening the vise with every passing second as he dragged Ghazi across the room, never allowing his scrabbling feet to gain purchase on the floor.

It took almost a full minute before his death throes subsided. His entire body shook as neurons fired wildly inside his brain as it begged for oxygen, begged its host to do something—anything—to forestall the inevitable.

And finally, he went limp.

2

Khirbet-Al-Jeer Air Base, Northeastern Syria*

THE TAN-COLORED UH-72 Lakota touched down on the Syrian airstrip for a matter of seconds, barely long enough to discharge its sole passenger before lifting back up into the air. Its pilot punched half a dozen flares as it rose into the sky, which burned bright ahead of a tail of hissing smoke.

A man named Jason Trapp strode across the dusty asphalt, pausing only to nudge aside one of the still-smoking expended flare canisters with the toe of his boot as he approached. It rolled off the side of the runway, where he hoped some private would find it before it ended up as FOD in the engine of the next chopper that landed.

He stood well above six feet in height and moved with a feline grace, though his body was hard and rough with years of accumulated scars. A close observer might notice that when he turned his head, his eyes flashed in the sun, each glinting a different shade. He had been to this part of the world before many times, first as a soldier, then as a spy. The violence and despair never changed, only the identities of those responsible for it.

His host was leaning on the hood of a mine-resistant armored vehicle, the shape of a Humvee but boosted several feet off the ground in order to propel the blast of an explosion away from the precious cargo carried within. The machine dwarfed her. He couldn't tell whether she really was that short, or whether it was just the gigantic reinforced tires that made it appear that way. He came to a stop a little in front of her, letting his duffel bag slide off his shoulder before he lowered it to the ground.

"Hell of an entrance," the woman remarked as the howl of the Lakota's engines faded into the distance.

She was young. Hell, not even that young. Trapp was just getting old. If he had to guess, he would peg her as being about a decade shy of him, though she looked at least two. She was dressed in desert boots, tan fatigue pants, and a pale denim shirt that was tucked into a canvas belt. She looked every bit like every other OGA type that seemed to sprout from the earth full-grown in places like this.

It was her hands that gave the game away. They were too soft. No calluses. They painted her as an analyst of some description, not an operator, though nothing else in her demeanor made the distinction.

"You mind telling me what the hell I'm doing here?" Trapp remarked in an even tone.

"Get in," she said, pushing herself up off the armored vehicle and jerking her thumb at the passenger door. "I'll catch you up on the way."

Trapp raised his right eyebrow as she walked away. "What about a name?"

The woman stopped, turned back, and shot him a grin.

"Right. We skipped that part. Feels like I know you already. The name's Madison. Madison Grubb."

Stooping to pick up his duffel, Trapp remarked, "That must've been hell in high school."

Madison grinned. "Why do you think I joined the Agency? Figured I'd get a fresh identity. Something cool, you know? Like Hawk. Madison Hawk. It has a ring to it. Instead I got a Dell laptop, a security clearance, and a shitty pension."

"You're telling me," Trapp chuckled back. He pulled the car's heavy armored door open and slung his duffel inside before climbing up and slamming it closed behind him. He liked this woman, even if he didn't yet know why she'd dragged him halfway across the world without even a hello.

Madison gunned the vehicle's engine. She looked like a doll behind the enormous steering wheel, but she maneuvered the car without trouble. Trapp was glad he'd resisted the male urge to offer his help when he saw how neatly she handled it.

The makeshift air base was a far cry from the enormous quasi-cities he'd found when he was first stationed in this region as a young grunt almost two decades earlier. It was little more than a strip of asphalt surrounded by a ten-foot wall of HESCO barriers topped by a few low guard towers. No Starbucks, no Pizza Hut. Not even a PX.

"I'm sure you're wondering why you're here," she said, slowing the vehicle as she approached the outer gate. She thumped her fist on the horn to signal to a waiting Bradley fighting vehicle that was pumping out thick clouds of black exhaust from below a limp Stars & Stripes affixed to its armor. "That's our escort, by the way."

"That's probably because I asked you," Trapp said. "Escort to where?"

"Fair point," Madison conceded. She didn't speak for a second, concentrating as she pulled their ride in behind the

Bradley, moving into a tight formation as both vehicles rolled toward the gate. "The flag is so that the Turks don't shoot us, by the way. Or the Russians. Not much stops Assad's guys, or what's left of ISIS. But they don't like to get too close on account of getting hosed when they do."

"Yeah, I've read a little about what's happening out here," Trapp replied. "Seems like a real crapshoot. And that wasn't an answer."

Madison stepped on the gas as they sped out of the airbase's gates, which were swiftly pulled shut behind them. "What does the name Khaled al-Shakiri mean to you?"

Trapp's gaze snapped to his left. He hadn't heard that name in a long time, but he felt a familiar surge of rage overcoming him at the mere mention of the man. "Why?"

"Answer the question first," Madison said, glancing in the mirror for a moment to study Trapp's face.

Despite his shock at hearing the name again after all this time, he had to admire the analyst's composure. She was preternaturally confident compared to most of the young analysts he came across. Most wilted when they came face to face with the men at the coal face, those tasked to carry out the invariably lethal recommendations written in dry bureaucratic prose from some windowless office in Langley.

Trapp took a moment to order his thoughts. He didn't know much about her, but he knew that she was cleared to be told about pretty much everything he'd ever done. Well, almost everything.

"He's a killer. A real sick bastard. And a true believer, to boot. The kind of guy who doesn't think twice about killing. If he needs to slit the throat of an innocent kid to achieve his objective, he will do it without losing a moment's sleep. When I was in Iraq ten, no—eleven years ago with Delta, we started to wonder whether he was even real or just a ghost."

"I can assure you that he is," Madison said, her tongue touching the left-hand corner of her mouth as she wheeled the armored car around a particularly narrow corner.

"I know," he replied with a decisive nod of his head. "I never doubted he was. I saw him once. At least, I think I did. We had him located to a market in Basra. Real busy place. Must have been a thousand people crammed in there. You know what they're like, those bazaars. They're not real big on personal space out here. Couldn't evacuate the joint, not without blowing our cover. So we had to make our move in broad daylight."

"What happened?" Madison asked, her tone sharp.

"I chased him through a stretch of fruit stalls. Ended up with a few crates of oranges pulped on my boots. Before I could get a shot—at least, without risking putting a bullet through some innocent trader—he grabbed a kid. She was maybe three years old. Put a gun to her head and fled."

"Hell," Madison said, sounding shocked. "Did they find the girl?"

"A couple days later." Trapp nodded, staring blankly out at the barren wheatfields on either side of the dirt road they were traveling down as the memory grew in intensity. "He just dumped her on the side of the road about ten miles from the market. They found her two miles from the nearest village without even a drop of water. She almost died. Spent two weeks in a coma after they airlifted her to Germany. And I never caught the asshole."

"But you'd recognize him?" Madison asked. "If someone put you in a room with him?"

Trapp stared at her. "Are you that someone?"

"Answer the question."

"Mine first."

Madison grimaced, drumming her fingers against the

steering wheel before she came to a decision. "Fine. I've been hunting this guy for two years. I think I might have tracked him down to al-Shaddadi Prison. That's why I brought you here—to confirm it's really him."

Frowning, Trapp asked, "The SDF only just caught him? What's he been doing all this time?"

"No, they've had him since the back end of 2017. Since the liberation of Raqqa. Records are pretty spotty from back then. It's not exactly clear when they captured him, but he wasn't in great shape. He gave his name as Nasser al-Ismaili. According to his prison file, he had an untreated shrapnel wound on his abdomen that almost went septic. They didn't transfer him to the prison system for almost three months."

"So how did you find him now?"

"Our friends at Fort Meade picked up some chatter about three months back, from a compromised cell phone somewhere in northern Syria. Three calls over seven days, all of which referred to something or someone called the Hand of God. Does that mean anything to you?"

Trapp shook his head. "Nothing."

"Me neither. But our database flagged it as a nom de geurre used by Khaled al-Shakiri when he was just a teenager in Indonesia posting on extremist forums before he joined the caliphate. It triggered a flag I'd set up, and I started digging."

"That's flimsy."

"You think I would drag you all this way for nothing?" she asked as the truck hit a bump, rocking Trapp into the air and reminding him to buckle his harness. The canvas strap caught on the pistol holstered at his waist, and he pulled it up and over before fixing it into place.

"I don't know you," he pointed out.

"Mmmm," she said. "Well, I've heard of you. And trust me, calling you out here wasn't a step I took lightly. The world is changing, in case you hadn't noticed. Washington thinks that the fight against ISIS was already won. They don't know what we're doing out here, and frankly, they don't care."

"So tell me."

"I'm trying," she quipped back. "Okay, here's the thing. The cell phone the NSA was listening into, it was used by a man called Usman Tariq. We had his voice print from interrogations carried out at al-Shaddadi a few years back."

"So this Usman guy, he got released?"

"Bought his way out," Madison said, her lips tightening. "It happens. Like I said, nobody's paying much attention to what happens out here. We've got 50,000 men, women, and children locked up in fucking concentration camps—the detritus of the caliphate—and nobody knows what to do with them."

"Easier to leave them to bake under the desert sun," Trapp remarked in an off-handed tone designed to gauge her response.

"Yeah, until the whole damn thing boils over," she snapped, punching the horn hard enough for it to emit a low groan. "If you'll forgive me for mixing metaphors, this whole country is a tinder heap. It's been baking under your desert sun for five years. It's smoking in places. Won't take much for that smoke to turn to fire, and when it does..."

"We're all screwed," Trapp finished.

"Something like that."

"But you're here," Trapp said as in the distance, above the haze of the sun baking the potholed asphalt, the top of a razor wire fence came into view. "The whole world hasn't forgotten. Not quite."

"Yeah, well, hell if it doesn't feel that way," Madison said. "If this really is al-Shakiri, then maybe we got lucky. It wouldn't take much for him to have escaped just like his buddy. And then where would we be?"

"Why do you say that?"

"You've looked into his eyes. Tell me if you think jail will have shown him the error of his ways."

Trapp shook his head.

"I didn't think so."

3

President Charles Nash swept into the glass-walled conference room overlooking the Potomac River with all the assurance of a politician riding high in the polls. His signature legislative achievement—the REBUILD Act—had cleared the House and was on course for Senate agreement any day now. As the name suggested, it was intended to fix the forgotten parts of America that had been torn asunder during the opioid crisis that had raged through the previous decade.

A crisis that had even cost him the life of his own son.

The bill imposed a punitive tax on the pharmaceutical companies that had done so much damage and spread the money out across innovative treatment programs, investments in policing and community support, and grants to students, schools, colleges, and universities in order to rekindle a belief in aspiration that had left too many such places behind.

And better yet, it didn't just fulfill a promise that Nash had made to his own family; it was wildly popular across the country. It had passed the House with enough bipartisan support that voters were beginning to believe that maybe, just maybe, America was still a country in which big things could get done.

"Harry," Nash said, eyeing up a man he'd once before, briefly, at a party fundraiser before he stretched out his hand. "I'm told you're my Creep."

"Mr. President?"

"Well, that's not a promising start." Nash grinned as he shook the hand of the man who'd been selected to run his reelection campaign. "Don't you read your history?"

Harry—the former senator from Wisconsin, Harry Hoffman—blinked, then understood. "Right, Nixon. The Committee to Reelect the President. I'm hoping we steer a path away from some of the controversies that attached themselves to that particular campaign."

"Just some?" Nash said, pulling a chair back and taking a seat. "Hey, they got him reelected, didn't they?"

Eyeing the nervous expressions on the faces around the table, the president focused on the young sharp-suited intern he figured had been detailed to take minutes and said, "For the record, that was a joke. You should write that down. I fully expect to win reelection without needing to bug the offices of the party across the aisle. But if you *have* to bug the offices... No, I'm just kidding. No bugs. No breaking and certainly no entering. Just clean, honest fun. That's an order."

"Yes sir," the intern said, underscoring the word *honest* twice. "But I'm just an—"

Nash cut him off. "Your job is to keep Harry in line. Apparently he's forgotten more about campaigning than you'll ever know."

"Cut the poor kid a break," Hoffman chuckled, drawing a chair of his own and taking a seat opposite Nash. "It's bad enough that he has to deal with my terrible sense of humor, let alone the president's too."

"I apologize." Nash smiled. "I'm sure you're doing a hell of a job."

"He is," Hoffman replied. "Now if you don't mind, I've been reliably informed that I have all of twenty-two minutes of your time, and you've already wasted one of those. Sir."

"Cut that out," Nash said, gesturing at Hoffman to continue. "We're going to be working pretty closely together. Well, just so long as you keep me above water, of course."

"Oh, you can rest assured," Hoffman said with the wry smile of an old pro who understood how the world worked. "If we start to dip, I will scrape my own barnacle off."

"Well, just make sure it doesn't come to that, Harry." Nash grinned, stealing a glance at the intern whose indecision about whether to write their musings on his boss's potential seppuku was visibly written on his face. "Now tell me how we going to win."

"We'll announce in a fortnight," Hoffman said. "We've leaked that it's happening already, to head off any potential primary challenge. I'm not expecting one—with your numbers, it would have to come from someone with a few screws loose—but I always prefer to be good rather than lucky."

"Any rumblings?" Nash asked. He tried to keep himself out of the cut and thrust of day-to-day politics, especially now that he was president, but he was still a canny operator. He wanted to know if there was anyone in his caucus who was beginning to have second thoughts. It was easier to catch a sickness like that before it began to spread.

"None, but I'll keep my ear to the ground," Hoffman replied. "Now, as for the announcement itself—I want to hold the launch rally in Baltimore."

Nash's eyes flicked up. He fixed his gaze on Hoffman and gave it the full force of an intensity that had been known to bowl away lesser individuals. He held it there for a few moments before speaking, his tone hard enough to crush gravel. "Do you understand what you're asking me?"

Hoffman, to his credit, didn't look away. "Mr. President, I know that's where George, ah, passed away. If you say no, I'll back your decision every step of the way. But I think this is something we should do."

"You know I prefer to keep my family out of politics."

"Nothing is outside of politics," Hoffman countered. "And frankly, sir, your family's tragedy is one of the planks that your popularity with ordinary Americans is built on. Everybody has lost someone. A mother, a father, a brother, or a child. They understand your pain. But you didn't just grieve; you decided to do something about it. And the REBUILD Act will be the crowning achievement that says you succeeded. It's important that you own it. Personally."

"I don't like it," Nash groused, knowing that the idea made good sense and yet finding that something about it instinctively prickled the back of his neck. "A rally, fine. But there? I'm not sure."

"Think about it, Mr. President. It wasn't just George who got hooked in Baltimore. Thousands of people did. I think it would mean a lot to their parents and children if you stood there and told him that their hardships were not in vain. That somebody noticed their pain."

Nash glanced at his watch. Barely five minutes had elapsed, but he decided it was time to go. He stood abruptly, knocking his knee against the conference table in the process. "Okay, Harry, time's up."

"But you'll think about it?" Hoffman pressed.

"I'll—" Nash paused, unaccustomed to the swirl of emotions that had suddenly risen inside him. George's death still hit him hard, even after all this time. He steadied himself. "I'll give you an answer by the end of the week."

4

Khaled al-Shakiri's shoulders were hunched as Omar approached. Sweat beaded his back and torso. He wrapped his arms around his body and clenched his jaw tight as another wave passed. He dug his nails into the scar tissue that marked his stomach hard enough to draw tears from his eyes.

"How is the pain this morning?" Omar asked, kneeling beside him. He sounded worried.

"Do I look that frail to you, Omar?" Khaled replied, hissing his friend's name as another torrent of pain washed into him. "I've never felt better."

"You don't have to hold out much longer," Omar murmured. He glanced at the scars on his torso. "Can you feel it?"

Out of sheer force of will, Khaled dragged his arms away from his body and straightened himself. He shook as he did so but continued, as much to prove to himself that he could as to show Omar. He reached for his friend's hand and pulled it toward his rib cage, stopping only when his fingers touched the skin.

Khaled closed his eyes and drew Omar's hand down,

guiding it to the point of greatest pain. Despite the agony it caused him, he pushed the man's digits into his flesh, as close as he could to the inch-long piece of shrapnel that was still stuck in his belly. "There."

Omar drew his hand away as though he'd been stung. "You shouldn't do that."

"But you felt it?"

"I did. It's... hard."

"Sharp," Khaled agreed. Talking helped. It kept his mind from circling back to its endless fixation on the pain that wracked his body. At least for a little while.

The prison doctor had been clear that he needed an operation to remove the shrapnel piece left inside him—and equally clear that one would not be forthcoming. There were barely funds available to heal the SDF's casualties, let alone the prisoners of the broken caliphate whom they guarded. His one and only consultation had been years ago, and the damage had grown worse with every passing month.

"It won't be long now," Omar assured him, leaning in close so that they would not be overheard. "Our friends will have arranged for a doctor to see you, I'm sure of it. You're too important to the cause to be allowed to die because of this. Allah will not allow it."

"Quiet," Khaled said, bringing his frame upright and looking around the room. "How are the boys?"

"Ready," Omar replied confidently. "They don't know what for, but they know that something big is coming. They are willing to do whatever it takes."

"I know they are," he said, recognizing the anxious faces on those around him of boys and men that he had known for years. He had fought alongside many of them, back when his body wasn't yet a broken thing.

He didn't doubt they would stand with him now. Not for him, but for the cause in which they all believed.

Omar turned away from the nearest camera, shielding his right thigh from its view. He reached into his pocket and pulled out a small black cell phone with a gray LCD display. He connected the battery, then wrapped an elastic band around the device to hold it in place, the case long since having broken.

"Careful," Khaled counseled.

The cell phone had taken them years to acquire. First, the inmates had scraped together enough funds to bribe the prison's administration to release just one of their number, a man named Usman. Naturally, after they demonstrated they had access to money, the price for the next had skyrocketed.

But only one was needed.

Even after that, it had taken months before their help on the outside had succeeded in smuggling a cell phone into the camp. On several occasions, inmates—the nominal recipients of previous attempts—had been snatched from the cell and interrogated brutally after a guard had taken a bribe and failed to deliver.

None cracked.

They would have been able to divulge little of the plan even if they had. The only man who knew its totality was Khaled himself, and he kept himself isolated from everybody except Omar, who he implicitly trusted would never break.

His friend powered up the device and waited for a few moments for it to acquire the only bar of cell signal that was able to penetrate this deep into the concrete structure. It buzzed in his hand as it received a succession of incoming text messages.

His shoulders bowed for a second with relief before he nodded and said, "They are in position."

"You deleted the messages?"

"Of course."

At the entrance to the cell, two prisoners started howling curses into the hallway. They wrapped their arms around the bars, twining themselves against the gate to prevent it from being opened.

"Hide it," Khaled snapped, the warning as always proving its worth.

The inspections had been more frequent since Ghazi's body was extracted several days before, though the guards themselves did little more than poke their heads into the cell to assure themselves that no more violence was in the offing. Khaled guessed that they didn't much care whether the inmates in their charge lived or died.

Omar disappeared into the crowd to do as he was told. Every prisoner surged to the front of the cell and began waving their fists at the approaching guards, forming an impenetrable wall of human flesh that blocked their view until the deed was done.

"Get back!" the onrushing guards yelled, beating their batons against the bars and not caring how many of their prisoners' fingers they snapped in the process. Others drove the feared black truncheons through the bars as if they were Roman legionaries slicing barbarians through a shield wall.

Cries of pain now mingled with the anger the prisoners' throats were generating. Slowly, inch by inch, the crowd was driven back.

As Khaled watched a guard stepped through his colleagues, calmly drew a pistol from the holster on his belt, and aimed it toward the ceiling of the cell. He didn't hesitate long enough to consider the consequences of a ricochet before smoothly the pressing the trigger. Nor—apparently—did he care much for either his own hearing or that of the men with whom he served.

The crack silenced the melee instantly.

Omar's eyes met Khaled's, a quick nod of the head confirming that the cell phone was safely hidden. The latter man felt a wave of relief wash over him, the endorphins quenching some of the worst of his everyday agony. His friend was right: They were close—if not to the end, then at least to the end of the beginning.

If his plans came to fruition, and Allah willing they would, then the former Islamic caliphate's initial emergence would seem like a mere footnote in history compared to what followed.

"Stay away from the gate," the guard called out diffidently. Behind him, his colleagues slid their batons back onto their belts and drew matching pistols as the key turned in the lock and the door swung on its hinges.

They trusted too much in those weapons, Khaled thought. They had grown fat and lazy, confident in the knowledge that the men they guarded were unarmed. It wouldn't take much to change that equilibrium.

He was counting on it.

Half a dozen men in a patchwork of black and tan masks stepped into the cell. Two of them were armed with automatic rifles: sufficient firepower to inflict a bloodbath in a matter of seconds.

Khaled watched as Omar stepped out of the crowd.

"I apologize for our anger," he said smoothly. "It's hot in here. And we are hungry. Still, that is no excuse for our behavior."

The guard who appeared to be in charge—it was difficult to tell one from another behind the masks they wore—ignored him. He reached into his fatigue jacket and pulled a folded piece of paper.

As he smoothed it out, he called loudly, "I'm looking for Nasser al-Ismaili. Step forward. You are wanted for questioning."

A chill ran through Khaled at the mention of the false name he'd given to the prison authorities so many years before. Omar stiffened.

"Why?" Omar demanded. "Who is this man?"

"Who are *you?*" the guard retorted. "If you can't help find the man I'm looking for, then you are no use to me."

He finished straightening the piece of paper in his hands and flipped it around. Khaled squinted from the back of the room. It was difficult to be sure, but it looked like the photo that had been taken of him during intake. Still, in the half-starved, bedraggled state he'd been in following the siege of Raqqa, the man in the image resembled thousands of other similar fighters.

"Nasser al-Ismaili," the guard repeated. "Somebody must know who he is. It will be easier for all of you if he simply makes himself known. If not... there will be consequences."

Punishing a group for the sins of an individual was against both the Laws of War and contravened the Geneva Conventions, Khaled knew. But such things were unheard-of in this place. This would not be the first time that an entire cell had been deprived of food and water until they cracked and gave up the information the guards were looking for.

It wouldn't even be the first time for *this* cell.

Khaled's cheeks flushed with a heat that was, for once, entirely unrelated to the injuries that had crippled him. This could not be a coincidence. In five years, he'd never once been singled out by the prison administration. He'd carefully fashioned a character to wear in front of them that was entirely unremarkable, just another broken ISIS fighter in a place that was bursting with such men.

And it was today, of all days.

"We are not leaving until we have the man we want," the guard insisted.

"Then we have a problem," Omar said. He glanced to his left and right, meeting eyes with men he trusted. "I don't recognize such a name. But even if I did, I wouldn't give him up to you animals. Not for all the treasures of paradise."

"Those can be arranged," the guard snapped, his fingers twitching around the grip of his pistol. He raised it in the air and aimed it at Omar's forehead. The photograph shook in his other hand. "If that's what you want, keep talking."

Khaled's throat ran dry as he watched the scene unfold. He needed Omar if his plan was to succeed. His friend wasn't just strong; he was smart. But he was also loyal to a fault, and he had no doubt that he would sacrifice his life if he thought it would help the cause.

Around Omar, the other prisoners began to grow restless. They were with him, Khaled could sense it. This could become bloody—and fast.

He couldn't allow that to happen. If a fight ensued, the guards would lock this cell down tighter than Fort Knox. And that would put months of careful planning at risk. There would be no better chance than this. Possibly no chance at all, if they had connected his alias with something more concrete than mere suspicion.

Khaled began to walk through the crowd, at first pushing against bodies whose owners' eyes were focused on the commotion at the front of the room but which parted as others recognized who he was. He aimed for a pocket of prisoners he knew he could trust, men who would give their lives up for him in a heartbeat.

"I am the man you are looking for," he said as he neared the front. He stopped, leaving a line of three men ahead of him. Enough to hold off the guards, if that proved necessary. "And I will come with you."

"Good," the guard snorted. "At least one of you sees sense."

"On one condition," al-Shakiri clarified.

Though he could not see the guard's face, his tone was one of stunned disbelief. "You're in no position to make demands."

"My friends are angry," he said in a conciliatory tone. He looked to his left and right, drinking in the righteous determination on the faces around him. "They are simply worried about what will happen to me if they trust you with my care. They want to know that no harm will come to me."

"Step forward immediately," the guard snapped. "Enough of this nonsense."

Khaled held his position. "I can't do that."

The guard switched his pistol aim from Omar to him. "Then we will come and get you."

"You must know it will not be bloodless," Khaled replied. Prisoners bristled at his sides. They were itching for this fight. Some of them probably believed that this was the moment they had been waiting for, the one they'd been warned to prepare for. "You will get me, but many of your friends will die in the process. Why not simply give mine the comfort they are looking for?"

"Just ask," one of the rifle-wielding fighters blurted out. "It can't hurt."

With the façade of unity broken, Khaled's interlocutor had no choice. He gritted his teeth. "What is it that you want to know?"

"Simply where it is that you plan on taking me," he replied smoothly. "And for how long."

He waited with bated breath for the response. If they planned on taking him beyond the prison's walls, then they would need to move the schedule up. That was a risk, but not as great as the destruction of all their planning.

And if they intended merely to transport him somewhere else within the wire, then Omar would know what to do. He would find him.

The guard jerked his pistol to the ceiling. "Up there," he said. "I don't know how long. A few hours, maybe. Some people want to speak to you. Americans."

"Why?"

"That wasn't part of the deal."

"It's a simple question."

Khaled could tell from the guard's body language that he didn't know the answer. He was simply a lackey doing the Americans' bidding. Just like all his colleagues.

But he had the answer he wanted. Other men had been to the interrogation rooms on the converted school's second floor. He had quizzed them endlessly on their recollections, and both he and Omar knew as much as there was to know about its layout.

He spread his palms as the guard struggled to form a response. "Never mind. I will come with you. I'm a simple man. I have nothing to hide."

5

Trapp had barely passed through the prison's outer gate when the smell hit him. It was a combination of backed-up sewage baked under the desert sun and the stench of men who were evidently afforded access to neither showers or even basic sanitation.

"Nasty," he said.

"You get used to it." Madison shrugged casually. Trapp noticed that she seemed to be breathing from her mouth rather than her nose.

He appraised the makeshift facility in a single glance as the armored car slowed to a stop. It was surrounded on all sides by flat farmland sown with swaying wheat. The SDF had built a double wall around the converted school. Each was constructed out of concrete breeze blocks and raised to a level about ten feet high before being topped with razor wire. Guard towers stood on stilts just outside of the walls on all four corners. Guns pointed both inside and out.

"I thought the Brits paid for a new maximum-security wing somewhere out here," Trapp asked, finishing his appraisal of the prison's security and coming away without much confidence.

They had passed checkpoints manned with SDF fighters on the main road that led from the city of al-Shaddadi to the prison that bore its name that were patently not staffed by the organization's best. The situation was no better upon arrival. The guards wore a muddled variety of uniforms and carried weapons that were, if anything, even more disparate and unkempt than the clothes on their backs.

"They did."

"So why haven't our Syrian partners already moved al-Shakiri, or whatever he's calling himself these days? They can't have many more dangerous ISIS leaders in their custody."

"Politics," Madison said as she pushed her door open. Trapp followed her lead. "Just like always. First of all, we have no solid proof that Nasser al-Ismaili and Khaled al-Shakiri are one and the same. Just phone chatter and a partial facial recognition match. We don't have any biometric data for al-Shakiri before his supposed capture to confirm it."

She raised her arm and greeted an approaching welcome party, lowering her voice as she continued. "Which means Washington doesn't want to share what we have with our *partners*. And on their side, they've been slow-walking all of our requests for months. They want more funding which, frankly, I can understand. These prisons are held together with a hope and a prayer. They don't have enough fighters to man the ones they've got, and there's still a trickle of new inmates from the ongoing battles with ISIS's remnants. The problem is: nobody back home wants to pay. So it's a stalemate."

"Understood," Trapp said.

He fell silent as the welcome party approached—noting the masks worn by all the guards. If they didn't even feel comfortable revealing their identities out here, what did that say about the conditions inside?

Madison greeted their hosts in fluent Arabic. Trapp caught a few words here and there—he'd picked up enough over the years to get by, but he was out of practice, and the rapidfire exchange mostly passed above his head.

Still, the meeting appeared to go off without a hitch, and they were led into the main prison building and immediately up a flight of stairs after passing through a heavy iron gate at the bottom of the stairwell that had clearly been a later addition to the pre-existing structure. Their hosts locked it before proceeding up to the top of the stairs, where they repeated the procedure with a second gate.

"They seem professional," Trapp commented as they were left on their own for a moment.

Madison nodded vigorously. "You can't fault their heart, that's for sure. Just their resources. If it really is Khaled al-Shakiri they're holding, you can be sure they'll extract a pretty price if we want to do anything with him. And I don't blame them."

The man who appeared to be their primary liaison returned, holding a pair of white lanyards marked with blue letters that spelled out LOCKHEED before the second half of the familiar logo disappeared behind his grip. Trapp wondered how this defense industry swag had made it all the way out here. He wagered that the SDF weren't negotiating for a $5 billion tranche of F-35s any time soon.

He stretched out his hand to offer them to his guests but then paused. He gestured at the weapon on Trapp's hip and said something in gruff Arabic.

"What's he saying?" Trapp asked. He had a general idea but wanted to be certain. After all, this was Madison's show, not his.

"He says no weapons in the interrogation room," Madison replied. "He will station a guard inside the room for our protection. But no guns. It's prison policy."

"Okay," Trapp said, unbuckling his holster and drawing the

pistol free. "But I'm fond of this one. Tell him to leave one of his guys outside the door. He can keep our weapons safe."

"I'll *ask* him," Madison replied. "We are guests, remember."

Trapp stifled a grin. She was good. Most analysts—particularly ones her age—never ventured far enough from their cubicle farms to make connections with the boots on the ground. He liked that she was different. The Agency needed people like her.

She conferred again and flashed their host a smile. If it wasn't for the mask, Trapp would've sworn the guy blushed. "Okay."

Trapp handed over his weapon grip first. Madison did the same. The guard gave a lanyard to each of them in turn, then spun on his heel and marched down the corridor.

"I guess we should follow?" Trapp said.

Madison shrugged and started walking. "Guess so."

The first floor of the prison building was a hive of activity. Dozens of guards and administrative staff sat behind desks in rooms that still bore signs of their previous life as classrooms despite all the years that had passed: maps on the walls, filing cabinets decorated with Post-it notes that had been scrawled in childish fonts. They were mostly unmasked, more confident in their privacy up here.

The guard led them to the end of the hallway, where a classroom had been subdivided into two interrogation rooms. An additional door had been driven through the hallway wall to access the second. Nobody had bothered to match the paint jobs afterwards.

I doubt it was a priority...

"Wait here," their host said in rough English as he unlocked the door. "We will bring the prisoner up."

He turned on his heel and left without a second word.

"I guess he understood me after all," Trapp remarked as he peered inside the drab interrogation facility.

The wall that separated the two rooms was made of bare concrete, and little light entered the small window at the far end, less still after it passed through the close-hemmed steel bars that had been welded to the frame. A single surveillance camera was attached to the wall, though it didn't appear to be functioning.

In the center of the room was a steel table. There were two wooden chairs on one side and one on the other. A heavy metal bolt had been welded to the tabletop.

"I guess so," Madison agreed. "You know, it wouldn't kill you to be a little more polite."

Trapp gestured for her to enter ahead of him and then followed. She took a seat at the table. He walked to the window instead. In the distance, he could just barely see the town of al-Shaddadi. On this side of the prison the wall was unbroken, unlike the side which hosted the main gate. Down below was a dusty exercise yard. It seemed barely used.

"I try. It doesn't seem to stick."

"I see that."

The two of them fell quiet as the seconds stretched by. Trapp sat down, then stood back up. As the wait hit the ten-minute mark, he paced back to the window. He wondered what was taking so long.

Finally, Madison spoke. "Do you think it's him?"

Trapp considered the question. He wanted Nasser al-Ismaili to be Khaled al-Shakiri. Desperately so. He'd forgotten how much hate he'd developed for the man over those long and unfulfilled months spent hunting him so many years ago.

"I think it looks like him. But I'm not sure. It has been a long time."

Madison sighed. "Me neither. Listen, I want you to lead the interrogation."

He frowned. "Why?"

"I'm a woman, for one," she said. "In my experience, these

guys don't even want to look at me, let alone answer my questions. But mainly it's because he saw you once before. I'm hoping that'll be enough to unbalance him. My research suggests he will be a tough cookie to crack. This is—"

Whatever she was about to say died in her throat as an enormous explosion rocked the prison. The shockwave was powerful enough to make the whole building shake underfoot. Trapp flung himself away from the window, fearing a second explosion.

"Down!" he yelled, his ears ringing. "Get under the table, now."

He scrambled on his hands and knees to join her. Another blast detonated the very second he did. It blew the windows out and sent a hail of shattered glass flying through the air where he'd just been standing. The shockwave sucked the air from the room as Trapp clamped his palms over his ears—knowing he was already too late to stem the damage from the first explosion but fearing a second.

Smoke filled the interrogation room as numerous sirens and fire alarms rang out around the building. The walls seemed intact, barring a few superficial cracks, but chunks of plaster had fallen from the ceiling, and the dust now coated the floor like snow. Glass was everywhere. Trapp wiped a trickle of blood off his forearm where a shard must have caught him as it scythed through the air but detected no other signs of injury.

"I'm okay," Madison said for her part as she rolled onto her back and started patting herself down. "My ears are fucking ringing, but apart from that, I think I'm okay."

"Yeah, me too," Trapp said, coughing from the dust as he clambered out from underneath the table. He edged toward the window, able to see even from this distance a thick plume of black smoke that was rising from just outside the walls.

Well, from outside where the wall *had* been.

As he approached the damaged window frame, he saw that

a huge hole had been blasted through the outer of the two prison walls, and a smaller—man-sized—one through the inner. Car parts were scattered all around, including a huge sheet of thick, contorted steel with a vision slit cut into it that resembled either a medieval knight's armor or an early prototype of a World War I tank.

Worse, armed men were flooding through the gap they'd created. He gave up counting when he saw a dozen of them.

"Shit," he muttered.

Madison limped toward him. She wasn't injured physically, but the shockwave had clearly done a number on her.

"Shit," she echoed, pointing at an identical cloud of smoke rising from al-Shaddadi. "VBIED. A few of them. Looks like they hit the SDF garrison in town, too."

Trapp nodded. The acronym stood for 'vehicle-borne improvised explosive device.' In this case, the platform that had carried the bomb had been up-armored, though since he hadn't heard any sound of alarm before the explosion, the terrorists' DIY efforts had proved unnecessary. They'd managed to drive a vehicle that looked like a medieval tank right up to the walls without anyone seeming to give a damn.

"Inside job," he said. "No way they got a vehicle large enough to hold a bang that size close enough without anybody raising the alarm."

Madison patted her empty holster. "Shit."

It was Trapp's turn to echo her.

Gunfire was already crackling all around the prison grounds, accompanied by the repeated, irregular thump of smaller explosions—the impacts of rockets and grenades. He squinted up at the nearest guard tower: the one that should have been observing the Eastern approach to the prison to prevent just this kind of attack.

It was quiet. Empty.

That cemented the situation in Trapp's mind. The attackers

had definitely had support from the inside. Either the guards in the towers had been turned, whether by stick or carrot, or they had already been taken out. Either way, the high ground was already lost.

His throat tightened as a familiar rush of adrenaline flooded through his system. Life was about to get real hairy, but he was back in his element.

He moved swiftly to the door. “Keep away from the window,” he said, gesturing her toward him. “What have you got in that satchel?”

Madison looked up at him quizzically, but to her credit quickly adapted to their new reality. “Um, files, mostly. Shit, they’re all classified. I shouldn’t have brought them with me.”

“What else?” Trapp asked as his hand closed around the door handle’s cool metal. He recognized the incipient signs of panic in Madison’s voice.

She looked down, holding the two sides of the bag open. “A satellite phone,” she said.

Trapp grinned. “See, things are already looking up.”

He pointed to a corner of the room which would be protected from any stray gunfire by the thick concrete walls. “Hold tight there. See if you can raise the alarm. I mean, I’m guessing the good guys already know that shit just hit the fan, but a little reminder that it’s splattering all around us wouldn’t go amiss.”

“Where are you going?” Madison asked anxiously.

“To get my gun back,” he said as the smile faded away. “And yours, if you want it.”

“Please. Don’t go far, okay?”

“Don’t worry, I won’t.”

He twisted the door handle slowly and smoothly so that the mechanism barely made a sound as it clicked open. He pulled it open an inch, listening as much as searching with his eyes for what was on the other side.

The answer was chaos.

As far as Trapp could tell, the SDF guard who'd been left there with their weapons was long gone. He pulled the door back another inch to confirm his suspicion, then tugged it fully open. There was no one there. Sheets of paper thrown by the shockwave scattered the space. The clang of fire and smoke alarms was louder out here, and the smell of smoke even more intense. His throat felt ragged already.

It was too thick to be left over from the car bombs. Something was burning. Something big.

Great.

He stepped out and quickly closed the door behind him. The hallway ended in a blown-out, barred window to his right, so he turned left instead and headed for the offices. At the far end, he saw a dozen armed men facing the gate that led to the stairwell. Some kneeled as others stood. Some trembled, others prayed.

Strangely, he caught a flash of orange in their midst. There was a prisoner among them, his wrists and ankles chained to a heavy leather belt around his midriff. A pair of guards flanked the man on either side.

And then it hit him.

It was al-Shakiri, it had to be. They must have been transporting him to the interrogation room when the attack began.

Now he was marooned up here, just like the rest of them, as the prison burned and attackers flooded its grounds.

6

"Do you want the good news or the bad?" Madison asked as he reentered the interrogation room, now loaded up with an M4 rifle taken from an armory cabinet and a pair of pistols. She was squatting on her haunches, local-style, underneath the window with the satellite phone's antenna extended so that it aimed directly up.

"Good," he replied, walking to her and handing over one of the sidearms, along with several spare magazines of ammunition. She nodded her thanks.

"Help's on the way," she said. "ETA five minutes."

"That's quick," Trapp observed.

"Yeah, that's the problem." She grimaced. "It's fast air. A single RAF Typhoon on combat air patrol. It's loaded out with five-hundred-pound Paveway Mark IVs, but unless you have a runway and a sled hiding out in one of your pockets, it's not going to give us a ride out of here."

"Ground support?"

"At least an hour out. And that's if we get lucky. Looks like there's another major assault going down in al-Shaddadi. Any serious relief effort will have to wait until that's mopped up."

Trapp peered out of the barred window. As yet, none of the figures streaming across the prison grounds appeared to have noticed their presence, but it couldn't last. There were more of them with every passing second. At first, he'd seen mainly black-clad ISIS fighters surging through the breached outer wall, but now those black dots were swallowed up by a sea of freed orange.

Worse, the initial attackers had brought with them large bundles of weapons. The large canvas bags they'd used to carry them were now scattered across the dusty courtyard below and resembled dark puddles. A few still held their shape, but these too were being stripped with every passing second as orange jumpsuit-clad prisoners equipped themselves with a mix of Kalashnikovs, pistols, and rocket-propelled grenades. There had to be dozens of armed killers down there now, if not hundreds.

"Looks like we're on our own," he murmured.

"I heard that's the way you like to operate," Madison said, forcing a smile.

"You heard wrong," he replied. As he scanned the exercise yard below, he saw a flash of movement and jerked back just as a volley of poorly aimed gunshots cracked through the smashed window frame. "Come on, we need to get out of here."

Madison shoved the satellite phone back into her satchel and tossed the extra pistol magazines in with it. He grabbed her hand and pulled her toward the door. Coils of smoke had begun curling underneath it—not yet enough to make it difficult to breathe, but certainly sufficient to tar the throat. It was hot, too. He hoped that was just the punishing climate and not the fire down below.

The two Agency officers stepped out into the hallway and collided with a wall of chaos. The guards nearest the gate were firing wild volleys of gunfire through the bars and down the stairs.

"Dammit," Trapp muttered.

"That doesn't look good," Madison agreed. She held her pistol like she mostly remembered what to do with it.

"Stay close," Trapp said. "We don't want to get separated. Here's the situation: This building's on fire. It's a concrete shell which should slow things down, but"—he gestured at the offices on either side of the hallway, where huge stacks of paper rested on thick wooden desks that also supported computers and all manner of flammable office equipment—"I'm guessing there's enough kindling down there to barbecue us all."

"So staying put isn't an option," Madison agreed, raising her voice over the sound of wild gunfire as they approached the gaggle of guards and support staff around the gate. She stopped dead. "Shit—is that him?"

"Yup," Trapp said softly. "It's definitely the same guy I saw. That enough of an ID for you?"

"I'll need you to write it up in a report," she said. The two of them shared a wry smile. The chances of either of them surviving long enough to get tangled up in Agency bureaucracy seemed remote.

At best.

They gravitated toward the individual who appeared to be in command. He was standing about ten yards away from the gate, alternately listening to a handheld black radio and barking commands into it. Unlike most of his fellow guards, he wasn't wearing a mask. As they approached, Trapp recognized his uniform as the one their host had been wearing.

"Nice to put a face to a name," he said.

Abdul turned sharply and let the radio fall to his side. "Yes," he said gruffly. "I have more immediate concerns than worrying whether these animals will hunt me and my family down."

"What's the situation?"

"Snafu," Abdul said with a grim smile. "I learned that from an American."

"Situation normal—" Trapp began.

"—all fucked up," Madison finished.

"The enemy is in control of the grounds, along with all four guard towers. I've lost many of my men. I have no contact with any of those who were stationed in the hallways. The only remaining strong point is right below us, in the center of the prison. About twenty of my fighters are barricaded in the control room there. They have no way out."

"Looks like we don't either," Trapp remarked, nodding at the gunfight occurring so close to them.

Abdul shook his head. He was a brave man but looked resigned to his fate. His uniform was smeared with plaster dust, and beads of sweat ran down the side of his face. "Not unless you have any friends coming to save us."

"A fast mover is going to buzz the jail about—" Trapp began before the shriek of a low-flying jet aircraft momentarily rendered any further conversation pointless, "—now. But if you're asking about a relief force, we're shit out of luck."

"It is the same on my end," Abdul agreed dolefully. "There is fighting all over the city."

Trapp glanced at al-Shakiri, who was a few feet farther away from the stairwell gate and noted with some surprise how *zen* he looked. Like some kind of freaking Buddhist monk. He didn't flinch at the sound of either gunfire or explosions, unlike the civilian support staff who had been herded to roughly the same point in the hallway. Nor did he appear excited. He just...was.

He put it out of his mind for the time being, figuring to survive five years in a jail like this, you would have to take up meditation so that you didn't go insane. Still, there was something weird about it. As though he wasn't surprised.

"Coming up behind," he called out, pressing his rifle's stock tight to his shoulder as he advanced through the crowd of guards. The floor was scattered with brass shell casings, but there were surprisingly few bullet holes in the ceiling, given the intensity of outgoing fire.

He hoped that meant the escaped ISIS fighters downstairs were more interested in freedom than vengeance.

The gaggle of SDF prison guards around the gate parted ahead of him without complaint and allowed him to approach the bars of the gate. He stood a head taller than most of them, and a foot taller than some, which probably played a part in their acceptance of his authority.

Three bodies lay on the other side of the gate at the foot of the stairs. Two belonged to jumpsuit-wearing prisoners and the third to one of the black-clad militants who'd attacked the facility. He watched as an armed prisoner nudged into view of their elevated position before jerking back as several chunks were torn from the concrete floor around him.

"Smart move," he muttered. "Now if you could tell the rest of your buddies it isn't worth it, that would be great."

Unfortunately, they didn't get so lucky. At once, half a dozen automatic rifles opened up downstairs. The sudden increase in chatter caused most of the men around him to instinctively retreat, firing wildly themselves as they did so. As one of them withdrew, he swept the barrel of his rifle across Trapp's bulky frame.

Trapp reacted quickly, allowing his own weapon to fall against its sling as he grabbed the fighter's trigger hand with one of his own, then knocked the barrel downward and grabbed the rifle entirely in the same movement.

"Do that again," he snarled, "and those assholes down there will be the last of your worries. Capeesh?"

The masked gunman stared wildly back at him for a few seconds before nodding, understanding his tone if not the actual words. Trapp handed the man his weapon back, hoping he wasn't making a mistake, then turned and fired several neatly spaced three-round bursts of fire down into the stairwell.

He turned and beckoned the guards back toward him. They obeyed, if a little reluctantly. "Keep their heads down, understood? Make them decide whether they want to choose freedom or a shot at paradise. I don't care how devout they think they are. Most will take the first option. Believe me."

Madison translated his words quickly, raising her voice to be heard over the roar of battle.

There was something curious about the way the freed prisoners were shooting, Trapp thought as he backed away. They surely had enough firepower to drive back the guards above them, despite not holding the high ground. It was almost as though they were holding back. He'd seen the RPGs they had brought into the prison. Just one of those was enough to end this. And yet they weren't simply ending this.

But why?

"Kill him!" one of the gate guards yelled in high-pitched Arabic—Trapp understood that much—just before he and all his friends opened up in a barrage of automatic gunfire that wouldn't have looked out of place on the first day of the Somme.

Another cried out with jubilation, punching his fist into the air.

"Suicide vests," Madison translated, clearly hearing something amid the maelstrom that he had not.

"Peachy," Trapp muttered. That probably explained the earlier reticence of the gunmen. They were simply holding back and waiting for the heavy artillery.

Well, two could play that game.

"Abdul," he called out, twisting his neck as he searched for the commander. "Do you have any grenades?"

The Syrian looked up from his radio. He frowned. "Grenades? I think—"

The answer came too late.

An explosion rocked the floor beneath them, forcing a hail

of shrapnel up the stairwell that sent the guards behind the bars stumbling back, clutching their faces and chests and screaming in pain.

"Get forward!" Trapp yelled, grabbing an uninjured fighter and physically propelling him toward the gate. He'd instantly understood what the explosion heralded. The first gate was likely breached. What mattered now was who would be first to react.

He sprinted to the gate, emptying most of his magazine down into the dust-swirled stairwell. But it was too late. As his weapon clicked dry, half a dozen orange-clad prisoners staggered out of the smoke and fell on the gate, some collapsing from the wounds he'd inflicted and sliding down the steel bars.

Trapp stepped back, letting the rifle fall against its sling and drawing the pistol from his hip. He squeezed the trigger reflectively, not flinching as one of the rounds sparked off the steel gate and ricocheted wildly back against the wall beside him. The guard at his side was firing wildly, but most of his shots were going high.

Then his rifle, too, ran dry.

Oh, shit, Trapp mouthed, taking another step back.

He kept his finger on the trigger but didn't fire. There were three rows of armed prisoners now: the first dead on the floor in front of the steel gate, the second kneeling, and the third standing. The latter two ranks each numbered five armed men. There were more of them behind, faces unseen. To shoot now would have the same result as suicide by cop.

For some reason, the prisoners didn't open fire. And as if by divine intention, neither did the Syrian guards behind Trapp.

It was a good old-fashioned standoff.

7

"Abdul?" Trapp called out, barely needing to raise his voice now that the most immediate sounds of battle had faded. "About those grenades?"

There was a brief pause, presumably as the Syrian collected his wits. "No luck. We don't store them up here."

"No," Trapp agreed. "That would have been too easy."

"Jason?"

It was Madison's voice. He didn't turn but kept his pistol aimed at the far end of a randomly-chosen ISIS prisoner—now *escaped* prisoner—instead.

"Yeah?"

"There's something off about this, right?" she asked, giving voice to the same worm of intrigue that had been burrowing into his brain for the past ten minutes. "What are they doing?"

"What's on your mind, Madison? Talk it out."

"They should be running, shouldn't they?"

Trapp's gaze swept across the stacked prisoners. They appeared surprisingly calm, despite the unsettling shriek of the Typhoon's jet engine in the sky overhead. He could tell a couple of them were itching to open fire, but they had good NATO-style trigger discipline, fingers kept agreeably far from the triggers.

"Should be."

"And if they wanted to go out in a blaze of glory instead, then this is the perfect opportunity. But they aren't doing that either. Even though that whole first row is wearing suicide vests."

"Nope."

"So you think they are here for a reason?" she continued, clearly building to something and just as clearly continuing to talk because if she didn't then she might simply break down from fear.

"Yep," Trapp agreed, the same thought crystallizing in his mind.

"You think that reason is al-Shakiri?"

A tall, broad prisoner shouldered his way through the crowd. His orange overalls were filthy from both incarceration and combat. Gun oil streaked the already stained fabric. His face was coated with smoke and dust. His eyes flashed with intensity.

"Just might be," Trapp agreed, dropping his pistol to his side and spinning in the same movement.

He marched toward the zenlike prisoner on his side of the barrier and grabbed him by the thick leather belt around his waist. Next, he brought the pistol back up and jammed it against Khaled al-Shakiri's temple. There was no longer even a scintilla of doubt in his mind over who it was he was dealing with.

For a moment, he dreamt about pulling the trigger and splattering the evil sonofabitch's brains across the concrete. The bastard deserved it, for what he'd done to that little girl, her family, and all those thousands of others. There was no sin in killing a man like him. It was justice.

Perhaps al-Shakiri sensed the urge traveling his captor's

veins, because for the first time, he displayed a hint of nervousness, pulling away from the gun barrel pressed against his temple and swallowing hard. Both men panted with a mix of stress and exertion as they stared the other down.

"Fuck," Trapp snarled, knowing he couldn't do it.

Not now.

Not yet.

He dragged the former ISIS senior commander back toward the gate instead, where the tall prisoner was waiting calmly. Trapp didn't like that part. It suggested that the man thought he was in control, rather than the other way around.

And hell, he wasn't exactly wrong.

After all, now that the worst of the battle din had faded, it was easier to hear the crackling of the fire still burning somewhere down below. It sounded big. And hot. And with hundreds of armed and escaped prisoners on the loose in the grounds, there was likely no way out whatever happened.

"Madison," he said softly. "Come here."

She jogged to his side. "What is it?"

He spoke out of the corner of his mouth. "You think our British friend up there might be interested in giving us a hand?"

"How?"

Trapp squinted as he pictured the layout of the prison compound. He felt al-Shakiri's heat on his skin. "Ask him to level the northeastern guard tower. Quickly. I want to spook them. It's a long shot, but..."

"Yeah, we don't have many other options," she agreed, reaching for the satellite phone and searching for a window in view of the sky. "It'll take a minute. I don't have a direct line to the pilot."

"Don't wait too long," Trapp said as he secured his grip on the thick leather restraint belt and began to slowly shuffle him to the top end of the hallway.

"No pressure, huh?"

"Something like that," he muttered.

Al-Shakiri walked leaden footed for a man of his diminutive, shrunken size. Trapp figured almost immediately that his prisoner was slow-playing him.

"I know you speak English, all right?" he murmured for his ears only. "Just know if you fuck with me, it'll be the last thing you do. Right now, my working hypothesis is that everybody outside of this gate is already dead, and we're all that's left. That's Hail Mary territory, you understand?"

The terrorist didn't respond but—even if almost imperceptibly—picked up his pace.

So you are listening, Trapp thought. There was something interesting about this, too, but he couldn't place his finger on exactly what it was.

He frogmarched the terrorist toward the gate. Thick smoke was now curling through the bars, causing both the prisoners on the opposite side and the friendlies on his to cough uncontrollably. He felt a rough tickle at the back of his throat but ignored it. There was something undignified about giving in to that kind of impulse. Weak.

And besides, the tall man in the orange jumpsuit certainly wasn't.

"What do you want?" Trapp said as he came to a stop. "Seems like neither of us have much time."

His opposite number was about the same height, and at the time of his capture likely of a similar build. Perhaps even stronger. Years of prison food and lack of opportunities to exercise had done a number on his physique. Still, he didn't look like the kind of man you picked a fight with if you had any other choice.

"Open the gate," the man said in thick, scarcely comprehensible English.

Resisting the urge to check on Madison's progress, Trapp quipped, "I don't think that would be healthy for either of us."

His new friend squinted in confusion. He stabbed his finger at the steel bars in question. "Gate!"

"Who the fuck taught you to negotiate?" Trapp asked, cocking his ear to one side and listening for the telltale scream of the Typhoon's engine. "A grizzly bear? You need to show me a little give and take, you know? Fluff me up a little bit."

It was definitely up there, though it was difficult to figure out how far out through the muffling of the thick concrete shell that surrounded him in every direction and the ever-present thud and crack of nearby explosions and bullets. There were clearly pockets of resistance scattered all around the prison. That was no surprise; the guards were fighting for their lives.

When they had first been imprisoned, these men were already fearsome, brutal individuals. Now they were driven by five years of added hatred.

"Open the gate!" the tall man screamed. He raised his weapon and thrust it through the bars.

"Now, now," Trapp replied, stalling for time. "There's no point in either of us getting angry. You have something I want, and I have someone of value to you. We can do a deal here."

His interlocutor reached down and grasped the shoulder strap of one of the suicide vests being worn by one of his fellow prisoners. Trapp resisted the urge to wince at the casual handling of the no-doubt poorly-wired and volatile explosive mix. A malfunctioning suicide vest detonating would be a hell of a disappointing way to go out.

"Open gate," he shouted. "Or you all die."

Trapp started, "If you planned on killing us all—"

But he never got to finish. There was no warning. At first each man was standing, and then nobody was. The detonation of the 500lb Paveway Mark IV ripped the ground from underneath all of them. In the blink of an eye, a storm of dust was whipped up and tore through the prison's already-shattered windows and then the hallways beyond.

Despite likely being forewarned after eavesdropping on his conversation with Madison, the sudden detonation appeared to have taken al-Shakiri by surprise. His reactions were dulled, and it took him two full heartbeats before the idea of trying to wrest the pistol from Trapp's hand seemed to occur to him.

By that time, it was too late. Trapp secured his grasp, tightening his grip on the prisoner for added measure.

"—you would already have done it," he finished, this time unable to resist the urge to cough as thick, no doubt asbestos-ridden dust mingled with the smoke already hanging thick in the air.

He paused for a second to observe whether the explosion—which was still reverberating the prison underneath their feet as though a thunderbolt from the gods had struck the earth—had had the desired effect.

Unfortunately, the prisoners arrayed opposite him appeared equally determined to stay the course, if a little dustier.

Worth a shot.

Trapp shrugged. "So why don't we make a deal, like sensible people. You guys back the fuck up, and I'll send your friend here down to meet you."

"Jason—!" Madison protested from behind.

"We don't have a choice," Trapp said harshly. "It's either this or we all die. And we can't catch him if we're dead."

He shifted his attention to al-Shakiri. "You heard all that, right? Why don't you convince your friend here that the smart play is to work *with* the Great Satan for once? A bit of compromise never hurt anybody."

After his brief attempt at escape a moment before, al-Shakiri had once again fallen still. Even serene. The prisoner said nothing for a few moments, then finally bowed his head. He spoke in calm, lilting Arabic to the large prisoner on the other side of the bars, who grimaced at the prospect but acquiesced with a quick nod.

Interesting, Trapp observed. The big guy clearly wasn't in charge here. Something to dig into. If he survived, that was.

"We accept your offer," al-Shakiri said. "Omar will remove all of his men from the hallway. All except him. You will do the same, barring yourself. Then you will unlock the gate and send me down the stairs."

"What assurances do I have that your friends won't attack the moment you're free?"

"I did not ask them to come for me," al-Shakiri said. "They have an... emotional attachment to me. A spiritual one, you could say."

"Yeah, and pigs can fly," Trapp said, loosening his grip on the prisoner and spinning him around so that he could get a read of his face. "But whatever helps you sleep at night."

"Once I'm downstairs, you will have the high ground, correct?" al-Shakiri said, eyeing Trapp directly as the RAF jet buzzed the prison once again.

"I will."

"And I believe you know how to use that weapon?"

"I do."

"Then you should have no trouble holding my friends at bay. As I said, their only concern was what you might do to me up here. But besides, they will not harm you. I give you my word."

As the terrorist stopped speaking, a hail of bullets penetrated the windows of the office to Trapp's left and embedded themselves in the ceiling, tearing away what chunks of plaster remained and scattering it across already-ruined workstations. Thankfully, the angle of the incoming gunfire was too acute. Without scaling either the walls or the guard towers, it was impossible for the escaped prisoners or their accomplices on the outside to accurately deliver fire. And Trapp guessed that the leveling of the first tower had persuaded most of them to discount that option. Still, it was a reminder that al-Shakiri's rescuers were not the only threat they faced.

"Fair point," Trapp agreed, jerking his head toward the source of the gunfire. "What about the others?"

"I would be lying to you if I said I had control over them. I only know those men who were placed in my cell. We became... extremely close over the past few years. That's why they came for me."

Bullshit, Trapp thought.

These men had known an escape attempt was going to happen. There was no other way of explaining the suicide vests, or the way they moved in practiced formation, rather than as a ragtag group of incarcerated killers tasting freedom for the first time in years.

"Okay," Trapp said. "You make the first move."

"Two Apaches inbound," Madison called from behind him. He knew she was trying to dissuade him from this course of action, but he was equally certain that it was the only way to save her life, not to mention the dozens of other support staff cowering behind him.

"What about ground support?"

She said nothing for a few seconds. "No news."

"Is bad news," Trapp finished. He grinned at al-Shakiri. "Maybe I'll get lucky and one of those choppers will ram a Hellfire down your throat as you make your escape."

"If Allah wills it." The prisoner shrugged. "I accept your terms."

He turned and spoke to the prisoner named Omar again. The second man grimaced but agreed, directing the men around him to retreat in a harsh, irritated tone. He gripped the iron bars as the largely barefoot fighters behind him shuffled backward, occasionally flashing his weapon just so Trapp knew it was there.

"I kept my word," al-Shakiri said. "Now it's your turn."

The clatter of rotors in the distance made its way to Trapp's ears. The aircraft sounded as though they were nearly in firing range. They would help turn the tide of the battle in the open spaces both inside the prison and beyond. Hell, the SDF's prison overcrowding problem was about to get a whole lot less urgent. This was the kind of target that gunship pilots dreamt of in their cots.

Grudgingly, he spun and indicated for Abdul to move his men back. He caught Madison's eye as he did so. Her jaw muscle was tense, popping out of the side of her chin, and she was gripping her pistol so tightly he worried that her fingers might go numb. She stared malevolently back at him, her eyes screwed up with rage.

He shot her a look that he hoped said, *I'll make it up to you.*

It didn't help.

As the guards moved backward, the RAF Typhoon dropped another guided bomb. The destination sounded several hundred yards farther away, and Trapp guessed that the pilot had been targeting an escaping vehicle. The accompanying rumble caused more dust to pour from the damaged ceiling.

"Okay," Trapp said, turning back to the gate. "You kept your word. Now I'll keep mine."

Abdul approached, holding up a key. "I think you will need this," he said, his own expression taut.

"I'm sorry," Trapp said.

"It's the only way," the guard replied, the humiliation of being forced into releasing one of his prisoners clearly rankling deep inside. He placed the key into the lock.

"Back!" Trapp said, aiming his pistol at Omar, whose knuckles were still white around the steel bars. "I said I'd release your friend. I never said anything about you."

Al-Shakiri stiffened but said nothing. Abdul turned the key. The mechanism squealed, then clicked.

Trapp watched as the prisoner pushed the gate open, then stepped across the threshold to join his friend. The two men embraced, and then the larger man ducked his head underneath al-Shakiri's arm and helped him down the stairs. He kept hold of his pistol, never fully pulling his attention away from where Trapp and Abdul stood.

He didn't turn away, not even after both men disappeared out of sight. Abdul gestured for several of his colleagues to join them at the precipice of the stairwell, and they formed two ranks of rifles, aping the earlier tactics of their former prisoners as they waited for an attack.

But it never came.

What the fuck was that about?

"Jason!" Madison called, breaking him from his reverie. "We've got a problem!"

8

Trapp handed Madison a rifle along with a frayed ammunition belt from one of the office's armory cabinets. "You know how to fire one of these things?"

"I've seen it done on TV," she said in a mock-girlish voice as she loaded a magazine and racked a round into the chamber. She shot him a withering look that told him she was still burning up with rage. "Does that count?"

He turned away, catching sight as he did so of the smoke now billowing out from underneath the closed door to the interrogation room where they had waited for al-Shakiri when he was still going by an alias before everything went to shit. It was the problem that Madison had been referring to. The ceiling underneath must have been weaker than the rest of the structure, or perhaps the room it stood over was used to store something flammable.

Either way, the fire downstairs was now raging through it, out of control. The door would hold it back for a few more minutes, but no longer.

"Let's go, people!" Trapp yelled. Abdul's guards were arranged in two parallel lines on either side of the prison's two dozen support staff, who to their credit had so far resisted the urge to panic. They knew to keep their heads down and to go wherever they were told.

Still, he was pretty sure that this was a suicide run.

"Back into the frying pan?" Madison said grimly, apparently deciding the time to have it out could come later.

"Something like that," Trapp agreed as Abdul shot him a thumbs-up. "Okay. Time to move."

He led the way downstairs, resisting the urge to cough on the noxious smoke that now billowed from every direction. He pulled his shirt up and breathed through it, not that the porous scrap of fabric did much to help. The sound of dozens of footsteps behind him was like nails on a chalkboard to a man who'd spent most of his career in special ops trying *not* to be heard.

"Quiet," he hissed as he came to the bottom of the stairs, lifting his left hand up and making a fist. Madison was right behind him and translated the gesture in hushed, whispered Arabic to those civilians who didn't understand.

He paused at the bottom of stairwell, half expecting Omar's men to open fire. But the space was empty. Apparently even the escapees, drunk on their newfound freedom, weren't foolish enough to stray this close to an uncontained blaze. From beyond the prison walls, he heard the thump of incoming rocket rounds. The Apache gunships were really going to town on the escaping prisoners, but there was only so much two of them could do.

Somebody needed to get boots on the ground. Enough hardened fighters had been incarcerated in this facility to, if not reignite the entire caliphate, then at least light the match that got the blaze going.

A few of them lay dead on the floor around his feet, but not nearly enough. The scent of blood and death was almost thick enough down here to block out the smoke.

Almost.

Trapp spied a handful of grenades scattered on the floor on and around one of the corpses. He knelt and stripped them, then stowed them in his pockets.

"Okay," he whispered. "Let's keep moving. Stay tight."

Abdul pushed his way through the crowd. He gestured into the depths of the prison, right where the smoke was thickest. "We have to go that way!"

"Why?"

"I told you, I have men in the control room. They are surrounded. These animals will slaughter them if we don't do something to help."

Trapp paused and took a knee. To his left, he could see an exit to the courtyard. The bars on the door now hung askew, blown open from the outside.

"We need to get these people out first," Trapp said, jerking his thumb at the civilians. "They'll slow us down."

Without waiting for a response, he rose and ran in a low crouch toward the door to the courtyard, gesturing at the others to wait. As he reached it, a hail of gunfire strafed the concrete at his feet, tearing up chunks of rubble and dust. He spun and threw himself behind the protection of the wall.

The rate of incoming fire doubled, then tripled. Trapp waited for it to slow, then dared to take a peek outside.

He didn't like what he saw.

"Shit," he muttered before making his way back to where Abdul was still crouched. "Okay, we do it your way."

"What about the secretaries?" the Syrian asked.

Trapp pictured the dozens of armed prisoners he'd just seen roaming the courtyard. There was simply no way to escape by that route. It would be like lining up for a firing squad. The prisoners were arranged along a broad front and had the advantage of cover to hide behind. By contrast, if he tried to shoot back, he would be able to call on no more than a couple of guns at a time, given the constraint forced by the narrow doorway.

"They look fit and healthy," he lied about a group who looked anything but. "Besides, either they keep up or..."

"They die," Abdul finished. "They understand that already."

"Okay. You lead the way," Trapp said.

"You know," Madison whispered at his side as they fell in behind the guard, "I was just joking about the frying pan."

Trapp looked up at the thick blanket of smoke that coated the hallway they were heading for. It looked like it led directly to the center of the prison. Abdul had explained upstairs that when the SDF converted the school for its new function, they'd hollowed out the center and created a strong point around which the cells were arranged.

Four hallways led into this central stronghold, one from each point of the compass. Prisoners were at the gates of all four of them, and though each still held, they were raining fire at the guards left behind—who were spread too thin simply holding the line to think about driving any particular group back.

Trapp caught up with Abdul. "The men in the control center—do they have a link to the outside?"

"Yes. A hardwired one." He nodded, eyes roving either side as he padded down the hallway. Flames crackled in an emptied cell that they passed on their right. "At least as long as it wasn't knocked out in this attack."

"Find out," he said, knowing he needed a way to contact whatever force was gearing up to take back the prison. Madison's satphone was useless through the thick concrete.

Abdul lifted the radio handset off his belt and pressed it to his lips. He relayed the question in Arabic. It was answered by a panicked colleague, the man's words barely audible over the relentless crackle of gunfire.

"Yes," he replied, his lips pressed grimly together. "It's still functioning."

"Good," Trapp murmured, closing his eyes for a second and picturing the layout of the prison. "I need them to get in contact with whoever's running JTAC out there. Our air support needs to focus all its efforts on clearing a path out for us through the southeastern corner."

"But there's no gate on that corner," Abdul replied quizzically.

"Tell them to make one. And while they're at it, get them to smoke every last one of those orange jumpsuit-wearing assholes they see. It's our only hope of making it out."

He turned, acid boring a fresh ulcer into his gut as he saw the positioning of the guards at the back of the slow-moving column. It was clear they were used to herding unarmed prisoners, not high-intensity combat. It was no surprise. The SDF had plenty of the latter on its hands outside the prison walls. No sense detailing its best fighters to stand watch when they were needed elsewhere.

Catching Madison's eye, he said, "Stay low, understand? Move nice and slow. Don't be stupid. If you see anything up there dressed in orange, put a bullet through it just to be sure."

"I don't think those are the rules of engagement, Jason," she replied with a tight smile. "I'll be okay. Go."

He left without another word, muttering encouragements to the guards at the edge of the procession of civilian staff. Most had by now lost their masks. They came from the entire spectrum of society: some barely old enough to be out of school, others well past retirement age. They were short and tall and young and old and fat and thin, and they were all as terrified as each other.

Trapp stopped short about halfway down the line, grabbing one of them by the arm and physically removing his finger from the trigger of the man's shotgun.

"You want to get all your friends killed?" he whispered, his throat hoarse from the smoke as he manipulated the man's digit and laid it flat along the trigger guard. "Keep that thing aimed at the floor unless you're prepared to kill the person on the other side. Got it?"

The man glanced down at his rearranged grip, then looked back and nodded. Whether he really did understand was unclear.

Trapp moved on, slowing as he reached the back of the line. Half a dozen uniformed guards were bringing up the rear. The only problem was that none of them were actually covering the retreat.

Which was... kind of a big deal.

"You," he said gruffly, grabbing one of them by the shoulder and physically spinning him around. He stabbed his finger down the murky, smoke-obscured hallway. "I want you looking that way. No matter what happens behind you, don't fucking turn around. Got it?"

The guard looked shocked by Trapp's sudden appearance, but eventually nodded. He spoke shakily. "Yes."

"Good," Trapp said, tapping the two men beside him in turn. "Them too. They speak English?"

The Syrian shook his head, switching his attention between Trapp's face and the murky hallway. "Just me."

"Tell them to do the same. You guys are all that's standing in the way of a couple of these ISIS punks from coming up behind us and slaughtering us all, okay? That includes you."

The guard swallowed, and though it was difficult to see his expression underneath the coat of plaster dust and grime and ash on his face, Trapp guessed that the blood had just drained from his cheeks.

"But you can stop it, right? You're the only one. Someone comes up behind us, light them up."

"Light?" the man said, screwing up his face in a quizzical expression.

Trapp tapped his weapon, lifted it up so that it was parallel with the hallway, and mimed pulling the trigger. "I don't care what paradise they think they're going to. No one runs directly into automatic gunfire, not them, not anyone. I've been around the block before, trust me."

"Okay," the man said, nodding seriously, a fresh resolve showing on his face. "I can do it."

Trapp slapped him on the shoulder. He saw that the gap to the rest of the column had grown as they talked. "I know you can. Come on, let's catch up."

He spent another minute getting the three guards behind the first rank of shooters to hold on to their buddies' ammunition belts and guide them backward so that they could focus their entire attention on protecting the rear. Then he returned to the front of the line.

"Nearly there," Abdul whispered, slowing as they reached a bend in the hallway. He nearly needn't have bothered. The rattle of gunfire from up ahead was incessant now. So too were the panicked squawks issuing from the guard's radio.

Catching the man by his wrist, Trapp gestured at the black handset. "Turn it down," he hissed. "What are they saying?"

Abdul flushed with embarrassment and hurriedly turned the volume knob all the way down. He brought the device up to his ear and listened intently.

"Three more dead," he said with a pained expression on his face. "Ten of the guards are alive and unhurt. Five are wounded."

"Can they walk?"

"At the moment." Abdul nodded.

Trapp grimaced. "Then we need to move fast. Every second we waste, the odds turn further against us."

"What is your plan?" Abdul asked, instinctively deferring to the more experienced fighter.

"Ask your men to turn as much of their firepower on the gate we're approaching as they can spare while holding the others at bay. Tell them to start in"—he glanced at his watch—"ninety seconds. Can you do that?"

He received a firm nod in response. There was nothing cowardly about this man, that much was clear. Nor most of the guards under his command. They weren't expert fighters, not trained for this kind of combat, but they were brave and prepared to die to protect their friends and families.

And that was what it would come to, Trapp knew. There was a reason they had all taken up arms in the first place—ISIS had come for their homes and loved ones once before. Every escaped prisoner, every one left alive at the end of this, represented a chance for that horror to happen again.

They didn't need him to tell them what was at stake.

"Good. Make that two minutes," Trapp said, glancing at his wristwatch. "I'm going to go up ahead and take a look. If I'm not back in time, you know what to do?"

Abdul inclined his head. "Go with Allah, my friend."

"I'll go with whoever keeps me alive." Trapp grinned in response. He squeezed Abdul's shoulder. "I appreciate it."

The Syrian didn't seem to take much offense at the jocular response with which his prayer had been answered. Imperfect vessels, and all that.

"I'm coming with you," Madison said.

"No," Trapp said harshly. "I'll move faster alone. And besides, one of us needs to make it out alive. There's something going on here. You feel it too."

Madison gritted her teeth but shot him a curt nod.

Figuring that was about as friendly as she was going to get, Trapp got moving. He pressed himself against the inner edge of the hallway before it kinked to the right up ahead. The closer he got to the turn, the more distinct the sound of men's voices became. They were stressed and excited, and one of them was firing his Kalashnikov on full auto.

Amateurs.

That appraisal was enough to get him moving. He doubted any of the escaped prisoners were standing watch to their rear. Maybe if they had fresh combat experience, it would've been different, but they'd been behind bars for years, their skills eroding away. The unparalleled excitement of battle—the flood of adrenaline that accompanied the fear of death—would have washed away whatever hard-learned tactical sense was left.

He poked his head past the corner, taking in the scene for only a second before jerking back, the move smooth and practiced. Closing his eyes, he processed the scene. At least fifteen prisoners, the precise numbers were hard to guess, armed with a variety of weapons, mostly Kalashnikovs and a few American-made M4 carbines taken from dead guards.

No vests.

The absence of explosive material explained why the prisoners hadn't simply blown open the gate to the control center as their colleagues had done when springing al-Shakiri. It was strange that one group had been so freely equipped with the devices and not the rest, but right now, it was a gift horse.

The key was that he'd guessed right: None of the prisoners were watching their rear.

"Well, let's not look y'all in the mouth," he murmured.

Trapp peered around the edge again, this time moving slower, allowing himself to drink more of the scene in. He felt the seconds ticking away in his mind but sensed instinctively he still had a minute and a half remaining.

He counted fourteen.

Several more escaped prisoners lay either dead on the floor or bleeding out beside the corpses of those whom they would soon join. He didn't see any heavier weapons than rifles and the occasional pistol. Nor were the besieging prisoners armed with huge quantities of ammunition, only what they could carry themselves.

The attack on the control center seemed unplanned and ad hoc, unlike the rescue of al-Shakiri, which had been anything but. Escapees had found guns and turned on their tormentors without needing encouraging.

Trapp retreated. He'd seen what he needed to.

They were ripe for the taking.

9

A dozen armed guards, accompanied by Madison and Abdul, approached Trapp as he urged them toward him. The rest remained with the civilians to guard against an attack from the rear—though the truth was that if the attempt to fight their way through failed, then their deaths would only be delayed.

"The others know what they need to do?" Trapp whispered. The gunfire from around the corner was growing more infrequent, which he hoped meant the prisoners were running out of ammunition.

"They do." Abdul nodded.

Trapp glanced at his watch. Thirty seconds remained. Probably not enough time to call off the covering fire, but he didn't think he needed to.

"Tell your men to stick to the walls and not to get in each other's way. There's going to be a lot of lead flying through the air."

"They understand," Abdul muttered.

"Good," Trapp said, turning grimly. He fished the grenades

he'd taken from the body earlier out of his pockets. "Don't start shooting until the guys in the control room do. And good luck."

They lined up on either side of the hallway. Trapp went first on the inner edge, around which he'd just looked, hoping like hell that he wasn't going to catch a stray round in the back. The position would buy him maybe an additional half second, and he intended to use it.

"Ten seconds," Madison said in a low whisper.

A huge explosion shook the prison, followed by the muffled sound of rocket fire. It had to be the Typhoon and the two Apaches getting to work clearing them a way out of the prison. Despite the high-risk tightrope act that was their current predicament, he still wouldn't trade places with the escapees now taking fire from above.

Trapp moved a full two seconds before the others, pulling the pins from both fragmentation grenades and lifting his arm back as he strode around the corner. He held them for a couple of seconds then launched them high one after the other so that they wouldn't bounce off the concrete floor and warn the enemy about what was coming. They each had four-second fuses.

The moment they were out of his hand, he dropped back behind the wall and brought his rifle back up to his shoulder, lightly depressing the trigger but not pulling it all the way back until he heard a thunderous hail of gunfire ring out from the other side of the bars.

It didn't seem polite to wait a moment longer.

Stunned by the renewed ferocity of the gunfire coming from a group that the prisoners manifestly believed they had successfully pinned back, they ducked behind cover. The reaction—a perfectly natural one—only served to herd them into a funnel of death. The two grenades detonated about two feet off the ground on either side of the hallway. A tornado of destruction scythed through the assembled ISIS fighters, instantly killing at least three of them and wounding just as many.

As though reacting to the firing of a starter pistol, Trapp spun back into the hallway and squeezed his rifle's trigger. He ignored the destruction ahead of him and fired in taut three-round bursts, locking on to a target, firing, and moving on without a second's hesitation.

He had no other choice. It was either them or him, and if he went, so did two dozen innocent civilians.

By the time the rest of the ambush party opened up around him, Trapp was already halfway through his first magazine. As spouts of fire blazed from the muzzles of the rifles to his left and right, in one case erupting almost two feet ahead of him—the result of an improperly filled cartridge that could as easily have blown the shooter's rifle chamber apart—the enemy began to drop in swathes. It was like harvesting corn.

In truth, they never stood a chance. The guards didn't need to be trained operators; they just needed to be able to pull a trigger and stand in the right place. The cramped hallway did the rest, funneling a hail of death toward the escaped prisoners.

And most of the guards did a whole lot better than that.

At long last, the gunfire fell silent. Orange-clad prisoners, their uniforms now stained red or simply ripped clean off by the force of the explosions, littered the floor, surrounded by hundreds of brass cartridge casings and pools of blood.

Trapp ejected his magazine and let it fall to the floor. The metallic clank as it bounced and skidded to a halt acted almost as a reminder to breathe. As he sucked in oxygen, nausea gripped his stomach. A guard to his left collapsed onto his knees and proceeded to be violently sick. Abdul barked into his radio, and after a few more scattered rounds, the gunshots from the control center fell silent.

"Keep moving" was all Trapp said as he held the wall for support, a wash of acid surging up his own throat at the charnel house of death ahead of him. He gritted his teeth and pushed off the support. He didn't have the luxury of giving in to his emotions.

At least, not now.

He picked his way through the slaughterhouse, spent rounds clinking underfoot as they rolled away from his boots, and stopped to the left of the steel gate, sheltering behind the concrete doorjamb for cover.

It wasn't necessary. The central hall in which the concrete and glass-surrounded control facility had been constructed was laid out so that he didn't have line of sight from his current vantage point to either of the three remaining entrances. He wondered whether it was an intentional security measure or just a fortuitous twist of fate.

Abdul rushed up beside him, his teeth seemingly gritted in an attempt to stave off nausea. He fumbled with the keychain at his belt, numbed fingers losing the correct key several times before he was finally able to insert it into the lock and twist.

The gate's hinges were well oiled, and it pulled open easily. Trapp glanced back, noting a mix of emotions on the faces of the guards behind him. There was disgust, terror, but anger too. These men wanted revenge for what had happened to the place they were sworn to guard.

Their eyes widened one by one as they saw the destruction that lay ahead. The control center's windows must have been bulletproof because they just barely held even as they had turned opaque from the effect of hundreds of discrete impacts. One of the heavy panes had been pushed backward and was hanging from its frame, like a smashed windshield after an auto wreck.

"Take half your guys down this wall," Trapp said, pointing to his left. "Stay real tight. Follow it all the way to the corner, and then do the same when you hit concrete on the other side. Tell your people inside that thing to concentrate their fire on the two lateral entrances. If they can keep them occupied while we get into position, we have good odds of taking them both out."

"What about that one?" Abdul asked over the echoing crack of gunfire. He gestured through the control hub to the gate Trapp knew lay on the other side.

"Keep a couple of guys on it. It's a risk, but if we can take out these two entrances, then we won't have a problem mopping up the last on the way out."

Abdul nodded resolutely. Trapp clapped him on the shoulder. "Atta boy. Let's go."

He grabbed half a dozen guards for himself and pushed them into position. He held up three fingers, then two, then stepped through the gate, pressing his right shoulder against the wall the second he was inside. He set a fast pace, not looking back to see if the SDF fighters were keeping up.

Twenty paces.

Corner.

Turn.

Ten paces.

Trapp slowed as his target came into view. His stomach was knotted with tension. The hulking control hub was to his left, standing like some besieged medieval castle keep. The walls left and right of the gate he was approaching were scarred with bullet holes. Every few seconds, a fresh puff of dust erupted from either side as the surrounded guards kept up their relentless covering fire.

He held up his left fist, halting the procession behind him, then waved at the control room. This was the hard part. Abdul had a radio. He could warn the guards on his side to cease fire as he made his move.

Trapp wasn't so lucky.

He didn't need long. Just a couple of seconds. Finally, someone inside responded. A face appeared in the exact spot where he'd seen a muzzle flash a moment before. The shadowed face squinted, then appeared to ascertain his intentions.

Here's hoping.

He held up three fingers, just like he had before.

Two.

One.

His boots crunched over dust and debris as he sprinted toward the gate. A fresh puff of dust fell from the opposite side as a gunshot cracked out. His primal brain stem screamed for him to stop, that this was suicidal, but he ignored it.

The gunfire fell silent.

And then his own began. He slowed two paces from the gate, took a step to the right, and squeezed his trigger just as a flash of orange came into view, cowering behind the door frame. The man fell, now just another corpse. Trigger squeeze, three rounds, trigger squeeze, three rounds. He was panting hard, forgetting to breathe despite all his experience. Sweat dripped down his temples and ran freely down his back.

He took another step to the left to open up his firing angle and allow another gun space to shoot at his side. He didn't aim at anyone or anything in particular, just squeezed and fired until his magazine ran dry. Another pace to the left as he slotted in a fresh magazine and squeezed.

To his right, one of the guards that had followed him into the control hall spun and toppled to the floor as a round took him in the hip. Trapp ignored it, stepping closer toward the gate —heedless of his own safety—and pressing the barrel of his rifle through the bars. He emptied the entire magazine. The other SDF fighters around him did the same.

Just as before, the untrained, inexperienced and—most critically of all, out of practice—ISIS prisoners collapsed under the weight of fire from this fresh attack. Just seconds before they must've believed they were on the verge of victory.

Not anymore.

Trapp's shoulders sagged as the sound of firing fell away around him. A moment later, the guns fell silent on the opposite side of the hall. Abdul had succeeded.

Only one enemy strongpoint remained now.

And it didn't stand a chance.

10

President Nash stepped out of the Beast and into the manicured grounds of the cemetery in which he'd buried his son. The Secret Service agent holding the limo door open for him stared dead ahead as he stood, unmoving, for a few moments. Her hair was tied back in a tight bun, but a few stray strands flickered in the breeze.

There was no privacy in his life, he reflected.

The usual retinue of aides, assistants, advisors, and other assorted hangers-on had been left back at the White House, along with all the chaos they brought with them. This morning's visit was not their concern. But his Secret Service detail traveled alongside him wherever he went. There had to be, what, fifty of them scattered around the cemetery?

And those were just the ones he could see. Dark-suited agents stood guard in a wide perimeter like ghosts among the dead. The highly trained and well-armed Counter-Assault Team, the quasi-SWAT unit charged with fending off an all-out assault on his motorcade, remained in their SUVs, a lurking presence at the back of his mind. It felt somehow wrong to bring all these implements of death and destruction to such a peaceful place.

Nash shook his head, knowing that if he committed to seeking reelection—a decision that was still very much up in the air in his mind—then he would have to bear four more years of this. Four more years of not being able to visit his own son's grave in peace.

Was it all worth it?

"Thanks, Kate," he said softly as he stepped away from the door. The agent closed it gently behind him.

"No problem, sir."

As he walked away, Nash thought he detected a hint of sympathy in the young woman's voice. He couldn't decide whether he appreciated the thought or hated the fact that so many others were aware of his family's tragedy at all.

"Hey, George," he murmured, looking down at the headstone on which his son's name was inscribed, along with the date of his death.

2018.

Nash's eyes focused on the year, a wave of anguish tearing through him. His throat grew tense, and a muscle pulsated on the side of his jaw.

You never recovered from losing a child.

He certainly hadn't. George's death, hell, and the years-long battle with opioid addiction that had preceded it, hadn't just cost him a son; it had stolen his entire family from him. He and Holly had never been the same after that.

Maybe there were things that he could have done differently.

You know there were.

He grimaced from the truth of that thought. He'd thrown himself into work as George fell ever deeper into his addiction. Perhaps he'd hoped to distract himself from the failures in his personal life with success in gaining public office. In reaching the very presidency itself, something he'd dreamed about his entire life.

Reality had turned out very different from those dreams. He'd always pictured stepping out of Marine One onto the White House's South Lawn, his son on one side and his wife on the other.

But when he'd first entered the Oval Office, he did so alone.

"It's been a while," Nash finally continued, squatting down onto his haunches in front of his son's gravestone. He reached out and brushed a few fallen leaves onto the grass on either side.

"I'm sorry I haven't visited. I've been—" He gritted his teeth, swallowing hard as he heard the words out loud. "Damn it, I won't blow smoke up your ass. Coming here still hurts."

The first couple of times he'd visited this place, he'd just stood here silently, bottling up the rage and guilt that still bubbled up inside. All those opportunities to change George's path in life, those roads not taken, they had all led here in the end. He'd been unable to save his own son, his only son, from ending up in an early grave.

Whatever other achievements he had in his life, they paled in comparison to that terrible failure.

Nash fell silent for a few moments, gripping the side of his son's headstone and half-imagining he was squeezing the kid's shoulder. The stone was colder than his memories. He shivered.

"I came here to ask your advice," he whispered. "I've always kept what happened to you to myself. Never spoke about it in public. Hell, even with your mom, I could never find the words. People know. Of course they know. But I never said a thing. Now I wonder if I was a fool all along."

He rubbed his palms together, staring at the ground, a prickle of shame on his cheeks.

"I'm not angry with you, George. I never have been, and I

never will be. You are my son, nothing changes that. And I don't want people to read into my silence, to think that you're something I want to forget. To think that I'm *ashamed* of you."

He exhaled angrily at the thought of it, then scanned the endless headstones ahead of him on the undulating ground. A shadow swept across the grass as a cloud scuffled across the sky.

"But I'm afraid," he admitted, his voice barely audible. "I'm not sure whether I'm more worried about using your memory for political gain or having people think that's what I'm doing. I don't know what to do."

Nash closed his eyes and tipped his head up to the sky. The cloud lifted, and a few rays of fall sunshine warmed his cheeks. In the distance, a single bird squawked angrily.

When he opened his eyes again, he knew.

He patted the top of the headstone once, shaking his head sadly. It was a strange tradition. He remembered tossing a football with George in the backyard. Driving him to tennis practice every Tuesday and Thursday in midwinter and sitting in the parking lot until it was done. But now, as then, he wouldn't trade it for the world.

As he walked back to the Beast, a newfound lightness in his step, he paused for a moment and squinted at one of the agents on his Secret Service detail. The man was about fifty yards away, at the very edge of the perimeter. He was holding a device that looked like a cross between a rifle and a shoulder-launched antiaircraft missile and sweeping across the sky. Nash watched him for a couple of moments, squinting as he tried to work out what the hell he was doing.

When he arrived back at the limo, he smiled at Kate as she pulled open the door. Before he climbed in, he gestured into the distance and asked, "Say, what is that thing?"

She turned and held her hands over her eyes to block out the sun as she worked out what he was referring to, then looked back. "Anti-drone countermeasure, sir. The service has been testing it out the last couple months. Manufacturer claims it will disrupt communications with pretty much any radio-controlled UAV on the market."

"Something I should be worried about?"

"No sir," she said, shaking her head. "That's our job."

"So it is."

11

They passed abandoned, emptied cells on either side as they moved quickly down a trashed hallway that led to the southern exit into the prison grounds, and hopefully the freedom that lay beyond. Trapp's unevenly shaded eyes took in the scene in one of them to his left. A prisoner had taken advantage of his emancipation to set fire to a stained, thin rollup mattress that still smoldered in the center of the room.

The material had mostly failed to light.

"Of all the things," he muttered, shaking his head.

He now had a radio handset shoved into his jacket, taken from the control center after they were finished relieving its defenders. The damn thing barely functioned from inside the prison's thick concrete walls. Occasionally, it squawked a fuzzy blast of static, behind which he could just barely make out human design.

He gestured for the procession to slow as bright sunlight blazed through an open doorway up ahead. The thump-thump-thump of the helicopter's rotor blades reverberated through their feet. The damn thing had to be hovering close enough for its skids to kiss the ground.

"Nearly there," he called out. "Let's stay focused." Abdul and Madison relayed the command in Arabic at the front and rear of the line respectively.

"Friendly forces inside al-Shaddadi," Trapp's radio squawked. "Aerial support has cleared the path you requested. Repeat, friendly forces, we've got your ass covered. If you're hearing this, please respond. Over."

Something about the voice rang a bell in Trapp's mind. He'd heard it before, he was sure of it. But where?

He grabbed the radio and squeezed transmit. "This is Hangman," he said. "Who am I talking to?"

There was a brief pause before the voice responded. Its owner sounded startled. "Hangman?"

"That's right," Trapp agreed.

"Well, no kidding," the voice said. "Long time no speak."

"Who is this?" Trapp demanded.

"Muniz."

"Shit," Trapp said, a genuine smile of relief and happiness springing unbidden to his lips. "You're still kicking?"

"Just barely," Muniz replied. "No thanks to you. And it's Master Sergeant now. *Sergeant*."

"I'll make it up to you with a beer when this is over," Trapp said. "It's good to hear your voice. Seriously. But right now, I could use a sitrep. We're almost at the southern exit. Do those choppers know they have friendlies inbound?"

Another short pause. "They do now. Stick to that side, okay? Air support blasted a nice easy path for you to follow, just out to your right. We've got a few more birds covering the remainder of the prison. It's like the first day of hunting season out there."

"Good to hear," Trapp said. "We're on our way out. Did any prisoners make it past the walls?"

"We've got runners everywhere," Muniz sighed. "At least a hundred, maybe more."

"Tomorrow's problem."

"It always is. See you on the flipside, brother."

Trapp clicked the radio transmit button twice in response, then thrust the handset back into his jacket. He had noticed that Madison had sidled up to his side as he talked.

"Old friend?"

"Something like that," he agreed, refocusing his mind as he eyed up the sun-draped exit. The route behind them was clear. Every prisoner inside had fled, and Abdul's men had locked the gates behind the procession as they passed through the hallways.

But outside was a whole different story.

"Keep your men tight, understood?" he called out to Abdul. "Follow me and head straight for the wall. We're home free once we reach the breach. But we have to make it there alive, okay?"

Abdul nodded.

Trapp strode forward. There were no more cell doors on either side of the hallway, so he kept his eyes glued to the exit. It appeared to have been opened manually, rather than with explosives, but a thick layer of dust and debris now coated the concrete floor from the helicopters' rotor wash.

He pressed himself against the doorframe and scanned the exercise yard. It was empty of shooters, although the bodies of at least a dozen prisoners and guards lay on the dusty soil, their posture contorted in death. Smoke streamed out of the building's upper windows to his right, and occasionally a burning streak of ash was coughed into the sky. He heard a loud crack as something structural deep within the building's bowels failed. It caused a whimper of fear from the civilians lined up behind him.

Ahead, the walls lay in tatters. Two huge breaches had been

chewed into them. One of them Trapp recognized as the handiwork of close air support. The RAF pilot had been busy. The other was presumably an entrance blown by the prison's attackers during the early part of their raid.

It was smaller, and they'd leaned a ladder against the outer side of the inner wall, which hadn't been so comprehensively destroyed. Trapp could see the topmost rungs peeking out from over the shattered concrete.

"We head for that breach," he said, stabbing his finger at the enormous hole for good measure. "Move fast and don't stop for anything. Copy?"

Abdul and Madison both nodded. Trapp waited as the Syrian translated the message for his men and coaxed the terrified civilians into one final effort.

"Ready?" Trapp asked tersely.

He moved the second he received an affirmative response and stepped out into the prison grounds. The rubble-strewn soil crunched underneath his boots. The air swirled with dust blown by the rotors of the powerful, insect-like Apache helicopter gunship that was hovering about fifty feet up, rotating slowly as its pilot and gunners searched for targets.

Trapp *really* hoped that Muniz had told them what was about to happen.

He tasted burned aviation fuel on the back of his tongue as he moved through the chaos, pivoting left and right, his eyes never stopping their roving. The enemy could be hiding behind any chunk of rubble, stretch of wall, prison window, or guard tower. There were too many innocent lives on the line to slip up. Adrenaline flooded his veins, drying out his mouth and spurring his heartbeat to unsustainable levels.

At the halfway point to the wall, he slowed, spinning on the sole of his right boot to check the status of those behind him. The civilians were keeping a surprisingly neat line—the fear of death will do that to you—though they'd strung out a little more than Trapp would've liked.

Still, he didn't detect any signs of danger.

Until he caught a flash of orange at the far-right corner of his vision. His gaze snapped toward the threat, and he brought his rifle up the second it was clear of friendlies. He spied a large group of gunmen exiting a door about fifty yards farther up the prison. Several strode out and took up firing positions as others filled in behind.

"Hangman," his radio blurted. "Aerial support says you've got company."

"I see it," he replied, bringing the radio up to his lips with his left hand as he kept his right steady on his weapon. "Big group. I count at least fifteen."

"Stay back," Muniz warned. "Choppers are about to engage."

Trapp dropped his eye to his rifle's optic. The borrowed weapon was old and hadn't been particularly well maintained. It was an AK-47, which meant that it would keep firing even if some young, dumb boot decided to urinate down the barrel and then fill it in with sand, but the scope was poor quality. Moisture had intruded, making his vision fuzzy.

Shit, he mouthed, pressing the handset back to his lips so hard the flesh smarted.

"Wave off, wave off," he shouted, still watching as more bodies stepped out into the sun. "They've got hostages. At least half a dozen. Two women, four men. Scratch that, make that three women."

"Copy," Muniz said tersely.

The Apache's nose lifted just in time. Its cannon could easily have chewed every scrap of human flesh in its sights into a fine mist in a matter of seconds, but instead it hovered in place, hocking menacingly over the field of battle, its rotors buzzing like an angry hornet.

"Keep them moving," Trapp shouted as he glanced back at the line of fleeing civilians, some of whom had stopped to gawk at this new threat as though they were rubbernecking the site of a highway crash.

He dropped his eye back to the Kalashnikov's scope, breathing deeply as he focused on mentally cleaning up the image it produced. The mist coating the lens wasn't thick, but it was enough to obscure minor details like faces and the precise details of weapons and clothing.

But the identity of the man in the middle was immediately clear. It was his shape, his posture, the way he held himself.

Trapp brought the radio to his lips. "It's him," he transmitted, forgetting that Muniz had no idea what he was talking about.

"Who?" came the quickfire response.

"Khaled al-Shakiri," he radioed.

"You're shitting me," Muniz replied, the radio's tiny speakers barely cutting through the tornado being whipped up by the Apache's rotors. The name was familiar to most in the special operations community. Al-Shakiri had been high on their target list for almost a decade. "What the fuck is he doing here?"

"Guess we had him all this time," Trapp replied, his index finger caressing the warm metal of his trigger. It would be so easy. Even though the rifle's sights likely hadn't been zeroed in decades, if ever, he had the innate ability to make the shot 99 times out of 100.

But he pulled his aim. Because he'd seen something else, a detail he'd somehow forgotten in the adrenaline-soaked, action-packed moments that had preceded this one.

"His guards are wearing suicide vests," he said through gritted teeth. "Do you have any boots on the ground this side of the prison? Tell your boys to keep their distance. I already watched one of these fanatics blow themselves up today."

"Copy that," Muniz replied grimly. "And negative on your last. ETA 15 minutes, minimum. It's chaos out here."

"Dammit," he said.

A quick peek to his right revealed that the first of the civilian support staff had reached the breach in the prison's walls and were beginning to clamber over chunks of debris and rubble that in some cases lay at hip height. Madison was kneeling about ten yards away from him, her rifle's stock at the crook of her shoulder.

The group containing al-Shakiri started to move. Trapp kept the terrorist at the center of his scope's crosshairs, watching as the big man—Omar—shouldered the weight of the injured prisoner. They were heading for the smaller breach.

"What's on the other side of the wall?" Trapp radioed.

"A gap of about a hundred feet, then a small town. Census records say it has about ten thousand inhabitants, but it's been a long time since the Syrian government was in any kind of position to count its citizens. When you add in displaced persons, you can triple that and add another few thousand for good measure. It's a rats' nest. A warren of narrow streets and newly built temporary housing. We don't go in there. Not if we want to come out."

"Great."

He took a pace to the right, keeping his weapon trained on the group of escaping prisoners. They were smart. The hostages were mingled among them, some of them held in place by the ISIS fanatics in explosive vests. He figured the devices were rigged with failsafe switches that would detonate the moment their wearers were killed.

Or maybe not. Maybe they wouldn't risk al-Shakiri's life like that.

But that was a choice that no man could make. Not if he wanted to sleep easy at night. It was an impossible, unknowable question that carried fatal consequences for the person who got it wrong.

"It's him, isn't it?" Madison called. She was coated with yellow sand and dust to the point that he barely recognized her.

"It's him," Trapp agreed. He took another pace to his right, then another, speeding up now in order to keep up with the prisoners. They were halfway to the wall already.

"We have to go after him," she said.

"Muniz," Trapp radioed. "I need you to spare an airship. Target is heading for the wall. I need him followed."

"Can do," came the reply. "Rerouting an asset now. But Hangman, once he reaches that town, he's as good as gone."

Trapp strode forward, moving both toward and alongside the group of prisoners. The first of them had reached the wall now. One gave another a boost, holding both their weapons as the second scrambled up onto the mangled top of the wall and hauled the ladder back down.

"Jason, take the shot," Madison called out. Al-Shakiri was just a few feet from the base of the ladder now. Omar was practically carrying him. He was right in the center of Trapp's sights. It was an easy shot. No more than a hundred feet.

He wanted to. God, he wanted to. Nothing would give him more pleasure than seeing that monster's brains splattered across gray concrete. But a civilian was momentarily manhandled in front of Khaled. Trapp couldn't see the precise details of the terror on the woman's face, but he knew it had to be there.

If he took the shot, then she would die. They would all die. The good and the innocent alike. And that was an outcome that he could not—would not—have on his conscience.

"You know I can't," he replied as he side-stepped toward her, almost turning his ankle on a stray chunk of concrete in the process.

"He's getting away!" she protested. "This might be our only chance to bag him."

Trapp switched his gaze between Madison's expression and the distant enemy. About half a dozen wary gunmen ringed the base of the ladder, some kneeling, others standing. Mostly their attention was focused on the two of them. They were too experienced to open fire and tempt fate. But they were sending a clear message that they were there.

Madison's rifle trembled. He could almost feel the emotional turmoil raging inside her. He didn't know exactly what it was she was holding on to, what had driven her to this point, but he knew how dangerous a situation it had created. Her finger twitched.

Crap.

He couldn't let her pull the trigger, and he sensed that was exactly what she was about to do. She wasn't thinking rationally. He watched as a muscle trembled on the side of her jaw. Sensed she was building up to the moment.

Trapp dropped his own weapon against its sling and dived toward Madison instead. He pushed her rifle down, seizing it firmly and snatching it away from her grasp. As he pulled it from her hands, he saw her trigger finger jerk reflexively—mere inches away from condemning them all.

He ejected the magazine, cleared the chambered round, and kicked both far away before dumping the rifle onto the dirt. Madison stared up at him, for a moment too stunned to feel anger. But it followed.

"What the hell are you doing?" she whispered, clamping her teeth together as she shot to her feet. All sense of place and time forgotten, she reached out and shoved him violently in the chest. He allowed himself to be pushed back, though the force of the impact was hardly sufficient to warrant it.

"Why did you do that?" she said, the anger fading and exhaustion—and shock—taking over. She sank back down onto her haunches, tears streaking through the dust on his face. "Why?"

Trapp turned away, aware that the threat wasn't yet over. He picked his rifle up once more and watched as the last of al-Shakiri's party disappeared over the top of the wall. They had taken the hostages with them. He jogged toward the ladder, leaving Madison in the dust.

By the time he reached the top, al-Shakiri was gone.

12

A machine gun mounted on a mine-resistant armored vehicle swung to cover the approach of Trapp's party. Most of the civilian staff they'd escorted out had disappeared into the warren of housing near the prison, but several remained—mostly those too wreathed in shock to comprehend that they were now safe.

"Nearly there," Trapp said as the exhausted survivors staggered toward the makeshift command post set up by the SDF militia and their foreign special forces counterparts.

A hive of activity swarmed around the warehouse that had been commandeered for the purpose. Looking up, Trapp made out the faint outline of half a dozen uniformed military personnel on the corrugated iron roof. The soldiers were seated on folding camp chairs, just like you might see at a cookout back home. They were leaning forward into observation devices mounted on tripods in front of them. He knew that they were conducting the orchestra of destruction that coalition aircraft were currently inflicting on al-Shaddadi Prison. A fresh explosion echoed across the dry countryside every half minute or so, followed by the screech of a jet engine or the low whir of helicopter engines.

About a dozen MRAPs surrounded the entrance to the warehouse, and a combination of SDF fighters and discreetly uniformed Western special forces types were building checkpoints and firing positions around the building.

The vehicles mostly belonged to the latter and sat underneath flags of their respective countries. The Brits, the French, and even a handful of Italians had shown their faces, but the biggest delegation by far belonged to the United States of America.

Trapp limped inside the security cordon. His mouth was parched, and he gratefully accepted a canteen offered by a British SAS operator.

"Thanks," he coughed as he sluiced the brackish water around his mouth. It tasted better than any crystal-clear mountain spring ever could. He spit the first mouthful out, then drained the canteen with his second.

"No problem," the Brit replied. "Keep it. You fellas look like you just crawled out of hell. Least I could do."

Trapp saw out of the corner of his eye that Madison was being similarly cared for. The Agency analyst had been almost silent since they'd left the burning prison behind. He suspected that she was in shock. He resisted the urge to offer some meaningless platitude. She had the kind of expression on her face that suggested the first person to approach her would leave with a bloody nose.

"Yeah, something like that," he agreed, sipping from the canteen now. "They've been planning whatever the hell that was for a long, long time."

"Hey," the SAS guy replied with a laconic shrug. "At least this gives us an opportunity to clean house."

Trapp nodded. "You seen Master Sergeant Muniz?"

"He's somewhere around," the Brit replied. "Probably inside. The general likes to keep him close."

"Doesn't sound like the guy I knew." Trapp grinned.

"I guess people change."

Trapp strode into the warehouse, ignoring a French soldier who asked him for ID. The young private trailed behind awkwardly, not knowing what to do with the big American who wouldn't take no for an answer.

"Hangman," Muniz roared, spreading his arms wide as he caught sight of his old squad mate. "You picked a hell of a day to go sightseeing. I should've known you had something to do with that mess."

Smiling wryly, Trapp accepted his old friend's embrace. "Been a long time."

"That it has," Muniz replied, standing back and examining Trapp critically. "You look like shit."

"Thanks."

"I mean, I don't think it has anything to do with what you just went through. You always looked a bit worse for wear. Only back then you were young enough to pull it off."

Trapp rolled his eyes. He straightened slightly and got down to business. "So how are things going out there? Any sign of my guy?"

Muniz shook his head. "Like I said, we got runners in every direction. ISIS hit both the local SDF garrison and our base with a truck bomb at the same time as the attack on the prison. It wasn't clear for at least fifteen minutes which the actual target was. Our local partners took at least thirty KIA straight off the bat, so even when the picture cleared up, we were slow to roll into action."

A pair of jet engines rocketed past somewhere overhead, sounding like they were flying only a couple hundred feet off the ground. Trapp counted a couple of beats in his head and wasn't surprised when a pair of massive booms erupted a moment later.

"There won't be much of that prison left by the time this is over," he commented.

"Not if I can help it." Muniz shrugged. "But it's not up to me. General Espinoza doesn't want to take this to the mattresses, and I don't blame him. It was a meat grinder the first time we beat ISIS. Real house-to-house Stalingrad shit. The SDF lost thousands. The local balance of power isn't exactly stable. Our partners and friends don't have too many more fighters to lose."

"So the more of them you can wipe out from the air..." Trapp started.

"Yep. The fewer we have to mop up later."

Trapp nodded. It was smart and probably the way he would have wanted it done if he was in charge. But it didn't do his chances of finding Khaled al-Shakiri any good.

"What about checkpoints on the roads out of town?" he asked. "I take it you've got surveillance assets up?"

"Yeah," Muniz said, leaning over a wooden trestle table and grabbing a ruggedized tablet computer. He pulled up a map of the area and tapped it in several places in a rough circle around the prison. "The locals are setting up checkpoints all over the shop. But it's probably too late for that."

Trapp nodded. He knew it too. The escaped prisoners would by now already have traded their orange coveralls for civilian clothing and dumped their weapons. There was no way to lock down a civilian population that numbered into the thousands spread across dozens of settlements. "What about a door-to-door sweep? We must have biometrics on everybody inside al-Shaddadi."

"Be my guest." Muniz laughed before his expression grew more serious. "But you'll be on your own. We don't have the manpower to step one foot inside that ghetto without provoking a bloodbath. I'm sorry. I know you want this guy. But

I have to be honest: Finding him is going to be like looking for a needle in a haystack."

"I appreciate the honesty," he replied.

"Why are you looking for him anyway?" Muniz frowned.

"I wasn't, really. I was just down here doing a favor. Providing an ID for—"

"Madison?"

"That's right. You know her?"

"We've bumped into each other from time to time. I know her reputation, mostly. She's like a dog with a fucking bone. Once she gets something between her teeth, ain't nothing getting in her way until she's crunched right through it."

"Yeah," Trapp chuckled. "I get that impression."

"Gets under the general's skin something fierce." Muniz shrugged. "But then, she's usually right. She's helped us take down a couple real nasty ISIS cells before they spread into something big."

Trapp nodded thoughtfully. "See, that's the thing. I came face to face with this guy, Muniz. Looked him in the eye. Saw the way the others reacted to him. Like they worshiped the ground he walked on. I think this whole operation was designed to free one man. And it succeeded."

Muniz hiked his eyebrow. "You got any proof? That's a big call."

"Nope. Just my gut."

"Far be it for me to second-guess your internationally-renowned stomach." His friend grinned. "But you think that stacks up? My memory on your guy is a little hazy, but he wasn't top of the pile in the caliphate, was he?"

Trapp closed his eyes and tossed his head back, picturing the file that Madison had handed him and then pulling his memories back further to the time he'd spent hunting al-Shakiri in this region years before.

"A senior military leader, but not in their top command structure, no. At least, not that we knew of at the time."

A muffled explosion rang out. Muniz jerked his head in the direction from which it had come. "This op was a big one. Half a dozen VBIEDs at a minimum, probably close to a hundred fighters, as well as enough hardware to arm several hundred more prisoners. Maybe freeing al-Shakiri was *an* objective, but I'm not buying he was the whole show. At least not without something concrete backing it up."

"Then let's go get it," Madison interjected. Trapp hadn't seen her approach. Judging by his reaction, neither had Muniz.

"How you doing?" he inquired. "That was some real shit in there."

"Fine," Madison replied harshly. Her voice shook with repressed emotion, but she held it together. "What's happening in the prison?"

"A small pocket of escapees is holed up in the east wing," Muniz said, drawing a circle around the section of the prison on the tablet map he was still holding. "There might be a few loose elsewhere, but we don't have any solid intel on that yet. The SDF is putting together an assault force as we speak to go in and mop things up."

"I need to go in with them," Madison said.

"Hold up," Trapp interjected. "Why? It's not safe. And besides, you should get some rest."

"I don't need it," she snapped. "I need to go back. There has to be something in there, something I missed."

Trapp and Muniz exchanged glances. The Latino operator nodded and faded away, leaving him alone with Madison. He gestured toward the warehouse's wide exit. "Come on. Let's go get some fresh air."

"Jason, stop trying to take care of me," Madison said through gritted teeth, though as he started walking, she nevertheless fell in alongside him.

"I'm not," he said firmly, putting his arm on her lower back and pushing her outside. "But you're not in the right place to go back inside, and if you were thinking clearly, you would see that."

"Go to hell," she said bitterly, wrenching herself away from him. She stood three steps away, her hands bunched up into fists.

Trapp watched her carefully. She was trembling, on the verge of an outright fit of shakes. Coupled with her reckless behavior when they reached the prison's grounds, he grew certain that there was more to this story than he knew.

But she wasn't a kid. And he couldn't treat her like one. He chose a tone that was firm but not harsh. "If you go in half-cocked like this, you'll put other people's lives at risk. Someone has to watch your back. And you could get them killed. Is that what you want?"

Madison said nothing. But as he watched, her shoulders rounded. She didn't seem so thoroughly consumed by anger anymore. This was different. Sadness.

"I didn't think so," he said softly. "But I think you're not telling me something. What makes this so personal?"

Her head swept jerkily left and right, as though she was taking in her surroundings for the first time. He watched the muscles on the side of her neck tense as she swallowed. "Not here," she said hoarsely.

Trapp followed in silence as Madison led him around the corner to a mostly empty side of the warehouse. A handful of SDF fighters and foreign advisors were digging firing points, but they were well out of range—and mostly looking in the opposite direction.

Finally, Madison turned to face him. They were standing right by the warehouse's corrugated iron wall. She started to shake and reached out and held it for support. She opened her mouth to speak, but no words came out.

He reached out and squeezed her shoulder. He knew better than to gather her into an embrace. She wasn't looking for physical comfort, just support as whatever she'd repressed shook itself free.

"That wasn't me," she whispered at long last, her eyes downcast, her chin angled toward the floor. "The person you saw in the prison grounds. I don't even recognize her myself."

Trapp stayed quiet. She was talking.

"God, I could've killed those people," she said, her voice jumping several octaves. "If you hadn't stopped me, I think I would have done it. I would've pulled the trigger, and all those innocent people would have died."

"But you didn't," he said to steer her away from entering a negative reinforcement loop. "You had the chance, and you didn't. That's what matters. Not what went through your head. Not what you dreamed about. What you did."

"But I didn't stop myself," she protested. "You did."

"Before I stepped in front of you, you could've pulled the trigger. Why didn't you?"

"I wasn't ready."

"You didn't want to," he countered. "And you wouldn't have gone through with it whether I'd gotten in front of you or not."

He didn't think so, anyway. But the mind was more powerful than most understood. A person could convince themselves of damn near anything given the right motivation.

She gritted her teeth but didn't respond. There was a war going on inside her head that he wasn't privy to.

"Tell me why, Madison," he prompted. "Help me understand what happened in there."

It took her almost a minute to open up. She started out tense, a tic on her jaw twitching, her knuckles white, a rictus of anger on her face. But as she spoke, the tension uncoiled within her.

"He killed a friend of mine," she said. "A good one. He sat

on the desk next to mine at Langley for two years. Brought me coffee every morning. I brought doughnuts."

"What happened to him?"

"He was posted out here back in 2017. The targeting cycle was too slow for the operators. They were missing high-value targets, sometimes by a matter of hours. Mark was sent out here to close the loop. It worked, for a while. I guess ISIS figured it out. They managed to insert a guy in a suicide vest. A local. He blew himself up in the cafeteria."

"The Al-Tanf attack," Trapp murmured, a hazy memory shouldering its way forward in his mind. "He was there?"

"Yeah," Madison whispered. "I've watched the footage more times than I can count. Cameras are such high quality these days, you know? He'd just racked his dirty tray and was heading for the exit when the bomber walked in. A few more seconds and he would've made it out."

"I'm sorry," Trapp said softly. He'd felt her pain before, more often than he cared to remember. It never got easier.

"Don't be," she said coldly, resolve replacing her pain. "It wasn't you; it was him. I worked night and day for weeks after the attack piecing together what happened. Al-Shakiri's cell coordinated the whole thing. He penetrated our militia partner in the area, figured out how to smuggle explosives into the compound without being detected, even picked the time, day, and exact location for him to strike."

She paused. Not for long. "I listened to the intercepts, Jason. I heard that monster planning my friend's death. And I won't stop until he pays for what he did."

13

President Nash didn't look up from the policy brief he was absorbed in until the assistant had already knocked on the door to his private study, entered, left a fresh stack of paperwork on his desk, and departed. As the door shut behind her, he finally tore his attention away.

"Thanks," he muttered, realizing only after he said the words that she was long gone.

He leaned back in his chair, reaching for the glass of scotch he'd been sipping all evening. It was down to a mere miasma of alcohol. He angled the glass and watched as the last few drops trickled to the corner, light from the desk lamp refracting in the amber liquid.

What time was it?

Nash glanced at the grandfather clock hanging on the wall, surprised to realize that it was past midnight. He shook his head, chiding himself for working so late. It was easy enough to do in this job. There was always a pressing matter to attend to, either firefighting some fresh crisis, or else an upcoming policy that would affect the lives of untold millions of Americans for which he was expected to pick a side after reading little more than an executive summary.

He didn't know how the hell previous presidents managed to hold down both the job and a family life without losing their minds.

He closed his eyes for a few moments and contemplated rest but decided he was still too wired to sleep. He pushed the policy brief aside and reached for the fresh paperwork instead, flicking through each document in turn to see if anything required his immediate attention. It was mostly dry, technical stuff. At the very bottom was the nightly document his staff put together that contained clippings of the next day's first editions.

These days, the articles were mostly screenshotted off the Internet before being pasted into a PDF and printed. He still remembered spending long hours as a junior aide, not long after he left the Marines, cutting out actual print newspaper articles from the papers, gluing them to a sheet of card, then photocopying them so that his boss—a first-term House representative—could use them as a coaster for his morning cup of coffee.

Okay, Grandpa.

Nash grimaced, the thought just another everyday reminder of what he'd lost. What he would most likely never have. He couldn't see himself starting a new family. Not at this age. Let alone having another kid. There was too much hurt. Too much water under the bridge. And besides, how old would he be by the time grandkids came along—eighty?

He snorted as he dropped his gaze to the page.

Nash Mulls Reelection Bid, the first headline read.

"Not exactly Pulitzer material," he muttered to himself, scanning the first couple of paragraphs without expecting to read much of interest. Upon reaching the third paragraph, he froze, a sudden flash of anger burning away the alcohol in his veins. He reached forward and stabbed the button on the intercom on his desk.

"Kathy?"

"No, sir," a female voice and said, presumably the assistant who'd dropped off the press clippings. "She went home. How can I help?"

"Get Harry Hoffman on the line," Nash said, hearing the audible anger in his voice and forcing himself to calm down. The young woman on the other end of the intercom didn't need to take the brunt of his rage.

"Yes, sir."

"Wait. What's your name?"

"Miranda, sir."

"Miranda, I'll take the call in the Residence, okay?" Nash said, remembering even in his anger the strictures of the Hatch Act.

"No problem. I'll connect you now."

Nash drew his chair back, stepped out onto the hallway and walked to his bedroom, which was equipped with a small seating area. Despite the fact that the Residence was in the White House itself, a legal fiction existed that exempted it from the requirements of the Hatch Act, which forbade the undertaking of party-political activities on federal property.

Placing the phone call from his private study next to the Oval Office would have been only a minor twisting of the guidelines, but Nash was a Marine, once and always.

Rules mattered.

He entered his bedroom and closed the door behind him with a little more force than either needed or anticipated. A red light was already blinking on the phone's base station, indicating that the White House switchboard lived up to its usual quick and efficient reputation.

"Harry. Did I wake you?"

"Not at all, Mr. President," Hoffman replied sleepily, self-evidently lying.

"What's this I'm reading?" Nash said, gripping the press book so tightly he tore the topmost pages.

"I'm sorry, sir, can you be more specific?"

"*President Nash is expected to announce his candidacy for a second term in a little under two weeks*," Nash read, his gaze burning holes in the paper. "*More interestingly, it is believed that his campaign team has chosen Baltimore's Oriole Park as the destination for his campaign's first rally, a location which holds particular resonance for—*"

Nash stopped reading. "Are you trying to roll me into something, Harry?"

"Of course not, sir. I honestly have no idea how this got out. It's a big campaign team, and it's hard to keep things like this under wraps."

"Find out," Nash growled. "I don't want anyone on the boat who isn't rowing in the right direction. That includes you. I specifically made it clear that I would give you my decision on this when I was damn well good and ready. If I find out you had anything to do—"

"Mr. President," Hoffman interjected firmly. "I promise you I did not leak this. When I learn who did, they'll be out of a job the very same minute. I respected your decision then, and I respect it now. Just give me the word, and I'll cancel the rally at Oriole Park. We have a backup location already in the works."

Nash gritted his teeth and chewed on an invisible wasp. He replayed Hoffman's words in his mind and concluded in spite of the blood pumping in his ears that he detected no dissembling.

"Okay," he said in a calmer tone. "I believe you. I'm sorry for waking you up."

The anger and adrenaline that had fueled him until now faded away. He remembered the calmness he'd felt in the cemetery just a couple of days earlier. He knew which path he wanted to take.

"No problem, Mr. President. Will that be all?"

"One last thing, Harry."

"Of course, sir."

"I want to do it."

Hoffman's response was wreathed in genuine confusion. "Do what, sir?"

"The rally. Oriole Park. The whole thing."

14

Trapp stepped over an orange-clad body as he re-entered the hall that contained the prison's control room, his face screwing up with distaste. The constant flow of air strikes had ceased about an hour before, and the joint SDF/SOCOM command had finally granted them permission to return—under clear instructions to bug the hell out the second they were ordered to do so. They were among the first to enter and were doing so well before anyone had figured out what to do with the corpses.

An occasional rattle of scattered gunfire broke out from within the prison building, but it was sufficiently muffled by many layers of thick concrete for Trapp to be sure that whoever was responsible was far enough away that he didn't need to worry about them.

Bodies of both guards and prisoners still lay where they had fallen. The prison had no air conditioning—at this point, the rubble barely had electricity—and the heat outside was pushing ninety. The scent of death was already unpleasant, but in a few hours, it would be positively unbearable.

"Watch your step," he muttered.

Madison followed a pace behind him. She had a pistol on her hip for self-defense but hadn't trusted herself to carry a rifle. Trapp thought differently but didn't push the issue. He was pretty confident that the storm that had swallowed her was now broken. And since they were surrounded by a detail of half a dozen SDF fighters, one extra-long gun didn't seem worth pushing for.

The steel door to the control center had been left ajar after the guards besieged inside had finally been relieved. It was scarred and dented from the impacts of repeated bullet impacts and bent in places, but somehow it had held. Trapp pulled it back.

Inside was a surprisingly modern office space. It could have been the control room for a power station or a data center. The electricity miraculously still functioned, and bright strip lighting blazed overhead.

"You know how to use this thing?" Trapp asked, gesturing at the computer equipment.

Madison nodded. "Abdul gave me his login details. Full access. He wants to catch these guys as badly as I do."

"I doubt that," Trapp replied as Madison pulled an office chair back from her chosen desk. A metallic tinkle sounded as the rollers pushed dozens of brass shell casings out of the way.

He took a position to her side but reserved most of his attention for the door. He'd already checked that the other entrances to the control room were still locked. If any prisoners had miraculously managed to evade capture this long, he was confident they wouldn't make it through him.

"Okay," Madison said, chewing her lip as she worked the prison's computerized surveillance system, her right hand switching from the arrow keys on the keyboard to the mouse every few seconds. "He was in cell 16. I think that's right."

"Rings a bell," Trapp agreed, recalling scanning al-Shakiri's file earlier that day. If he read something, it usually stuck. At least for as long as it was needed.

"Looks like the guards keep a log," she said, rapidly working her way through a computer program that looked like it was designed for Windows 95. At least the machine it was running on was significantly more modern, so there wasn't much of a delay between each mouse click and the required action.

She pulled up an Arabic-language document that was organized by date and time. The less said about Trapp's written Arabic, the better. He waited to be told what she was reading, alternating glances between the computer screen and the door. She scanned through it quickly.

"Nothing too interesting," she murmured. "Definitely nothing referencing either his real name or his alias."

Madison pulled up a search box and typed in a query. Trapp was at least able to recognize al-Shakiri's name written in Arabic. She hit the return key but was quickly greeted with an unfriendly chime. She ran the same query for the escaped terrorist's alias, as well as a variety of spellings that might've been used.

"Okay, so it looks like he stayed pretty much under the radar." She returned to the main document. "Wait, there's something here."

Trapp turned to the computer monitor. "What am I looking at?"

"Looks like the guards moved a new prisoner into cell 16 about a week ago. An internal transfer. The guy was causing trouble in his previous cell. There's basically no record of violence in 16 as far back as I can see. I guess they figured moving him in there might round off his rough edges."

"Did it?" Trapp asked turns Madison's fingers flew across the keyboard once more.

"Not exactly," she remarked dryly, double-clicking on the mouse and expanding the video file that appeared. It was taken from inside a prison cell—he guessed 16—from somewhere up high. Either the ceiling or the wall.

Madison scrolled through the video until she found the timestamp she was looking for, then pressed play. Both watched in silence as several of the prisoners kicked up a ruckus, then as guards entered and placed the new prisoner into the cell. They retreated, weapons drawn, and locked the gate behind them.

"Not exactly surprising they rioted," Trapp murmured.

Many of the ISIS fighters who had been incarcerated in this prison were no doubt responsible for heinous crimes. But they had been locked in this place for five years without any hope of even trial. Al-Shaddadi made Guantánamo Bay look like the Ritz-Carlton on Central Park. At least prisoners there got their own cell.

The ones left to rot here, by contrast, were treated worse than battery-farmed chickens. It would drive any sane man to seek revenge—if only to make the pain end.

"Nope," she agreed. "What's he doing?"

The prisoner swaggered around the room, dropping his shoulder and barging men out of his way.

"Spoiling for a fight," Trapp observed, remembering the few weeks he'd spent in a Siberian work camp not so very long ago. "To prove that he's a bad motherfucker."

"Spoiler." Madison smiled grimly, evidently pleased with her play on words. "It doesn't end so hot."

No, Trapp thought as he watched the prisoner choke out, before his neck finally snapped. *It doesn't.*

The rest of the footage was uneventful. In fact, al-Shakiri only appeared in a couple of seconds of the footage. He was mostly shielded from the cameras by groups of inmates, who were deliberately positioning themselves in front of him.

"This is coordinated," he said. "They practiced doing this before. Everybody knows where to go."

"Right. And it's all done to hide al-Shakiri from the camera. You can even briefly see the big guy, Omar, looking to him for instructions. He was in charge in that cell, not this new guy, not the muscle, not anybody else."

"You say the record showed cell 16 was unusually peaceful?" Trapp asked.

Madison clicked away from the video footage and queried the computer system. "As far as I can tell, no trouble before this. At least not for several years."

"How does that stack up to the others?"

"It's an outlier. A big one," she replied over the sound of keystrokes. "Most of these cells lose a prisoner once every three months or so. A stabbing here, a brawl there. But not 16."

"So he kept them in line somehow," Trapp mused. "He had the big guy for muscle, but that wouldn't have been enough. The others could have overpowered the two of them if they really wanted to. Forty to one is bad odds no matter how tough you are."

"I'll take your word for it," Madison said. She pushed the keyboard away. "I'm not going to find anything else here. At least, not without siccing a team of analysts on this database and whipping them for a month. We're looking at six angles per cell, 24 hours a day for years. It might as well be a black hole."

"I agree."

"Then let's go take a look at his cell."

As they followed their SDF-provided escort through the prison's hallways, the sound of battle began to fade away. It seemed that finally, after almost a day of intense fighting in the jail's grounds, the hard part was over.

Trapp knew that wasn't the case. The hard work was only just beginning. Several hundred inmates had successfully escaped. It was unlikely that every single one of them would return to fighting for the so-called Islamic State. Some of them would have been so shocked by the sheer brutality of life inside al-Shaddadi's walls that they would go straight.

But he doubted that would account for many.

It was much more likely that they would return to the only life they knew, tempered and hardened by the horrors of their experience. A fresh wave of horror was about to be visited on a region which had already seen so much pain.

And all because some jackass in Congress had balked at spending a few measly dollars to help the Syrians keep this problem in check. Trapp was an American exceptionalist, and he wasn't ashamed to admit it. It was fashionable these days to claim that America should step back from its commitments around the world. That she was overstretched. That she had no business in the business of empire.

But he knew better. Because what happened on the frontier inevitably its way home. And if there was one thing worse than fighting your enemies abroad, it was brawling with them on your front doorstep.

"This one," one of the Syrian escorts said as they approached a numberless cell door. The gate had been opened, and the set of keys used to do so still dangled from the lock.

Trapp crouched, lifting the keychain toward him with the nail on his right index finger so as not to disturb any fingerprints that might be recoverable. He examined the ring of keys. They were shiny, and though it was impossible to be absolutely sure, looked recently cut.

More evidence that this was an inside job.

Madison stepped through the open doorway, and he followed quickly behind, wrinkling his nose as he encountered the room's thick scent. This end of the prison had escaped the fire, which had eventually been stopped by the structure's concrete and rebar construction that left nothing else to burn.

Right now, Trapp would have welcomed the return of the

smoke that had scoured the back of his throat just a few hours earlier. The stink of sweat, bodily fluids, feces, and rotten food seemed to be impregnated into the cell's walls. There was only one toilet, and it appeared to be out of commission. A large white bucket set next to it, flies buzzing at its rim.

"How the hell did anyone live like this?" Madison asked, covering her mouth as if she was about to be sick.

"You get used to it," Trapp said off-handedly. "Eventually."

"I won't ask," she said, speaking as though through a blocked nose. She closed her eyes, her eyelids flickering, then turned as she opened them again. She pointed at the far wall. "I think he slept over there."

"Looks as good a place as any to start," Trapp said, stepping over a thin, stained mattress pad as he walked to the spot Madison had picked out.

He tossed the entire area as she did the same with Omar's section behind him. He winced as he lifted a set of stained white underwear from the top of a folded prison jumpsuit, wishing he had a pair of nitrile gloves. There was no telling what he might catch in here.

He patted the jumpsuit down, squeezing the material between his fingers, but came away empty-handed. The prisoners were allowed few creature comforts—barely even a change of clothing—and slept either on the hard ground or on a scattering of thin pads. There weren't nearly enough of the latter to accommodate all eighty-plus inmates.

The two of them silently divided the cell into quadrants and divvied them up accordingly. They worked for about fifteen minutes in silence as they searched the space thoroughly.

"Anything?" he called out, lifting one of the pads and finding an orange toothbrush that had been snapped in half and filed against the concrete into a shiv. The makeshift weapon was only a couple inches long. It would hurt like hell if someone stabbed you with it but was unlikely to kill you.

"Nothing interesting," Madison replied.

He glanced over to her and watched as she shuffled from side to side on her haunches by the wall, lifting items of clothing and other miscellaneous possessions, searching them thoroughly, then placing them back down.

Her breath caught. "Wait..."

Trapp stood, scanning the ground around him one last time for anything he might have missed. There was nothing. "What have you got?"

"I'm not sure," Madison replied haltingly. She was crouched by the wall, scrabbling at it with her fingers. "Maybe nothing."

He walked over to her. *Maybe* was a whole lot more promising than what he'd found. He stopped a couple of feet behind her and watched as she worked a seam in the concrete wall. It was circular, about the size of his spread palm, located only a couple of inches above ground level, and looked to have been repaired with mortar.

Madison broke off a piece and lifted it to her nose. She gave it an experimental sniff, swallowing uncomfortably as that inevitably reminded her of the cell's foul stench.

"It's mint," she said with a hint of surprise. "I thought so."

"Toothpaste?" Trapp asked.

"Yep. Mixed with concrete dust. I almost didn't notice it. It was covered with a stanky-ass T-shirt."

She fell silent as she continued to excavate the seam. Once she'd removed a section about two inches long, she was able to pull full chunks of the toothpaste mortar out. This revealed a chunk of concrete shaped like a brick that rattled now that it was no longer held in place.

"Here goes nothing," she said, pulling it free and tossing it aside.

"Jackpot," Trapp said, accidentally slapping her on the shoulder hard enough that she nearly rocked over. He held on until she steadied herself, then let go.

Madison extracted the cell phone. It was a Chinese model, a burner, held together with an elastic band. She turned it over in her fingers.

"We need to get this to tech. It might be the break we're looking for."

15

Adnan Gulen looked up from his workbench in some surprise, noticing for the first time that he was alone in the large aerospace test facility. The workspace in front of him was scattered with tools, electric motors, wiring, microchips, and an endless supply of electronic components used in the design and manufacture of advanced unmanned aerial vehicles.

Drones.

"Crap," he said under his breath as he realized that—once again—time had kept on ticking as he was lost in his work. A large digital clock hung on the wall on the opposite side of the enormous converted hangar. The numbers, stark and red, told him that it was almost 9 p.m.

Double crap.

His wife Esra would kill him. It was only Wednesday, and this was already the third time he'd worked long past the end of his shift this week. Worse, the kids went to bed at 8 p.m. He wouldn't get to speak with them until morning.

Adnan pushed himself away from his bench, setting the recalcitrant motor down with a heavy sigh. The component was running too hot, burning through electricity fourteen percent faster than its design specifications indicated it was supposed to. It was a conundrum, and he'd always been fascinated by such things. Though self-taught, he was an engineer at heart, and once a problem presented itself to him, he was rarely able to pull himself away until he'd solved it.

He reached automatically into his pants pocket for his cell phone before realizing that he was no longer allowed to bring it inside the design hall. Security had been ramped up over the last few years, though Adnan still remembered the days when the then-small Turkish drone manufacturer was mocked at trade shows.

When *he* was mocked.

Now Baykar was the jewel in the Turkish military-industrial complex. But when he first joined, it had been just another startup. It was easier now. If he needed a specific—usually expensive—microchip, all he had to do was pick up the phone, and someone in sourcing would acquire it for him. If he needed a motor flown in from Germany or a tungsten casing 3D printed overnight, these things would happen just like magic.

The National Intelligence Organization—known locally by the acronym MIT—Turkey's version of both the FBI and CIA in one simple package, now performed regular monthly security sweeps at the company's test facility. Even his home was occasionally swept for bugs.

But when he'd started sketching little unmanned aircraft on scraps of paper, the company was barely making enough money to meet payroll. Back then, if he wanted to build something, he was forced to scrounge batteries from scrapheaps, microchips from kids' toys, and somehow fashion them into a version of Frankenstein's monster that the company's executives could pitch to the Air Force as a futuristic, high-tech prototype.

And he usually succeeded.

Adnan shook his head. He needed to get home. He scribbled a few notes on his progress onto a pad he kept for just that purpose—for all his undoubted strengths, short-term memory wasn't one of them—then half-jogged to the door. He punched the green exit button with the base of his palm, waited for the buzzing sound to indicate that the security system had disengaged, then burst back out into the lobby.

He retrieved his cell phone from the night shift officer at the security station, then headed for his car. He squeezed the key remote, and an orange flash to his far left indicated that he was heading in precisely the wrong direction, despite the fact that almost every worker had already returned home, and the parking lot was correspondingly empty.

Right, that's where I left it.

Adnan readjusted his direction smoothly, climbed into his car, and managed to reverse out of the space without hitting anything. Another win. Despite being both the foremost designer and builder of the company's most advanced prototypes, he wasn't any good at actually *operating* them. Whenever he tried, the test drone usually ended up smashing into the runway's asphalt, getting caught in a tree, or simply not taking off at all.

Precisely how he'd managed to retain his driving license this long was a matter of fascination both among his colleagues and even within his own family. Esra rarely permitted him to drive the kids, unless it was on the Dodgem cars at the fairground.

And often not even then.

He flashed his lights as the guard lifted the outer gate for him as his car approached, then jerked the steering wheel to the left, avoiding clipping the man at the last moment. He winced, considered raising his arm in apology, and then thought better of it. He indicated, looked carefully right and left, and then once more just to be safe, and then turned onto a dark, empty street.

The Baykar development facility was deep in the Turkish countryside, about 150 miles from the company's commercial headquarters in Istanbul. These roads rarely saw any traffic past seven in the evening, when the company's employees—most of them—ended their shifts.

As he drove, Adnan realized that he'd forgotten to send a message to Esra to let her know he'd be late. Well, she already knew that part. He thought about stopping, but it was only a twenty-minute drive to his house. If he wanted to make it back before she fell asleep, he didn't have much time to waste.

A flash of bright white light filled the interior of his car as a vehicle seemed to appear out of nowhere behind him. He glanced up at his rearview mirror, frowning as he tried to work out where it had come from. Was there a road turning back there? He couldn't remember one, and he'd been driving the same route every morning and evening for over a decade, but then again, he didn't usually pay attention to such details. His mind was ordinarily too full with the schematics of his projects and endless, overflowing ideas about how to improve their aerodynamics, flight duration, and payload.

Grimacing, Adnan dragged his attention back to the road. *Don't get distracted*, he reminded himself.

Still, he couldn't help but pay attention to the car on the road behind him. It was unusually close to his own, almost tailgating him. The hair on the back of his neck stood on end. He slowed and flicked his indicator on once to let the driver know that they could overtake.

But nothing happened. Instead, the car behind sped up until it was only separated from his own by a few bumper lengths.

"What do you want?" he muttered, a faint sense of unease gripping his stomach.

Rationally, he understood that there was little to be afraid of. Keşan was a safe town. But there was no street lighting out here in the depths of the farmland, and the sea of darkness around the tiny island of light thrown by two sets of car headlamps felt all-encompassing.

"It's nothing," he said out loud, his voice reverberating around the car's cabin. "Just an asshole. Ignore him."

But was it nothing? That man from MIT had come to the office, what, a year earlier? He was an intelligence officer. A spy. He'd given a special contact number to all those present and asked them to report anything suspicious they came across, anything at all. That man had told him to trust the little voice inside his head, not ignore it.

"It might save your life."

Surely he was overthinking things? But as the car behind accelerated, its bumper practically kissing his own, Adnan felt sheer panic wash over him. He reached into his pants pocket for his phone, but the fabric was pulled taut now that he was sitting down, and he couldn't get his fingers into it.

At least not without adjusting his position and—

He nearly swerved off the road. Adrenaline battled panic in his body, a powerful flood of the stuff shocking him as it swept through his veins. He pulled his hand back up as though he'd been stung and slapped it onto the steering wheel, squeezing his knuckles tight around the scarred leather as he panted frantically.

"Think," he urged himself.

Deciding that he'd tried slowing down once already, this time Adnan stepped on the gas. His car—a sedate, slow sedan that his wife had decided was perfect for his particularly inept style of driving—took a few seconds to process the message before it began to accelerate.

It didn't help. The vehicle behind was much more powerful than his own. It was some kind of SUV, though it was difficult to be sure through the tiny mirror pane that sat above his dashboard. Adnan dared not take his eyes off the road for longer than a fraction of a second lest he plunge over the edge.

He was driving much faster than he ever had before. The speed terrified him, but not as much as whatever was happening behind.

And then there was another flash. Not just the bright white light of the chasing car's headlights, but a rotating blue.

Police!

"Thank God," Adnan moaned aloud, slumping forward for a second before straightening his posture behind the wheel. He was saved. Surely now this maniac behind him would give up his crazed pursuit.

Chips of stone and debris scoured the underside of his sedan as the distraction briefly caused him to dip off the side of the road, one tire clipping the dusty shoulder before he veered back onto the asphalt. He squeezed the steering wheel tight, clamping his foot all the way down on the gas pedal and peering out at the road ahead. There was a bend coming up, wasn't there? He couldn't lose focus now.

What's taking so long?

Adnan looked up at the review mirror once again, fear curdling into anger as he waited for the police car to stop—and arrest—the lunatic who was following him. His heart stopped. There was only one vehicle behind him. The SUV had a single blue strobe flashing on its dashboard.

He clamped his attention back to the road ahead. There it was, the bend, swinging around to his left. He braked sharply, and the SUV clipped his rear bumper, almost causing him to lose control of the speeding vehicle as he slowed. Everything he knew about driving was from playing games on his Xbox. These days he rarely found the time, but he'd played hour after hour of them during his twenties, even scouring the Internet for tips on how to drive better. He remembered that unless you accelerated out of a hard turn, you would veer off to the opposite side.

In the games, that only meant that somebody would overtake you. But since there was now a waist-high stone wall to his right, bordering a farmer's field, losing control would mean almost certain death.

Sweat trickled down Adnan's face. His mouth ran dry. He didn't have time to consider why this was happening; he could barely concentrate on controlling the vehicle itself with so much adrenaline flooding his system.

"Now," he yelled, reaching the apex of the band and stomping his foot on the accelerator once more. The sedan's puny engine didn't have the power of the imaginary race cars he'd driven all those years ago, but it gave him enough to yank him around the corner.

There was another couple of miles of straight road ahead, wasn't there? He thought so, anyway. The realization momentarily relaxed him and freed up some of his mental capacity for other thoughts.

Like: Why was a cop chasing him in the first place?

Some of his earlier panic started to fade. There had to be a simple explanation for this. At first, the unmarked police car had only tailgated him. The real craziness only began after the blue lights started flashing.

And then it came to him. Adnan felt so stupid he almost thumped his forehead against the steering wheel. If he had, the horn would have beeped a clownish groan, echoing the way he currently felt.

This was a test.

It was so obvious now. The security services had warned all of Baykar's key employees that they would occasionally have Turkish counter-intelligence agents following them, checking up on them, making sure they weren't being targeted by foreign spies.

They hadn't mentioned an event like this, but it was the only explanation now that he came to think of it. The only time the SUV had come close to actually endangering his life was when *he* had braked sharply as the bend approached. And then it had immediately backed off. Even now, it was tailgating a few yards behind—but if this was a real psychopath, wouldn't he be running into the back of him right now?

Adnan felt almost dizzy with relief. His palms grew sweaty as he began to wonder how he should apologize to the agents. Would he get in trouble for running? He would have to explain that he'd been terrified, that he'd misinterpreted the situation.

He could hear their voices already: "Don't you know you're supposed to stop when you're pulled over by a police officer?"

He picked his hand off the steering wheel and waved it between the headrests to signal that he'd finally understood, a broad, almost drunken smile now creasing his face as the panic faded. He reached forward and touched his hazard lights, and finally—almost surprised it was still pushed all the way down—lifted his foot off the gas pedal.

The sedan slowed, and he finally brought it to a stop about fifty yards ahead. The police, or was it the security services, SUV backed off the instant he indicated he was stopping, only confirming his earlier suspicion that he'd gotten it all wrong.

He practiced his apology in a low voice as the SUV rolled to a halt behind him. He grabbed his company ID badge from his pocket and clutched it in one hand. They would know who he was, of course, but it couldn't hurt to remind them that he was an important man. They would let him off with a warning. Heck, maybe they would even be impressed with his evasive driving.

Adnan glanced back up to the rearview mirror that had caused him so much stress over the past—how long? Was it really only a couple of minutes? It felt like a lifetime. Two were emerging from the unmarked car. It looked like they both wore windbreakers, like federal agents in American movies, but the SUV's powerful headlights were beaming into the mirror and made it difficult to make out anything more detailed than a pair of dark silhouettes.

"I'm sorry, officers," he repeated one last time. "I thought—well, I don't know what I thought. I was told I was a security target. I never believed it, not until you—"

The officers closed in. One walked up either side of his sedan. Adnan glanced past the passenger seat to his left, then heard tapping against the window to his right. His head turned naturally in the direction of the sound, and when he saw what was causing it, he audibly gulped.

It was a pistol.

They're overdoing it, aren't they?

Adnan wound down the window as he was directed, peering up at the cop's face. He could make out little detail in the dark. The officer flashed his ID too quickly to read and then said, "I need you to get out of the car."

"Of course," Adnan agreed instantly, reaching for the door handle before fully processing the man's words.

It was only after he was swinging his legs out of the car that something curious occurred to him. The cop's Turkish was accented, as though it was a second language. He sounded like many of the Syrian refugees that had settled in the area since that country's civil war.

But that didn't make any sense. Would the Millî İstihbarat Teşkilatı—the National Intelligence Organization—really hire a foreign citizen for such a sensitive role? Surely not.

Or maybe, he reassured himself, the man had simply been deployed in Syria. Some people picked up accents like a holiday tan, didn't they?

"Are you from the security services?" he asked in a low voice. "I'm sorry, I didn't mean—"

His voice fell away as the two men traded a look. It was

clear they had no idea what he was talking about. The officer on the passenger side opened the other car door, leaned across, and removed the keys from the ignition.

"What are you doing?" he protested.

"Is your name Adnan Gulen?" the man on his side asked, snapping his attention back.

He sounded official, despite the accent. Adnan replied automatically. "Yes. But—"

"I need you to come with us," he replied.

"But I'm going home. To my wife..." Adnan stammered, not understanding, his voice finally trailing away.

The cop reached into his pocket and pulled out a cell phone. He turned the screen on, then spun it around. There was a picture on the screen. No, a live video. Adnan frowned as he squinted at it.

"This is where you are going?" the man asked.

Fresh terror flooded Adnan's limbs. "That's my house. Why are you filming my house?"

The man—definitely not a cop—raised his pistol and placed it against Adnan's forehead. "You're going to record a message to your wife. Telling her you're not coming home. Telling her you're never coming home."

"But she's expecting me. I texted her..."

"Make a choice, Mr. Gulen. Your life or your children's?"

16

"You should get some sleep," Trapp said as he sidled up behind Madison.

She whirled around, almost sending the cell phone she'd been fiddling with flying across the spartan intelligence facility. She tightened her grip to prevent it at the last moment, taking a deep breath before setting it down on the trestle table in front of her, where it rested alongside a dozen or more similar devices, all hooked up to wires.

"You frightened me," she said, slightly breathless.

Trapp shot her an apologetic smile.

"Didn't mean to. I guess I can walk too quietly for my own good, sometimes." He frowned. "Have you even showered?"

Madison theatrically lifted her left arm and took a loud sniff. "Do I smell that bad?"

"Not *that* bad," Trapp laughed. "But pretty ripe."

"Thanks," she fired back. "That's just what every lady likes to hear."

"What are you doing, anyway?" Trapp asked. He scanned the table in front of her, easily picking out the cell phone they'd found in al-Shakiri's prison cell by the elastic band that held the battery in place. His gaze passed across the other phones next. "Where did all these come from?"

"The dead." She shrugged. "Muniz and his men have been bringing a new one in every couple of hours. Mostly from the bodies of the ISIS fighters who attacked the prison to trigger the escape. The SDF don't have the resources to exploit them."

"You've been here all evening?"

"What time is it?" Madison inquired absently, turning back to her work.

"Almost midnight. I figured you were in bed."

"I probably should be," she admitted, relaxing back into the wheeled office chair she'd burst out of when he first entered. "But I think I'm on to something."

She rolled left along the table to a large, curved LCD screen. It was the kind of device you expected to see in a high-end electronics shop, not an austere converted hangar in the back end of nowhere. Trapp followed, observing how the rat's nest of black wiring attached to each of the cell phones fed into Madison's computer.

"Show me," he said.

"I was getting to that."

She shook her mouse, waking up the screen to reveal a computer program that Trapp didn't recognize, then tapped a few commands into her keyboard. The software was some kind of data visualization tool. To the left of the screen, he saw icons representing each of the recovered cell phones with faint dotted lines drawn between them. The right hand of the screen contained a dense text box filled with phone numbers, addresses, and geographic coordinates.

"I cross-referenced the data on both the flash memory and SIM cards found in each of these phones," she said, indicating the devices taken from the fallen ISIS fighters, "with the one we think is linked to al-Shakiri."

Madison tapped another command into the computer

without looking at the keyboard, bringing an icon that Trapp figured represented that cell phone into the center of the data view. The other devices orbited around it like planets around a sun.

"And?" Trapp prompted.

She snapped around, fixing him with a cold glare. "I was getting to that," she said.

Not for the first time.

Trapp held his hands above his head. "I surrender."

Pointing at the cell phone he recognized, Madison said, "That's the one we took from al-Shakiri's cell. I'm calling it Object A."

"Okay."

"Object A hasn't made a single call to any of these numbers," she said, waving her hand across the other cell phones.

"Damn."

"But..." Madison grinned, tapping a line of text on her computer monitor. "It did place repeated calls to *this* number, each usually only lasting a few minutes. But that's happened over two dozen times during the last two weeks."

"Why that timeframe?" Trapp wondered aloud. He snapped his fingers. "His counterpart got a new burner."

"That's my best guess," Madison agreed. "The interesting thing is that Objects D, G, and K were all in contact with that same number at least once in the past seven days."

"You work quick," Trapp said, impressed.

"It's mostly the software," she said modestly. "All I did was plug in the wires and wait for it to spit out its analysis. But it confirms what we thought all along. Our guy didn't just take advantage of a prison break—he planned it."

Trapp nodded. "I agree. This phone number has to belong to an individual that al-Shakiri was using as a messenger, an in-between. Maybe Usman Tariq, maybe someone else. If we find that person..." he said, spreading his hands.

"Maybe we find our fugitive," Madison said. She moved her mouse and double-clicked an icon. "Luckily for you, I've got more good news."

A satellite map appeared on the computer monitor, overlaid with map data and other annotations that Trapp didn't recognize. It took several seconds to fully render on-screen. Madison worked the scroll wheel on her mouse until the picture zoomed into a grid square that the scale in the bottom right told Trapp was a mile on either side. The image showed a town surrounded on all sides by desert. Probably a few thousand residents.

"What am I looking at?"

"We have a line into the cell network in this region. Metadata only. We can't listen into phone calls, but we can tell roughly where the phone was located when it placed a particular call."

She typed a command into the computer, and two dozen red crosses appeared on the map overlay, mostly clustered around one apartment block on the bottom right of the grid square.

"These are all the triangulation points for our target's cell phone. Some of them are fuzzier than others—usually when the call only lasted a few seconds. His—or their—phone always placed the calls. Powers up, places the call, powers down. Rarely turned on long enough to get a good fix. Except the ones from Object A. He always *received* them. Right on the hour, same time every day."

Trapp raised an eyebrow. "You think our guy's a woman?"

"Not likely." Madison snorted. "You know what these misogynistic assholes are like. They wouldn't know talent if it hit them in the mouth."

"Preach," he replied dryly before tilting his head to his right shoulder and stretching out his neck, then repeating the stretch on the other side.

"That's better," he groaned, refocusing his gaze on the apartment building now outlined in red. "This is great work. This looks like the location this whole prison break was planned from. If we get lucky, someone there might know what happened to al-Shakiri."

"So what we do now?"

"We need to hit that building. Tonight."

~

THE MARINE GENERAL leading the special forces taskforce in the region swept into the airbase's cramped conference room with little ceremony, followed by a menagerie of staff officers and other aides. Muniz brought up the rear. He was dressed in casual clothing and clutched a can of energy drink, the metal slightly crumpled by his grip. Trapp recognized a few faces from the makeshift command center near the prison, now etched a little more deeply with exhaustion.

General Eric Espinoza showed no such human frailty. He looked almost a foot shorter than Trapp, his head so devoid of hair that he wondered whether he'd shaved it just before stepping into the conference room. He had that kind of ineffable mix of energy and ambition that propels so many Type A personalities through their lives. Trapp guessed there wasn't an obstacle in his entire career that the diminutive yet powerfully built Marine hadn't either dismantled or simply barreled right on through.

"At ease," he said, irritably gesturing for those arrayed around him to be seated. "Someone tell me what this is about."

"Thanks for arranging this, brother," Trapp murmured as Muniz took a seat beside him. "I owe you one."

"If your intel's good, I'll give you a pass," his old friend replied. "I want this guy as badly as you do."

"It's good," Madison said firmly, her voice cutting through the background murmur of lower-pitched male tones. She was standing in front of the projector screen on the far end of the room, a laptop poised on a stand by her side.

"I'll be the judge of that, Ms. Grubbs," General Espinoza said without cracking a smile. "Proceed."

"Yes sir." She nodded, lifting her laptop screen up and tapping the space key to bring up the first slide.

The projector took a couple seconds to warm up before the beam of bright white light shot out its front end. The slides that appeared on the screen were typically CIA-drab, though Trapp appreciated that Madison had resisted the urge to fill up the white space with al-Shakiri's shoe size, the name of his childhood doctor, and his wife's blood type. She understood what many analysts didn't: Less is more.

"This is Khaled al-Shakiri," she said, drifting a red laser pointer over the terrorist's prison intake photograph, then a fuzzy image of the same man taken from one of the cell's overhead surveillance cameras.

She gestured at Trapp before continuing. "It is the Agency's working theory that al-Shakiri was responsible for planning and executing the assault on al-Shaddadi yesterday morning."

"Was it yesterday already?" somebody quipped from the back of the room, drawing an irritated grimace from Espinoza.

"Let the woman speak," he said, rapping his knuckles on the table in front of them to reinforce the point.

"Sir." She nodded. "In the days and weeks leading up to yesterday's assault, the NSA picked up a number of phone calls from insurgent communities inside Syria. Where it was possible to intercept the contents themselves, they used coded language which analysts at Fort Meade have as yet been unable to decipher. However, they all had one thing in common: They referred to someone or something known as the Hand of God."

"And you think that's what they call your guy?"

"That was my theory, General," Madison agreed. "It was on the basis of this intelligence that my colleague and I were due to interview—and hopefully confirm the identity of—this individual yesterday morning."

"Quite the coincidence, don't you think?" one of Espinoza's aides asked. "He's been sitting in that prison for five years, and then the same day you turn up, he manages to break free."

Madison raised her eyebrow before Trapp could intervene on her behalf. She fixed the man with an icy stare. "Are you implying I had something to do with his escape, Captain?"

"Of course not," the man blustered. "It's just—"

"Interesting," Madison said drily. "So you said. It's not interesting at all, at least not to me. It's downright obvious."

"How so?" the officer asked, white-lipped now that he knew the attention of the entire room—and of his commanding officer in particular—was turned on him.

"I'm surprised you need me to walk you through it, Captain," she said. "But we like to offer the platinum package here at the Agency. So here goes: It's not a coincidence that I was there the same day as the escape. The intercepted phone calls are *why* I was there. Hand of God is a known nom de guerre of Khaled al-Shakiri—"

"Move on, please," General Espinoza murmured, flicking his hand as if bored. "What do you have for me that is operationally relevant *now*?"

Madison tapped her keyboard once more, and a fresh slide appeared: a map of the region, with a grid square of ten miles by ten miles marked out in red. Another tap, and half a dozen similarly-colored dots blinked into life.

"These are the locations of the calls we intercepted in the weeks leading up to the attack. My theory is that these were recruiting efforts. The person responsible for coordinating the attack needed enough warm bodies for a reasonable chance of success. And to get them, he needed to trade on someone else's reputation."

"Al-Shakiri's," Espinoza said.

"Exactly." Madison nodded. Trapp sensed she was pleased by the general's contribution, though she hid it well. You always wanted your principal engaged, even if they were firing critical questions your way. Because the alternative was boredom, disinterest, and bureaucratic torpor, and those enemies were more lethal than any weapon.

"After the attack," she continued, tapping her laptop one final time to display the smaller grid square that Trapp had first seen a couple of hours before, "we discovered a phone in the target's prison cell. It had only ever dialed one number, which we've geo-located to this building. We believe that's where al-Shakiri's partner—the individual who likely coordinated this attack—is located."

"Do you have a name?"

"Some suspects, but nothing definite," she replied.

Trapp leaned forward over the lip of the desk and set his elbows down on top of it. He clasped his hands, then cleared his throat. "General, we need to hit this building immediately. There's a chance that the fugitives don't yet know we're on to them. It's possible that al-Shakiri himself might be at that location."

Espinoza studied the map in silence for a few moments. "I find that unlikely."

"General—"

Holding up his hand to forestall Trapp's protests, Espinoza said, "Before you say anything else, Mr.—" He paused, reframing before continuing. "I intend to approve this strike. We got lucky intercepting these calls once. Maybe our adversaries are sloppy enough to allow that to happen again. Maybe we pick up al-Shakiri's partner, a phone, or a computer. But you know as well as I do that the man himself is long gone."

"Thank you, sir," Trapp replied, consciously having to force himself to relax after pumping himself up with adrenaline in preparation for a cockfight. He pushed his chair back, already mentally going over the equipment and kit he'd need. "I appreciate it. I'll need to see an armorer before it goes down."

The general didn't react. "I don't see why."

"I thought I was coming here for a vacation." Trapp grinned in response. "Answer a few questions, confirm an identity, then spend a week in the sun. I didn't think to bring my rifle."

"Perhaps I misspoke. I meant to say: I don't see why you'll need one," Espinoza replied, standing and turning to leave. "Staff Sergeant Muniz and his team will handle the operation. You and Ms. Grubbs can observe it from right here on base."

"No way," Trapp snapped, biting down a sudden burst of rage. "I need to be there."

"I don't give a damn about your intentions," Espinoza replied. "My men will handle this. You do not have my consent for a ridealong. My decision is final."

"This was our catch," Trapp protested, making a note to apologize to Madison later for stealing her glory. "We have a right to be there when it goes down."

"You don't have a right to squat. Not on my base. Not in this country, you understand?" Espinoza said, shooting Trapp a glare that might have turned a boot private to stone. "This is my turf. I don't know you from Adam. My boys train every day as a team to be the best at what they do. Are you on that team? Because I sure haven't seen you at the range. You being there, no matter how good you are, puts my boys in danger. And for that I will not stand."

Trapp bristled at the perceived slight to his professionalism. His fists clenched. He was about to say something he would probably regret when he felt Muniz's hand closing around his forearm.

"It's okay, brother," his friend said. "I've got this. You know I'm good for it."

Memories of al-Shakiri's crimes the last time he was out here in the desert invaded Trapp's mind. The terrorist deserved to die—and he wanted to be the one who put a bullet between his eyes. But as he cast around the room in search of support, he caught Madison's instead. She shook her head ever so slightly, and instantly he felt himself relent.

The tension held for a moment longer, but finally it broke. Espinoza seemed satisfied that he'd made his point.

"Dammit," Trapp breathed as the general marched out of the room. "What an asshole."

"He's not," Muniz said with a smile creasing his features. "He just doesn't know you. Once he does, there's no battle he won't fight on your behalf. But until then, there's no changing his mind."

"I see that," Trapp replied, shaking his head as he reflected on how he might have handled the conversation better. "I blew that, huh?"

Muniz stood and slapped him on the back. "You make a hell of a first impression, man. You really do. But if it helps—he ain't the type to hold a grudge."

17

"Comm check," Master Sgt. Muniz said into his throat mic, transducers converting the vibrations in his larynx into a digital signal before it went out over the encrypted radio.

He listened as the members of the operation's various strike teams checked in. He was at the top of his game, he knew. But he was also uncomfortably aware that his hot streak couldn't last much longer. He was nearly forty years old.

Thirty-six, he reminded himself.

But the two ages weren't so different. Maybe the Army would allow him to do this job for another two or three years before they tried to stick him behind a desk. He'd rather join the Marines and chew crayons eight hours a day than suffer that fate.

"Copy," he finally murmured. "Flight time's under fifteen minutes today, gentlemen. I expect to see you all safe and sound back at base tonight. Happy hunting. Out."

A separate radio channel to command constantly filtered useful—and sometimes not so useful—information in through his earpiece. A surveillance drone operated by the Air Force was in a holding pattern thousands of feet above the target location, sending a constant feed of high-quality video back to Khirbet-Al-Jeer Air Base.

As far as the reconnaissance analysts could tell, the apartment was still occupied. An hour ago, a military-age male had exited the building, climbed onto an ancient motorcycle, and disappeared before returning fifteen minutes later with a pair of gallon-drums of drinking water strapped to his bike and hauling them back through his front door.

Since they'd only acquired the target location a few hours earlier, there hadn't been time to run a full pattern-of-life analysis. That precluded ordering a kinetic strike to simply wipe whoever was unlucky enough to reside inside off the face of the map.

But Muniz never liked that kind of job. He preferred to get up close and personal with the bad guys his unit hunted day after day, night after night. Explosives got messy. Not usually literally, since the fissile component of a JDAM was usually sufficient to convert an insurgent's body into pure energy, but because you never learned who had gotten hit.

Could be the guy you were hunting. Could be his wife.

Or his kid.

No, this was where Muniz came alive. Dropping out of the belly of a Blackhawk as the chopper decelerated from cruising speed to a dead stop in a matter of seconds, rappelling down a rope, and sticking the muzzle of his rifle in the face of the men he was there to kill.

Not tonight.

"Remember, this is a rollup job," he radioed. "If we can take our targets alive, we do. They can't talk if they're dead."

A stream of acknowledgments—and ribald jokes—followed his urging but died away quickly. He knew why. Every man was currently in the grip of his own private ritual. Some prayed. Some tried to block all thoughts out of their mind.

Some nearly shit themselves. Muniz had cycled through each method in turn at some point in his career.

Right now, he liked to talk.

"Jealous yet, Hangman?" he transmitted over the command channel, knowing that the man he'd cut his teeth under in the special operations world had to be on the other end, choking down crude-oil coffee and fuming that he wasn't involved.

"Fuck no," Trapp replied a couple of seconds later in a tone of studied indifference. "I always saw myself as officer material, you know? Hang back at some nice air-conditioned base with my feet up. Get my nails done. That's the life."

"That's a lie." Muniz grinned. "This is killing you. Don't try to deny it."

"Yeah," came the grudging response. "Maybe you're right."

"Maybe," he repeated as the nerves returned. Overhead the thump-thump-thump of the rotor blades cutting through the air fell into time with his breathing. Too fast. He had to master the anxiety, not give in to it.

He closed his eyes, taking in deep, steady breaths through his mouth and exhaling them through his nose. For a time, nobody spoke, not inside the chopper, and not on the radio. Even command seemed to be holding its breath.

The nerves faded. They always did.

"Two minutes out," the crew chief transmitted over the bird's internal channel.

"Go time," Muniz murmured to himself.

"Street's still clear," came the confirmation from command.

It was good news. Muniz's chopper was to stop over the target building itself, but the second Blackhawk was tasked to land on the road outside to disgorge its cargo so that the two strike teams could hit the building simultaneously from different infiltration points. If the drone operator had reported that the road was now blocked, the operators would have had to rappel onto the asphalt—dicey with an unknown vehicle in the way.

"Copy," he radioed before switching channel and transmitting a final message to his men.

"Mission is go as planned. Happy hunting."

TRAPP TENSED his legs as he stood in the back of the command center in a forlorn attempt to stop them from shaking with adrenaline. The wall opposite him, on the other side of a line of desks occupied by smart, hard-working young men and women tapping away on keyboards, looked like something out of *Call of Duty*.

Nine huge television screens had been fastened together to form one single unit. It was mostly dominated by the live feed from the surveillance drone, which was currently feeding infrared image back to base. It was 5 a.m. Not yet light.

Between the high-fidelity footage and the terse radio transmissions that he'd spent most of his adult life making—rather than being on the other end of—he almost felt like he was in combat himself.

"You okay?" Madison asked, apparently detecting a change in his breathing. She was standing alongside him, equally useless to the final outcome of the operation. They had each done their part. Now it was up to Muniz and his elite team of special operators.

"I don't like sitting on my hands," Trapp groused.

"You're standing," she pointed out dryly. "And besides, I was in that room. It didn't sound like you had any other choice."

"I guess not."

"You ever think about working on your people skills, Jason? I know someone. She does NLP. Have you heard of it? It stands for—"

"Neuro-linguistic programming," Trapp replied, shooting Madison an icy stare. "I'm not letting some quack poke around in my head, not for all the gold in Fort Knox."

"How do we know there's any gold there, anyway?" she replied, cocking her head quizzically. "Maybe Jimmy Carter stole it all, and the government's spent the last fifty years covering it up."

"Carter? I have my doubts," Trapp replied.

"He was into peanuts, right?" she continued. "Looot of money laundering in the peanut game."

Trapp frowned. "Seriously?"

"No, not seriously," Madison laughed quietly. "And Carter of all people? Crappy president, but he's practically a saint. Took your mind off things, though, didn't it?"

"Yeah," he admitted. "I suppose it did."

"Just let me know when you want my friend's number. I won't tell her what you said about her." She winked.

Then she straightened, instantly becoming all business, and nodded at the screen. "Looks like this thing is happening."

Two balls of white fire streaked across the bottom right of the drone's infrared feed. The Blackhawks. Their engines glowed like supernovas against the cool of night. They flew in tight formation. He could picture what the men inside were seeing, a composite built from hundreds of similar missions in his own past.

As Trapp watched, he heard the radio transmissions from the ground support team as they reported they were on schedule. He could see the GPS dots that represented their vehicles on a map to the right of the drone feed. They were speeding toward the target building with sufficient leeway built into their timings that they would arrive five minutes after the choppers. Enough breathing room to make sure that they didn't accidentally tip off the bad guys that something was happening, close enough behind to secure the scene for the intelligence teardown.

And in case shit hit the fan.

"Thirty seconds," a female voice said over the command center's speakers. Trapp could see her lips moving as she dipped them to the microphone. It was delayed by about half a second. Long enough to lend it an uncanny valley sensation, as if he was watching a movie rather than real life.

As her voice faded away, the command center grew oppressively silent. Dozens of men and women all brought together for one purpose, and in that moment entirely and uniformly impotent.

"Ten seconds."

The nose of the lead Blackhawk shifted almost imperceptibly upward on the drone footage. Trapp could feel the stomachs dropping out from underneath the operators currently inside as the powerful helicopter bled off speed and altitude. His trigger finger itched from the desire to be doing something useful instead of sitting here, riding a desk.

They didn't even give you one of those.

Several bright flashes strobed on the infrared footage. Trapp tensed.

"What is it?"

Before he had a chance to answer Madison's question, one of the pilots radioed, her tone rising in inflection as the stress washed over her, "This is a hot LZ. Repeat, hot LZ. I've got incoming!"

"I guess we know it's the right place," Trapp murmured, briefly tipping his head back and whispering a silent prayer for the safety of the men currently putting their lives on the line for a public who would never know their feats.

Or fates.

"Somebody doesn't want to be found," Madison agreed, her lips pursed with anxiety. "Let's just hope it's the right someone."

He nodded. There were a lot of people in this part of the world who would prefer to stay hidden. Most of them would rather take their chances in a gunfight rather than handing themselves over to suffer an unknown fate.

"Suppressing fire," a voice ordered. The throat mics didn't pick up gunfire, so Trapp could see the occasional muzzle flash erupt out of the side of the two Blackhawks, but not hear the familiar sound. After a couple of seconds of shooting, the chopper tasked to hit the roof moved into position.

"Alpha, go," came a terse command.

Trapp could have described the scene on that rooftop with a hundred percent fidelity even with his eyes closed. A pair of thick, curled nylon ropes were launched off the chopper's side, uncoiling as they tumbled to the deck. Before they finished unspooling, the first pair of operators already had their gloves clamped around the thick cables and the ropes threaded through their thighs. The second two operators followed before their colleagues hit the deck, and then two more after that.

"Boots on the ground," Muniz's voice reported.

The Blackhawk immediately arrowed off to the side of the drone's coverage, rapidly gaining altitude and speed. In the street below, the second helicopter was almost finished unloading the other strike team.

But Trapp's eyes were focused on his friend's progress. He watched as all six operators converged on the trap door that led down into the apartment building. One of them affixed a precut length of det-cord and called out a warning a second before a bright flare showed up on screen.

"Flash out," came a second call a moment later. The detonation of the stun grenade inside the building was more muted on the footage. Before the monitor's pixels had adjusted to the illumination, the first of Muniz's men had launched himself inside.

"Clear," a tense voice reported.

Then silence. Trapp knew how events would unfold.

Muniz's team would proceed through the building, hunting for the insurgent who'd opened fire on the helicopters. They would move both fast and cautiously, as their colleagues did the same on the floor below.

"I see kids' toys," one of the operators warned. "Careful."

"This place is a fucking maze," another added.

"Hallway's clear."

"Taking fire!"

Then, "Tango down."

"Dammit, there's a kid in here. I repeat, there's definitely a kid in here. Another shooter too. They're in the same room."

Madison breathed out heavily. "Animals. What's going to happen?"

Trapp's jaw was clamped tightly shut, his eyes focused on a screen on the wall that was no longer telling him anything useful. The entire strike team was inside the target building. The ground support units would arrive at any moment.

He opened his mouth to reply, but by the time he'd formulated the first word, it was already too late.

The entire building exploded.

18

The chopper touched down in an empty field a five-minute walk away from the crater in order to avoid disturbing the ongoing rescue efforts.

But every single person involved knew that it was fruitless.

There were seven survivors. Only one of them was from Muniz's squad, and he'd already been medevacked out, his legs missing, and was probably already on a flight to the Army hospital in Germany.

None of the seven would be able to talk. At least not for a while. Their list of injuries was as severe as it was extensive. It was unlikely that many of them would ever return to active duty again.

"It was a trap," Madison whispered, sinking down onto her haunches as they approached the epicenter of the devastation. Only a third of the apartment building was still standing. It must have been packed with an almost incomprehensible weight of explosives.

Trapp remained standing, a muscle pulsating in his jaw. He swept his eyes across the rubble, knowing better than to hope that Muniz might be pulled out from its depths. "No shit."

She choked but said nothing. What was there to say? This was on both of them. They had found the cell phone, they had connected it to al-Shakiri's escape attempt, and they had done their damnedest to convince General Espinoza not just that the operation needed to happen—but that it needed to happen now.

Maybe with a little more due diligence, Master Sergeant Eddie Muniz might still be alive.

And the others.

Two dog handlers in US Army combat fatigues jogged through the rubble, their charges racing ahead of them. The dogs ran in wide arcs, doubling back on themselves over and over again, sometimes spinning in circles and eddies as they hooked on to some faint scent. They were trained to detect signs of life—breathing, movement, the human voice.

But they didn't alert once.

A line of black body bags studded the dusty ground beside a large tan MRAP. There were four of them. They were zipped, but not full. Trapp had seen that before, too. It was what happened when there wasn't enough left. It would take months of DNA analysis for forensic technicians to identify which part belonged to which body.

And only then would the families be offered any closure. Most wouldn't find it. Not now, not ever.

"How could you have been so stupid?" Trapp whispered to himself, his head sinking to his chest.

He should have found a way of being on that helicopter, no matter what Espinoza said. This was his play. Muniz had died because of him. And it should've been Jason Trapp who was first through that trapdoor because if anyone had to die for his call, it should have been him.

Rationally, he knew that his own death wouldn't help anyone. But at least there was no one left to mourn him. Muniz had family. He had friends. He was a damn fine soldier, and he didn't deserve to go out like this.

Trapp wandered through the rubble, searching for evidence, for any clue that might lead him to the man who had set all this in motion. But it was hopeless. The explosion had been so powerful, chunks of debris were turning up in fields half a mile away.

He replayed the final radio transmissions in his mind as he tried to picture what had happened in that building. They were garbled, tense.

"I see kids' toys. Careful."

"This place is a fucking maze."

"Hallway's clear."

"Taking fire!"

"Tango down."

"Dammit, there's a kid in here. I repeat, there's definitely a kid in here. Another shooter too. They're in the same room."

What was it that Madison had said about their enemy? She'd called them animals. And she was right. What kind of monster would use a child as bait to lure the operators hunting them deeper into their mousetrap? To do so knowing that an innocent would die as a result?

"Animals," he repeated aloud.

And that was exactly what had happened, he knew. Al-Shakiri hadn't just planned his own escape from prison; he'd played out what would happen after as well. He knew that America wouldn't stop hunting him just because he'd like it that way, so he'd drawn up a scheme that would allow him to strike back.

But that was his mistake.

"This is my fault, Jason," Madison whispered.

He turned, not realizing that she'd sidled up beside him until now. Her clothes were coated with dust, and she was holding her elbows, arms clamped around her body. She was trembling.

"It's on both of us," he said gruffly. There was no sense shying away from the truth. Better to face it head-on, no matter how much it hurt. It was only then that you could look to the future. To payback. "We sent these men to die."

Madison flinched at the impact of his words. If she'd come to him for comfort, she hadn't found it. But he sensed that wasn't why she was here.

She swallowed. "No. I did this. I thought I had it all figured out. I didn't stop to think that maybe that bastard was one step ahead of me."

"We sent these men to die," Trapp repeated. "And that's on us. Eddie was my friend. I've known him a long time. And you want me to tell you something?"

She nodded.

"Every day he laced up his boots, he knew it might be for the last time. You have to if you want to survive in this business. You start thinking any other way, you'll lose your mind. Better to just accept it. Yeah, we sent him to die. But if it wasn't us, it would've been some other jackass. Maybe it's better it was people he knew who did it."

"How—how can you say that?" Madison asked haltingly, stumbling over her words as though she was drunk. She was in shock.

Trapp finally tore his gaze away from the destruction and turned to face her, an agony deep within his chest, like vinegar pouring into an open wound. He thought about embracing her but decided against it. That wasn't what she needed right now. Better to tell her the truth. It was the only way to see what she was made of.

Or maybe you're just lashing out…

"Because it doesn't matter what we did. You and I, we'll both hold on to that pain the rest of our lives. What matters now is what we do next."

"We've got nothing," Madison hiccuped. She pressed her hand across her mouth, embarrassment briefly overcoming shock. "He's long gone, and we don't have a single other lead."

"You're wrong," Trapp said.

Maybe it was his tough love, or maybe it was just Madison's natural personality breaking through, but she screwed up her face with confusion—and hunger. It was being a dog with a bone that had gotten her this far. And she hadn't lost the scent.

"What are you seeing that I'm not?" she demanded, glancing around as though she expected to see something she'd so far missed.

"Nothing," he said.

Her expression darkened. "Jason—!"

He held up a finger. "Nothing here. And there won't be. He's too clever to lure us to a place where there would be anything to find. But he made a mistake. Hubris drove him here, not strategy."

"I don't understand."

"He should have just disappeared. He would have been a needle in a haystack of escaped terrorists. You could merge all the three-letter agencies, and there still wouldn't be enough resources to track them all down. After a week without a sniff, we'd have given up the chase."

"The hell I would," Madison snorted.

"You," Trapp said, his face breaking into a one smile. "Maybe not. Me neither. But I guarantee the rest of the world would have moved on. There's always another threat. Another fire to fight, and never enough water. You know how it is."

"Let's say you're right," she admitted grudgingly. "I still don't understand where you're going with this."

"He thinks he's smarter than us," he said, dragging his incisors across his bottom lip almost hard enough to tear the skin. He gestured at the devastation in front of them, savoring the metallic taste of blood. "Maybe he was right. *Once.* But now he's on the run. He has to bat a thousand every single day. It's our job to make sure that's not good enough."

Madison nodded slowly. "But why go to all this trouble? Why not just run?"

"First," Trapp said wryly, "we're infidels. I'd be more worried if he wasn't trying to blow us up."

"And second?" Madison asked quickly, not buying Trapp's weak attempt at humor. He wasn't fooling either of them. This one was going to hurt for a long time.

"He's angry," he replied. "He was in that prison cell for a long, long time. A man like that, it's gotta hurt. He thinks he's smarter than the rest of the world. And yet the rest of the world got to live their lives while he rotted behind bars. This was him trying to get revenge. And it's going to be what helps us catch him in the end."

19

"Thank you, Abdul," Madison said, pulling a thin silk shawl from her head as a heavy metal door swung shut behind her. She arranged it around her shoulders. "You didn't have to do this."

The militia prison commander wore a sweat-stained uniform that clearly hadn't been washed in days. It was marked with rubble, dust, and the grime of combat. Trapp immediately respected the man for joining his soldiers on the front line rather than leading from behind a laptop screen.

"I didn't," he said. "And yet I had to. I've lost many friends over the previous two days. I want to know why."

"That's what we intend to find out." Madison nodded. "And thank you anyway. I appreciate it."

"Your general is looking for you," he replied obliquely.

"So we hear," Trapp replied.

Abdul exhaled. His face was lined with wrinkles, and the bags under his eyes were as black as mid-winter mud. But then, Trapp realized, so were his. And Madison's. All three of them looked like they felt. There was only so long you could push the human body before it visibly started to fall apart.

Facial exhaustion was merely a leading indicator of system collapse.

"Then I pray you get what you need. My men know to help however they can."

"Whatever we find out, we'll share with you, Abdul," Madison promised.

The commander reached out and grasped her hands. He squeezed them softly, then said, "I know you will. I have enjoyed working with you, young lady. I suspect it will not be for much longer."

He turned on his heel and left the temporary holding facility. It was a warehouse that had had been converted into a prison in which to hold and process inmates that had escaped from al-Shaddadi. The captured prisoners were audible through the thin corrugated iron wall that separated the holding area from the section of office space they were standing in.

Madison walked to a trestle table stacked with manila folders containing what—usually little –was known about every recaptured inmate who had ever crossed paths with al-Shakiri. No matter how briefly. They were arranged in two piles, one half the size of the others. She started leafing through them.

It was grunt work, but they had no other leads. And right now, grunt work was exactly what they both needed. Anything to distract the mind from endless recrimination.

"If the scuttlebutt has reached him..." Trapp remarked, shrugging his shoulders as his voice faded away.

"I know. We don't have long."

"Then we'd better get started."

Madison nodded. She pushed the larger of the two stacks of folders toward him.

"Did I lose the toss?" he protested mildly.

She tapped the smaller pile in response, then gestured at

the shawl around her shoulders. "These belong to the wounded. From what Abdul told me, half of them have lost limbs. The SDF doctors didn't have the time to try and save their legs and arms as well as their lives."

"Or the inclination," Trapp interrupted darkly.

"Or that," she agreed. "But they've pumped the invalids full of painkillers. Strong ones. They might talk to me."

"But the others won't," Trapp said, understanding. The rest of the inmates would be tired, hungry, and most of all angry that their short-lived break for freedom had been exactly that. It was unlikely he would be able to convince any of them to talk. And for Madison?

Impossible.

"Exactly."

"So what am I working with?" he asked, appreciating that the captured prisoners' mental state, despite everything, wasn't completely against him. The inmates would be bereft, their hopes of escape, perhaps fanned over many months or years, shattered in an instant. "I need something to offer them."

Madison reached into a thigh pocket in her pants and pulled out a small pair of pliers. She offered them to him. "Abdul gave me these," she said.

"Very funny."

"He really did offer," she said, her expression betraying her confidence about what came next. "I'm pretty sure he was joking."

"Not in this part of the world."

"We don't exactly smell of roses either," she pointed out.

"Fair point."

She shot him a wry smile. "Since we can't offer them a reduction in their sentence, Abdul told me I can at least promise anyone who talks their own cell. Better food. Maybe even a phone call to relatives once every few months."

"Generous," he replied, realizing that in comparison with

the conditions in genpop, it truly was. He picked up his stack of files and held them against his torso, large enough that he could barely fit his right arm around them. It was going to be a long day.

Madison shrugged. "Better than a kick in the teeth."

THE FIRST PRISONER said nothing as a pair of balaclava-clad SDF guards roughly dragged him into the interrogation room and manacled him to the table, the chain links pulled so tight he was forced to slump across it, his wrists stretched out.

Trapp raised an eyebrow but said nothing.

He scratched the side of his cheek with an extended index finger as one of the guards left the room, leaving the other to translate. The itch didn't fade. A thin manila folder rested on the table in front of him. Not the prisoner's. He reached down to the stack that sat on the floor to his lefthand side and plucked the topmost off it, spreading it out across its sibling.

The inmate photo that stared up out of it could—just barely, if you squinted in the right kind of light, be said to resemble the man chained opposite him. In the intake photo, the prisoner's head was covered in a thick carpet of black hair, and his beard had grown long. By contrast, this iteration's scalp had been roughly trimmed, and only a few days' stubble covered his chin.

Trapp tapped the file. "Your name is Mohammed, correct?"

Before the translator was halfway finished composing his sentence, Mohammed tossed his head back as far as the chains around his wrists allowed. Trapp saw what was coming an instant before it happened, but his chair leg caught the rough concrete ground, and he was unable to push it back in time to avoid the thick slug of saliva that the prisoner sent hurling through the air.

It landed on his left cheek, thick and warm, and hung there for a few seconds before it started to drip. It clung to his skin as it did so, coiling snakelike.

"Delightful," he murmured, reaching into his pocket for a rag with which to clean himself.

The translator-cum-guard sidestepped the table with surprising speed and slammed the prisoner's forehead against the steel. The ensuing crunch left no doubt as to the outcome for the soft cartilage and bone in his nose.

"Just take him," Trapp said tiredly.

"You don't want to talk?" the man inquired. "He will answer your questions. I promise."

Shaking his head, Trapp said, "No. He won't."

Minutes passed as the second guard returned, unlocked the prisoner's cuffs, and helped his buddy drag the insensible man away. Trapp leaned forward to wipe the blood from the table, and after a moment's consideration, decided to leave it where it was. He dumped the first file onto the floor on his right side.

The next prisoner carried in to meet him couldn't keep his eyes off the pool of blood, though that perhaps had something to do with the fact that he was bound even closer to it than his predecessor. The only problem was that he didn't know shit.

Nor the next, or the one after that.

In fact, Trapp was already almost a third of the way through the stack of files already, and the blood was only just starting to congeal. The little notepad he'd set alongside the folder in front of him, a ballpoint pen resting in a diagonal slash on top of it, was still empty.

He watched as his latest appointment was brought in. The only advantage of the repeated interrogations was that, despite their present lack of success, he was at least getting the chance to refine his technique.

"You want a coffee?" he asked, rubbing his eyelids as the interrogation room's gloom seemed to press down on his shoulders. "I could use one myself. I think it's the lack of natural light in here."

"I don't drink coffee," the man replied. In English. "It is haram."

"Your English is great," Trapp remarked. "Fine, no coffee. What about water?"

The inmate straightened as much as the chains would allow. It seemed to Trapp as though it was done with a sense of pride. "I am—was—an English teacher. I'm not thirsty."

He was talking, which Trapp took as a good sign. Most of the others had either kept their mouths clamped shut, or instead, their eyes had darted nervously around the room, often drifting across the masked face of the guard standing behind him. It was no surprise. Trapp suspected that everything said in this room would be reported back to Abdul the moment the session was over.

Or he's just listening in...

That option would be more efficient, though Trapp didn't voice his suspicion. Still, he wanted to put his new friend at ease. He twisted in his seat and eyed the guard. "Well, I could use a pick-me-up. I've been at this for hours. You mind?"

When the man made to lift his radio off his belt, Trapp shook his head. "You get it. And one for yourself while you're at it. I take it black, no sugar."

"What do you want?" the prisoner asked bluntly as the guard tramped from the room, his boot steps heavy. "I don't know who planned the breakout. I promise you this. I didn't even leave the prison grounds."

Trapp frowned with surprise. He opened the man's file but found that it was sparse. Little more than a photo, processing dates, and a list of cell numbers the presumably corresponded to where he'd stayed. He'd been incarcerated for five years. The last two of those had been in al-Shakiri's cell. He dragged his finger across the paper until he found the man's name.

"Really?"

"You sound surprised," Haidar said, the metallic chain links rattling against the steel table.

"Wouldn't you be?" Trapp asked. When he received no response, he continued, "Okay, I'll bite. Why didn't you try and escape?"

"I am an honest man. I was never guilty of the crimes I was accused of committing. But I was sentenced. I respected my sentence."

"So you stayed inside your cell?" Trapp asked, knowing full well that Haidar hadn't. "Must have been terrifying."

"No," he replied, passing a test he didn't even know he'd been set. "When the others escaped, I went with them. I wanted to see my daughters again. My wife. I don't even know if they're alive."

Trapp leaned forward. "But you didn't go through with it. You had the chance. Many others did. Even from your own cell."

"Maybe I should have," he replied morosely, slumping toward the table. "How can I ever look my daughters in the eye again, knowing that I could have seen them again, if only I had crossed through that hole in the walls? Will they ever forgive me?"

"I can't answer that. Tell me what held you back."

"I told you already," Haidar said, a flash of anger glinting in his tear-filled eyes. "I am not guilty. In fact, the guards here never accused me of a crime. I was in the wrong place at the wrong time, just trying to fetch water when I was captured and brought to that prison. I am not guilty, but when it came to it, I respected my sentence."

Trapp leaned back, impressed by the moral character of the kind of man who would tread such a path. Assuming, of course, that it was true.

He flipped open the other folder in front of him, revealing a page-sized photograph of al-Shakiri face down. It was the first time he'd made it this far with any of them. He turned it over and slid it toward Haidar.

"Do you know this man?" he asked simply.

"Of course," came the reply, though Haidar had barely glanced at it.

"Why do you say that?"

"I was in a cell with him for… months. Longer. I don't know how long."

"Two years," Trapp said, providing the answer.

Haidar's shoulders slumped. "If you say so."

"What is his name?"

"I don't know."

"You say you were in a cell with this man for two years and you can't tell me his name?"

Haidar's eyes flashed. "You said it was two years, not me. Besides, why should I tell you anything?"

Trapp paused a moment to consider his response. He sensed that bribery wasn't the correct path here. Every inmate ever sentenced proclaimed that they were innocent, and yet miraculously, in this case, he suspected it was the truth.

"His name is Khaled al-Shakiri," he said. "He is a very dangerous man. I'm trying to find him before he hurts somebody."

Haidar stiffened at the mention of al-Shakiri's name.

"You know him?" Trapp asked quickly.

"I've heard the name. Before."

He fell silent. Trapp didn't have to ask before what.

"So you know the kind of man he is?"

Haidar nodded. "I do."

"Then you know I need to find him. Will you help me?"

He held his breath as he waited for a response. He had conducted many interrogations across a long career, and there was always a moment when the subject decided to cooperate—or not. Trapp sensed he had reached it.

"I can't help you," Haidar replied, though in an almost disappointed tone. "Mostly he spoke to the big man. Omar. I knew he was in charge, but I tried to keep myself to myself in there. Many of the other prisoners were...unpleasant men. We only spoke once. He seemed pleasant. Well read. I didn't know who he really was then."

The lock on the metal door at the other end of the interrogation room clicked, and a moment later the heavy slab squealed open. The guard appeared holding a cup of coffee, bracketed in its frame. Trapp winced and held up a hand to forestall him.

"What did he say?"

A commotion echoed through the open doorway after he asked his question, and Trapp squeezed his thigh underneath the table in an attempt to hide his irritation. He wanted the door closed to block the source out, but not enough to distract Haidar from speaking.

"He just talked about... About home. He said he would go back there. I laughed, told him that this was the only home he would ever know. But he was insistent. He said that he would be back. He really seemed to believe it."

Raised voices carried through the open doorway. They grew louder and carried with them the unmistakable tone of argument.

"Did he say where home was?" Trapp asked, eyes flicking to the door, then back.

Haidar was distracted. He kept looking at the door and seemed anxious. The spell was broken.

"Anything you can remember," Trapp said softly. "Just tell me. You know the kind of guy al-Shakiri is. What he's capable of. You can help me put him away."

"Indonesia—"

The door to the interrogation room started to open, hinges squealing from the force with which it was pushed. Haidar shut down instantly, clamping his mouth shut. He retreated in on himself.

Dammit, Trapp thought, grinding his molars together. He had to fix this. Why now of all times?

He got his answer a moment later. General Espinoza stormed through the door, practically pushing the SDF guard out of his way. Madison trailed behind him.

"Trapp!" Espinoza shouted, his face red with anger. "Pack your bags and get the hell out of my sight. You're gone."

20

Trapp shot Haidar an apologetic glance, hoping to all hell that Espinoza hadn't blown the entire interrogation. Once they got talking, subjects rarely thought about stopping. Unless they were given an opportunity, neatly ribbon-tied, to reconsider whether it was really in their best interests.

He made for the door, passing the general's outstretched finger without reacting and not stopping until he was on the other side. The unexpected paucity of his response seemed to briefly take the wind out of Espinoza's sails. The three of them reassembled on the other side. Trapp got his shot in first.

"General, he's talking," he said in a low voice, hoping that it wouldn't carry through the warehouse's thin corrugated iron walls. "I don't know what he knows, but I'm certain we want to find out. Let me do my job."

The moment the words left his mouth, he sensed that he had said something wrong. Espinoza turned even more puce-red than he was before.

Not possible.

"I didn't ask you here, Trapp, but I'm damn sure going to be the one who orders you to leave. I lost good guys out there. Doesn't that mean anything to you?"

"Of course it does, General," Trapp said, knowing the officer wasn't in his right mind. This was special forces. He would have known the men he ordered into battle far more intimately than any ordinary commander. Grief was talking, not good sense.

"Eddie was my friend," he continued. "I've known him for years. Since he was just a kid starting out in the Army. I never wanted him to die. If it could have been me in his place, I would've traded gladly. But he knew the risks. Just like I do."

"I don't give a shit," Espinoza said brusquely, seeming to take criticism from Trapp's words rather than compassion. "You're done here, Trapp. Both of you. My people will take it from here. Langley's already been told. They concur with my assessment. You're on the next ride out of here, and if you think this is an ass-chewing, you have no idea what's coming. Now get out of my sight."

~

THE WHIRLWIND CHOPPER ride from Syria to the Iraqi Al-Harir Air Base, and the subsequent civilian contractor-operated passenger turboprop journey to the sprawling Al-Udeid Air Base in Doha, Qatar left little opportunity for Madison and Trapp to debrief on what the other had learned.

Nor did the trip afford the privacy in which to do so. Trapp had little doubt that eyes and ears on the various aircraft had been instructed to report anything they said back to General Espinoza. The man was angry, but he wasn't an idiot.

It wasn't until they landed in Qatar, where they waited for the next C-17 back to the United States operated by the 816th Expeditionary Airlift Squadron, that they found the opportunity to speak.

At least, Trapp did.

As they sweated in hundred-degree heat on the concrete floor of a tan-painted hardened aircraft hangar that wasn't equipped with air conditioning—but did have Wi-Fi—Madison pulled out her laptop.

"You aren't worried about that thing overheating?"

She didn't respond to his lame joke as her fingers sped across the keyboard. The computer's speakers emitted a continuous series of chimes as her email inbox connected with the Agency's secure servers.

"What did you learn?" Madison asked without looking up.

"Not much," Trapp admitted before filling her in on what he'd learned from the truncated interview. He suspected there was more that Haidar might've told him, but no smoking gun.

"Indonesia," Madison muttered, putting up a notetaking app on her laptop and typing a quick note. "It's worth looking into."

"You ever been?"

She shook her head.

"It's a big place. Covers a tenth of the world's landmass—at least it feels that way. Doesn't narrow things down much at all."

"It's a long shot, but we need to cover our bases."

"Did you get anything?" Trapp asked, slumping back against the concrete base of the hangar's wall. It was impossible to get comfortable no matter how he shifted his position. He held up his finger to forestall her answer. "One other thing—I need a favor."

She hiked an eyebrow. "Shoot."

"You and Abdul seemed to have an understanding. You think he'd take another look at the last guy I interviewed? I have his inmate number."

"To what end?"

"He's not guilty of anything other than being picked up in the wrong place at the wrong time. He's served five years for that crime. I'd like to see him walk. If not that, he should at least get his own cell—for his own protection as much as anything else. Word gets out that he talked..."

Trapp spread his hands. He didn't need to explain what would happen next.

Madison nodded. "I can ask."

After twisting his frame yet again, Trapp nodded his thanks. "Sorry, I interrupted you."

"No problem. I think I've got something, though I'm not sure what."

"Go on."

"It might just be rumor, but a couple of the guys I interviewed remembered al-Shakiri. From before, not just al-Shaddadi. It seems that he was assigned to some secretive operational cell."

"Doing what?"

"Best guess? International terrorism. Shock and awe kind of shit. Remember back at the caliphate's peak there was a series of terror scares? Explosives hidden in printers and laptops and that kind of thing. The idea was to ship them in aircraft cargo bays and have them detonate at 30,000 feet."

Madison made a muted explosion sound, then spread her palm flat and dove it toward the ground.

"Rings a bell." He nodded. "But I don't remember they had much luck. Mowing down pedestrians with a truck on a leafy boulevard in Nice isn't exactly 9/11."

She nodded. "Rumor is the NSA had them penetrated from day one. We were two steps ahead of them the entire time. That's why they had to resort to lone wolf attacks like Nice."

"So that was al-Shakiri's gig?"

"Not exactly. Seems he took over later on, after the worst of the previous cell's failures. After that, things went quiet. No attacks, but not because of anything we did."

"You think he was planning something big?" Trapp asked.

That was his operating assumption. The attack that had cost Muniz's life confirmed that for him.

"I do. I managed to get a list of three names, all known to have worked closely with al-Shakiri in the last few months of the territorial caliphate. All three of them were engineers."

She double-clicked her laptop's trackpad, then turned the screen so that he could see it. "This guy, Mihzir Khan, graduated the College of Aeronautical Engineering in Risalpur, Pakistan in 2014. Confirmed killed in the fall of Raqqa. The other two are whereabouts unknown. Likely dead, but we have no way of knowing for sure. Record-keeping wasn't exactly top of mind when the Coalition was pounding ISIS into dust."

"What do we know about them?" Trapp asked.

"I'll spare you the gory details. One dropped out of Al-Furat Al-Awsat Technical University in Najaf, Iraq, the other graduated second in his class at the National School of Civil Aviation in Toulouse, France."

"There's a common thread," Trapp murmured, feeling enlivened by the information, even if he didn't yet see where it led.

"Yup. All aerospace. My best guess is they were identifying weak points in passenger aircraft. Where to place explosives for maximum effect, that kind of thing. But that's all it is—a guess. Anyway, it's likely they are all dead. The question is: Did they finish their work before we slotted them?"

The pace of incoming messages to the laptop, at least judged by the irritating series of chimes, slowed as both fell silent to digest her question. It was replaced by a piercing whistle from an Air Force crew chief, who waved at them from the opposite side of the hangar, then jerked his thumb toward the runway.

"Looks like our ride's here," Trapp said, exhaustion returning after a brief flurry of excitement generated by Madison's revelations. There was definitely something here, but it was thin at best. A link to Indonesia, maybe something to do with passenger aviation. Whatever the through line was, it was harder to decipher than the Zodiac letters.

Madison's computer pinged one last time. She stood up, carrying it in one hand and swinging her rucksack over her opposite shoulder. Trapp grabbed her bags along with his duffel—which he'd barely had the opportunity to unzip, let alone unpack—ignoring her protestations.

His longer stride carried him a few steps ahead of her, helped by the fact that her eyes were glued to the laptop's screen. The crew chief yelled a second time for them to hurry up, his voice barely audible over the roar generated as the C-17's engines began spooling up behind him.

"Wait, I think I've got something," she said.

"Tell him that," Trapp said, jerking his thumb at the Air Force NCO. "Because I get the sense he doesn't plan on sticking around."

"I'm serious."

"So am I," he replied, taking in the crew chief's increasingly frantic gesticulations. He grabbed Madison's arm. "Fill me in en route."

They boarded and were unceremoniously shown to a row of airline-style passenger seats bolted on to the Globemaster's floor and sandwiched between lines of large steel cargo pallets. In lieu of a business class-style amenities kit, they found two sets of ear defenders lying on their seats. Trapp wondered if Espinoza had arranged for treatment this spartan, or whether the Air Force's logisticians were just having a particularly bad day.

"Better get comfortable," he remarked as the warning tone for the C-17's rear door sounded. "Gonna be a long flight."

Madison, eyes still glued to her laptop screen, made a generic murmur of agreement. She glanced around to see if anyone was listening in, then appeared to decide that the airmen and women tightening straps and checking cargo would be unable to hear what she said over the aircraft's powerful jet engines.

"I got a bulletin a couple of days ago from MIT, the Turkish security services," she said.

"I know them." Trapp nodded. "But damned if I can pronounce their real name."

"It's *National Intelligence Organization*." Madison grinned.

"That easy, huh?" he said wryly. "So what's eating them?"

"I put flags on all of al-Shakiri's known associates a while back, no matter how tenuous the link, and wherever they are in the world. At least, where those locations correspond with friendly intelligence agencies. Reasonably friendly, anyway."

Trapp knew that US relations with Turkey generally, and the Turkish MIT in particular, had been flaky for some time. The Turks likely only shared intelligence so they could be seen to do so, which meant information they deemed as unimportant. But then, the same could be said of the CIA.

"And?" he prompted.

"We got a hit. A week or so ago, two men known to have run with al-Shakiri lost their tails and disappeared. MIT was only checking in on them a couple days a week, often by video-link. Too many potential targets mixed in among all those Syrian refugees. By the time they realized they were in the wind, it was too late to track them."

"Anyone I recognize?"

Madison shook her head. "Nobodies. At least that's what we thought."

"Any idea what they plan on doing?"

"None. Just that they're gone. Five years they've been living in Turkey, getting up to no trouble—"

"And the week al-Shakiri goes missing..."

"They disappear right along with him," Madison finished grimly.

Both fell silent for a moment as the windowless cargo aircraft swung around a turn as it proceeded across the runway. The metal cargo pallets creaked from the momentum. The plane stopped and started to build up engine power, trembling slightly as the jet thrust battled with the landing gear's brakes.

Trapp raised his voice to be heard over the engine squeal as the C-17 started rolling. "Hell of a coincidence," he said.

"Yeah. If you believe in that kind of thing."

21

The man shivered in the pitch darkness. His eyes were open, but he saw nothing save vague shapes, brief flashes of white and color as his brain struggled to make sense of the endless nothingness around him. There was another in there with him. He smelled familiar, an old friend. In the background, there was a harsh, chemical stink and a strange vibration that never seemed to cease.

"We're almost there," his friend whispered. His voice was tender and caring. He stroked the sick man's hair, which the latter realized was in his lap. He was lying on his friend. "Don't give up now. Not now we've come all this way."

He knew they had traveled a great distance, though in that moment he was sure neither how far, nor either the names of their destination or port of embarkation. All he remembered was that they were engaged on a mission of great importance. Something that would change the world.

His friend dipped a cloth into a pail of water, wrung it out, and wiped the sweat from his forehead. For a moment, he felt cool, but then the shivering returned. He was burning up.

There was a click, and suddenly the darkness was

vanquished by a bright glow. The sick man instinctively squeezed his eyes shut as a peal of agony surged through his mind. The beam of light danced around the narrow space. His friend lifted his head and held it gently as he maneuvered himself out from underneath him.

"It's going to be okay, Khaled," the man whispered.

That's right, they had to stay quiet. The journey had lasted several days already, during which they had barely spoken to one another, only rarely even tasted fresh air. But where were they? And who were they hiding from?

He screwed his eyes tighter shut as he battled for understanding. The answers were in his mind somewhere, but try as he might, he couldn't reach for them. Another wave of nausea swept through him.

"I'm going to give you another dose," his friend said softly. "Before we move. It will help."

It was too early, wasn't it? But his friend's voice was so compelling. And he hurt. Everything hurt. His stomach, his head, every limb. It was as though he was wearing a blanket of lava, the heat searing every inch of exposed skin.

Slowly, haltingly, the man opened his eyes. The world wobbled in front of him, a fit of dizziness overcoming him so powerfully he thought that an earthquake must be shaking the world beneath him.

A word that his friend had spoken echoed in his mind.

Khaled.

That was his name. He remembered now. What they were doing. And why he needed to live to see it brought to fruition. He watched as the beam of Omar's flashlight danced across the small space. The man moved excruciatingly slowly, always careful not to knock into the corrugated steel that formed three of the four walls that imprisoned them.

Noise would kill them both.

A small cool box was stacked on top of a larger one at the

far end of the space. Omar moved slowly toward it, able to stand fully upright yet needing to keep his body hunched to avoid knocking into the walls. He lifted the lid and extracted a plastic pouch from inside, along with a length of clear medical tubing.

He knelt by his friend's side, pulling a rubber cap from the end of the line and attaching it to the cannula running into a vein on the back of Khaled's hand. Omar lifted the pouch and hooked it onto a bracket that was screwed into the steel above. It hung there, feeding desperately needed intravenous antibiotics into Khaled's bloodstream.

"See," he murmured. "Better already."

Khaled looked up at his friend, marveling at how their roles had reversed. For so long, he had been the leader, and Omar his flock, despite their disparity in both physical size and prowess. In the cell they had shared for so many years, he was the one who had first brokered the uneasy truce between the various inmates that had allowed them to thrive as a community, hanging together instead of hanging apart. Omar had enforced that truce when necessary—but it had rarely proven so.

That was his doing. He had found a group of lost souls and given them purpose.

But now Omar led him.

The escape from al-Shaddadi was Khaled's idea, but Omar was the one who had made it happen. He had practically carried Khaled over the wall in his arms, driven the vehicle that had spirited them to freedom, taken him to the doctor to have his long-ignored wounds cared for.

And he still cared for him now.

"If I die," Khaled whispered, reaching up and gripping his friend's stained T-shirt, "you need to see it through."

"That won't happen. Allah will see to that."

"I do not judge his will. If he sees fit to take me, then I will go willingly. But the mission must succeed, you know that? And other than me, you are the only one who knows every detail. So it must be you."

"You won't die!" Omar hissed. "Stop talking this way. You need your strength."

Khaled grew quiet for a few seconds. His friend shook with repressed emotion. He looked as though he wanted to scream —which would be a natural enough reaction after the horrors they'd both survived over the previous five years, not to mention the stresses and torments of just the past few days. He watched as Omar slowly relaxed.

"But if I do, you'll do as I ask?" he ventured. "I need to know, Omar. Give me the strength I need to continue."

"You know the answer already," his friend replied through gritted teeth.

"Thank you."

The two men drifted into silence, at first tense, then companionable. Khaled stopped sweating, at least for a time. His fever felt as though it was breaking, though it had given him many false dawns before. Perhaps the antibiotics were finally beginning to win their battle against the tiny devils in his bloodstream. He was certain that the fight inside him was between good and evil, just as the struggle he'd committed his adult life to was.

He was not, of course, an uneducated man. He understood the basics of germ theory, of bacteria, genetics, DNA, and all the various intellectual building blocks that undergirded modern society. But his understanding of the world was also a more ancient one. There were things—too many to count—that man's science could not explain. And those realms could only be attributed to Allah—and, no doubt, his nemesis.

Satan.

But Khaled knew which force was stronger. The only question was whether Allah would see fit to save him, or whether he had other plans. Neither outcome concerned him greatly. He was a servant. His only purpose in this life was to see that Allah's will was done.

Omar reached out and touched him gently on the leg, lifting his index finger to his lips with his other hand and gesturing for silence.

Khaled complied instantly. Even during the glory days of the Islamic caliphate, when he'd led large paramilitary taskforces, he'd known to trust Omar's instincts. The large man was a natural soldier. He was as proficient with firearms, blades, and explosives as any Western special forces operator and combined those skills with a natural, unerring nose for trouble.

It took him another ten seconds to detect the sound that had alerted his friend. Even then, the sound of footsteps on the iron decking outside was scarcely audible.

He lifted his hand and rested his palm against the cool steel. It was dripping with condensation as the relatively chilled air within the container came into contact with the warm tropical heat on the outside. It was barely an inch thick. Less, even. That was all that separated their hiding place from the sailors who worked on the other side.

They rarely came down into the cargo compartments—that was what their contacts had promised. And experience had shown that it was the truth. The problem wasn't that the rare visits happened, it was that it was impossible to know *when* they might occur. Sailors got bored. There was little to do at sea. Every day they had heard a loud thumping on the deck outside at the exact same time and puzzled over it for hours.

It wasn't until the third repetition that Khaled figured it out. Someone was going for a run. And apparently they chose not to use the treadmills in the container ship's tiny onboard gymnasium. Or else the fitness equipment on the Malaysian-flagged rust bucket was out of order. In fact, that was likely.

But this new sound was different. Quieter. Perhaps the individual responsible had a slight build, or maybe he was walking far away, and the sound was somehow traveling through the ship's steel floor.

Or—

A heavy thump rang out as someone rapped against the steel container's exterior. Three times, then a pause, then three times more.

It was the signal. They had arrived.

Even though both men had been expecting it, they flinched. They had spent several days in almost complete darkness and silence as Khaled sweated through a vicious infection. Likely septicemia. The tension that had built was almost indescribable. All that was left to occupy either mind—at least when Khaled was conscious—was daydreaming of everything that could go wrong.

Omar reacted first. He lifted his hand, formed a fist, then hesitated for a second.

Khaled nodded.

He rapped his knuckles against the corrugated steel. Just once. As they had agreed.

Nothing happened for a few seconds. Footsteps echoed around the container. Omar stood, quickly maneuvering himself toward the end where the cool boxes and other supplies that had sustained them through the long journey were stacked. He squatted, rummaging inside one of them before emerging with an object in his hand.

A knife.

On one side, the blade was smooth and sharp before tapering to a vicious point. The other was ridged like a saw. It was seven or more inches long, sufficient to reach deep inside a man and gut his organs. Khaled had seen it done. Had seen Omar do it.

He prayed he would not have to see it done again. He took no pleasure in causing the deaths of other Muslims. It was a sin, though one he was sure that Allah would forgive in service of his greater goal.

A lounder, metallic squeal. The bolts on the front end of the container were being tugged open. Khaled winced, fearing that others would hear the sound and investigate, despite knowing that it was unlikely that one such sound would draw any attention whatsoever on a vessel where such noises were common at every hour of the day and night.

A thunk sounded as the bolts were pulled back and down. He detected the faintest change in pressure as the doors were pulled open and air rushed toward the exit. Then footsteps inside the container.

Omar positioned himself beside the low entrance to their hiding place. It was two-thirds the width of a door and about the height of a man's waist. On the other side of the wall was plaster, in front of which stood racks of refrigerated medical supplies. It would—should—be impossible to spot even if you knew it was there. He stood over it with the weapon poised to strike.

Acquiring a refrigerated container had been hard work. But surviving the first part of the long waterborne odyssey—sailing out of the Persian Gulf into the Arabian Sea—in hundred-degree heat inside an airless steel box would have been suicide. Especially after a surgery to remove the fragments of shrapnel that had scarred him so long ago—desperately needed, and yet an equally desperate risk. The container had been modified by a friendly engineer, the far end pulled forward just enough to create a hiding space, but not so shallow as to draw attention.

The man had been smart. He'd known that it was easy for the eye to miss inconsistencies that sat below its ordinary level. And if it made a forced entry a little more difficult for the attacker, that was only a benefit.

Khaled pictured his friend bringing the blade down in a fast, vicious strike on an unsuspecting customs inspector's neck. It would sever spinal column and arteries alike. The victim would die without ever seeing the face of the man who had killed him.

He swallowed. His mouth was parched. He needed water. The fever was back.

Another two knocks. Whoever was on the other side of the plastered and painted drywall knew the correct sequence. But that didn't mean they were who they said they were. Men were imperfect beings. Even those who professed to be resolutely committed to their faith, who claimed they would give everything in the service of their religion, could break when confronted by earthly consequences.

That was the hand of Satan at work.

It was the implacable force against which Khaled al-Shakiri fought so hard. He was Allah's servant. He was the hand of God.

Water.

It was all he could think of now as the fever raged inside him. The doctor they had consulted after the prison break had told him that he wouldn't survive the coming journey and all its hardships without surgery to remove the shrapnel fragments. One was perilously close to an arterial blood vessel in his intestines. It was a miracle, the doctor had said, that he'd survived this long.

The doctor had put it down to Khaled's sedentary life inside the prison cell. But he knew better. It was Allah's hand at work.

He raised his hand to signal Omar, momentarily forgetting where he was and what was happening around him. He tried to speak, but his throat was too parched to form words.

He was so thirsty.

Khaled heard scratching on the other side of the drywall, then a scrape as something heavy was moved. Tiny thumps as items—his conscious mind would've known these were pharmaceutical boxes—toppled onto the container's floor. Then a louder crash as a hammer smashed against the drywall, puncturing it and emerging through the other side.

Both stowaways stared at it, watched it withdraw then once more cut through the thin wall with ease. Over and over again the man wielding it beat the drywall down. It was impossibly loud inside the container. Finding his way back to consciousness, Khaled feared that someone would stumble across them at any moment.

And finally it was done. The hammer swept up one side of the small entranceway, then the top, then back down the other side, clearing debris and kicking up pale dust that floated in the dark.

A head poked through. It was swathed in dark hair, its cheeks coated white and panting hard from the exertion. Its owner looked right, meeting Khaled's glazed eyes, then left. He saw Omar's legs first and followed them upward, flinching as he saw the knife poised above him and ready to strike.

"What is the password?" Omar whispered.

"The surat," the man said, stumbling to speak.

"Which one?"

"Al-fath," came the reply, laced with relief.

Khaled closed his eyes. He recited the Quranic verse known as surat al-fath in his head.

Surely those who pledge allegiance to you, O Prophet, are actually pledging allegiance to Allah. Allah's hand is over theirs. Whoever breaks their pledge, it will only be to their loss. And whoever fulfills their pledge to Allah, He will grant them a great reward.

Omar relaxed. "It is time?"

The sailor nodded. Neither man had met him before. Their contact was the ship's captain, but he could not move around the vessel as easily without drawing attention. His role was to organize the crew so that they never came to notice the precious cargo they carried in their midst.

"He is weak," Omar said. Khaled noticed with some

surprise that his friend was gesturing at him. "You must help me carry him."

The sailor nodded. "We must hurry. The captain has stopped the ship's engines for a few moments. But we don't have long."

"The plane?" Omar said. "Is it waiting for us?"

"I don't know anything about that. All I was told was to get you down to a boat."

Khaled caught flashes of medication boxes on either side as they manhandled him out of the hiding place and through the container, then rusted steel as they half-carried, half-dragged him through the aging ship's gangways.

What plane? he wondered.

The plan he had labored over for so many years returned slowly to him. They'd travelled overland through Syria and Iraq. A container ship had carried them from the Persian Gulf to Pakistan, and an ambulance plane would carry them the rest of the way. The journey already had cost the better part of a week, and there was still much hardship to come. But every step of the way, true believers had helped smooth their path. Even after so long, after so many false dawns and broken promises, they were still out there.

It was sunset when they emerged into the open air. The sky was clear, and the most glorious ocher warmed the base of the horizon as the sun broke on a new day. As Khaled locked his eyes on the ball of fire rising from the east, he found himself unable to breathe. It was surely a message of divine favor.

For though it was still many thousands of miles distant, he knew what lay at the very end of that path.

Home.

22

The Air Force bird carried Trapp and Madison to the enormous US military hub at Ramstein Air Base in Germany, where they boarded a regularly scheduled Patriot Express 737 that touched down at Joint Base Andrews almost twenty-eight hours after their journey began.

The DOD-contracted commercial airliner even offered its passengers booze, which was a risky move given that most of those on board were Army enlisted. But neither of them were in the mood for drinking.

"I feel like crap," Madison admitted as they stepped onto the runway. "I think I would kill someone for a shower. At least maim somebody."

Trapp, who didn't feel a whole lot better, murmured his agreement. His attention, though, was consumed by a black sedan that was sitting on the runway. Its driver, a trim man with close-cropped blond hair wearing a dark suit, leaned against the hood. He was wearing shades, despite the thick band of murky cloud that sat in the sky overhead.

"You might have to," he said.

Madison opened her mouth to reply, then noticed where

his gaze was focused. "Well, that screams government, wouldn't you say?"

Trapp nodded. "I guess we should get it over with."

"Yeah," she agreed ruefully. "But I could have really used that shower."

The drive to Langley via the Beltway, then the Richmond Highway hugging the Potomac most of the way, took about an hour. The traffic was first thick and then inexplicably disappeared.

"You got a name?" Trapp asked the driver. He was CIA, that much was certain. Most likely from the agency's Security Protective Service. They were the guys who protected the director, and apparently they also ran errands like this.

"Mark."

"A real one?"

He didn't get a response to that.

They entered the Langley compound through a side gate that was no less secure than the main entrance. Despite the fact that they had an escort, Trapp was still forced to stare at a facial recognition camera that was no less janky than when the devices had first been installed almost five years earlier.

By the time Mark, or whatever he was really called, pulled the car up in visitor parking, it was almost dark. He climbed out quickly and opened the door for Madison, who smiled her thanks.

"Hey, Mark," she said as Trapp swung himself out. "You mind telling me what all this is about?"

"Not my job."

She pasted her most disarming smile on her face and gently brushed his arm. It was a remarkably familiar gesture, the kind that female operatives were trained to use at the Farm, though Trapp knew that Madison—as an analyst—had never taken such a course. She was all natural.

"At least tell me who you are taking us to see," she said. "I mean, look at me. I look like I've been dragged through a cornfield by my hair. I just want to make a good impression, that's all. You know how it is."

It wasn't the way that Trapp would've gone about extracting the information, but it worked.

"Mr. Richards told me to bring you to him," Mark said. He coughed quietly, almost sounding embarrassed.

"As in the head of the Terrorism Desk?" she replied, adding a slight laugh. "I'm either in a lot of trouble or about to get a promotion. Let's hope it's the latter."

"That's him." Mark nodded.

Trapp kept quiet. He was pretty sure that Richards wasn't Madison's direct boss. It wasn't a good sign, that was for sure. On the other hand, he didn't care much for bureaucratic dick-swinging right now. Not after everything that had happened.

"Great," Madison said brightly. "Hey, one other thing. You mind if we go through the lobby? I just want to pay my respects. It's a personal tradition. You understand, right?"

It was the second time that she'd used the same trick, but it seemed to work. Though maybe it wasn't really a trick, after all. The gold stars in Langley's lobby held an outsized importance in the mind of every last one of its employees. They were a daily reminder of the ultimate sacrifice made by those who put their lives on the line and the consequences for others of them screwing up.

"Sure."

The marble-floored lobby was busy despite the late hour. Trapp paused for a second as he stepped over the Agency's eagle-headed seal and realized that he'd fallen in step with Mark, who appeared equally unwilling to interrupt Madison's private tradition. The Memorial Wall glowed on the opposite wall, almost seeming to beckon him toward it. He hadn't been this close since they'd added Ryan's star.

Madison stopped in front of the goatskin-bound memorial

book. She reached out to it hesitantly before turning the pages with great reverence. She stopped when she found the one she was looking for and dragged her finger hesitantly across the paper.

In honor of those members of the Central Intelligence Agency who gave their lives in service of their country, the inscription above her read.

Trapp knew it by heart. Ryan's wasn't the first memorial service he'd attended. It was unlikely to be the last. There were 139 stars on that wall now. More with every passing year.

The brothers he'd lost weren't named in that book, though their star was engraved forevermore on the marble above. And if he were to one day fall beside them, neither would his. He would remain classified in death, as in life.

Trapp found himself by her side. He didn't really remember walking over. Madison's eyes gleamed with emotion.

"We'll get the bastard," he murmured softly, unwilling to disturb the peace of the place. He didn't face her as he said the words. He focused instead on just one of those marble indentations, the last resting place of the best man he'd ever known.

"Sure we will," Madison replied, her voice choked. She turned away.

~

"WHAT THE FUCK WERE YOU THINKING?" Clark Richards said.

He was a man of average height, build, and complexion. He wore a neatly trimmed beard, the kind that had become popular over the past few years. Trapp guessed he'd chosen his glasses after watching Ben Affleck in *Argo*.

Before they'd entered his office, Madison had told him that she would handle things. This was her case, so he was happy to defer to her judgment. Well, not happy. He wanted to push

Clark Richards against a wall and tell him to get the fuck out of the way so they could do their jobs.

But it was Madison's case. Her call. So he just stewed beside her.

"What do you mean?" she asked.

"Who authorized you to go into combat?" Richards said, eyes flashing from behind those large, square glasses. "Because it certainly wasn't my office."

"It wasn't something I did intentionally," Madison fired back frostily. "I couldn't have known that al-Shaddadi Prison was going to be attacked on that day."

"We'll get to that."

Trapp sat quietly. He'd taken an instant dislike to Richards. There was something about the Central Intelligence Agency—or maybe any large bureaucracy—that allowed second-rate individuals like him to rise through its ranks. They were desk warriors, trained mainly in the art of forging razor-sharp memos and using them to stab their fellow candidates for promotion in the back.

Even in the National Clandestine Service, the Agency's operational arm, the waters were fouled with seaweed of his kind. But there was less of it to cut through. Especially in the Special Operations Group, Trapp's real home.

The Intelligence arm, which was home to analysts like Madison, was a different kettle of fish.

"You could've been killed," Richard said. "Imagine how that would reflect on the department."

"Syria *is* a war zone, sir," Madison replied coldly.

In case you hadn't noticed, Trapp thought, detecting her subtext. He wondered if Richards had also.

"Oh, believe me, I'm aware. My office will be closely examining how you were able to worm your way in there. Protocols exist for a reason."

A muscle on Madison's jaw pulsed intensely. Trapp could

tell that she was biting her tongue, not giving voice to what she truly wanted to say in case it rebounded to her disadvantage. Richards seemed like the kind of man who would stand in the way of good intelligence work only to prove a point.

"Can I brief you on what we've learned, sir?"

"How did you miss an impending attack on this scale?" Richards asked brusquely instead. He removed his glasses, extracted a polishing cloth from his jacket's interior pocket, and began to clean them. "It's acutely embarrassing."

"I thought you didn't want me there in the first place?" Madison said, unable to hold her tongue any longer. "Sir."

He sniffed. "If you had to be there, you might as well be useful."

"I was working on how we missed it when I was ordered to return to Washington, sir," Madison said. "If there's blame to be apportioned, I'll be the first to put my hand up and accept it."

Unlike you, Trapp thought. This wasn't a debrief, it was a shit-shoveling session, and Richards wanted to make sure it didn't land on him. Anger flickered inside his chest. He wanted nothing more than to punch the insufferable desk-jockey in the middle of that smart face.

"For now, what we know for certain is that this was meticulously planned. I became aware of insurgent chatter referring to someone or something known as the Hand of God in the weeks leading up to the attack. I traced that chatter back to its source—Khaled al-Shakiri—when the attack took place. I was just a few hours too late."

Her face displayed genuine anguish at the lives lost as a result of her—perceived—failure. Trapp knew it was nothing of the sort. You couldn't prevent every attack, no matter how hard you tried. It was a miracle that Madison had come as close as she had.

"And you let him get away," Richards said, confirming Trapp's guess as to the purpose of the meeting.

"What's important now is finding him, sir," Madison said. She unfolded a manila file on her lap. "I have reason to believe that his escape was in service of some larger plan—"

Richards held up a finger. "You'll hand off your work to another analyst. My office will be in touch with the details in due course."

"Sir, this could be time critical!"

Richards replaced his glasses. He peered down at Madison. "Ms. Grubbs, I'm not presently minded to place much weight on your analysis."

Trapp stood up. His chair scraped against the floor behind him. Richards looked up at him, his eyes startled behind those ridiculous thick-rimmed frames.

"Well, you should be," he said. "Without her, we wouldn't know anything at all."

"And what do we know? Because so far, I'm not hearing—"

"Oh, shut the fuck up," Trapp said, luxuriating in the shocked expression that appeared on the department head's face. He stepped toward the man's desk, looming over him. "You're not hearing because you're not listening. Well, here's the thing. We have a senior ISIS commander who engineered a daring escape from prison. His known associates are dropping off the grid after years of inactivity. You know what that smells like to me?"

Richards didn't answer.

"It smells like they're planning something big. And I sure wouldn't want to be the asshole hauled up in front of Congress for missing it when the shit inevitably hits the fan. That tends to be a bad career move. You know what I'm talking about, don't you, Clark?"

Still no answer.

Trapp eased himself back into his seat and adopted a more reasonable tone.

"So here's the thing. I can either write up what I just said in a memo. And you know, I'm no wordsmith, but I've been working here long enough to have a real thick Rolodex. Long enough that somewhere in there I'm pretty sure I have the director's email address. A memo like that could have wide circulation. Not the kind of document that's easy to sweep under the rug. You choose."

23

Adnan Gulen started awake from a torment of half-remembered nightmares as a cold slap collided with his face. His eyelids sprang apart to reveal a blurred face peering down at him. He tried to speak, but his mouth was desert-dry.

In that moment, Adnan had the sensation of waking in a hotel room in the middle of the night—a strikingly childlike fear, a desire to be reacquainted with the familiar. But the sensation did not fade. It only grew more powerful, more disorienting, with every passing moment.

"Wake up," a rough voice said as a powerful hand closed around his arm and shook him violently. "You have work to do."

"Wha—?"

Why couldn't he see? Where was he? More importantly, how had he come to be in this place that he did not recognize?

As consciousness slowly returned, Adnan realized that the blurriness in his eyes was a result of a cup of ice water—complete with cubes—that had been thrown into his face to wake him. He lifted his free arm, the one the man's fingers were currently clamped to, and dragged the back of his hand to clear his vision.

Despite the heat—the unfamiliar, tropical stickiness of the room that he had awoken in, Adnan shivered. Though his mind was still befuddled by whatever chemical substances had been pumped into his veins, he knew that all was not right with his world.

He sat up, greedily reaching out for one of the already-melting ice cubes that lay on the plain surface of the olive-green camping cot on which he'd slept. He thrust it into his mouth, not caring who saw. Adnan dared not meet the gaze of the man standing over him.

When his mouth was sufficiently lubricated to speak, he croaked, "Where am I?"

"Arabic," the other man said in response.

Adnan blinked. What the hell was that supposed to mean? And why was his mind operating so slowly?

Flashes of memory came back to him, kaleidoscopic in their lack of order. In them, he was sitting in a wheelchair, and his face itched. Oh God, but it itched. What did that mean? Someone had wheeled him onto a plane. He didn't remember the destination written on the ticket, if he'd ever seen it. But he remembered the cool, icy sensation of another hypodermic syringe of sedatives being depressed into his veins. The cramping around his heart, and then only blackness.

He reached up and patted his face. It was wet but also sticky, as though still coated with an adhesive residue.

Realizing that the man had woken him in Arabic, his second language, rather than Turkish, Adnan rephrased his question in kind. "Where am I?"

"That is not your concern," came the swift response. "Do you need food?"

The very idea of eating sent an intense wave of nausea cascading out from Adnan's gut. He doubled over, his stomach spasming, and emptied its contents onto the floor beside his cot. The vomit was thin and watery and had a pinkish tinge. He'd only seen that color once before, after a week of food poisoning that had left him vomiting up his stomach lining.

I haven't eaten in days, he realized.

He clutched his stomach and moaned, only half in an attempt to buy himself a little time to think. This had to be a test, he decided, if only to hide from the truth. MIT wanted to know that he wouldn't break if a foreign intelligence agency ever captured him. He hung on to the notion that this was his own country's doing even as, deep down, he knew the idea was ridiculous. The alternative, though, was too horrifying to even conceive.

"Get up," the man said brusquely, plucking at the cloth on Adnan's shoulder to encourage him. "I will show you your lab. We have provided all the tools that you will need."

"To do what?"

"No questions."

Why would MIT go to these lengths, though? He was a Turkish citizen. Surely there were laws against this kind of thing. Of course, the security services operated by their own kind of rules, but they couldn't simply kidnap him, could they? The company would surely have been informed ahead of time, and his bosses would've protested. He was too valuable to the project he was working on to simply disappear for days at a time.

How long has it been?

Adnan rose slowly, his mind still whirling with a mixture of emotion, memory, and the sluggishness that comes of days hooked to IV sedatives. He remembered now why his face was so sticky. They'd made him wear a mask. He'd been awake for that part before they'd put him under once again.

He took in the man who'd woken him for the first time. He was enormous, standing almost a foot taller than himself, and significantly broader. Even so, he looked as though he'd recently been sick, like he was still filling out his frame after a period of illness. He was naturally dark-skinned, perhaps Syrian or Iraqi by the look of him, but his skin was pallid. It had been refreshed by a short period of sunshine, but the tan hadn't yet baked in.

"I want a lawyer," Adnan protested. "You can't do this."

The big man turned, eyed him up with a chilling coldness that sent ice through his veins, and then punched him in the stomach with such speed and ferocity he didn't see the blow coming. He collapsed to the ground, all air driven from his lungs, and clutched at his throat as he struggled to breathe.

Panic welled up inside him as the oxygen deprivation threatened to slip him back into unconsciousness. Acid from his earlier vomit stung his throat. He filled his mouth with air, sealed his lips, and compressed the gas in attempt to force it down into his lungs. It succeeded, barely. But even that little oxygen helped stave off the blackness consuming his vision.

Slowly, Adnan regained the ability to breathe. His eyes were thick with salty tears, and saliva dribbled from his nose and mouth. Getting hit never looked like this in the movies. He looked up at his captor, his body language signaling that he was beaten.

"No more talking," the man said simply before turning away.

No further response was necessary. Adnan understood now that this was no test. No government agency would act this way, not even MIT. He'd been kidnapped.

He followed his guard out of a corrugated-iron door and emerged into what Adnan could only describe as a tropical paradise. For a man who had been born, raised, and spent most of his life in the dry Turkish heat, the thick humidity was oppressive. But the air was fresh and smelled of plants that he did not recognize. It was better than being inside that drab, airless shack.

As the two men walked through the jungle, he tried to discern clues that might help him work out where he was. There was nowhere in Europe with vegetation like this: thick vines, leaves the size of men, and trees heavy with fruit. He recognized bananas growing overhead and remembered vaguely that the banana plant was an herb, not a tree.

"This way," his captor grunted, gesturing to the right where the path forked.

Why was he focusing on such details? To distract himself from whatever fate his captors had planned for him?

Where did bananas grow? India, he was sure of that. And South America too. He'd seen the words 'Product of Brazil' on those little stickers. The climate and vegetation would both fit the Amazon, that was for sure.

And a hundred other places, he thought hopelessly.

The big man stopped so suddenly that Adnan, in his reverie, almost collided with him. They had entered a clearing in the jungle. The trees had been felled in such a way that though a large section of ground had been cleared, the canopy was barely broken overhead. In the center of the clearing was a large, surprisingly modern building constructed of concrete blocks and a solid roof—entirely unlike the shack he'd awoken in.

He could hear the hum of a diesel generator and taste the burned fuel on the otherwise pristine air. Additional solar panels sat on the roof.

His captor pushed him in the direction of the door on the outside of the structure. It was open, but as they passed through, he saw that it was equipped with an electronic keypad lock. The frame was extra thick, like those at the laboratory in Turkey. He guessed that meant the locks would be essentially impregnable.

"You're awake," a voice said as he stepped inside.

It took Adnan's eyes a few moments to readjust to the light inside the building. There were no windows, though an air conditioning unit mounted on the wall kept the space pleasantly cool. He realized that rivulets of sweat were already streaming down his face from the short walk.

Two men were already inside the building. One was thin, almost starved, and sat hunched over in a wheelchair. The other wore jungle-pattern fatigues and carried a military-style automatic rifle which was finished in a similar camouflage. Adnan flinched as he realized that the man dressed as a soldier was one of those who'd kidnapped him.

"He will not hurt you," the wheelchair-bound invalid said, speaking so quietly he was barely audible. "I apologize for the way you were brought here. If there had been an alternative, I assure you I would have taken it."

"Who are you?" Adnan asked, his terrified mind choosing the first question that sprang to mind.

"My name is Khaled. Khaled al-Shakiri," he replied. "The man who woke you is Omar, my good friend."

Was it a good thing that they were so free with their identities, Adnan wondered? Or were they false names?

He swallowed, hoping resolutely that it was the latter option. He nodded, realizing that Khaled seemed to be expecting a response.

"Why am I here?" he asked next, for the first time truly taking in the contents of the room.

It was equipped much like his laboratory back in Keşan. A powerful-looking computer sat on the desk behind Khaled, a screensaver lazily bouncing around the screen. There was a 3D printer—an expensive one, at least a quarter of a million dollars' worth, still wrapped in the manufacturer's plastic wrap. Parts bins rested against every well, their clear plastic containers almost overflowing with electronics, motors, wiring, and computer chips.

Hell, he even saw an electron microscope.

At the other end of the room, two enormous wooden crates rested lengthwise along the wall. The outsides were covered with writing—presumably directions to shippers—that he didn't recognize.

"I need you to build something for me," Khaled said before catching himself. "Well—finish something. *Two* somethings. I had them brought here at great expense."

Adnan nodded, again sensing a response was expected.

"What?"

Khaled gestured toward the two crates. The guard behind him shouldered his rifle and placed his hands on the wheelchair's handles. Adnan followed with Omar in tow.

"Open it," Khaled ordered. It was clear that he was in charge, despite his obvious frailty.

Omar bent over and picked up an iron crowbar. He grunted as he popped the lid of the nearest crate, levering the nails out in a dozen separate places. It took him a few minutes, and when he was finished, he signaled to the guard to help him lift the wooden slab. They left it leaning against the nearest wall.

"Take a look," Khaled instructed.

Adnan gingerly stepped toward the open crate, nausea still swirling inside him from his prolonged sedation and probably from the lack of calories over the previous few days. He didn't know what he expected to see. But whatever he'd anticipated, it wasn't something so familiar.

He looked up, eyes clouded with confusion. "What am I supposed to do?"

"Finish them."

"What for?"

"That is not your concern."

"But what will you do with them?" Adnan pressed.

These men were not good people. They were criminals, probably terrorists. Why did they need drones, let alone ones this large? It was difficult to be certain, given their unfinished state, but he guessed the UAVs he was looking at would be capable of carrying a significant payload. Perhaps a hundred pounds of explosives. Enough to inflict serious damage.

"Not your concern," Khaled repeated, this time in a steely tone despite his slumped posture.

"I—I can't do this. If you needed these for legitimate purposes, you would have bought them on the open market."

"You will," Khaled said softly. Almost sadly, it seemed to Adnan.

"You can't make me. This is difficult, technical work. You can't force me to do it."

Khaled reached into a pocket and pulled out a photograph. He handed it to Adnan, who recognized the image immediately. It was taken from the frame on his bedside table. He remembered taking it, remembered the way that the children had squirmed and squiggled in Esra's arms. A chill ran through him, nausea replaced by sheer terror.

He turned it over and saw the date and location the photo had been taken on, written in his own hand. These people had been inside his house. He stumbled and almost fell.

"Think about it," Khaled said, signaling to his aide to wheel him away. "I think you will find the work quite rewarding."

24

"What the hell is this?" Trapp groused as he flicked the light switch on the wall—itself made of a yellowed, faded plastic—to reveal a windowless basement conference room whose décor didn't appear to have been updated since at least the Iran Hostage Crisis.

"You're telling me it took two whole days for them to find us a secure location to work out of, and this is the best they could do?"

The windowless part went hand in hand with the room being two floors below any source of natural light. But what was unforgivable was the lack of any visible attempt to remedy that problem. The overhead lighting was weak and feeble and scarcely penetrated the gloom.

"I believe it's known as malicious compliance," Madison said with a wry smile. She set her bag down on the conference table, pulled back her chair, and made a face when she saw how thick the coat of dust on it was.

Trapp looked around, taking in the rest of the room. Corkboards covered most of the walls that weren't already occupied by empty filing cabinets. Tiny scraps of paper were still pinned to it, left when the paper they had once been attached to was torn away.

He wondered what answer he would get if he asked one of the wizards in Science & Technology to carbon-date them.

"Asshole," he said, an image of Clark Richards' unsettling, bearded face filling his mind. "He's just ticking boxes."

"Oh, you can be sure he doesn't believe us," Madison agreed brightly. "But he's been in the Agency long enough to know the three most important letters."

"CYA," Trapp agreed.

Madison pulled a photograph of Khaled al-Shakiri from her bag, levered a couple of pins from the corkboard, and pinned it up. She took a step back to admire her handiwork.

"You know, I think I like this way better than doing everything on computers. Gives a better sense of perspective."

"Welcome to my world."

"I'll be stringing twine around the room, *A Beautiful Mind*-style soon." She grinned before growing more serious. "Okay, what do we have?"

Trapp snorted. He stuck up two fingers and counted them off. "Turkey and Indonesia. You know what that adds up to? Sweet fuck-all."

"Yeah, with that attitude. I've got an MIT contact at the Turkish embassy here in DC. He owes me a favor."

"I know a guy in Detachment 88," Trapp said, his mind swiftly casting off its earlier frustration as it tangled with the mystery in front of them. "I'll reach out, see if I can get some background."

Madison raised an eyebrow. "You're going to have to give me a little more than that."

"Indonesian counter-terror squad. Best of the best over there. We fund it. Least, we used to. I helped them out on a job a few years back."

"Very mysterious." Madison smiled.

She checked her watch. They'd only stopped long enough to shower and find a fresh change of clothes before getting to work. "Nearly eight p.m.," she said. "I'll give my guy a call."

"Makes it eight in the morning in Jakarta," Trapp said. "But if I know Adi, he'll be sleeping off one hell of a hangover."

"He's not a Muslim?"

"Oh, he is. A devout one. But it's like with Catholics; sometimes the ones you see most often in church are those begging forgiveness for their sins."

"When was the last time you went to confession, Jason?" she asked as she leaned over to check—he figured—whether the secure telephone on the table still functioned.

"Not really my style."

"I think the Agency has a priest if you want to change that," she chuckled, bringing the handset to her ear. "Top Secret clearance and everything."

~

"So what now?" Trapp asked as he put the phone down. Adi had—as expected—sounded like he was sleeping off a three-day bender when he finally managed to reach him. But the Indonesian police officer was nothing if not diligent and agreed to look into the matter.

While he was on the phone, Madison had set up her computer and spent the previous half hour typing diligently into it. Her own contact had agreed to investigate the disappearance of the two refugees his own agency had been sitting on. *When* he planned to get back was another question entirely.

"Seems we're all out of leads," he continued. "At least until either the Turks or the Indonesians come through. And there's no guarantee on either."

"That's where CASPR comes in," Madison said without looking up.

"Who the hell is Casper?"

"It's not a person, it's a computer program. Computer-Aided Search Parameter, in full. The acronym is a bit of a stretch."

"You can say that again," Trapp agreed. "What does it do?"

"As the Coalition was rolling up ISIS, NSA, CIA, a bunch of other three-letter agencies all sent intelligence-extraction teams in the wake of the military advance. The caliphate was operating as a full-blown nation-state, which meant unlike the usual ad-hoc nature of most terrorist cells, much more day-to-day administrative work was centralized and needed to be reported to superiors. All that work creates a paper trail, and we wanted to sweep up all the crumbs they left behind. At least, that was the theory."

"So what happened?"

"The teams went in, photographed millions, probably tens of millions of recovered documents. Uploaded every official-looking computer, smart phone, and thumb drive they came across into a secure cloud. There are over a billion separate data entries. CASPR is just a search tool that can help us sift through it."

"And how do we get started?" Trapp said, standing and walking over to her. He peered down at her laptop screen.

Madison hit the enter key and leaned back. With some satisfaction she said, "He already is."

"I thought you said it was a thing, not a person?"

"I never said I was intellectually consistent."

"So how long will 'he' take?"

She grimaced. "That's the thing. If this was a priority investigation, we'd get all the server time we needed. Unfortunately..."

"It isn't."

"And then some. Plus we don't really know what we're

looking for. I've set up search queries for al-Shakiri, his bodyguard, every name that came up in the interrogations, plus anything relating to aircraft, aviation, or aerospace engineering. To complete all those on the amount of bandwidth I'm allotted? Maybe a week. If we're lucky."

Trapp hid his frustration. He'd worked in the intelligence field long enough to know that nothing ever happened quickly. The only consolation was that it was extremely unlikely that, whatever al-Shakiri had planned, it would come to fruition in the next few days.

"Then why don't we go get a bite to eat? I'm starving."

He wondered if he'd imagined the fleeting, pleased expression that washed over Madison's face, and on reflection, hoped he hadn't.

"Yeah, I guess we may as well," she said, gesturing at her computer screen.

He squinted at the progress bar on the screen. CASPR's total estimated search time ran into weeks. "Seriously?"

"It'll come down," she said, not sounding too convinced. "At least a little bit."

They grabbed burgers and fries in a staff cafeteria that had space for hundreds of simultaneous diners but presently only seated about six. Trapp chose a table far from any inquisitive ears, near a window that looked out over the Original Headquarters Building. Though the night sky was pitch-black, enough light shone from the vast office complex to make out the lush green thicket of trees that grew in the concrete courtyard outside.

"So what's our next move?" he asked once he'd polished off the first half of a surprisingly moist burger. He'd asked the server to let the chef know he preferred his meat to be griddled sufficiently lightly that even a veterinarian who graduated at the bottom of her class would have a decent chance of resuscitating it.

For once, the request had borne fruit.

Or meat.

"Because the way I see it," he continued, "we can't wait for CASPR to come good. Feels like a race between that search completing and the Rapture, and I'm not sure which I have my money on to finish first."

Madison stuck out her tongue. "You got any better ideas?"

Unfortunately, he didn't. Only a restless urge compelling him to do anything other than sit on his hands and wait.

"There were a whole lot of prisoners we didn't get a chance to interview," he finally said.

"Unless you have a way of sweet-talking Espinoza into going along with that request, I think that option is a bust."

He slapped his palm down flat on the table, sending a sound like the crack of a whip bouncing around the vast dining hall. The frustration—and guilt—swirling inside him was threatening to boil over. The sound drew a few interested glances, which quickly faded away as he did nothing more interesting than sit there stewing. "You're right. But where does that leave us?"

Madison's phone rang, disturbing the silence that had begun to develop. She glanced at the screen, then put her finger over her lips. Trapp nodded his understanding as she accepted the call and put it on speaker.

"Erol," she said, injecting warmth into her tone. "That was quicker than I expected."

"I'm sorry, Madison," came the immediate and airy response in a British-educated accent. "I'm afraid I have very little for you. I've emailed you the surveillance reports for the past five years, but you won't find much. As far as we could tell, they were both very dull individuals. The agent in charge assures me that it's most likely that your subjects returned to Syria. It happens all the time."

"Both of them?" Madison said doubtfully. "At the same time?"

"Of course, my dear. They say there's no such thing as a coincidence, but we've both been in this business long enough to know that isn't the case. I'll let you know if either of them pop back up. We should do dinner. Soon?"

Madison and Trapp traded glances. She replied, "Of course, Erol. It's been too long."

"Ciao," the Turkish intelligence officer said before hanging up the phone.

"He's hiding something," Trapp said the second the line went dead.

"No shit. Burying us in paperwork. You think there's anything in those surveillance reports?"

"Doubt it."

"You're right. Erol's too smart for that. So what's he up to?"

"Could just be embarrassment at losing two tails in quick succession?" Trapp posited. "The intelligence world is no different from any bureaucracy. Nobody likes being seen with egg on their face."

"I don't buy it. Subjects slip surveillance all the time. Especially long-term check-ins like our guys. Even if they were being watched around the clock, after that long without putting a foot out of place, whoever was watching them wouldn't have expected them to run."

"Maybe they're planning an attack in Turkey?" he suggested next, playing devil's advocate.

Madison shook her head. "Then they would want our help, not to stonewall us. We're missing something here."

"You're right," he said, pushing his chair back. He gestured at her half-eaten burger. "You done with that?"

"Apparently," she said, arching an eyebrow.

"We're not going to figure things out by sitting here," Trapp said. "Why don't we go blow off some steam? I find that usually helps me think."

The search for a place to do just that led them to a cramped shooting range in the bowels of the Original Headquarters Building that was primarily used by the compound's Security Protective Service guards to keep their eyes in, and for former field operatives now condemned to soul-crushing desk jobs on the seventh floor to pretend their lives still had meaning.

It was empty at this time of night, but the front desk was manned. Trapp checked out a pair of pistols and half a dozen loaded magazines.

"You held yourself together in Syria," he said as they reached a shooting booth. He placed both weapons down and turned to face her. "I was impressed. How often do you come down here to practice?"

"I didn't know I was being graded," Madison replied archly before admitting, "not as often as I should."

"The best day to change that was yesterday. But today will do just fine," Trapp said, sliding the mag into the pistol and chambering a round. "We both got lucky in Syria. Next time we might not."

"I'm an analyst, not an operator," Madison protested.

"You think the bad guys make that distinction when the bullets are flying?" Trapp replied.

"I guess not."

"I want you to become an expert shot with this thing. Keep one in both your house and your car. Get so comfortable drawing and firing it that it becomes second nature. So you don't end up as another star on that wall."

Madison's expression deadened. She swallowed but said nothing.

Trapp held up his free hand. "I'm sorry. I didn't mean to bring up your friend."

"No, you're right," she said in a voice that was barely more than a whisper. "My pride won't do Mark's memory any good. And me dying if I could've prevented it sure won't either."

He nodded.

After the moment passed, he grabbed two sets of ear protection and prepared one of the pistols. He handed it to Madison, grip first. "Show me what you've got."

She took the task on with gusto, chambering a round, then assuming a broad shooting stance, feet wide apart and the pistol held level in front of her. She closed one eye as she lined up her shot. Trapp said nothing.

After several seconds, Madison pulled the trigger. She fired again and again, spacing the shots out about a second apart until the magazine ran dry. Pulling the cans off her ears, she called out. "How'd I do?"

Trapp looked downrange. Most of her shots had hit the target, which was pock-marked from repeated impacts. They were largely grouped in center-mass, albeit with a wide spacing.

"Not bad," he acknowledged, holding out his palm. "You mind?"

Their fingers brushed one another as Madison passed over the gun. He was surprised by the rush of interest he felt rising within him.

Easy...

As he loaded a fresh mag, he said, "That was good shooting. But the bad guys won't give you that long before they start shooting back."

"So what do you suggest?"

He pulled the ear protection into place, holding the pistol down at his side. He didn't have a holster, so he simulated pulling the weapon up, found the target, and fired five close-spaced rounds into center-mass in quick succession before inching the barrel up and delivering the sixth into the head of the now-ragged target.

Madison's eyes went wide.

He held out the gun. "Your turn."

As her next set of rounds echoed in the confined shooting range, the phone buzzed in Trapp's pocket. He pulled it out and glanced at the screen. "That was quick," he said under his breath.

Madison looked back. Her hearing impeded by the bright-yellow ear defenders clamped to her head, she half-yelled, "Did you say something?"

Trapp held up his phone to show Madison the message he'd just received. He spoke loud enough to be heard. "It's from my Indonesian contact. He's got something for us."

25

The kid in the seat behind scrunched his knees to his chest, took a deep breath, then jackknifed out to ram his heels into the seatback. The blow sent a judder of pain through Trapp's aching shoulder, a relic of an old injury that only played up these days when he sat on his ass for too long. It wasn't the first time the boy had kicked him. He suspected that it wouldn't be the last.

Closing his eyes, Trapp pictured unbuckling his metal seatbelt, reaching over to the row behind and grasping the child by his collar. What was he, ten? Light enough to dangle from one ankle and shake him until he agreed never to fly again.

Damn Richards, he thought grimly.

The New York to Jakarta plane route was the longest scheduled commercial flight in the world. It took a grand total of twenty-two hours, and Trapp was doing it in the back. It was the quickest route, but the Agency could at least have sprung for business class on a flight that long.

You're getting soft.

Not soft, just old, he thought. There was a time when he wasn't much out of his teens that he would simply have slept through the entire journey. Even with some pissant child doing his best to get himself thrown out the emergency escape.

Wouldn't that be a treat.

He pictured the little boy tumbling head over heels, punching through clouds, imagined his terrified scream as he plunged toward the Pacific Ocean below—

"Another whiskey, sir?"

Trapp opened his eyes and nodded. Singapore Airlines was at least efficient, regularly trundling the steel refreshment carts up and down the aisles and inquiring whether the benighted passengers on board needed anything. He didn't understand how she looked so damn fresh after fifteen hours in the air.

That gave him an idea.

He jerked his time at the seat behind. "Can you give it to that asshole?"

The flight attendant knowingly raised her eyes and glanced at the child behind, who was limbering up to belt Trapp in the back once more. She lowered her voice and said, "I'm afraid not, sir. I would offer you another seat, but we're fully booked on today's flight."

"It's no problem," Trapp said as he accepted the liquor. In a plastic cup. "I've slept in worse places."

She moved on to the next passenger. The thing was, it was true. He'd slept in many worse places. In tropical jungles with cockroaches and millipedes crawling over his sweat-soaked skin and scorpions burrowing into every open crevice in his clothing and rucksack. In Alaska on a training mission, where he damn near froze to death.

But usually he didn't have a face on which to ascribe his misery. Fifteen hours—and counting—of dreaming up ways to kill a minor wasn't exactly the pinnacle of healthy self-care.

He returned to the idea he'd had when the attendant was serving him. The reason she looked so perky. On a flight this long, there had to be at least two, maybe even three sets of different crewmembers so that they could rotate in and out while still complying with international crew rest regulations.

Which meant they had to have somewhere to sleep. It would probably be cramped, claustrophobic, stink of sweat, and have no more room for his extensive frame than an enlisted sailor's bunk on a Navy frigate.

All in all, it sounded like heaven.

They wouldn't be able to stop him busting his way in, he was sure of it. The Singapore Airlines stewardesses were polite, friendly, and to a woman about five foot high. It would be like one of those YouTube videos of a hundred kindergartners going head to head with two NFL pros.

And worst case, there might be an air marshal on board. At this point, he'd practically beg the man to put him out of his misery.

Instead, he sipped the plastic cup of cheap scotch and drifted into an uneasy sleep.

~

"JASON!" Captain Adi Rahman called out with altogether too much energy for whatever ungodly hour it was as he emerged into the jetway that led into the terminal at Jakarta's international airport—which bore a name that Trapp was certain he was unable to read, let alone say out loud. "Good to see you."

"You know," Trapp replied, smiling at his old friend as he extended a hand in greeting, "there are islands off the coast of India home to tribes that have never made contact with modern man that I could've reached quicker than Indonesia."

"The usual way these things go is, 'Good to see you too.'" Adi grinned. "How was the flight?"

"Don't ask," he replied, narrowing his eyes as he saw his tormentor deplaning, clutching a stuffed toy. The child's mother looked unnaturally well-rested. It probably helped not bothering to do a moment's parenting.

"Do you want the good news or the bad news?"

"You pick."

"I sent a couple of my men to your fugitive's home village, a place called Tadjau. Nice and discreet, don't worry."

"I don't need to. I helped train you, remember? What did they learn?"

"Not much yet. They've set up a surveillance post to see if al-Shakiri turns up. I doubt it, but you never know."

"That's the good news?"

"I see your patience hasn't improved. I was getting to that."

Trapp grumbled a half-hearted apology.

"It seems like a few of the locals disappeared over the past few days. Mostly young men, in their late teens and early twenties."

"Prime age for radicalization," he commented.

"The local police and security services have had an eye on one or two of them for a few years. Nothing concrete. Memberships of radical Facebook groups, occasionally showing up in the company of militant Islamist recruiters, you know the drill."

Trapp hid a smile. Adi had picked up all the lingo from the succession of foreign trainers that had passed through Detachment 88's headquarters over the years. Not to mention the uniform. He was wearing tan hiking pants and an olive-green T-shirt and had his bronze POLISI badge clipped to his belt on the opposite side of his torso to his holster. Forget Hollywood's so-called soft power. The greatest exporter of American cultural ideals were the men and women who worked in the Department of Defense's foreign military training programs.

"Any idea where they went?"

"We haven't gotten that far. They are on the island, that's all we know. None of them were picked up at airports or boarding ferries."

"Which island?" Trapp asked, knowing that Indonesia was an archipelago composed of almost 17,000 individual isles spread over an area more than three million square miles. The haystack just kept on getting bigger.

"That's the bad news," Adi laughed, taking in his guest's unkempt appearance. "Sumatra."

Trapp groaned. He'd visited once before on a training op. Sumatra was almost the size of Texas and composed of volcanic, tropical terrain that was twenty times more difficult to penetrate than desert scrub. An entire battalion could evade detection for decades inside a single square mile.

Adi reached down and picked up Trapp's duffel bag. It was all he'd brought with him. "Chin up. We can be there in eight hours. Seven if we're lucky."

"The engineer," Omar said, "he's good. Better than promised."

Al-Shakiri nodded, wincing as the slightest of movements generated a flash of pain from the wounds that covered his torso. Tropical air was, in hindsight, a poor choice of environment in which to recover from the back-alley surgery to remove the shrapnel from his body. The two men sat in a cramped temporary office in one of the buildings that made up their mountainous compound. Omar was on the sofa on the opposite wall, a tiny laptop balanced in a ridiculous fashion across his massive thighs.

In truth, Adnan's performance so far had come as a great relief to him. Omar was right: The Turkish engineer was better than they had had any right to expect. It wasn't just that the man had been given the correct motivation, but that he was a hacker at heart. It seemed as though he had been able to subsume his misgivings about the project in favor of the sheer mechanical delight of getting the two unmanned aircraft working.

"How long?" al-Shakiri breathed.

"The first test flight could be tomorrow. Maybe the day after that. He says it depends how long it takes to validate the flight control software. But the components held up better than we expected after so long in storage. The desert air helped. And we have spares for those parts that did fail."

"And the boat?"

"It is waiting in Padang Harbor. The captain is one of us. He will remain there as long as we require. The journey to Malaysia will take little more than a day."

"Make sure the transport is in place. We leave the moment the engineer is finished."

"We?" Omar repeated. Al-Shakiri detected the slightest hint of his most trusted lieutenant holding his breath as he spoke. "Are you sure that's wise? The doctor gave strict instructions that you should rest. The journey will not be easy. It was a miracle you survived this long."

"Allah will protect me. Or he will not. But it is in his hands. I do not presume to know what path he has chosen for me."

"Of course not," Omar conceded. "But you could come later."

Al-Shakiri opened his eyes. He caught his friend's gaze and held it while slowly shaking his head. "I cannot. I must see it."

Omar bowed his head. He understood. This was both of their life's work. To not be there to see it come to fruition in person would feel like a dagger to the heart.

"There is news from our friends abroad," he said. "In America and Syria both. The same names keep popping up. The infidels who came to interview you."

Al-Shakiri smiled to himself at the memory of the trap he'd laid for those foolish and arrogant enough to believe they had the right to come after him. He'd watched a video clip of the explosion once he was well enough to open his eyes after the operation. It was grainy and taken from a distance, but he was sure that dozens of Americans must have died.

But those numbers paled in comparison to what was to come. Picturing the completion of his plan had kept him sane in al-Shaddadi. Now, as then, it also helped distract him from the pain that wracked his frame.

"Go on." He gestured before exhaustedly dropping his arm back onto the rest bolted to his wheelchair.

Omar spun the laptop around to reveal a photograph taken during his greatest triumph—for now. It was of a burning prison. Smoke rose in the background of the shot but didn't obscure the subjects: two Caucasians, one male, one female. Both were armed. A rifle looked like a toy in the former's hands.

"Our friends in Syria have not yet been able to identify the man in this image," he said. "But we have an identity on the woman. Her name is Madison Grubbs. She is a CIA analyst from their Counter-Terrorism Center."

Al-Shakiri snorted at the title, though a smile tugged at the corners of his mouth. This very photograph was another of his triumphs—though on a far smaller scale than what was to come. That was one thing he had learned from the Americans: You couldn't win unless your intelligence was better than your enemy's. He hadn't known that the photographs would prove useful when he'd instructed someone in the teaming tenements that bordered al-Shaddadi to capture them, but he'd always understood there was a chance.

That was why he would beat them.

First he would cut off the head of the snake. And then the Islamic world would rise up for the final battle in the fight of good against evil.

"Our source in the SDF says the two Americans were in Syria to interview you alone," Omar continued in a concerned tone. "And since the escape, it is you that they are searching for above all others. Is there any chance that they have caught wind of our plan?"

"None. Only you and I know the full details, and I'm sure that I have not betrayed us."

Omar's face reddened. "Nor have I!"

"I know that, my brother."

Al-Shakiri kept his face expressionless. It was good to test your people from time to time, even those as loyal as Omar. It was the only way to ensure they remained that way.

"This Madison and the other American interrogated prisoners who failed to escape. We don't know if any talked, but it seems as though one was moved to a private cell."

"So we can guess that somebody did."

Omar nodded. "Do you see why I'm concerned?"

His fingers starting to tremble as the pain medications wore off, al-Shakiri slumped against his wheelchair. He inhaled a deep breath before he was able to speak.

"Have our people in Washington watch her. She will be our canary in the coalmine."

26

"How do you want to play this?" Adi inquired in English, raising his voice to be heard over the engine noise of the small convoy of unarmored black Land Rovers, their sides now splattered with mud, that was carrying them into the hills of West Sumatra.

"It's your turf." Trapp shrugged. Adi was a good guy, and they'd spent enough time drinking some of Jakarta's seediest bars dry a few years back that he thought he knew him well. But playing the role of the loud, brash American who swaggered into somebody else's home and told them how high to jump never sat right with him.

More importantly, it rarely worked. As long as the locals weren't irredeemably corrupt—and Adi certainly wasn't—then it was better to work with them than in spite.

"He's your suspect," Adi replied graciously. "I am happy to follow your lead. My men will do the same. Besides, if we catch him, I doubt the CIA plans on taking the credit. And the man who caught an internationally wanted terrorist would merit a promotion, don't you think?"

He grinned.

"You're right about that." Trapp nodded. "And if you bag this prick for me, I'll write the letter of recommendation myself."

He glanced around the Land Rover's cabin. It was configured with two benches which faced each other, and in addition to him and Adi also contained two Detachment 88 commandos. They were kitted out in black fatigues, complete with balaclavas, helmets with eye protection resting on top, and automatic rifles. Their upper arms bore the unit patch: an owl on a yellow background surrounded by a red border.

He wondered how that had come about. Did they even have owls in this part of the world?

In total, Adi had brought along a dozen of his paramilitary police officers, as well as a driver for each of the four vehicles. The village they were heading for was small and nestled deep in the mountains. Census information wasn't exactly perfect out here, but there were likely no more than fifty inhabitants. The ratio was more than sufficient to deter trouble.

"You said al-Shakiri's parents are still alive, right?" Trapp asked as he mulled things over.

"According to the locals." Adi nodded. "You think they know where he is?"

"I want to set a fox loose in the hen house," Trapp decided. "You have foxes out here?"

"Flying foxes," Adi said. "Bats. Not quite the same thing, but I understand the metaphor."

Trapp continued, "From what we know of al-Shakiri, he's detail-oriented. Hell, he planned the largest ISIS attack in Syria in the last three years using a twenty-dollar burner phone. I'm guessing he has at least one set of friendly eyes in the village. If not his parents, then someone close by."

And, he thought, the kind of man who'd planned a follow-up attack like the one that had killed Eddie Muniz had at least one of the deadly sins: pride. It was time to throw him off balance. See what happened when not everything went to plan.

Adi shot him a thumbs-up. “My men will interview the families of the suspects who disappeared over the past couple of weeks. They might know something. I doubt it, but these Islamists aren’t always...”

He trailed away, seemingly searching for the correct phrase in English. Trapp finished for him. “The best and the brightest?”

“Exactly. It’s possible they’ll let something slip. You and I will speak to his parents.”

The Land Rover hit a pothole, throwing them all a few inches up off the bench. Trapp landed heavily. The roads this far from the port city of Padang barely deserved the name. They were dirt tracks, turned coal black by the monsoon rains. Trapp guessed the mud ran deep enough to swallow the vehicle he was currently riding in whole.

And yet every few minutes, the convoy was forced to stop, engines idling as an impossibly overburdened truck chewed through the mud heading in the opposite direction.

“They won’t stop,” Adi said as one such vehicle, laden with a dozen tree trunks each too wide for a man to close his arms around, nearly sheared the Land Rover’s side mirror clean off as it sped down the hill.

Trapp twisted to look out of the rear window, wondering how the driver managed to keep it under control. It reminded him of a soapbox car, rider long since pitched out, tumbling toward a certain collision.

“I figured,” he said wryly, still staring out of the raindrop-soaked rear window.

Another hour and they reached the village. It was a collection of mostly wooden structures, some roofed with corrugated iron, others a latticework of palm leaves. Many of the buildings were raised off the ground on stilts, presumably to save the contents from monsoon flooding.

It didn't look like a pleasant place to live. But Trapp wondered what about al-Shakiri's upbringing had driven him into the arms of militant Islam, instead of the ranks of millions of migrant workers who moved to the country's cities each year in search of a better life.

He climbed out of the Land Rover, losing his right boot to four inches of mud. He pulled it out with an audible pop.

"At least it isn't raining," he said, glancing up at the foreboding dark sky.

"For now."

Half of Adi's men took up positions at the exits of the village to catch anyone who chose to run. Trapp privately thought it was hopeless. The jungle swallowed the settlement on all sides. These people would know where to hide better than anyone. And they would be impossible to find.

The rest, Adi and Trapp included, entered the village.

In front of each of the homes was a square freestanding porch. It seemed to be where the entire family hung out during the day. A few kids were playing buck naked in the rain but were quickly gathered up by their parents and older siblings. Some displayed no interest at all, and others stared resentfully at the newcomers.

Adi held up his badge. He raised his voice and spoke in rapid-fire Bahasa—the local Malay dialect. Trapp didn't listen. He studied the faces of those watching his, searching for anything that didn't belong, anyone watching just a little too closely.

But they all were. He wondered when the last foreigner had visited this place. Maybe not for decades. Perhaps not since the Dutch left.

Stop flattering yourself, he thought.

Adi let out a low whistle, and his men separated, going door to door to interview the families of the suspects. Trapp wished he'd asked them to take off at least some of their battle rattle. They resembled heavily armored cyborgs. There was a reason detectives back home wore civilian clothing, after all.

"It's this one," Adi said after consulting what appeared to be a hand-drawn map of the village before slipping it back into his pocket. He pointed at a ramshackle dwelling. Unlike the others, nobody was sitting on the porch. One of the Detachment 88 commandos followed, eyes roving for threats to his boss's safety.

"You think anyone's home?" Trapp asked, wondering if al-Shakiri was one step ahead of him.

The Indonesian police captain called out in his native language instead of answering. A voice answered from within the one-roomed home. It sounded thin and weak.

That answers that.

As Adi negotiated entrance to the meager dwelling, Trapp examined it. He wondered if the prodigal son had ever returned, or if he'd ever even planned to. He certainly hadn't sent any money back to his parents to allow them to move even a few steps up from crushing subsistence poverty.

Maybe this was a dead end. If he cared this little about the people who had raised him, was it likely he had anyone watching this place now?

Adi gestured for Trapp to join him. In place of a door, there was a curtain of blue plastic sheeting to ward off the rain. The creases were white with age and use, making it resemble the surface of the ocean. It was pulled aside from inside, revealing a gloomy interior. There wasn't much more room than a two-man tent. On the wooden floor lay two sleeping mats, on top of which sat an elderly man and his wife. She was veiled and stared at the floor.

"Ask your questions," Adi said. "I will translate."

Trapp reached into his pocket and flashed the intake photo

of Khaled al-Shakiri. Adi said something he presumed was, "Do you recognize this man?"

The father, his hair white with age and dark features creased from decades spent working in the sun, peered at the image. The whites of his eyes had a yellow tinge. He didn't react but spoke quietly.

"He confirms it's his son," Adi translated.

"When was the last time you saw him?"

"Many years, he says. Whenever the police last came."

"Not this week?" Trapp pressed, studying the old man's face for any sign of recognition. "He's back in Indonesia. Did he visit?"

Once Adi had finished translating, the man's eyes flared wide with shock, for a moment revealing a sense of the vitality and curiosity he must have had as a young man. Life had beaten all that out of him.

"It is news to him."

For the first time, al-Shakiri's mother stirred. Like her husband's, her eyes appeared jaundiced. Trapp wondered if there was something in the water. They were about all he could see of her. Despite her age and wear, her eyes flashed with intensity. She looked from Adi to Trapp and settled there, fixing him with a vicious glare. She stabbed her finger as she spoke.

"She says he's not welcome here," Adi said. "He never gave her a grandchild. He abandoned them to this life. He has the devil in him."

That was true enough, Trapp thought. He was sure now that this was a dead end. It had been worth a shot, but these people knew nothing.

"Thank them for their time, will you?" he said with a heavy sigh before turning away. He caught himself and reached into his wallet. He didn't have any Indonesian rupiah, but he had a few hundred bucks in greenbacks. They would probably prefer it that way.

Trapp felt the back of his neck prickle as he withdrew about half the cash and pocketed the wallet. He folded the bills between his fingers and thrust them through the opening into the shack. The old man protested, but al-Shakiri's mother shot her husband a withering stare.

I know how that feels, Trapp thought.

He turned away for good.

"What did you do that for?"

"It's the government's money, not mine," Trapp said, glancing around surreptitiously as he tried to work out what had set off his instincts a moment before. "Maybe I'm growing soft."

"Sure," Adi laughed.

Then Trapp caught it. A teenage kid was hiding in the gap between two of the houses. His feet were swallowed in mud all the way up to his ankles. He was staring at the newcomers, neck hunched forward with interest.

He turned to Adi. "Don't look now," he said softly, "but I want you to send your guy behind those two houses. Someone is watching us. I want to find out why."

Adi laughed and slapped him on the back as though they were sharing a joke. He turned to his bodyguard and issued the instruction, and then started walking with Trapp in front of the two shacks.

"Could be nothing," he said as they walked.

"Yeah, could be."

Trapp slowed his pace as they approached the spot in which the lookout was hiding. They would cross him laterally if they continued on this path. The kid had no reason to suspect they had any nefarious intentions toward him. He waited until he judged that Adi's guy had sufficient time to get in place.

"Now," he said, spinning and lurching toward the kid, whose eyes went wide as he backpedaled hastily, then started to sprint between the two houses, throwing up sprays of mud in the wake of his light, quick feet.

Only to run headfirst into a Detachment 88 commando who had at least a foot and a half and eighty pounds on him. It wasn't a fair fight.

"You'll learn, kid," Trapp murmured. He waited with Adi as the bodyguard slapped a pair of plastic zip-cuffs on the teenager's wrists and marched him toward them.

Adi frisked him quickly but professionally. He pulled a cell phone wrapped in a plastic bag from the boy's back pocket, along with a thin wad of local currency. He flicked through it.

"A fortnight's wages out here," he said to Trapp when he was done counting.

"Seems like a lot," he agreed. "And that's a nice phone."

As they spoke, their captive stared sullenly at the ground. Adi pulled the cell phone out of the bag.

"You're right. It's an iPhone. An old one, but it works."

Trapp waited as Adi questioned the boy. He didn't attempt to interfere. This was terrain his friend was much better suited to than a foreigner, ignorant of local customs. It took a few minutes. A crowd gathered around them, watching silently, but did not protest.

Finally Adi turned back.

"He says his cousin gave him the cell phone and the money. He was to watch over the village and report anything unusual."

"To who?"

"He doesn't know. He was given a phone number, that's all."

"And did he?"

"Apparently not."

Trapp raised an eyebrow. "You believe him?"

"Not really," Adi said. "I think he's lying about that part. Not about the cousin, though. He seems like a simple kid."

He issued a command to the bodyguard, who cut the boy's restraints but kept a tight hold of his shoulder. Adi removed the phone from the bag, took one of the boy's fingers, and used it to operate the fingerprint reader. He glanced down at it, then flashed the screen at Trapp.

It was open to a messaging app. The picture was grainy but clear enough. It had been texted to a number which was not in the phone as a contact. It showed Trapp reaching into al-Shakiri's parents' home. The money was just barely visible if you zoomed in.

"That should do it," Trapp said with some satisfaction. "Keep the phone. Maybe a technician can pull something useful off it."

"What about the boy?"

"Cut him loose. He's given up all he knows."

27

By the time Madison hung up the phone, it was almost 11 a.m. in Virginia. Jason had been gone for almost four full days, and she'd barely left the office in all that time. Their most recent call had lasted almost an hour as he filled her in on his investigations in West Sumatra, they bounced ideas off each other regarding next steps, and she brought him up to speed on her own progress stateside.

Synopsis: not much.

The Starbucks cup that sat on the table in the dingy, windowless Langley conference room was almost as long as her forearm. She'd requested two extra shots of espresso from the barista, one of the few in the country whose job required a security clearance and an in-depth background check. She opened the plastic lid and peered inside. There was still about three fingers of brackish black liquid left. She screwed up her face but drained it anyway.

Jason hadn't sounded overly hopeful that he would be able to track down al-Shakiri, despite being almost certain that he was somewhere on the enormous Indonesian island. He'd mentioned a cell phone that was being analyzed by Detachment 88's technical people, but so far, that lead hadn't gotten anywhere.

Despite the stacks of files weighing down the conference table and sheets of loose paper in the shape of rolling sand tunes all around her, Madison wasn't having any better luck. She'd decided to take her investigation back to first principles: examining what little was known about their target's childhood in Indonesia and then how he had been radicalized in the hope that she might uncover a clue that she'd previously missed that might help Jason run the bastard down.

But two days in, an idea which had seemed full of promise now appeared hopeless.

She leaned back in her chair and massaged her temples as the extra kick of caffeine began to dump into her system, tag-teaming with the morning's previous infusions to send her heart rate racing. With her eyes closed, she ground her teeth together in frustration—and almost missed the quiet ping from the other side of the room.

Madison lurched upright, automatically checking the table for her cell phone, despite the fact that it was presently securely locked up in a Faraday cage several floors up that prevented all electronic signals from going in or out. Strangely, she realized that she'd been hoping it signaled news from Jason, despite having only just gotten off the phone with him.

Those things are worse than cigarettes, she thought irritably as she looked around in search of the source of the noise. Her cheeks flushed with warmth.

For a long moment, it didn't occur to her that it might be from the laptop running CASPR, since the machine had quietly chugged away at the tasks set by its human overlords for several days now without so much as a peep.

"That better not be an error message," Madison grumbled as she pushed her chair back and walked to the other side of the table.

After this long, she'd mostly given up hope that CASPR would produce anything actionable—hell, that it would find anything at all. She straightened the laptop screen and squinted down at it.

The results screen on the janky Windows XP-style program read: *Links found: 1.*

She navigated the mouse over to the document listed underneath and hovered it there for a second before double-clicking—not wanting to build up her hopes only to be disappointed.

A fresh window opened up. On the left-hand side was an image that was slowly populating on the screen, dial-up-style, and on the right was the metadata associated with it: where the document had been found, who by, when it had been scanned into the system, and so on.

Madison took this in while she waited. The document had been found along with several thousand others in a house in Raqqa in 2018, at which point they had been transported to a warehouse on the outskirts of Baltimore containing millions more, where a private firm had been contracted by the NSA to restore, sort, scan, and ultimately upload the recovered intelligence to a secure cloud network.

After the fall of the territorial caliphate, the work—and most importantly, the funds appropriated—had been put on the back burner. It wasn't until just nine months ago that the document in question was finally scanned into the system. And by that point, nobody was interested.

Except her.

Finally, the file finished downloading onto her laptop. It was three pages long, printed onto pink carbon paper, the kind used for invoices and waybills. The writing was so faint Madison had to zoom in to make out anything at all. Even then she was forced to squint.

The form wasn't written in English, nor even Arabic.

Japanese, maybe. Or Korean? Madison thought. The only part she recognized was a date: March 11, 2016. The rest was a mystery.

Unconsciously, her right hand formed a fist, and she thumped the table, causing the laptop to jump half an inch. Why could nothing about this damn investigation come easily? What was an invoice—or whatever the document was—written in an Asian language doing in a building linked to the Islamic State in Syria?

CASPR could have answered that question for her—it was designed to machine-translate every file it reviewed for search keyword purposes—but the lowest-bidder government contractor clearly hadn't thought it necessary to provide that information to the end user.

Me.

Madison chewed her bottom lip as she tried to work out what to do next. She wouldn't be surprised if the lead meant nothing at all. It wouldn't be the first time that CASPR had added two and two and made forty-one.

She leaned over the table and pulled the secure phone toward her, frowning for a moment as she remembered the internal extension she was looking for. It took a second. She sat back down as she punched it in.

The phone rang three times before it answered. "You got Blaise."

"Blaise, it's Madison Grubbs. How are things?"

"Madison!" Blaise Jacobs, an analyst on the Agency's Asia Pacific desk, said with genuine warmth. They'd worked together when they were both early in their careers, before she had been posted to the Terrorism beat, and had always gotten on well. "I'm doing great, thanks. This is a nice surprise. I haven't heard your voice in what, six months? It's been too long."

"Right," she replied hurriedly, cursing herself the moment she heard the tone of her response.

Blaise took the hint without any sign of hurt. "I'm guessing this isn't a personal call?"

"Sorry," she said with a flush of embarrassment. "But no. I'm running down a case, and I got a hit on CASPR but—"

"Let me guess," came the reply, accompanied by an audible eye roll. "It's all in foreign. Typical."

Madison grinned. Blaise was a polyglot, fluent in pretty much every language known to man. "You got it. You mind taking a look? I'll owe you one. I'd put a translation request through the ordinary channels, but—"

He interrupted again. "You want it done sometime this century. No problem, send it over."

"Thanks, Blaise. I owe you one."

His tone shifted to one of mild embarrassment. "Nah. Remember that time with the Uber? You know, outside of Scott's Taproom. We're even."

She stifled a laugh. "Rings a bell. Thanks anyway. I'll send you the file now."

"Ciao. And don't be a stranger, okay?"

"I won't."

She fired over the email and had a response within fifteen minutes. Blaise had typed out a translation. She started reading.

'Not sure what I'm looking at here. Seems to be a waybill from Wonsan Agritech, a North Korean black-market arms manufacturer based out of South Pyongyang. Looks like whatever you're dealing with landed at the Port of Beirut on the date listed and was then trucked overland through Syria. I've translated the full document in the attachment. Hope it means more to you than it does to me. Blaise.

PS: don't forget that drink.'

Madison let out a sigh, the mild buzz of excitement she'd

had until now fading as quickly as a burst balloon. Was this just another dead end?

She copied the manufacturer's name from Blaise's email and began searching through the Agency's databases. It didn't take long to get a hit. Wonsan Agritech, she read, was purportedly an agricultural equipment supplier primarily focused on delivering low-tech solutions to developing economies that couldn't afford John Deere, or at least those developing economies that were willing to do business with a sanctioned North Korea.

In reality, Wonsan Agritech's tractor sales were merely a front for international arms trafficking. There were very few industries beyond methamphetamine production and currency counterfeiting in which North Korea was anywhere close to world-leading, but arms trafficking was one.

Pyongyang was willing to sell to pretty much anyone, so long as the price was right. They sold high-end ballistic missiles to the Eritreans, and sometimes their bitter rivals in Ethiopia, too. They shipped automatic rifles to every conflict spot in Africa and everything in their inventory to the many troubled states in the Middle East, from Yemen to Iraq.

Madison scanned Wonsan Agritech's list of known products.

"What the heck?" she murmured.

Primarily, it seemed that the company designed and sold computer chips, optics, and weapons sensors. It wasn't the smoking gun that she'd been expecting. She let out a sigh. It was probably unrelated to al-Shakiri anyway. The US Navy had intercepted at least a dozen shipments of arms to Syria that were believed to be North Korean weapons shipments to ISIS. It was believed that many more had slipped through the net. Mostly it was low-tech equipment: ammunition, rifles, grenades, and rockets. She would need to double-check, but she hadn't heard of anything more advanced than that.

But it didn't make sense. Unless US intel on Wonsan Agritech's activities was plain wrong—always a possibility when dealing with a hermit state that didn't admit outsiders—then why would they have shipped anything to ISIS at all?

Madison felt that little itch in the back of her mind that she always got when she was on to something important. It might or might not be related to al-Shakiri at all, but if North Korea had once supplied advanced munitions to international terror organizations, wasn't that worth checking into?

She reread Blaise's email, then double-clicked the attachment he'd mentioned. The itch was still back there, unscratchable through hard work alone, just as it was impossible to make the discomfort of a mosquito bite go away no matter how good the scratching felt. Blaise had superimposed translations in white text boxes over the pink form, which contained both the original Korean and its English translation.

As Madison scrolled through the translation, her eyes widened. She'd missed something. The original manifest had a product description: RK6998B. Blaise had even circled it for her.

It might be nothing, but…

She copied the Korean text into a search box and hit the enter key. The program spat out a response in under a minute. A near record. She opened a neatly typed memo written a couple of years earlier by someone on the Arms Control desk.

It appeared that the Kenyan Coast Guard had intercepted a suspected shipment of North Korean weapons bound for Somalia, and then likely on to Ethiopia. The crew had scuttled the boat in deep water before it could be inspected, but after interrogation, the captain revealed that the bulk of the cargo had been composed of missiles, launchers, and spare parts produced by Wonsan Agritech. It wasn't clear which bucket RK6998B fell into, but the descriptor had been listed in a recovered manifest book.

It all fell into place.

The team al-Shakiri had constructed was heavily composed of aerospace experts. Either he was using them to put together a missile system using parts purchased from Wonsan Agritech or to identify how to target the airplanes themselves. That had to be it.

Adrenaline flooded her system as she imagined what the world would have looked like if they'd succeeded before the caliphate collapsed. The 9/11 attacks had depressed international air travel for years, but there were countermeasures that could and had been implemented. TSA screening, air marshals, increased cockpit security.

"Game over," she muttered.

If al-Shakiri's cell had acquired high-end antiaircraft missiles—and demonstrated the capability to use them—the airline industry would have been toast. What family would book tickets for their precious kids if there was a chance of being blown out of the sky? Insurance rates for business travelers would skyrocket—if the employees even agreed to travel at all.

It wouldn't just be the airline industry either. The entire global economy would take fright. And with good reason.

I need to tell Jason.

Madison glanced at her watch and was surprised to find out how much time she'd lost. It was past midnight in Sumatra. Jason had sounded exhausted when she'd spoken to him over two hours earlier. She thought about calling him anyway but decided that it could wait. It was only early afternoon where she was on the East Coast. She had time to do a bit more digging before he woke up in a few hours. Maybe by then she would have something more concrete.

It was time to pay Erol a visit.

28

"Is everything ready for the test flight?" al-Shakiri asked, anticipation running through every nerve ending in his body and for now at least quieting the relentless pain that dogged his every movement.

Omar nodded, but his expression seemed drawn as he entered the cramped office. He was wearing a traditional patterned batik shirt, its armpits stained dark with sweat. He was carrying a tablet computer.

"It is," he said.

"Good. And the transport? We must be ready to leave immediately. The engineer can complete the second device en route."

"It is in place. The captain has left harbor and is en route to the pickup point. Everything is proceeding to plan. But we have a problem."

Al-Shakiri's eyes narrowed. They were too close to the finish line for problems. He only needed a couple more weeks. Not even that long. "Tell me."

His lieutenant squatted down beside the wheelchair that

the man detested as an affront to his dignity. He'd acquiesced to it only because there was no other choice.

Omar turned the screen on and showed his boss a grainy image. "This was taken in Tadjau yesterday. Densus 88 were asking questions."

"What did they learn?" al-Shakiri hissed. He grabbed the tablet from Omar's hands and stared at the man from Densus 88—the Bahasa name for Detachment 88.

He hadn't been back to the village in which he'd grown up for over a decade, but he remembered what his parents' shack looked like. How could he forget? He'd hated that place for so many years, hated sharing a tiny room with those two frail, pathetic people who claimed to be his parents.

How could they be, really, when they'd long ago given up? There wasn't even a spark of ambition in either of them, let alone the relentless flame that burned in his own heart.

"I'm not sure," Omar admitted as he zoomed in on the image. "I had to travel to Solok to access the Internet safely. It's too risky to do it here. I've made inquiries, but—"

Al-Shakiri stopped listening. He focused on the image with renewed fury, realizing for the first time that it contained a second individual, a Caucasian rendered in sandy, indistinct pixels. Worse still, the man had a flash of green in his hands. American dollars, which he was thrusting through the opening into the shack.

Even after all this time, he felt a flash of filial guilt. Despite knowing that his fate was to serve Allah, to bring about his Kingdom on earth, al-Shakiri had grown up in a society in which male children were expected to care for their parents in old age. He'd left his to rot in the squalor of his own childhood.

The guilt turned to anger. It was easier to face that way.

"Who is he? The white one."

"We do not know. Perhaps the same man who was at al-Shaddadi. Perhaps not. There is no way to be certain."

"Find out."

Omar nodded uncertainly, perhaps startled by the intensity of his boss's rage. "If the Americans have made it to Tadjau, then they know something. They know that you are involved. Perhaps the ambush on their strike team was—"

"Choose your next words carefully, brother," al-Shakiri said coldly.

Instead, Omar reached for the tablet, which he was forced to almost pry from his master's grip. He spoke quickly, as if trying to dispel the awkwardness that now filled the room.

"Our people followed the CIA woman as you instructed. These were taken just a few hours ago."

He flipped through a couple of images, then handed the device back. Now it displayed a surveillance shot taken with a long-distance camera lens. The image showed a man and a woman, both holding coffee cups, sitting on a wide flight of stone stairs.

"What am I looking at?" al-Shakiri snapped, clearly still thunderous with rage.

"This photograph was taken on the Spanish steps in Washington, DC. The woman is Madison Grubbs. The man with her..." He paused to wring his hands before continuing.

"I do not yet know his name, but he works in the Turkish Embassy. It's only a five-minute walk from where they are sitting. I believe he may be the intelligence attaché. If I'm right, then the net is closing in. They found your village. For the woman to be in contact with Turkish intelligence indicates they must know about the engineer, too.

"Perhaps," he ventured, "we should pick another target. There are alternatives. The consequences of the Americans stopping us could cripple our movement. We have expended so much to get to this point."

Al-Shakiri stared at the image in silence for a long time. All his frustration, guilt, and anger over the situation with his parents boiled up inside him. His fingers blanched white around the tablet.

"Boss?"

He spoke softly. "We need to know what she knows."

Omar nodded, clearly deciding not to push his point. "I will keep the tail on her, but it is dangerous. The longer it goes on, the greater the chance of detection. DC and Virginia are infested with their FBI counterintelligence people."

"I don't want you to follow her," al-Shakiri said, thrusting the tablet back at him forcefully. "I want you to take her. She wanted to interrogate me. It's time to repay the favor."

Omar looked back at him, eyes darting nervously around the room. Finally, he gave voice to his concerns. "Kidnapping a federal agent is a risk. A big risk. They may know nothing, or at least have only a few pieces of the puzzle in their grasp. The fact that only the two of them are investigating suggests this, does it not?"

"Are you questioning my judgment, Omar?"

The man looked anguished. "Of course not. But are we burning down a house to fight an infestation of termites? That is my only worry."

Al-Shakiri fixed his lieutenant with a determined stare. He wondered whether his decision was being influenced by what he had seen. Perhaps, he conceded, but not greatly. He assured himself he would have made this choice either way.

"Take her. Find out what she knows, then get rid of her. The Americans are heavy-footed. They will throw all their efforts into finding her and pay no attention to our other plans. Allah wills it."

Omar bowed his head. "Of course. I will set things in motion."

"Quickly," al-Shakiri pressed. "Now, take me to the runway. I wish to see our eagle fly."

29

Trapp started awake the moment the first of three loud, successive knocks sounded on the door to the private room in the police barracks that Adi had arranged for him. He had pried open his groggy eyes by the time the door swung open, clattering against the wall, but hadn't yet sat up in bed.

"Put this on," Adi said, flinging a large dark object through the room's gloom.

Whatever it was weighed at least twenty pounds and landed painfully on Trapp's crotch before he had a chance to react. He looked down to see the Bahasa word POLISI stenciled in white letters onto the back of a ballistic vest. He rapped his knuckles against it, confirming that it was equipped with a thick set of Kevlar plates.

"What's up?" Trapp asked, reaching for his watch on the floor by the bed. He glanced at the dial. "It's 5 a.m. What's the fire?"

Despite the early hour, the Indonesian police captain looked wide-awake. His skin gleamed with health quite unlike Trapp's own weathered skin. He even looked like he'd shaved.

Asshole, Trapp thought sourly.

"You said that al-Shakiri was interested in aircraft, did you not? Perhaps missiles?"

"Yeah," Trapp replied, rubbing his eyes as the heaviness of sleep faded from his body. Madison had caught a break, and he'd passed it along. Adi's enthusiasm—whatever it was for—was catching.

"The Air Force picked up a strange radar contact in the hills about fifty miles southeast of Solok yesterday afternoon. I was only just told about it. Perhaps it is what you are looking for."

"Solok," Trapp repeated as he swung his feet out of the narrow single bed and onto the floor. The tropical heat now flooding through the open doorway had completely dispelled several hours of the aged air-conditioning unit's work. "That's the town where your tech guys detected the cell phone that picture message was sent to, right?"

Adi nodded. He gestured for Trapp to hurry up. "Correct. Come on, the Air Force is lending us a pair of helicopters. But we have to leave right away."

"That's more like it," he replied, enthusiasm building now. He shrugged on a pair of tan hiking pants that were lying on the back of a chair. "You think it's something?"

"Could be a flock of ducks." Adi grinned. "But it's in the right location if whoever was using that cell phone was attempting to cover their tracks. And the area has been known to harbor militants in the past. It's thick jungle. The roads are mostly known only to the locals. It's the perfect place to hide. It's worth taking a look, at least."

Trapp pulled the plate carrier over his shoulders. "I get a weapon, or are you sending me in cold?"

"We'll get you kitted up en route. But if there's trouble, let my men do the shooting. It will be better if you only fire in self-defense. Less paperwork."

DESPITE THE HURRIED START, it was a further two hours before the pair of Indonesian Air Force Eurocopter Caracal helicopters touched down at an airfield on the edges of the harbor town of Padang, and another thirty minutes before they were refueled and a fresh set of pre-flight checks completed. The delay gave Trapp the opportunity to download a recent set of satellite imagery of the target area onto a small tablet computer, though his sat phone's bandwidth was so low the job was barely completed in time.

"My liaison in the Air Force tells me we only have six of these things," Adi yelled as about a dozen men—a mixture of Detachment 88 commandos and local cops—boarded the two aircraft. "And only three of them are airworthy at any one time. We got lucky."

"Great," Trapp muttered, crossing his arms over his loaned M-4 carbine for comfort. He'd never liked helicopters. They were loud, fuel thirsty, and had a tendency to crash in austere environments, killing everybody on board. "You think they'll make it the whole way there?"

"Oh, I'm sure of it," Adi replied as the cargo door raised behind them, sealing them inside. He placed a set of ear protectors over his head, and Trapp followed. The second half of his reply came through the intercom. "The only question is whether they'll make it back."

Trapp shifted as he made himself comfortable on the bench against the chopper's outer wall. The interior was surprisingly roomy, and the aircraft looked relatively new. He knew the maintenance challenges Adi had referred to were no reflection on the local engineers tasked to care for them, but instead a result of the mere presence of rotors overhead.

His stomach fell away as the Caracal lifted into the air. He pulled the ruggedized tablet computer from a thigh pocket to take his mind off it and brought up a map of the area southeast of Solok in one window and the satellite photos in another.

"Show me where you guys picked up this radar contact," he said, showing Adi the tablet.

It took the Indonesian police officer a few moments, but he circled his fingertip in midair over a section of the map that appeared to contain no signs of human civilization, just rugged hills and the occasional volcanic mountain top.

Trapp switched between windows, using two fingers to drag the satellite photos across the small screen until he was looking at the right place. If the al-Shakiri task force had contained more than just him and Madison, an imagery analyst would already have examined the shots. But he'd seen enough of them over the course of his career to know what to look for.

He spent about five minutes zooming and scrolling across the screen before something triggered his interest. He waved to attract Adi's attention and then showed him the tablet for a second time, pointing out a long clearing in the thick jungle. "What does that look like to you?"

"A runway."

"Yeah, that's what I thought. Could be a logging strip, but I don't see any others in the area. What other industry is there up here?"

"Some mining." Adi shrugged, his voice tinny through the headphones. "Other than that, mostly subsistence farming."

"Could be a mine," Trapp thought out loud. "But I don't buy it. I think this is what we're looking for."

"I agree. I'll tell the pilot. My guess is that we are about thirty minutes out."

Further examination of the imagery revealed little. The jungle canopy was just too thick. There were two or three shadows that were possible indicators of dwellings or other buildings, but nothing certain. After a while, he gave up. Whatever was down there, they would have to discover it first-hand.

Trapp's headphones filled with rapid-fire Bahasa as they approached the LZ. He handled not understanding a word of it with a zen-like calm and focused on checking his weapons and equipment instead.

A voice that he guessed belong to the pilot sounded over the intercom as the chopper went into a steep, banking turn and circled over the area. He noticed the other Detachment 88 commandos glancing at each other with interest as the man signed off.

"He says there's smoke down there," Adi explained. "It might mean nothing, but..."

"I don't see many signs of life," Trapp replied, peering out of a porthole but seeing only a thick bank of gray cloud on the other side.

"No."

The pilot's voice came over the intercom again.

"Thirty seconds," Adi called out before repeating the command in his native language. "Get ready."

Trapp unbuckled his harness and checked his weapon and ammunition one last time, then tugged at the satellite phone attached to his belt to ensure it was securely fastened. He glanced over his right, then left shoulder to make sure that his ballistic vest wasn't caught on anything, and then did it all over again as butterflies flooded his stomach.

They were quickly swept aside as his gut pulled the opposite trick from the start of the journey as the helicopter rapidly lost altitude. The motor powering the rear door groaned, and the ramp swung open. At first, he spied only empty air on the other side, but within a matter of seconds, it was replaced with a thick wall of verdant jungle. He sucked in a lungful of thick, warm air.

A couple of seconds later, the Caracal's wheels touched

down with a thump which reverberated through the entire chopper.

Trapp was first out, his rifle's stock pressed against his shoulder as he ran in a low crouch to avoid bumping his head as he leapt out of the rear of the chopper. His boots thudded against firm grassland as he continued about twenty paces away from the aircraft, his eyes scanning left and right in search of danger. He stopped and took a knee, sweeping his rifle's barrel across the thick tree line.

About twenty yards to his left, the second Indonesian Air Force bird set down on the ground and disgorged its passengers. The other bird contained a handful of local cops, who were dressed in green fatigues, unlike the Detachment 88 commandos, who were attired in all black. They moved professionally, though without quite as much assurance as their better-trained colleagues.

Stalks of grass and wildflowers flew through the air before hitting a wall created by the powerful engine of the other chopper. They hung there for a few moments before swirling in place, tornado-like. Trapp squeezed his eyelids half shut to protect them from the assault.

The two helicopters lifted off. Within thirty seconds, the chaos created by their rotor wash was just a distant memory.

"There's the smoke," Trapp called out, gesturing into the thick jungle in front of him.

A pyre of black fumes thicker than a man's torso was gushing into the sky. It seemed too large to be the result of a cookfire, though perhaps there was an innocent explanation. His experience of Indonesia indicated that regular garbage collection was a rare thing. Most of the locals burned their trash. That could explain it.

"What do you think?" Adi asked.

"That way," Trapp said, picturing the strange shadows he'd spotted on the satellite imagery and lining them up mentally with the smoke. There was something behind the treeline, that was clear enough. But its exact nature wasn't, the jungle swallowing all light within twenty feet. An entire army could be camped in there, and they would have no way of knowing.

Adi issued a series of low commands, and his men split up into small units and advanced slowly toward the treeline. He and Trapp followed a couple of paces behind, falling into a command role and scanning ahead for any sign of danger. Every single man proceeded in silence, their tension palpable. Something about this whole situation felt...off.

Trapp took a deep breath through his nostrils and tasted the smoke on the back of his tongue. It was pungent and chemical. Could be trash, but he didn't think so. He couldn't hear any birds.

In fact, he didn't sense any animal life at all. No squirrels sleeping through the trees, not even the patter of rodent paws in the underbrush.

One of the Indonesian commandos called out a low warning.

He interpreted it without understanding the man's words. He sensed the cause a second later, hearing the sound of footsteps somewhere in the trees. He dropped to a knee and searched for the source of the disturbance. Blood pounded in his ears.

A crackle of gunfire erupted a moment later, its source invisible. The rounds chewed up the grass at the feet of three of Adi's commandos. They reacted instantly, returning fire without panic.

"Shit," Trapp swore, sweeping his own rifle left and depressing the trigger. A line of bullets spat out of the barrel, severing vines and sending leaves and branches coursing to the ground. There was no way to tell if he'd hit anything through the thick jungle. "I think it's only one shooter—"

His words were disproved before they'd finished leaving his

mouth. A second shooter opened up to the right of the smoke pyre. These gunshots sounded as though they were coming from deeper in the jungle. As far as Trapp could tell, neither gunman had hit anything.

That won't last, he thought grimly.

"I'm going in," he said, gripping his rifle tightly and rushing into the cover of the jungle before Adi could call him back. He figured there would be a whole lot more paperwork for the police captain to deal with if this mission ended up with half a dozen dead Indonesian cops.

"Jason, stop!" he heard the man call out, followed by, "Fuck!"

Trapp slowed as the jungle swallowed him up. It had rained recently, but the vegetation had absorbed up the excess moisture and left the jungle floor firm underfoot. Strangely—and in spite of the frequent precipitation—it was covered with fallen yellow and orange leaves, like the Virginia countryside in the depths of fall. There were bugs everywhere: beetles the size of a man's thumb, and long, winding, pink-flecked black millipedes. Moths fluttered around him, thick as falling ash.

He kept himself low. Adi's men were well-trained, but it was easy to get disoriented in an environment like this. Easier still to pull the trigger without being certain who was on the other side.

He stopped and sniffed the air, but all he smelled was the smoke. The echo of the helicopter rotors was incessant in the sky above. It made it difficult to focus on the little sounds, the ones that might save his life.

Trapp worked his way slowly toward where he'd heard the second gunman firing from. He chose every step carefully, placing his boot lightly on the ground to check for branches, twigs, anything that might snap and give his position away. The direction he chose was only a guess, but he stopped every few seconds to listen.

Twice he caught... something. Half sounds, perhaps only heavy breathing or the lightest of footsteps, but it was enough that he was sure he was on the right track. The jungle was now so thick that he barely had a couple of feet of visibility. Blood pounded in his ears, beating a tense drumbeat.

He ducked underneath a low-hanging vine. Just past it, a forest of thin, dry tendrils hung from a tree overhead, willow-like but for their dry, crisp texture. They whispered as he passed through them, like a chorus of women sighing. The sound was deeply unnerving, a reminder that there was nothing so terrifying as jungle combat, an environment where your enemy could be fifty feet away without you ever knowing.

Trapp stopped again, goosebumps prickling the back of his neck.

He heard breathing in here, somewhere. Then a crack as a twig snapped underfoot. He froze, craning only his neck in search of the sound. Whoever had caused it had fallen equally still, probably praying that they had not been heard.

It had come from the right. Maybe only a couple of dozen feet away. Perhaps less.

Trapp slowly rotated in that direction. He pressed his cheek against the side of his rifle and swept its barrel a few inches to the left, then the right. An isolated outbreak of gunfire sounded, the first shooter, followed by a sustained answering barrage from the commandos. Then that too faded away.

Seconds passed, then an entire minute. He remained entirely still, just listening, his wraithlike eyes interrogating the gloom for his enemy. He would wait like this for hours if that was what it took. He had done it before.

This time, he didn't have to.

A footstep sounded, slow and steady, like a hand pushing down into a mattress. It was close, not even a dozen feet away. Trapp turned his head slightly, the rifle following. He peered through the tendrils, which hung like a bunch of shoelaces off a cobbler's wall and almost as opaque and held his breath. His heart fluttered with the adrenaline flooding his veins.

And then he saw them. A pair of eyes staring back at him, wide with horror.

Both men squeezed their triggers at once.

30

Three rounds spat in quick succession from the barrel of Trapp's gun, aimed at center mass. He squeezed the trigger again as returning gunfire trimmed the vegetation around him. It came coursing down like snow. His heart beat thunderously in his chest. He squeezed again, no longer seeing a pair of eyes ahead of him.

His vision was narrowed from the adrenaline. He barely saw anything.

He kept firing until the entire magazine was empty. It might have been a waste, but in the dense jungle, there was no way of knowing. He dumped it, not bothering to retrieve the spent casing, and pressed a replacement home. His mouth was dry, and he tasted copper on the back of his tongue.

Was the other guy dead?

He paused, trying to listen over the beating of his heart and the hammering of blood in his ears. The jungle nearby was quiet now, no sign of life—either man or beast. Except him. His heartbeat slowed as he held his breath. Still nothing. Slowly, he took several steps to the right, keeping the barrel of his rifle trained on the spot in which he'd last seen his enemy.

He stopped and listened for movement. Nothing.

There was only one way of ending this. He had to advance and find out for himself. So he did. He crept through the jungle, knowing it would only take a few steps.

It did.

The body had been spun around when the bullets hit it. It was lying slumped over a fallen tree trunk. It belonged to a man wearing three-quarter length denim jeans and a white vest. The latter item was stained with yellow sweat and now soaked with blood. Without body armor, he hadn't stood a chance.

Despite knowing there was no chance that the man was alive, Trapp kicked away his fallen rifle. He patted the body down, discovering a handgun in the front of the man's jeans. He threw it into a nearby bush.

The radio handset thrust through a loop elastic on his ballistic vest crackled in Adi's voice. "Jason, was that you? Are you okay?"

Trapp panted. He realized that though time had slowed for him, it had kept on going for the rest of the world. He reached for the canteen at his waist and unscrewed the cap, draining a third of it to quench his fierce thirst before answering. It washed away some of the copper on his tongue, but not all.

"It's Hangman. I'm fine. Tango down."

"Ditto. We've entered the jungle. Don't get surprised."

He took a knee a few feet away from the body, covering the jungle ahead. The sound of a dozen of Adi's commandos padding through the jungle made it difficult to listen for dangers from the front. He panned his rifle left and right, still on edge as the adrenaline from his brush with death washed its way through his system.

Adi joined him less than a minute later.

"Looks like you were right," Trapp said in a low voice.

"There's definitely something here that someone doesn't want us to see. What's the status of your guys?"

"Alive," Adi confirmed. "One of them twisted an ankle, and another took a graze to the thigh. They'll both be fine."

Trapp nodded. It was about as good as could be expected in this kind of combat. It didn't matter how well-trained you were when you couldn't see, hell, even smell your enemy.

He glanced at the corpse lying face down next to him. It told its own story. Despite being equipped only with a worn, poorly maintained Kalashnikov and no protective gear, not even boots to replace a ragged pair of Nike sneakers, the man had likely known this jungle like the back of his hand.

And even he had fallen.

Adi split his men into three groups, tasked for the left and right flanks, and one for the center. Trapp attached himself to the latter. All three crept through the jungle as the smoke grew thicker around them. A light breeze pushed it from its source in their direction. Somewhere to the left, one of the Indonesian commandos stifled a cough.

"We can't be far now," Trapp whispered.

He was right. They stumbled into a clearing an instant later. One second, there was nothing but dense jungle ahead of them, the next a cramped space amongst the trees. It housed a small, corrugated iron building that still stood intact. It couldn't be the source of the smoke.

Adi detailed two of his men to clear it as the rest provided cover. The door was halfway open, and it didn't take long to confirm that no one was inside. Trapp approached and stuck his head into the unlit gloom. The space was configured as an office, though anything of value had been taken. A computer monitor rested on a battered desk, cables naked where the desktop box should have been. There was a scattering of empty folders and files on the floor.

"Shit," Trapp murmured. "Looks like they just cleared out."

"We still might find something," Adi replied. He didn't sound confident.

They exited the small shack. One of the Indonesian police commandos pointed at an electric cable on the ground. It looked like an industrial-grade extension lead. They followed it through another patch of jungle, only about thirty feet deep, before again emerging into a clearing. This one was larger.

"Maybe not," Adi muttered as they laid eyes on the shell of a much larger brick and concrete structure. The gray construction material was now as black as a satanic temple. The ground several yards around it had been baked dry by the heat. A scattering of gasoline cans told the story of what had happened here.

One of the commandos called for Adi and pointed out a path that led away from the clearing. It had been camouflaged by felled branches and smaller saplings, presumably in an attempt to disguise it from the air. The commando proceeded down it and reported that it led back to the runway. The concealment was thickest at either end. In mere months, the jungle would once more swallow it whole.

Trapp took the sight in and put the pieces together in his mind. Whatever had been happening here was important enough to hide. He had no doubt in his mind that al-Shakiri was responsible for it. Indonesia's militant groups were mostly quiescent, and besides, the timing was just too convenient.

The question was: What were they hiding?

He nudged Adi and jerked his head toward the smoldering structure. As they approached within a few feet, the heat inside was enough to pull them up short. Wincing, they covered their faces with their arms and kept going.

The interior of the building was burned to cinders. The floor looked like lava, where large fixtures and pieces of equipment glowed with heat.

"Any of your guys have a camera?" Trapp asked, not holding

out much hope that there was anything here still possible to identify. But he had to try. It would be hours, maybe a full day, before the structure cooled enough for forensic techs to dig through the ash and debris to make some sense of what had been here.

Adi whistled for a nearby officer, who handed over a small digital camera. Trapp circled the building, closing in as close enough that he was confronted with the noxious scent of the ends of his eyebrows and eyelashes igniting. He snapped pictures of every piece of machinery, zooming in as many identifying symbols—manufacturer logos, part numbers—as he could find.

There weren't many.

Plastic containers around the edges of the walls had melted and burned, entombing whatever had been stored inside of them in a hardened, black concrete—like flies in amber, only not nearly so transparent. Nuts and bolts and screws and hand tools stuck out of the oily mess.

"What do you think was happening here?" Adi asked when he was done.

Trapp shrugged. "Looks like a lab to me. Or some kind of manufacturing facility. But making what, your guess is as good as mine. I'm not sure we'll know for weeks. If ever."

"My men found a road down the mountain," Adi replied. "Just wide enough for a van. Maybe a small truck. It's not much more than a dirt track. But there are indications that it was used recently."

"They must've only just cleared out," Trapp said, scratching his forehead. It was possible that he had missed al-Shakiri and the rest of his crew by a matter of hours. He slapped his thigh with frustration.

"I've contacted local law enforcement. They are setting up checkpoints on every road."

"How far from here to the nearest port?" Trapp asked.

"On these roads? Maybe nine hours. But there are a thousand little coves capable of allowing a boat to shore. We can't cover them all."

A sense of pointlessness welled up inside him. They didn't know what kind of vehicles the enemy was driving. This far from a major city, it might take almost a day before a forensic tech could get out here, make plaster casts of the tire tracks and connect them to a specific make or model. And that was if the Indonesians even had a database containing that kind of information.

"They're long gone," Trapp said, drawing a look of agreement from the police captain. "Send your men to the ports. Have them search every vessel scheduled to leave in the next three—no, seven days. More if you can find the manpower."

"What are they looking for?"

"You said local industry mostly consists of natural resources and low-end manufacturing, right?"

Adi nodded.

"Then anything that doesn't fit that pattern. Machinery, computer parts, whatever. I'm guessing they'll have disassembled whatever it was they were building. I don't expect we'll just stumble onto a live missile."

"Okay" came the reply.

"You think you've got the pull to do it?" Trapp inquired. "Shutting down an entire port will ruffle a lot of feathers with the local bigwigs."

And some of them might have been bought off, he didn't add.

"I'll arrange it. I assure you, Jason, my government does not want to be known as the source of a weapon that brings down an American airliner."

"Didn't do the Saudis any harm," Trapp said viciously before shaking his head. "I appreciate it, brother. Once this thing—whatever it is—gets to sea, it's game over. They will sail to the next port, put it into a fresh container, and it will be gone with the wind."

Adi's radio crackled. He raised it to his lips and replied in Bahasa. When he was done, Trapp held up the digital camera. "You mind if I keep this for a bit? I need to get the photos back to Langley. Maybe they can make more sense of them from there than I can from here."

"No problem."

Trapp found a quiet spot by a felled tree trunk and sat down on it. He retrieved the satellite phone from his belt and powered it up. It was past midnight back home, but he guessed that Madison would be wide awake. She was like him in that way. Once she got the bit between her teeth, she didn't let go until the job was finished.

"Jason," she replied, sounding tired but not groggy. He'd guessed right. "What time is it?"

"Just past lunch."

"I meant here," she said. "Shit, I let the day get away from me."

"Is this a bad time?"

"No. I went to see my contact at the embassy today. Turned the screws a little bit, you know. Impressed on him the consequences his government might expect if they were found to have known something that could have prevented an imminent terrorist attack."

"He give you anything?"

"No. But he knows something, I'm sure of it. He said he would ask around, but I'm guessing he needs to take my request to his bosses."

"So whatever's going on, it's big. Something that matters to them, not just us. Shit."

Trapp leaned back, exhaustion now flooding his body. His neck and back were tense, as much from the frustration of not seeing how all these pieces fit together as the bumpy chopper ride and the rigors of combat.

"Yeah," Madison sighed. "What about you? Any luck?"

"They were here, Mads," he replied, unconsciously giving her a nickname. "We missed them by a hair's breadth. They burned everything they left behind. Adi's people are going to sweep the area, but—"

She laughed grimly. "They're looking for a needle in a... needle stack. It's like that, right?"

"Yeah. Listen, I've got some photos. I'll upload them to you now. I need you to get forensics to take a look. And get some techs down here. I'll send a location as soon as I get off the phone. Can you do that?"

There was no reply, just an empty silence. Trapp pulled the phone from his ear and checked the screen, wondering for a moment if the battery had died, but the LCD glowed back at him. He had plenty of signal.

"Madison, you hear that?"

Her tone, a terrified whisper, sent a chill running straight down his spine.

"Jason," she whispered from ten thousand miles away. "I think there's someone in my house..."

31

For a moment, Trapp's heart stopped beating. It was hard to believe that this could be happening. And he was on the opposite side of the Pacific Ocean, impotent to help. But somehow, he kept his voice level. If someone was after her, Madison needed to stay calm.

"Madison, where are you?"

"Home," she whispered. "I'm home."

"What room?"

Trapp gestured wildly for Adi. The Indonesian police officer shot him a surprised look, then seemed to recognize that something was seriously amiss. He came running over.

"I'm in my bedroom. I was working. Shit, Jason, I can hear someone at the front door."

"Stay calm," he said. "Is your bedroom door closed?"

"Yes. But it won't stop them."

"Turn the lights off in your bedroom, Madison," Trapp said, keeping his voice even and firm. He needed her to listen right now. "Turn the lights off and put something heavy in front of your door. Do it now and do it quietly."

"Okay," she said, her voice catching.

Trapp covered the mouthpiece of the satellite phone. Facing Adi, he said, "Call the duty officer at the embassy now. I need the CIA station on the line. It's urgent. Tell them an intelligence officer is in danger."

Adi nodded, clearly sensing that now was not a time for questions. He reached for his own phone and punched in a number. He spoke in Bahasa with someone Trapp guessed was an operator, then waited.

"I turned off the lights," Madison whispered. "I can hear footsteps downstairs. They're definitely in my house."

"The door, Madison," Trapp pressed. "Is it blocked?"

She paused a moment before replying, her voice breathy when she did. "I've pushed a dresser in front of it. It's not heavy, but it's the only thing I've got."

"That's good. Now do you have a weapon?"

"Not in here," she replied, shock and fear doing battle in her voice. "I'm such an idiot. My safe is downstairs. I never expected—"

He cut her off. Now wasn't the time to give in to panic. "It's fine. Look around, tell me what you see. I want something hard and heavy."

"I—" she panted. He heard rustling. "I have a pair of dumbbells. Small ones, about eight pounds. But they're iron."

"Okay. Pick one up."

"I have it.

"I'm sending help, okay?" he said. "The police will be there soon."

"How long?"

Trapp ground his jaw together and sent an inquisitive look in Adi's direction. Clearly understanding that something was horribly wrong, he wore an anguished expression. He gestured that he was still waiting.

Mouthing the word *fuck*, Trapp realized that Madison was on her own. If whoever had broken into her house wished her harm, then there was no way for help to arrive in time.

"Not long. I need you to get behind the door. Does it open inwards or outwards?"

"Why?" Madison choked.

"Just answer me."

"Inwards."

"That's good. They're going to have to break down that door and get through the dresser. I want you to hide behind where the door opens. The second you see someone, hit them with that weight as hard as you can. Aim for the head and don't stop until they're down."

"I don't think I can—"

He interrupted her. "I know you can. You didn't panic in Syria, did you?"

Madison's voice wavered. Eventually she said, "No."

"Then you won't now. Hit as hard as you can. I don't care how tough they are, no one survives a blow to the head."

"Okay. I can hear them," she said, her voice growing ever quieter until it was barely audible. "I think there's two of them. They're coming upstairs."

Trapp heard the banging all the way from Virginia. It sounded like a bull was on the other side of that door, ramming it so hard the earth shook. He felt sick with helplessness. This was all up to her now. It cut him up inside.

There was one final crash, the loudest of them all. Madison whispered, "God, Jason, what do I do?"

And finally, the phone went dead.

~

MADISON JUMPED with fright as the door splintered. She dropped her cell phone, and it tumbled underneath the dresser blocking the doorway. Terror gripped her stomach, and she stared down at the floor for a few mindless seconds as she figured out whether to go after it.

Stay where you are!

It was as though someone else was in her skull with her, as though the adrenaline coursing through her system was giving her fight or flight reflex sentience. She obeyed without question, holding her position, keeping the dumbbell raised high in the air despite the exhausted ache in her shoulder.

She worried she would be too tired to strike the blow required, but even as the concern came to mind, it seemed to float away. She could do what it took. She knew it.

Whatever the men were doing on the other side, they finally succeeded. The door shattered, falling in a shower of splinters and chunks of wood. What was left of it hung off its hinges. Madison held her breath, knowing that the next few seconds were going to be vital.

With one powerful kick, the dresser toppled over. The first of the two attackers clambered over it, turning his masked head as he searched the room.

Now!

Madison took a half step forward and brought the weight down as hard as she could. It seemed to whistle through the air. The man looked up at the last moment, his eyes gleaming with shock in the darkness. He turned, but too late. The dumbbell glanced off his temple with a heavy, sickening thump.

He crumpled.

"Shit," a voice swore.

For a moment, Madison didn't know whether she had uttered the curse. By the time she processed what she'd just done, the second attacker was scrambling into her bedroom. He came at her in a football tackle, catching her somewhere underneath her left shoulder and slamming her to the ground. As she fell, she dropped the weight. She scrambled forward, but in the darkness, she couldn't see where it had fallen.

She was no longer terrified. She was long past that stage. The adrenaline pumping through her system was sending only one message.

Fight.

The second attacker was heavier than her. Much heavier. His torso was surprisingly soft as she scratched and punched at him. He was straddling her, sitting on her chest. She wanted to go for his eyes, but her arms were too short. She looked up at him, her lungs screaming for oxygen. His masked face was only a silhouette in the darkness. He had a gun in his right hand and was wearing gloves.

"Stop struggling, you fucking bitch," he swore, his tone laced with malice, aiming the gun down at her.

Madison didn't stop, but her ordinarily analytical mind began to work at light speed. It was like the clarity she got following her morning coffee, only a hundred times as intense. She instantly understood that this struggle was hopelessly skewed against her. Her attacker wasn't just armed; he was both stronger and heavier. She could already feel exhaustion tugging at her muscles. Her stamina would fail before his strength.

But there was something else. If they'd wanted her dead, she already would be. He had a shot. All it would take was one trigger pull, and she'd be lights out.

They want me alive.

The thought should have been terrifying, but instead brought a startling lucidity. She couldn't win this fight, not unless the cops arrived in time. What mattered now was helping her pursuers find her.

And there was also the fact that these men had acted with surprising amateurishness. They should have waited until much later, when she was sure to be asleep. The thought gave her strength.

But as Madison considered this, her attacker adjusted his position and rammed his knee hard into her left side. Strangely she felt no pain, but the blow stole the air from her lungs. Her vision started to narrow. She knew she didn't have long. She needed to act now.

The hand with the gun was too far away to reach, she knew. But the other one was pushing down on her chest as the man tried to stop her fighting underneath him. If she could grab it, maybe she could break his wrist and even the odds.

She snatched for it, wriggling with all her fading strength so that he was forced to pull the hand back for balance. Madison snatched at it as he did, in the process ripping the glove from his hand and flinging it across the room, but her fingers closed on thin air.

A sense of helplessness momentarily overcame her at the failure of her plan, but she beat it back.

Her attacker's eyes followed the glove but alighted on something else. Madison followed his gaze and saw the dumbbell only a foot or so away. She went for it, but he was faster, scooping it up with his ungloved hand.

Holding it up over her head, he stared down at her malevolently.

"Last chance."

32

Trapp sat slumped in the back of a Gulfstream executive jet, his head still spinning. Beyond the low hum of the engines, there was no sound. No other passengers. No conversation, no stewards offering drinks. Just hour after hour of silence in which to contemplate his failure.

He replayed Madison's final panicked words in his mind over and over. *"God, Jason, what do I do?"*

But he had no good answer. By the time local law enforcement had arrived, Madison was long gone. The door that led from her small backyard showed signs of forced entry. Her bedroom was half-destroyed. She'd fought hard, that much was clear. But in the end, she'd been overpowered.

You should have done something different, he thought. *Given her the tools to survive.*

The fact that this was arguable, at best, didn't assuage his guilt in the slightest. Madison had been outnumbered. But he was the one who had been on the phone with her when her kidnappers came. He was the one who had failed to give her the tools to escape.

The only—slight—consolation was that it appeared she'd

been taken, not simply killed outright. Whoever had come after her wanted her for something: information, leverage, time would tell. But that gave them an opening. It was up to them to exploit it.

And yet for the next twenty-four hours, he was stuck in this damn metal cylinder as he crossed half a world. A vein pulsed on the side of his temple. He felt as helpless now as he had when listening to Madison's last words. Perhaps more. All he could do now was wait. Wait for the forensics reports to come back. Wait for local cops to pull traffic cameras and local CCTV. Wait for a lead.

Any lead.

It was then that thoughts of what might be happening to her invaded his mind. Trapp had been interrogated before. Beaten. Tortured. Not only after he entered his nation's service, but before, when he was only a boy. It had lasted longer then.

So he knew better than almost anyone else what Madison was likely experiencing. Understood the consequences that would dog her both mentally and physically for the rest of her life. She was a fighter. But every day her captivity dragged on, even every passing hour, would deepen that hole inside her. Make it harder to ever climb back out.

Which meant they needed to get her back. Fast.

The laptop in front of him finally pinged. His eyes snapped open. He'd been waiting for this. He pushed aside the emotional turmoil, squeezed it into a dense cube, and forgot about it. Wishing he could've done things differently didn't make it so. Madison was gone, and spinning in circles wasn't going to get her back.

It was almost dawn in DC. She'd been gone for more than six hours, long enough for Trapp to get on a borrowed private jet, long enough for the CIA, FBI, and local law enforcement to form a task force.

Intelligence officers had disappeared before. Even been

kidnapped. But rarely, if ever, on domestic soil. This was an affront to the entire intelligence community, and no expense or effort would be spared to get her back.

The video feed of the conference room that materialized on the screen in front of him made that plain enough. Equipped with multiple screens, whiteboards, video-conferencing equipment, and enough space for more than two dozen participants, it put the basement he and Madison had been assigned just a few days earlier to shame.

Trapp recognized a number of familiar faces in the process of sitting down: Mike Mitchell, deputy director of the Special Activities Group, several men and women wearing uniforms that marked them out as members of the FBI's Hostage Rescue Team, as well as many more who he either barely recognized or had never seen before.

"Jason." A voice greeted him, more circumspect than when they'd last met. It belonged to Clark Richards, head of the terrorism analysis desk. "I'm glad you could join us. It seems—it looks like you were right."

Flattening his palms against the table in front of him, Trapp physically restrained himself from shouting—and only because he didn't see the sense in totally derailing the meeting. Not while Madison was missing.

"You didn't listen, did you?" he replied. "We told you we were on to something big, and you shut us out. This is on you, Clark."

Richards grimaced. "Now isn't the time to point fingers, Jason. We need to row together on this one. All that matters is finding Madison. And besides, I gave you both room to run on this."

"Getting your excuses in early, is that it?" Trapp said through gritted teeth. "Fine. You're right. We need to get her back. We can park our personal differences until then. But be assured, I won't forget. Now what do you have?"

Richards hesitated for a moment before continuing, perhaps deciding whether or not to fire back. He glanced around the room and then looked back at the camera. "You've seen the photos?"

He had.

A crime scene photographer had meticulously documented Madison's entire house, from the entry point to the bedroom. An image of a bloodied dumbbell raced across Trapp's mind, artificially bright from the photographer's flash. Next he saw a black leather glove which had been found underneath Madison's bed.

And her phone. The screen was lit in the first of the pictures. It had three missed calls from a contact identified only as J. He remembered waiting helplessly for an answer that never came.

"I have," Trapp agreed curtly. "Are the prints back on the dumbbell? What about DNA on the blood?"

"Not long," Richards replied. "We put a rush on it."

"No shit."

"What did she say, Jason?" Mitchell, Trapp's direct superior, interjected, apparently recognizing that the current relationship between Richards and his subordinate was too fiery to be productive.

"There were two of them. At least two," he corrected himself. "She dropped the phone once they burst into the room. I couldn't hear much after that. Just scuffling, fighting. A man's voice—"

"Any accent?"

Trapp closed his eyes and tried to remember. He shook his head with frustration. "No. I don't know. It was too indistinct. Where are you with the traffic cams?"

"We've got analysts going through every second of footage from the area—but there's a lot of it. Half the local residents have doorbell cams. Add that to cameras at local retail outlets, we are talking about days' worth of footage."

"Then get everybody in the whole damn Agency out of bed. Go door to door if you have to." Trapp glanced at his watch. "It's been six hours now. Every minute we waste..."

He trailed off. Everybody knew the stakes.

"We are, Jason," Mitchell said in a considerate tone, doing his best to match his gaze through the camera. "But it's going to take time."

Trapp slammed his fist down against the table. To his immense frustration, the growl of the Gulfstream's engines mostly obscured the sound. "Dammit. Where the hell are those fingerprints? You need to cross-reference them against every prisoner database we have from Afghanistan, Syria, and Iraq. Al-Shakiri's working with people he trusts. They might have come across our radar before."

"We're on it, Jason."

He bit his lip and tried to think. Madison had been smart. He had no way of proving it, but he was sure that she'd intentionally snatched off her assailant's glove in a desperate attempt to help law enforcement identify him. She must have known her capture was inevitable.

Richards cut back in, interrupting his train of thought.

"Trapp, what were you chasing out in Indonesia? If the perpetrators were willing to go to the lengths of kidnapping a CIA officer to achieve their goals, we have to assume an attack is likely."

Narrowing his eyes, Trapp continued, "Our working theory was that al-Shakiri had put together a cell which aimed to attack passenger jets."

"How?"

"Madison found evidence that before its fall back in 2017, ISIS was working on building a surface-to-air missile. That's a low confidence estimate, but she found a connection between a North Korean arms manufacturer and the Islamic State that might have involved supplying missile seeker heads. The intelligence is unclear. You need to get that to the FAA immediately."

"To what end?" Richards asked doubtfully. "You're right, this intel is inconclusive at best. We can't exactly ask them to shut down domestic and international air travel on the basis of your hunch. Besides, this was all a long time ago."

Trapp glowered back at him. "It's not a fucking hunch. The site I took down with the Indonesians was being used as some kind of test facility. The Indonesian Air Force picked up a radar contact a day—no, nearly two days ago now. I think they were testing their missile. If I'm right, we don't have long."

"They sent us the data," Richards said. "Our people have reviewed it, and analysts at NORAD gave a second opinion. It's no more conclusive than the rest of it. For all we know, it was a flock of birds. Hell, it might be nothing at all. Indonesian radar coverage isn't designed to cover the interior. It might've just been a glitch."

"Do you believe in coincidences, Clark?" Trapp snapped. "You think it was just a freak accident that following the trail of this so-called *glitch* led us to al-Shakiri's hideout? Because if that's right, you're even more incompetent than I thought."

"This isn't getting us anywhere," Mitchell interrupted.

"You're damn right it's not," Trapp exploded, the frustration of being trapped in the Gulfstream and thousands of miles from the action surging out of him now. "We need to be focused on saving Madison, not dicking around with this moron."

"And we are, Jason. You said it yourself: The same people behind this plot are the ones who took her. Getting to the bottom of what they're planning is the only way of finding her."

Mitchell rubbed his chin and continued in a more mollifying tone. "You've been on this longer than anyone. You might know something that we don't. So help us out. We need all the details. Anything, even the most insignificant-sounding piece of information, might be the thing that cracks this whole thing wide open. Did you two have any other leads? Was there anything that might have precipitated this attack? We need to know why it happened—and why now—before we have any chance of figuring out where they might have taken her."

"No," Trapp said sharply, automatically. He consciously forced himself to relax. Much as he hated the idea of giving Richards what he wanted, Mitchell was right. They needed to work as a team. He couldn't do it alone. Especially not from here.

"Wait," he muttered. "She was hunting down some of al-Shakiri's known associates. Two of them disappeared from Turkey a couple of weeks back. The Turks either didn't know where they were or weren't sharing. It was probably a dead end, but Madison was trying to breathe some life into it."

Richards and Mitchell exchanged glances, as did several of the personnel behind them. Mitchell responded first. "Jason, you haven't heard?"

"Heard what?"

"An employee of the Turkish Embassy was murdered last night on his way home from the office. He was working late. Someone put three rounds through his back. The embassy hasn't yet released the name, but we believe he is, or was, Erol Aksoy, deputy chief of station for Turkish intelligence here in DC."

"God dammit," Trapp said. He lurched up from his seat, then realized he had nowhere to go and sat back down. "Mike, you need to put the screws on the Turks. There was a reason this guy was killed. Finding out what is how we get her back."

"This is going to be a delicate situation," Richards said. "Once the press finds out a diplomat was murdered, it will be front page news. If a reporter gets so much as a sniff of the fact he was an intelligence agent, it'll lead every news bulletin from here to Jakarta. We're going to have to tread carefully.

"Besides, we have time. If—and I repeat, *if*—this terrorist was building a missile over there in Indonesia, it'll take a month to ship it stateside. Probably more like two. There's no sense in treading heavily and attracting press attention just for every lead we have to go to ground."

"You never heard of airplanes, Clark?" Trapp said derisively, feeling a flash of satisfaction at the look this drew.

"Mike, do what I said, okay? Get the Turks to reveal what they're hiding. They should want revenge as badly as we do. And we don't have time, whatever this goon says. If the terrorists went to the lengths of kidnapping Madison, then their end game must be close. We don't have two months. We might not even have two days."

33

A searing cold broke through Madison's unconsciousness, bringing with it a startling clarity, like an early-morning ice swimmer washing away the thickness of night. She was soaking wet, and...

Naked?

She could feel cool air kissing the inside of her thighs, her bare stomach, and the nape of her neck, and the way individual droplets of water beaded on her skin. The way one joined a second, then a third, before the trio lost their battle with gravity and trickled to the seat underneath.

The information about her seated position came as a revelation. Had she fallen asleep at her desk? She'd been working long hours recently, though she could not yet remember why. But that clearly made no sense. She wouldn't be naked at work. Something else was happening here. She strained to remember what, battling against a body that seemed predisposed to fight her every wish.

Why wasn't it reacting to her commands? She just wanted to raise her chin. To look up and work out what the hell was happening.

Still her eyes stayed closed, as though pulled down by leaden weights. She heard raised, angry voices in the background, bringing to mind memories of listening to her parents quarrel as a young child.

Except this was different. She heard two men arguing, not a man and a woman. Why were they arguing? Was it over her?

Have I done something wrong?

Scenarios spun through Madison's mind with dizzying speed, each more fanciful than the last. Her brain went into overdrive, usually so adept at matching patterns, but not this time. She was working with too little information. If only she could lift her chin. Open her eyes.

Listen.

Something about the tone of the argument gave Madison pause as she felt the glue attaching her eyelids together begin to loosen. She could have opened them but didn't. Not yet. They sounded so unhinged that she held back. Just for a moment.

"How the fuck was I supposed to know it was different?" the first voice yelled. "I followed the instructions from the Internet, just like I was supposed to."

"We stole it from a vet, dumbass. You didn't stop to think the dose for a horse and a human might not be the same? Look at the bitch. It's been a day, and still she's barely breathing. What if she doesn't wake up?"

The first voice grew more defensive. "I'm the dumbass? I didn't allow myself to get knocked out by a five-foot nothing pencil pusher, okay? You were supposed to inject her, anyway. I did what I had to to get us both out of there before the cops arrived. A little bit of thanks would be nice."

"You think the boss is going to thank either of us for putting her into a coma?"

A short silence fell, giving Madison an opportunity to process what she'd just heard. Cold sliced through her, tinged with fear. It was freezing in here, wherever she was. She could feel herself beginning to tremble. But the prickling at the back of her neck wasn't a reaction to the temperature.

She was terrified.

Strangely, Jason's face swam into her mind's eye at that moment. He didn't say a word, though she desperately wanted him to, but simply met her gaze with steely determination. She seized upon it, resolving not to give in to her panic. It wouldn't get her anywhere. Instead she needed answers.

First on the list: Why was she so damn cold?

"Well, what the fuck do we do?" one of the voices asked.

Madison began to analyze the sounds around her, her brain falling into patterns she'd chiseled into it over the course of years. The act helped to calm her. The voice sounded American, which surprised her. The accent was difficult to place.

"Get some more ice. She moaned when we tossed the last bucket over her. Nearly woke her up."

"What if it was just her monkey brain?"

"What the hell are you talking about?"

The man sounded embarrassed. "I read a book once. You know you still blink if you slip into a coma? Some people even react to pain. Doesn't mean there's anything left of their mind. Just a hunk of nerve cells following old programs."

A short pause. Then, "You think too much. But hell, if you want to explain that bullshit to the boss, be my guest."

Madison flinched with excitement. They'd tossed a pail of ice water over her. It explained why she was dripping wet and freezing cold. Next question: Why soak her? What purpose could that serve?

They were trying to wake me up.

Why?

Because... I was unconscious.

Why?

They drugged me.

Instead of provoking another hit of adrenaline, the thought momentarily stunned her. She remembered now, could picture the two men breaking through her bedroom door. Hitting one of them—apparently not hard enough to put him down permanently—then failing to break free of his partner.

As the wave of revelations washed over her, Madison almost didn't hear the footsteps. She felt body heat radiating against her frozen skin as one of the two men approached. She willed herself to be silent, not to react. What was he going to do?

The reality of her nakedness brought a lump of terror to her throat. She was so tired. Could she fight him off, if it came to it?

And then he was on her.

Her kidnapper roughly pulled open her left eyelid and stared inside. The sudden rush of bright light burned her retina. She almost pulled back, as much from the shock of the rough treatment as from the unexpected pain. But somehow she mastered the urge, perhaps aided by the drugs still running through her system. She willed herself not to react.

"I think I got something," the voice said with a hint of excitement. He was peering at her, so close that his two eyes had formed one whole. All she could see through her unfocused pupils was a blur. He was Caucasian, she thought. A little on the chubby side.

"What is it? She awake?"

The first man pinched her cheek roughly. He pulled and twisted, searching for a reaction. Madison somehow forced herself to breathe slowly and steadily to avoid giving her captor the reaction he was probing for. He twisted harder, then gave up in disgust.

"Nothing. Just that monkey brain of yours. Fucking bitch. Let's get the ice."

The two men stomped away. Madison waited a few seconds until she was sure that it wasn't a trick, that they weren't secretly looking back to see if she moved, then haltingly inched her eyelids open. She looked out through a forest of eyelashes, not daring to push it any further.

It took her eyes a few moments to adjust. She was in, hell, she couldn't tell. A barn? A farmhouse, maybe. Her slumped position, chin on her chest, meant that she was staring at the floor. She took in the dusty flagstones, speckled with stalks and clumps of cut, dried grass. A few feet away, the legs of a wooden dining table rose from the floor.

Unable to look up any further without moving her head, and unsure whether she would be capable of doing so in any case, Madison explored her own body next. A wave of relief washed over her as she realized she wasn't naked, just stripped to her underwear. She wasn't sure why the revelation brought so much comfort, since she was almost totally exposed in any case. But she guessed it meant they hadn't...

Touched me.

Madison suppressed a shudder at the thought. But she couldn't focus on that for now. It was clear she was a captive: She could feel the plastic cuffs biting into her wrists and ankles. She had a brief window of opportunity as her kidnappers left to get ice. But there was no way of knowing how long it would last. She needed to make every second count.

She lifted her chin, quarters of an inch at a time, until the whole room came into picture in front of her. It was a farmhouse, that was for sure. An old colonial-style one, with an interior design that might have been modern in the sixties, but not since. The room she was in was the kitchen. Some of the counters were swathed in faded tarpaulins, and in the background, she thought she detected the low hum of a diesel generator.

This was good news, she decided. Construction this old was mainly confined to the Northeast. It also seemed likely given the appliances and electricity sockets she saw that she was still in the United States. She let out a deep, trembling sigh. For whatever reason, the thought comforted her, despite the fact that she was still in tremendous danger.

She slowly rotated her head, taking in the rest of the space, listening intently for any sign that her captors were returning. As yet she heard nothing. Most of the building's windows were boarded up, though a few of the planks used to do so had come loose, allowing chinks of light inside.

An abandoned farmhouse, then. Perhaps on the market—but for a considerable length of time, judging by the level of decay. She catalogued every detail, not knowing which would matter and which wouldn't, and not wanting to be caught out later on. Just a few feet to her left was a kitchen counter. There was no skirting board along the floor, and she could see a rusted and thankfully empty mousetrap peeking out from underneath.

She turned her neck back to the right. Finally, the table came into view. There was barely a square inch of its surface that wasn't covered in detritus. Madison's eyes passed over brown paper bags, bearing logos of McDonald's and Burger King among other fast food joints. Just the sight of them made her empty stomach rumble.

How long had it been since she'd eaten?

She'd heard one of the men say she'd been out for a whole day. And she wasn't even sure she'd eaten since breakfast on the day she'd been taken. Her body reminded her of that fact now as a wave of nausea passed through her. She fought it off.

Madison squinted as she tried to make out the other items on the table. Her eyes were still blurry from the drugs and probably the aftereffects of a full day of unconsciousness. They were so damn small. What were they?

Cell phones!

Her eyes shot wide open with sudden excitement. There had to be almost a dozen burner phones lying on that dining table. If she could only reach one, she'd be able to call 911. The operator would be able to trace the phone signal.

Shit.

She came back down to earth with a bump as the reality of her predicament struck home. She was still bound to this damn chair. Unless she could somehow free herself in the next few seconds, while her kidnappers were gone from the room, then they were nothing more than a temptation.

A scraping noise echoed through the farmhouse, causing her ears to pick up. She held herself completely still for a moment until she was sure that it didn't presage their immediate return. She fought off a growing sensation of despair. She couldn't—wouldn't—allow herself to give up now.

Madison jerked her arm back to test her restraints, but the movement was met with unceremonious failure. Her wrists were bound tight, one to either side of the chair. She ran the same test with her ankles a moment later with a similar result, only this time she realized that here there was a little more play. The soles of her feet were flat against the floor. If she tented her toes and pushed upward, she was able to make the chair rock—even move it an inch or so.

The realization gave her an idea. She was only a few feet from the table. Maybe there was a way she could push herself toward it. There had to be something over there that she could use to cut herself free. She couldn't see any obvious signs of weapons left around her, but perhaps a door had been left open. Failing that, a window.

I'll crawl through a damn sewer, if that's what it takes.

Madison started to push, wincing at the shrill squeal that echoed through the kitchen as the chair legs scraped across the stone floor. She tried again, managing to push herself a full three inches, only to almost tumble over as one of the feet caught against an exposed spur. She splayed her toes wide and dug her heels against the ground to steady herself, eyes wide with tension at the prospect of being caught.

Easy, she reminded herself, even her own inner monologue shaky with nerves.

She tried again, rocking the chair instead of pushing it. It was quieter that way.

Four inches. Then three. A full five. She pushed until her toes started to burn with lactic acid buildup and the arches of her feet cramped from the unaccustomed effort. She was more used to rolling her wheeled office chair a few feet to pour a fresh cup of coffee or check out a nearby computer screen than this. The drugs they'd pumped into her—she guessed ketamine, from the overheard description—had left her limbs like jelly.

But she didn't give up.

"Come on," she whispered, heart racing as she made it halfway to the table. She kept going. Finally, she made it. Her lungs pounded from exertion, as though she'd sprinted a full mile rather than pushed herself a handful of feet. The table was now right beside her.

Instinctively, Madison tried lifting her right hand, only to be brought up short by the restraints around her wrists. She bit her lower lip with frustration and turned her head to the side with impotent fury. She cursed the narcotic hangover dogging her thoughts. The burner phones were only a few inches away. How could she not have considered how she would actually pick one up before going to all this effort?

And what are you going to do with it?

The reality of her near-nakedness reared its head once again. Even if she managed to acquire one of those cell phones, she had nowhere to hide it. Her kidnappers were already perverted enough to strip her down to her underwear and would surely notice if she somehow grew a male appendage while they were gone.

How would you get it there, anyway?

Madison ground her jaw shut. She could figure out the details later. None of them would matter unless she managed to clear the first hurdle. She closed her eyes and urged herself to think, absent-mindedly extending her hearing as far as it would go. Still she heard nothing, no sign that her kidnappers' return was imminent.

But the reprieve could not last long.

Think!

She tugged at her zip cuffs until the pain of the plastic ties cutting into the flesh at her wrists was almost unbearable. A tear formed in the corner of one eye as she yanked again. She tried pulling it upward instead of to the side, but this only succeeded in nearly dislocating her right shoulder. The cuffs were pulled too tight. There was no way she could get enough leverage to break them.

Wait.

Frowning, Madison tried to figure out what had just occurred to her, an itch at the back of her mind. Her shoulder. What about it? It had risen up when she tugged. Unless her arm was made of elastic, that meant the cuff had to have slid up the wooden uprights that made up the back of the chair.

But what good was that to her?

Finally it struck her. If she pulled her right wrist up as far as it would go, until her shoulder almost cramped from the contorted position she was forcing it into, then she could bring her right elbow out and use it as a crude facsimile of her hand. It would only give her a few inches of reach, at most a foot, but that might be enough.

Footsteps.

Madison blanched with fear. What would they do to her if they discovered what she was doing? They surely wouldn't leave her unguarded again. This was her only chance.

No time to think.

She pulled her right wrist up until the elbow stuck out over the dining table. With her full weight, she rocked to the right. The chair would have fallen over without the table in the way. She rested her elbow on it, leaning on the chair's rightmost legs. The cell phone was just an inch or two away from the point of her elbow. If she only reached...

They were getting closer.

Come on!

Madison gritted her teeth. She pushed her elbow out a little farther, ignoring the pain in her shoulder as the nerves there fired off pain messages from its contorted position. At long last, she touched the cool plastic of the cheap burner.

She stopped dead, despite every neuron in her brain urging speed upon her. She was only going to get one shot at this. If she pushed that cell phone even a half inch farther away, it was over.

Lifting her shoulder until tears leaked from her eyes from the pain, she managed to bring the elbow up and over the cell phone. As soon as it came to rest on the device, she dragged it toward her, toward the edge of the table. It fell onto her lap.

Shit, now what?

Definitely no time to think. Madison acted on instinct. Her eyes glanced to the left, in search of somewhere to hide it, and settled on the mousetrap underneath the kitchen counters. She tilted the chair forward, using her elbow for leverage, straining until the burner began to slide. It toppled to the floor, thankfully coming to rest right by the tip of her big toe.

She could hear voices now. Her kidnappers had to be in the next room. No time. She brought her foot back as far as possible, tensed her thigh, and kicked out. She didn't wait to see what happened to it before she threw herself with all her strength to the left—away from the dining table, away from the evidence of what she had done.

Her head thumped against the hard stone floor. Her vision

flashed white. She heard running footsteps as the two men urgently entered the kitchen in search of the commotion she'd caused.

But as they roughly wrestled her back up, her eyes settled on only one thing. The phone, nestled in the darkness right where she'd aimed it.

Now what?

34

"We're making a habit of this, Jason," a familiar voice called out over the hum of the slowing engines as Trapp bounded down the staircase that had unfolded from the Gulfstream's side, fueled by a burning frustration that came of having been cooped up for over twenty-four hours while a manhunt proceeded without him.

He looked up to see Special Agent Nick Pope, an agent from the FBI's counter-intelligence division. In many ways, the two men were much alike. Military backgrounds, similar build, almost identical height. Pope was leaning against a Chevrolet Suburban with tinted windows and government plates.

"What are you doing here, Nick?" Trapp asked, his throat husky from the dry air on board as the aircraft's pilots joined him on the asphalt. "I don't need a babysitter."

"You sure about that?" the co-pilot groused, shooting him an exhausted, irritated look as they passed one another.

He replied with a withering stare of his own. "I appreciate the ride, gentlemen," he said. "Let's not make it a habit."

"What was that about?" Pope asked, following the two men with an intrigued eye.

"Comms setup died about halfway through," Trapp explained as he pulled the passenger door open.

Pope laughed, the sound punctuated by his own door opening. "And let me guess, you were in the cockpit every thirty seconds asking for an update? On the world's longest flight. Way to make enemies and alienate people, Jason."

"Can it," Trapp fired back. "And I meant it about the babysitting. I'm good."

"I know you are, Jason. Unfortunately, the United States is a country of laws, and they say that you don't get to operate on your own. Not stateside. Besides, you don't have a badge." He glanced across the center console, then cleared his throat, apparently amending what he'd just said. "Not a legal one, anyway. I can help. And you don't have a choice."

Trapp decided to pick his battles. He knew and liked Pope and decided the man could be useful. "Fine. What's the latest?"

The FBI agent took no offense from Trapp's brusque tone, either inoculated by previous exposure or willing to cut him some slack due to the circumstances. Or maybe he just didn't care.

"We put a name to those prints. Nothing on the DNA yet. We're running a familial match search using the commercial databases to see if it lines up with our suspect, but that will take time."

"Any sign of him?"

"His name's Ricky Cobb. Thirty-two years old, native of the district—"

"You're shitting me," Trapp interrupted. "He's American?"

"Born and bred." Pope nodded grimly. "We got a search warrant for his apartment. He's gone."

"Tell me about him."

"Nothing much to tell," Pope said, shooting him a sarcastic

look. "Oh, except he got kicked out of high school for writing a manifesto and bringing his dad's .22 to show-and-tell."

"They have show-and-tell at high school?"

"Well, he certainly wanted to talk about it. There's hours of interrogation tapes from back then. We pulled them out of cold storage. Kid's a real creep. Dead-eyed, you know?"

"What was the manifesto about?"

Pope lifted his hand from the wheel and waved it airily. "Usual shit. Jews this, tentacles that. Wrote about how he fantasized about executing every girl in his freshman class for not giving him the time of day."

He glanced up at the rearview mirror, his expression betraying how disturbed he was by what he'd read. "Wrote the same thing over and over, only changing the name each time. 'I push Becca to the wall. I pull the trigger, and she falls.' Rinse and repeat."

"Shit. How do you think he got mixed up in this? Not exactly my area of expertise, but the incel crowd usually lean more to white nationalism and Christian fundamentalism, don't they?"

"Usually. Garden variety nutbags like him are primed for radicalization. Guess he got reading a different set of forums and chose Islamic fundamentalism. He was listed several times in surveillance records after attending Friday prayers at radical mosques in the late 'aughts. Nothing actionable, and nothing we could do about it at the time. Ricky gets freedom of assembly just like every other red-blooded American.

"But get this: In 2014, he books a vacation to Turkey, then drops off the radar completely. No tax records, no bank transactions, not even a cell phone plan during that time. Then he pops back up four years later. Slots back into life like he never left. Except this time, he's a model citizen. Doesn't visit the mosque. Lives with his mom. Holds down a steady job."

"Girlfriend?"

"None we've been able to identify. Neighbors have never seen him with a woman. We subpoenaed the social media companies to get access to his accounts. No messages to or from any females that stick out. Though the kid has spent an ungodly—and I mean *ungodly*—amount of time browsing women's Instagram profiles. Usually the young and suggestively clothed kind."

Trapp fought against the exhaustion tugging at his eyelids. Despite being cut out of the loop on board the jet for the past twelve hours, he'd found himself unable to sleep. Now that unforced error was making him sluggish.

"Okay. So we've got a sexually repressed thirty-two-year-old Caucasian male with Islamic fundamentalist tendencies and an American passport. He most likely joined up with the Islamic State in Syria back in 2014, then slipped back across the border to lie in wait."

Pope nodded grimly, feeding the steering wheel through his hands as he overtook a school bus. "They trained him up. Kept him off the radar until he was ready. And then they sent him back."

"And he's been kicking his heels all this time. Not putting a foot out of place, doing nothing to attract law enforcement's attention. Until now."

"That's what we're thinking, Jason. If they've waited until now to activate him, whatever they're planning must be big."

Trapp fell silent for a moment as he mulled the thought over in his mind. Then, changing tack, he said, "What about the Turks? Do we have anything from them yet?"

Pope shook his head. "Nothing. The director called the head of MIT personally, but from what I hear, it was like talking to a brick wall. We're not exactly in their good books at the moment with the whole F-35 thing. Maybe they have something to share, maybe they don't. But I don't think they intend to no matter how politely we ask."

"Oh, they know," Trapp said grimly. "Anyone run them down on the consequences of holding out on intelligence that leads to a major terrorist attack on US soil?"

"They've been read the riot act. Didn't do a damn bit of good."

Trapp thumped the dashboard, dislodging one of the cupholders. He pushed it back inside, but it got stuck halfway. He pushed harder, and something snapped.

"Fuck."

"Forget about it. They'll just take it off my salary," Pope joked.

It didn't raise a smile. "There must be something else," Trapp said insistently. "Every second we sit on our hands, Madison's chances of survival get lower."

"We're not sitting on our hands, Jason. The CIA is on this. Practically every Bureau agent in the tri-state area has had their leave revoked. We are working night and day to get her back."

"But we don't have any leads, do we?"

Pope stayed silent for a few seconds before replying simply, "No."

"Then we need to shake things up. Go on the offense."

"You got any ideas?"

Trapp chewed on his lip. "Tell me about the suspect. Rick. What do we know about him?"

Shrugging, Pope said, "The profilers say he's likely unstable. His parents took him to a variety of therapists and psychiatrists in his teens. He never engaged with any of them long enough to come up with a diagnosis. From what we hear, they all agreed there was something wrong with him; they just couldn't agree on what."

"His parents are still alive?"

"His mom is. Dad died three years ago of a heart attack."

"They close?"

"Before he disappeared, no. They drifted apart. His pops

was former Navy, didn't like the idea of his only son converting to Islam. Made that opinion real clear. Drove a wedge into their relationship. But after he returned from—for argument's sake Syria—he reestablished contact with Mom. Never said where he went. But she speaks the world of him."

Trapp felt a glimmer of excitement ignite in his gut. Finally something he could work with. "Then let's turn that to our advantage."

~

MADISON LOOKED UP WARILY, the taste of copper on her tongue. The mere act of blinking now caused sharp spikes of pain to travel up the nerve endings in her face. Blood pooled in her mouth. There had to be a cut inside her lip somewhere. She played her tongue across the fragile flesh until she found it. There was nothing she could do to stem the flow. She waited until she had half a mouth full of the liquid, then spat it out of the side of her mouth.

"You're disgusting," one of her tormentors sneered, apparently forgetting he was the one who had cut her in the first place. "Look at you."

"I can't," she muttered pointedly in response, knowing she should be smarter than this, that she shouldn't bait them, and yet unable to resist. "Unless you untie me."

"Shut up," he shouted violently, his spittle flecking her face in a dozen places. "Tell me why you were meeting Erol Aksoy. I won't ask again."

This time, Madison resisted the urge to remind him that he'd instructed her to be silent. Maybe she was learning. After all, they'd only been working her over for what, three hours now? She had no way of knowing exactly. All she knew was that everything hurt. In a way, she was glad she couldn't see herself in the mirror. She could feel what her face must look like. Bloodied and bruised and puffy.

She wasn't sure how much more of this she could take.

"We're friends," she protested numbly in response. "We've been over this. I told you, we met at a conference about extremist radicalization four years ago. We kept in touch ever since. Sometimes he has something useful for me, sometimes—"

She fell silent, realizing she'd made a mistake. These men already knew who she was. They'd taken her Agency credentials from her bedside table, along with the files she'd been rifling through. After that, she hadn't seen much point in hiding the identity of her employer.

But now she'd stupidly drawn a link between her profession and the precise question they were answering. She quickly glanced between the two men. One was darker than the other and a touch taller. Perhaps half-Somali, though that was only an educated guess. He was the one asking most of the questions. The Caucasian terrorist spoke little and seemed less sure of himself, as though he was being carried along a river and not of his own choosing.

If only there was a way of separating them, she was sure she could work on him.

Or are you just trying to convince yourself of that?

"—sometimes we just meet for coffee," she finished lamely, hoping she hadn't left too long a gap in her speech. "And that's all we were doing yesterday. The other day, whenever you took me."

Madison focused her attention on the smaller man, matching his gaze without making it too obvious. She spoke in an almost motherly tone—hating the need to do so but doing it anyway. Her bloodied cheeks ached with every word.

"Listen, I don't know who you guys are or what you want. And I won't lie to you. You're going to do some prison time for this. Two years, maybe. But if you turn yourselves in now, I'll intercede on your behalf. Write a letter of recommendation to the prosecutor. You'll get out after a year. I'll make sure you don't get put in with the animals."

She tried to spread her hands before remembering with a jolt of pain they were still tied behind her back. Sensing the other kidnapper opening his mouth to speak, she continued quickly, "But if you let this drag on much longer, there won't be anything I can do to help. If you're lucky, you'll get stuck in solitary and slowly lose your mind. And if you're not... I don't envy the kind of things you'll see in maximum security. Or the people you'll meet."

A hard, painful slap collided with her cheek and whiplashed her neck hard to the right. "Shut up, bitch," her interrogator spat derisively. "What makes you think you have any right to speak to us like that? Like you're better than us?"

A flash of utter rage burned Madison from the inside. She vowed that if she survived this, she'd make sure that one went away for a very long time. Preferably somewhere where he didn't get the benefit of natural light until he was pushing seventy years old. And a walking frame.

But she focused instead on his quiet partner and murmured softly, "It's not too late."

35

"Elizabeth Cobb?"

A gray-haired woman pulled open her front door, the latch chain rattling as it pulled taut. She peered out of the two-inch gap, her face lined and deep bags underneath her eyes. She didn't look like she'd slept through the night.

"Are you the police? I already told you everything I know. I don't know where my boy is."

Pope flashed his badge as Trapp lingered behind, casing the modest home for anything that might have been missed. He didn't notice anything incriminating. The window frames needed replacing, and the small patch of grass in the front yard hadn't been cut in weeks. The whole place needed a fresh lick of paint, but in that it was no different from most of the homes on the street. It was a modest, working-class neighborhood.

"FBI, ma'am," he said. "We just have a few further questions. Can we come in?"

"I don't know," she said doubtfully, eyes following Trapp as he walked a few paces down her front porch and casually peered inside. "I'm not sure I have anything more to say."

"Ma'am—"

Trapp decided he'd had enough of playing nice. This was moving too slowly. He strode toward the front door and stopped directly in front of it. "Mrs. Cobb, has anyone explained to you what your son has gotten himself mixed up in?"

She touched her throat, eyes widening at the sudden shift in tone, then shook her head. "Not exactly."

"He kidnapped a federal agent," Trapp said without emotion. "It's our belief that he is working with ISIS to pull off a major attack on American soil."

"Ricky?" she said, once more shaking her head in disbelief. "I don't believe it."

"You better start," Trapp snapped. "Mrs. Cobb, your boy went to Syria to fight with the Islamic State. We don't know exactly what he got up to when he was there, but you can be assured it wasn't good. We have fingerprint evidence placing him at the crime scene. There's no doubt about this."

"I don't know," she said, taking an involuntary step back. "Maybe I need a lawyer."

"Here's how this is going to play out," Trapp continued forcefully. "I'm going to find where Ricky is hiding out, and I'm going to put a bullet through his forehead. I won't lose any sleep over taking him down, you understand?"

Pope said, "Jason—" as Elizabeth Cobb squeaked with horror.

"So you have two choices, Mrs. Cobb," Trapp said, ignoring his friend's intervention. "Get your lawyer, do whatever they tell you to do to try and keep your boy out of prison, only to bury him when I'm done with him—"

"Jason!"

"—or work with me," Trapp finished, modulating his tone as he threw the now tearful mother a bone. "Help us find your son, Mrs. Cobb, and I promise you I will do whatever I can to keep him alive. He's going to go to prison for a very long time. But it's better than ending up in a box."

He fell silent but stared expectantly at the trembling woman, his gaze unmoving and unmoved.

Pope's arm had sprung up, his fingers resting just under Trapp's shoulder, but he too fell silent, clearly sensing that the approach might be bearing fruit.

"I can't," Elizabeth choked. "I don't know how I can help you. I don't know where he is. He doesn't tell me anything. Hasn't in a long time. And even if I did, how could I?"

"What do you mean, Mrs. Cobb?" Pope inquired softly.

"What if I do something, help you somehow, and it gets him killed anyway? I don't care what he's done. He's still my child. I would never be able to live with myself."

Her trembling became more intense, and silent tears ran down her cheeks, glistening with the reflection of the sun that streamed through her front door. She reached out and gripped the doorframe and clung on to it as if it was the only thing keeping her upright.

"Elizabeth," Trapp said in a cold, controlled tone. "If you don't help me, you might as well sign Ricky's death certificate. If he goes through with what these terrorists are planning, hundreds of innocent Americans are going to die. If that happens, I assure you that every cop and federal agent in the country is going to have him in their sights. He'll be enemy number one. And they won't stop until they get their man."

She became ashen-faced as every word of Trapp's verbal assault crashed down around her, closing her eyes as she pictured the death of her only son.

"But if you help us find him, I can protect him. There are no guarantees in this world. But I promise you that I will do my utmost to keep him safe. This is your only play, Mrs. Cobb. It's the best deal you're going to get. So what's it going to be?"

Elizabeth's eyes were full of tears as she replied. She started to hiccup before clapping her hand over her mouth. "Okay. I'll do what you want. You have to promise to help him. He's a good boy, I know it. I don't know how he got himself mixed up in this. You need to keep him safe."

"I promise," Trapp said firmly.

"But I don't understand what it is you think I know," she said. "I don't know where he is. I told you already, he doesn't share things with me. Maybe he doesn't trust me. Maybe he never did."

"I know you don't where he is, Mrs. Cobb." Trapp said. "I want you to film an appeal. I want him to see what he's costing you. And what he might cost himself."

"I'M HUNGRY," Madison said, wincing as even the slightest movements pulled at the scabs on her split lip and made the bruises that littered her face smart with agony.

She was still in the kitchen of the farmhouse, where she'd been ever since she woke up, and her two captors were eating as they watched a news program on the television. Every meal was the same: PBJ sandwiches. Right now just the smell of the peanut butter was torture. She wanted a bite as badly as she had ever wanted anything in her life. It felt like days since they'd fed her last. Maybe it had been.

She was so exhausted she could barely lift her chin from her chest. Her shoulders had long ago given up protesting the contorted position they'd been forced into and had now gone numb.

"Give us something, then," the more composed of the two men said, tauntingly holding up half a sandwich. "It's all yours. Just tell us what you were doing with the Turkish spy."

"We've been over this," Madison said, her throat hoarse from dehydration. "He's a friend."

"And I already said I didn't believe you," her captor replied, grinning manically for a moment before taking a large bite of the sandwich. He held eye contact with Madison until he finished it off.

Asshole, she thought sourly. She decided to nickname him Greedy from now on.

Her stomach rumbled. She returned her gaze to the floor, knowing it was hopeless. At least they weren't beating her any longer. That had stopped earlier that same day. Her kidnappers appeared to have shifted to a new tactic: denying her food and water, and even adequate bathroom opportunities.

Well, it's not going to work.

"Hey, turn that shit up," the other man said. Madison looked up to see that all color had drained from his complexion. "That's my mom."

"What are you talking about?"

"It's my mom. That's her front door," the man said, his voice going up an octave. He pointed at the television screen. "Fuck, they must be on to us."

"We knew this would happen," Greedy said as his buddy jumped up off the chair and punched the volume buttons on the underside of the old television screen. "It was only a matter of time."

"You don't understand, man. They know my name!"

A fresh line of text flashed up on the news chyron. It read: 'WANTED FOR QUESTIONING: RICK COBB.'

"What did you think was going to happen?" Greedy said dismissively. "We both agreed to do whatever it takes. This country is sick. It needs to be cleansed."

"Yeah..." the other man said uncertainly. He seemed to be wavering. "But they know my *name*... Wait, there she is!"

Madison kept extremely still, moving only her eyes as she focused on the television screen. The last thing she needed right now was for her captors to remember that she was still in the room. This was the kind of moment she'd been hoping to engineer.

"Ricky, if you're listening to this, just come home," a gray-haired woman—presumably Ricky's mother—said, causing the Caucasian terrorist blanch. "I don't care what you've done. I just want you to be safe."

The camera focused on the woman retreating into her home, the door closing behind her as camera flashes ricocheted off the paint, before the feed switched back to the studio.

"Authorities aren't saying exactly what Mr. Cobb is accused of, but they repeat that he is to be considered armed and highly dangerous. The FBI task force hunting him down has set up a tip line, which should be at the bottom of your screen. If you have any information at all, don't hesitate to give them a call. Now let's go to Janie, with the weather..."

"There's no turning back now, Rick," Greedy said. "They know who you are. You'll spend the rest of your life behind bars. You want that? Me, I want to die. Paradise sounds a whole lot better than the life I got."

Madison now knew his name. That was something she could work with.

And the terrorist's mother had called him Ricky. She needed to get a moment alone with him to appeal to whatever was left of his conscience. Even his soul. If she did, which name should she use? It was a tough choice. She wanted to play on his childhood memories, use them to her advantage without making it obvious what she was doing.

And how are you going to do that?

Frustration flickered inside her. Ricky was hesitating, but Greedy knew it. She needed to separate them, but try as she might to wrack her brain to figure out how, she was coming up dry.

For now, she concentrated on memorizing the tip line

number that had popped up on screen. For half a second, she allowed her eyes to flash back to the cell phone's hiding place on the floor. So close, yet so far. She might as well be separated from it by the Grand Canyon. They almost never left her alone long enough to get to it.

"Who says we get to die?" Rick protested, sounding half-panicked. "They don't tell us shit. We gotta find this place, mow the fucking lawn. What's that about? That worth dying over?"

"Trust the plan, Rick," Greedy said. "The boss didn't do all this for nothing. You know what he's like. You remember, don't you?"

"Yeah," Rick replied, growing quieter. He squeezed his eyes shut and swayed, as if a memory was coming to the front of his mind. "I guess you're right."

"You know I am." Greedy grinned. He slapped Rick on the back, then searched for the jar of peanut butter to make himself another round. "Besides, the boss will be here any day now. We're in the end game. Have faith, brother."

"I guess," Rick murmured. "I just wish I knew what it was."

36

Madison awoke with a start to the sound of engines revving somewhere outside. She jerked upright, cursing audibly as her exhausted muscles and tender flesh protested the movement.

This was different. Something was happening.

For now at least, the farmhouse was empty. She looked around freely, eventually focusing on the small window at the far end of the kitchen. It looked out onto the drive that led up to the farmhouse. She saw a flash of white pass across it.

Momentarily, Madison allowed herself to believe that help had arrived. That her prayers had been answered. That any moment now the Bureau's Hostage Rescue Team would crash through the building's front door, pump a hail of lead into the terrorists who had taken her, and snatch her to safety.

It didn't last.

She slumped forward slightly, ignoring the pain this caused in her bound wrists as reality crashed home. Even so, she kept her eyes glued to the little glimpse of freedom she could see through the small window to the outside, drinking in every detail.

A sprinter-style van had just pulled up outside. Maybe two of them, judging by the dual engine sounds she'd heard. Despite the crushing, ever-present terror of her current situation, a gleam of interest fired up in her chest. At heart she was a detective. She liked solving problems. This was a fresh clue.

The engines cut out, and for a brief moment she heard only peace. Then the muffled sound of voices outside, and the clicks of opening car doors.

Okay, think, she urged herself.

It was already clear that more terrorists had arrived. She could hear at least three unique voices, though not what was being said. How many operatives did ISIS have on US soil? It was hard to believe that so many had been lying in wait all this time.

If they were gathering now, that surely had to mean that they were nearing the climax of whatever it was they had planned. It also fit with her own kidnapping. Drawing the wrath of every federal law enforcement and intelligence agency was too great a risk to take unless an operation was imminent.

But what the hell were they planning? Madison gritted her teeth with frustration as she attempted without any luck to force the jigsaw pieces to fall into place.

She heard the farmhouse's front door opening, then the scrape of footsteps on the ground. She craned her neck as the sound of voices grew louder, closing her eyes in order to help her focus.

A scrap of conversation floated through the air, the words spoken in Arabic, a language she translated easily in her mind. "Take me to her."

A second voice. Concerned. "Boss, you need to rest. You're not looking well."

"Now, Omar."

Madison's face drained of blood. This couldn't possibly be happening. How was he here?

She physically shrank away from the door into the kitchen, pressing her shoulders against the back of the chair. The role reversal couldn't have been starker. Only a couple of weeks earlier, she was the one planning to interrogate a prisoner; she was the one who thought she was in control.

Yet somehow Khaled al-Shakiri had been one step ahead of her this entire time.

She watched as the door handle started to twist. Her mouth went dry, and she would have started to shake if she hadn't squeezed her fists tight, digging her nails into her palms, and forced herself to maintain the barest semblance of control. As the door swung open, Madison was caught in two minds: whether to keep her eyes averted from the devil or to meet him in the eye.

She chose the latter.

The door opened fully, and she would have thrown up her hand to shield her eyes from the sudden brightness flooding through the open front door behind if they weren't bound. Her pupils narrowed, and it took a moment before her vision came back into focus.

Her breath caught in her throat.

It was him.

Strangely, Madison felt none of the sheer terror that she had imagined these last couple of days. She'd created a monster in her mind, and yet Khaled al-Shakiri was a pitiful, broken thing.

He was sitting hunched over in a wheelchair, sweat glistening on his forehead. He wore a wool cap over his head despite the mild weather, and a gray T-shirt clung to his torso. It was difficult to be sure, but she thought she detected a scent of sickness even at this distance.

She catalogued all this in an instant, her mind already whirring. Something must have happened to him in between his escape from al-Shaddadi Prison just a couple of weeks earlier and now. Blinking, she cast her mind back to his prison file, a document that she had studied countless times and had practically committed to memory.

Madison remembered that he'd sustained severe internal shrapnel injuries during the final days of the caliphate. He hadn't been finally processed into the SDF prison camp system for over three months, the intervening time spent in the hospital, and his injuries had never been fully treated.

With his hands on the wheelchair's handles, she recognized the powerful frame of al-Shakiri's chief lieutenant, Omar. It seemed he'd traveled a different path over the past couple of weeks: His frame had filled out rather than shrinking.

"I'm glad you could make it," Madison said, a strange energy flooding through her despite her precarious situation. She coughed as the words triggered a searing flash of pain from one of the many bruises on her front. "I wanted to register a complaint. Your hospitality is terrible."

She sagged forward as she finished speaking, the movement tugging against her zip-cuffed wrists, and grunted with discomfort. She willed herself back upright, not wanting to display weakness. As Omar pushed the wheelchair into the kitchen, the door began to swing closed behind him, but not before she caught sight of something interesting. Her captors were beginning to move boxes into the farmhouse. It was impossible to tell what was in them, but they looked happy. Just as the door clicked shut, she caught a glimpse of a man she didn't recognize.

She couldn't be sure, but she thought she glimpsed the same zip-cuffs on his wrists as she sported on hers. He looked terrified.

Who the hell are you?

"I take no pleasure in causing pain to a woman," al-Shakiri said, his voice barely audible. His face grew tense as he spoke, and she suspected that the words caused him as much agony as they did her.

"Doesn't seem to have stopped you," Madison replied.

"Show some respect!" Omar snapped as he brought the wheelchair to a halt a couple of feet from her. He took a pace closer, towering over her, rage smoldering on his face.

"Enough, brother," al-Shakiri said. "Leave me alone with her."

"But—"

"Look at her. She cannot hurt me. You can wait for me outside."

Omar gritted his teeth but obeyed.

"He's well-trained," Madison observed. Now that the terrorist she had chased for so long was right in front of her, she was sure that he was unwell. Hell, he looked like he was barely clinging to life.

"He believes in me."

"I can't imagine why."

Al-Shakiri frowned, then shook his head. "You wouldn't."

"What do you want from me?" she demanded, feeling a strange liberation from her current powerlessness. Nothing she could say or do was likely to alter her chances of surviving. So she embraced it. "Why am I here?"

"Why were you hunting me?"

"It's my job."

He shook his head. "I think not. I remember you from the prison grounds. I saw the look in your eyes. This is personal for you."

"It's just business," she lied, hatred swelling in her breast as she remembered what had happened to her former friend, Mark. "I'm good at my job. My boss tells me to hunt you down, you better believe that's what I'm going to do."

"Don't lie to me," he hissed.

Madison hated herself for flinching. She'd glimpsed true evil in his eyes. "Tell me why I'm here."

He changed tack. "You are CIA, correct?"

She nodded but remained silent.

"What do you know about what I have planned?"

"The walls are closing in, Khaled. You might as well give up now. We might not know everything, but it won't be long before we do."

He studied her intently for a while but didn't speak. "I don't think so."

"We found your hideout in Indonesia, didn't we?" Madison said, replaying her final conversation with Jason in her mind for anything she could use to convince him. "We know what you were building. Whether or not I survive, my friends will find you. And you will fail."

"Tell me, what is it you think I am building?"

Madison said nothing. She glowered back at him.

Al-Shakiri sighed. He spoke softly. "If I just say the word, Omar will come through that door, and he will not stop beating you until you break."

"Your people already tried that," she fired back.

"They are amateurs," he said coldly, his gaze still burning into her as though he was trying to interrogate her soul. "Omar is not."

"No, just a psychopath," she said dryly, recognizing the false bravado in her own tone.

"Do you think I will be able to strike the White House, Madison?" al-Shakiri inquired casually.

She replied before she had a chance to stop herself. "What?"

His gaze was still intent as he continued. "It is well-defended, is it not?"

Madison swallowed before replying, thinking fast. Something about his question struck her as off. Why attack the

White House? It had to be one of the most heavily defended sites in the country. She didn't buy it.

"That's not your plan," she said confidently.

"No, it is not. But thank you, you have told me exactly what I needed to know."

Panic washed through her. "What are you talking about?"

"You don't know my plan. At least, not enough to stop it. I congratulate you for coming so close, but it will not be enough." He paused, then raised his voice and called out, "Omar."

As the door opened, Madison yelled, "What are you planning to do, you asshole?"

Al-Shakiri smiled as Omar began to push the wheelchair out of the room. The thought seemed to give him fresh strength. "I intend to kill your president, Miss Grubbs. And I will make you watch."

~

TRAPP HAD BARELY SAT down after running down yet another fruitless lead submitted to the FBIs anonymous tipline when Special Agent Pope stepped into the break room in one of the vast exercise halls at the FBIs training facility in Quantico.

The space, which contained a smattering of furniture that looked as tired as they did, was just adjacent to a nerve center set up on the floor of a baseball court, where tables of agents analyzed every piece of information the Joint Task Force received.

And since the initial appeal on local news had been clipped and then gone viral on TikTok, that was a lot.

He lifted a paper coffee cup to his lips, wrinkling his nose with disgust as he discovered it was empty— though not before a couple of cold, acidic drops rolled down his tongue. "Anything on your end?"

"Squat," Pope replied with a grimace. "It's been, what, a couple of days and they're still flooding in."

"Yeah. I just got back. Guy saw a suspicious van parked up near Potomac Airfield. Turned out to be some hobo sleeping off a three-day bender," Trapp replied, venomously tossing the empty coffee cup into the nearest trash can. It bounced off the rim and a couple of drops splashed out and stained the nearby wall.

That about summed up the luck they were having.

Pope glanced at his watch. "Shit, it's almost midnight. I need to take my kid off the babysitter before she threatens to dump her with social services. Again."

Trapp looked longingly over at the coffee percolator. "Go. Anything comes up, I'll give you a call."

"Get some rest, Jason," Pope replied. "You've barely slept in forty-eight hours. You won't do anybody any good if you're too tired to think."

"You're probably right," Trapp said grudgingly.

"I know I am. See you back here at 5 a.m.?"

"You got it."

37

Madison started as she became aware of a presence in the kitchen with her. She didn't know how long she'd been asleep, but it was dark out. Once again, they had left her alone for several hours while they did God only knew what with power tools outside, though not before tightening her restraints and forcing her into an ever-more contorted pose. Every inch of her body protested with agony.

She looked up to see a familiar face in the gloom of the kitchen, on the other side of the dining table. He was staring directly at her, which explained the prickling on her skin. "Ricky?"

He flinched. "How do you know my name?"

Madison paused for a beat before replying, steadily meeting his gaze. Two days had passed since she'd seen the news report, but her chance was finally at hand. "I saw it on the television. That's what your mom called you, right? Ricky?"

"Keep her out of it!" he replied, raising his voice involuntarily before glancing around. He looked like he was falling apart.

"Okay, I will," she apologized, a muscle at the back of her neck spasming as she lifted her chin to keep her attention focused up at him. She thought quickly, sensing that she had a window of opportunity here which she needed to seize—but also that it was a fundamentally unstable one.

Ricky was searching for an out, she was almost certain of it. But that didn't mean she would be successful in offering him one. If she pushed too hard, he might as easily shut down, or she could trigger a self-defense reaction. It would be a narrow tight-rope line to walk.

When he said nothing, she probed gently. "What are you doing here, Ricky?"

Still he didn't reply. He took a few steps toward her, eyes flickering anxiously around the room and a muscle pulsating on his jaw. He seemed to half-close his eyes for a moment and just listen, then peered through each of the doorways that led into the kitchen. When he was satisfied that he was alone, he continued. As he passed the dining table, he picked up a half-empty glass of water and proceeded to her side.

"We don't have long," he whispered, his chest heaving. He seemed on the verge of hyper- ventilating.

"Okay," Madison said calmly, despite her own desperation. "I get that. So what do you want?"

"I want out," he said, his pleading tone almost a confession. "I thought once I got back from Syria that it was over. I did bad things out there. I wake up every night thinking about them. Shit, I was so dumb."

"So what are you doing here, Ricky?" Madison asked, glancing to the door but sensing that they were still alone.

"He pulled me back in," Ricky said, panting from the stress. "They sent me back after training—this was years ago. Told me to slip back into the country and live like I never left. They said they had big plans for me. But then the caliphate fell. I thought it was over. I felt, I dunno... *Relief*. Even when I was out there, I knew I had fucked up. ISIS wasn't what the forums said it would be, you know? I just thought I was going to get a wife. Have kids. Live in some kind of paradise on earth."

Madison sensed she was losing him. "Who pulled you back, Ricky?"

"The guy in the wheelchair. His name's—"

"I know who he is," Madison interrupted.

Rage flashed in his eyes, momentarily beating back fear. "Then you know what he'll do to me if he catches us talking. We don't have time to play games like this. I just need to know: Were you telling the truth about what you said? Can you help get me out of this mess?"

"Okay, okay," she said. She needed him scared, not angry. "You're right, we don't have long. Cut my wrists free."

He gripped her upper arm tightly and squeezed. The pressure on old bruises sent another wave of pain flashing through her nerves. She gritted her teeth.

"Tell me," he snarled.

"Of course I can. You know who I work for, right?"

He nodded.

"We can arrange a new identity. The Marshals will move you somewhere safe. Set you up with a new life, a job. You can leave all this behind. It'll be like a bad dream."

Ricky swallowed. He blinked a couple of times, as if picturing the vision she was painting, then nodded once. "What do I gotta do?"

"Like I said," Madison whispered, not daring to believe that she really had him. "Just cut my wrists free and help me out of here. You do that, I promise I'll help you out."

He shook his head violently, splashing a few drops of water from the glass in his free hand in the process. Madison reeled as she felt the hope die in her breast.

"It's too dangerous," he said. "The big guy, Omar, he scares me. He's, like, on patrol the whole fucking time. I'm only in here because I saw he was checking out the field. No way I get you out of here in time. I have to carry you."

"I can walk," Madison protested.

"Yeah, right. Not after what we did to you," Ricky said. "Besides, it's a long way to the road. No way to get there without being seen. There has to be some other way."

Madison's eyes widened. She remembered the cell phone she had kicked underneath the kitchen counter, and then the number for the tip line that she'd memorized. It seemed insane to share her backup plan with one of the men who had quite literally kidnapped her—in fact, the one who had held a dumbbell over her head and threatened to hit her with it.

What other choice do you have?

The answer was none.

"Do you have a cell phone?" she asked.

He shook his head vehemently. "I did. But when Omar arrived, he took them all."

Dammit, Madison thought. She'd hoped not to have to reveal her secret. But she was out of options.

"What about the address for this place, did you know that?"

He scrunched up his face. "Of course. I found it."

"Okay." Madison closed her eyes for a second as a wave of exhaustion rocked her. She prayed that she was about to make the right decision, that she'd correctly surmised the character of the man kneeling at her side.

She was under no illusions that he was somehow a good person. He had joined an international terrorist group of his own volition, gone to Syria and been trained by them, then returned to his homeland to lie in wait.

But he was also a scared, stupid young man. He'd probably figured he was in the clear for years after the fall of the Islamic State. The last few days would have been as terrifying for him as they had been her.

Almost.

"Under the kitchen counter," she pointed. "There. You see it?"

He turned his head. "Huh?"

"The cell phone. Quickly. Get it, and text this address to the tip line. When the cavalry arrives, lie down on the floor, okay? Make sure you aren't within a country mile of a weapon, and spread your arms and legs wide so that the agents see you're not armed. Do whatever they tell you."

"Where the hell did you find this thing?" Ricky whispered, scrambling toward the cell phone and dropping the glass he'd been holding. It rolled across the floor, sounding as loud to her as a fireworks display.

"Do you remember the number?" Madison whispered.

Ricky shook his head as he stuck his hand underneath the counter, and she reeled it off.

"What's happening in here?"

Madison froze at the unexpected sound. She hadn't heard anyone approaching, and yet somehow he was here, standing in the doorway.

Omar.

She watched in dismay as he examined her bound frame closely, then mounting horror as he started to turn his head in Ricky's direction. The young terrorist was crouched on the floor, the cell phone in his left hand, frozen with indecision and fear. She had to do something.

"He tried to touch me!" she yelled as loudly as she could, hoping to attract Omar's attention. "That sonofabitch tried to fondle me. You guys are creeps. You pretend to be religious, but..."

Tipping her head back, Madison collected as much saliva and spit in her parched mouth as she could, then aimed it toward Omar.

"Get away from me!" she hissed through gritted teeth.

She dared not look at Ricky. She needed Omar's eyes on her

for as long as possible, even though his implacable gaze terrified her. She had never felt more alone, more terrified than she did right now.

"Is this true?" Omar said, finally turning to Ricky.

Madison swallowed hard, realizing that her chest was heaving. She looked at Ricky, and almost fainted with relief when she saw that he was now standing, the cell phone nowhere to be seen.

"I was just trying to give her water," he said lamely, pointing at the stain on the flagstones.

The lie was paper thin. Madison could tell that Omar didn't believe it.

"Yeah, you gave me water," she added loudly. "Just so you could get close to me, right? Tell him that you touched me."

Omar grimaced. He pointed toward the doorway. "Out! Don't come in here again unless I directly instruct you to. Understood? And get some sleep. You have a big day ahead of you tomorrow. You need to be rested."

Ricky nodded hurriedly and beat a hasty retreat.

Madison held herself upright, not daring to heave a sigh of relief. She still wasn't entirely certain that Omar had bought the ruse. And even if he had, would Ricky go through with what he'd promised?

She shivered, realizing there now was an added tension. The terrorists were clearly closing on the climax of their plan. Perhaps this was what had driven Ricky to her.

We're in a race against time.

Omar walked toward one of the large watercooler bottles that the terrorists had trucked in, since the plumbing no longer functioned in the old farmhouse. He tilted it and poured a fresh glass, then brought it to her. He tipped it against her lips, and she drank greedily, hating how easily she gave in to the desperation of thirst.

He was surprisingly gentle in his actions for a man she

knew had committed so much horror. Just being a room with him made the hair on the back of her neck stand up.

He put the glass down and turned to leave. Before he walked through the door he said, "I'm sorry for him. It will not happen again."

38

"It's up here somewhere," Pope said, quickly glancing at the map on the SUVs dashboard to be sure. It showed a road surrounded by fields, deep in the countryside outside of Baltimore. He slowed the big vehicle a little but didn't stop. His voice was hoarse from exhaustion. They'd started early that morning, and this was already the day's sixth stop—all busts. "Tipline got an address, that's all. Probably nothing."

Trapp scanned the information packet the joint FBI-CIA taskforce had pulled together in record time. If he'd been in the right mind to take a step back and examine the big picture, he might have been impressed with the efficiency with which thousands of employees were running down even the longest shots, and the speed with which the analysis was being pushed out into the field.

"Maybe," he muttered, dragging his finger up the touch-screen of the FBI-issue tablet computer. "But I've got a hunch about this. The number that sent the text was clean. Like never been used before."

"Could be a burner," Pope said. "Or a crank."

That was the issue with going public. Even the most minor law enforcement requests to the public resulted in a fire hose of mostly nonsense tips from the borderline insane, and citizens who were more concerned about their neighbors keeping their front yards neat and tidy than wasting police time.

"Want me to call in and request backup?" Pope asked.

Trapp considered the idea, but just as quickly dismissed it. It would take at least half an hour and probably longer to spool up proper backup and get it out here. If she was in there, it was time that Madison might not have. "Let's take a look before we make that call."

"You got it."

"Park it up there," he said, gesturing at a pullout about twenty yards down the country lane. It was hemmed in on either side by thick branches and foliage that together cut off most of the view of the sky. "We'll go the rest of the way on foot."

"Sounds good," Pope replied.

That was something Trapp liked about working with the man. Despite the fact that ninety-nine times out of a hundred, this visit would end up with nothing to show for it, he didn't complain. He was old-fashioned like that. Preferred knocking on doors to the so-called 'policework' carried out from behind a computer screen which seemed to be all the rage these days.

"I need a gun," he said once the car was parked and the engine switched off. His tone brooked no argument.

Pope didn't bother trying.

As he opened his car door, he gestured toward the trunk. "In the back."

The FBI vehicle contained a hard case lockbox that was bolted to its chassis. Unlocking it required both a keypad and a corresponding physical key. Trapp let out a low whistle as he saw the reason for all the security. It contained a veritable armory. Two pistols—both Glock 19s, Bureau standard issue.

On top of that was a single Remington 870 12-gauge shotgun and a Colt M4 carbine.

Also in the back were a pair of ballistic vests and two FBI raid jackets, the letters stencilled in yellow on navy blue. After donning one of the vests, Trapp picked up the M4 and several magazines of ammunition. Pope wordlessly took the Remington.

Trapp also stuffed one of the Glocks through an elastic loop on the front of his borrowed ballistic vest as Pope shrugged one of the raid jackets on.

"I'd let you borrow one," he said while zipping it up. "But it's probably expressly forbidden somewhere in US Code. I'd have to look it up to be sure, but then again, ignorance is no defense against the law."

"But letting me use a Bureau weapon is fine, huh?"

"I don't know where you got that thing." Pope shrugged as he closed the lockbox and the trunk after it. "And if anyone asks, neither do you."

Trapp grinned. "Got what?"

The two men turned and surveyed the target. A few pale tufts of cloud scurried across the narrow patch of otherwise blue sky visible through the trees bracketing either side of the road. It was a pleasant October day, and despite their proximity to the urban crime and decay of the city of Baltimore, this far out from the center, the terrain was positively bucolic.

"What do you think," Pope murmured, reflexively lowering his voice, "down the road or across the fields?"

Trapp didn't like either option. The fields were likely too exposed from the farmhouse. But the road leading up to it was almost certainly covered by security cameras. He let out a puff of breath. "Let's take a look."

They crept toward the turning to the farmhouse. Thankfully, the backroad was quiet. They hadn't passed another vehicle in the previous twenty minutes, and none swept past now, alleviating the need to explain what they were doing with heavy weaponry in a place like this.

Pope pressed himself up against the fence, a few feet short of the turning. He craned his neck up and peered around. "I don't see any cameras," he said softly.

"Could be anywhere," Trapp replied.

To the left-hand side of the road leading up to the house was an open field. It didn't look recently tended, from what little they could see of it. The grass covering it had grown about knee-deep before becoming top-heavy and collapsing in on itself. Wildflowers had seeded the space and now provided flashes of color in random patches.

Trapp looked up and saw that one side of the farmhouse looked across the wide-open field. He cursed the fact that it wasn't planted with crops. Head-high wheat or corn would have been a treat right now.

"It's a risk," he said. "Someone looks out of one of those windows, and they'll see us coming half a mile out. We'd be sitting ducks."

"I agree."

The field to the right of the road was segmented with hedges and had partially been planted with fruit trees. They didn't provide complete cover, but it was better than nothing. More promisingly, Trapp couldn't see the farmhouse from this angle.

He jerked his head toward it. "That way."

Pope nodded. "Agreed. You lead. Remember, we're just taking a look. We don't have a warrant."

"Uh huh."

"Damnit, Jason, there are rules."

"I said uh huh."

"Yeah, that's what I'm worried about."

Trapp hid a smile at the banter. He needed it. He was running on empty. He was almost certain now that Madison was dead. The only reason he was still going was to bring those responsible for it to justice.

He hopped over the fence, wincing as the aged wood let out a crack. They were still at least half a mile from the farmhouse, and there was almost no risk of being overheard, but it was a good reminder to be careful even so. Pope followed, choosing a different spot.

The two men crept through the quasi-wood. Brambles caught on Trapp's jeans, the thorns digging in just enough to draw blood from his shins before the next step tore them loose. A few spikes broke off and remained embedded in his flesh, causing sufficient pain for him to grit his teeth without rising to the level where he needed to stop and do something about it.

Rotten apples and pears coated the ground underneath the orchard. Trapp half-expected to see wildlife passed out around his feet, blackout drunk from consuming the fermented fruit, but there was none. The alcoholic scent made its way up to his nostrils. He paused at the edge of the line of trees, crouching and gazing in the direction of the farmhouse.

"See anything?" he whispered, the first prickling of adrenaline starting to get to work in his system.

"Looks clear to me."

"Let's keep going."

"Roger that."

They stuck to the fence line on the left of the field, which ran parallel with the road toward the farmhouse, though separated by a section of untended land several feet wide that was thick with foliage and trees. Trapp paused after about five minutes and pointed toward the road, guiding his finger toward a metal post.

"See the cameras?" he whispered.

Pope made a noise of agreement.

"They haven't made much attempt to hide them. Hopefully

that holds true on the route we're taking. But keep your eyes peeled."

"This ain't my first rodeo, Jason."

They reached a hedge which acted as the boundary of the sub-divided field they were crossing. Trapp dropped to his belly and crawled underneath it, disturbing a thick pile of dried leaves that had accumulated beneath along with the thick colony of insects nestled within. He paid neither any attention, not stopping until he was able to see what was on the other side.

"Come see this."

It took Pope a few seconds to join him. Trapp gestured out at the field, which unlike the one to the left of the road, or the converted orchard they'd just passed through, seemed neatly tended despite its proximity to the supposedly abandoned farmhouse.

The half of the field closest to their current position was as wild and unkempt as the rest, but the grass nearest the building was neatly trimmed. A riding lawnmower was visible, parked near the fence to their left by a pile of what looked like household trash at the edge of the cropped 'lawn.'

"Interesting," Pope whispered. "Looks like someone's home."

Trapp flipped the plastic cap off his rifle's scope. It provided about four times optical zoom—only enough to give a little extra clarity to the picture his naked eyes were showing him. He swept the sight across the house first, searching for any watching eyes.

When he found none, he made a careful pass across the field. Only about half of it was visible from where they were currently lying, with the rest blocked off by a decrepit barn whose red paint had long ago been replaced by a darker shade of rust.

"Whoever cut that seems pretty anal," he observed. "Grass is cut closer than Fenway Park."

The scope passed over the pile he'd initially mistaken for household trash. Trapp stopped it dead. "Wait."

"What is it?" Pope asked.

"This is the place," Trapp replied slowly, wishing he had a bit more zoom at his disposal. The pile was composed of wooden slats that appeared to be parts of packing crates. A heap of polystyrene pellets, the type used to prevent damage to items in transit, had been swept a few feet in every direction by the wind.

Pope's tone grew excited. "You sure of that?"

"Call it a hunch," Trapp replied, delving into his memory to see if he recalled coming across anything similar on the raid in Indonesia. He grimaced after nothing came to mind. "Something about this feels off. Why cut the grass?"

"A hunch isn't enough for a warrant, Jason," Pope said.

"Who said I needed a warrant?"

"Jason—"

Trapp interrupted, frowning as a low roar from a passenger airliner echoed high above as it passed over them. "You hear that?"

"Hear what?"

"The airplane."

"Yeah, what about it?"

"It's too high up. Unless these assholes have somehow built a PATRIOT missile while living in their mother's basement, this farm is about the worst location possible to fire off a surface-to-air missile if you're planning on actually taking something down. We're missing something."

"It's underneath the flight path, no?"

Trapp glanced up at the sky. "Too high up. A Stinger would have trouble hitting that thing. No way a home-made rocket has a better shot. I'm not buying it. Besides, even if this was their planned launch site, why cut the grass? There's no need."

"Hold up," Pope whispered. "I see movement."

He swiveled the rifle scope back to the house, quickly catching side of what had attracted his friend's attention. One of the doors had opened. For a few seconds, nothing happened. Then two men exited, standing close together. One of them was enormous, perhaps even taller than Trapp himself. Or perhaps that was just an illusion caused by the slight build of the individual standing next to him.

"What do you see?" Pope said.

Trapp watched as the two men walked swiftly across the area of cut grass, heading toward the section behind the barn. "I'm not sure," he replied softly, squinting so hard that his forehead began to ache from the effort.

The larger man walked a step behind the other. His skin tone seemed darker than his partner's, but from this distance, it was difficult to be certain of that fact. His brain might as easily be filling in the details he wanted to see.

But he sensed it wasn't. That man was Omar; he was almost sure of it.

Almost isn't enough.

He focused on Omar. He was wearing dark jeans and a checked shirt. He looked like any other suburban dad at the school gate. His right arm was extended across the opposite side of his body, the hand hidden behind his bulk.

"What are you holding?" Trapp murmured, frustration building inside him. Without turning to Pope, he said, "Any way we can get some air support up here? Something that won't attract too much attention. Not a helicopter. You guys still operate those Cessnas, don't you?"

"ACLU's been right up our collective asses on those," Pope groaned. "Civil liberties lawsuits up the yahoo. But yeah, we have them."

"Do it anyway," he replied, still tracking the two men as they passed behind the barn. "Shit, I lost them."

"What do you want to do?" Pope asked, still lying on his front. "We know someone's in there. Maybe we send an agent in undercover. Parcel delivery guy. Hell, maybe a woman would be better. Less threatening. These guys don't seem to think they are worth much."

"Their loss," Trapp muttered, Madison's face swimming across his vision.

Another passenger jet passed overhead, the echo of its engines slowly building in intensity with every passing second. Pope wriggled to get some space in his front, then reached inside his raid jacket. A fresh sound joined the jet roar a moment later.

"What's that?" Pope said.

Trapp brought the rifle scope back across but couldn't see anything. He pulled his eyes away from it for a moment and checked that the lawnmower was still where he'd last seen it. It hadn't moved.

He shook his head. "Hell if I know. Sounds like a vacuum cleaner, but a bit louder. Leaf blower, maybe?"

Pope shook his head. He had to speak up to be heard. "Loudest blower I ever heard. No way."

Whatever the sound was, it was joined a moment later by another blast of noise. Trapp wracked his brain as he tried to figure out what the two men were up to but came up blank.

"We need to get closer," Trapp said, glancing left and right as he tried to figure out the best route. Was anyone left in the house? Maybe it would be best if they went right down the center of the field and headed straight for the barn. It was even money that they would remain undetected.

"Agreed."

But even as Pope spoke, the pitch of the sound changed. It almost reminded Trapp of a jet engine building to take-off velocity. But that was impossible. He pictured the map of the area in his head. He remembered the offset grid layout of the fields all around. There wasn't a runway for miles. At least not one he remembered.

"Oh, shit..."

"What?"

There was a runway after all, Trapp realized. It explained the cut grass. It explained everything. Al-Shakiri had never been building a missile. He was building...

A drone.

Two of them.

They emerged from behind the barn at the same time, their noses already reaching up into the sky. The rear part of their landing gears were still zipping along the bowling-green surface underneath, but as Trapp watched, both drones launched fully into the sky, almost immediately pulling up into a steep climb.

Each was about as long as the Suburban they'd driven here in, if a fraction of the bulk and weight. They were painted the same gray as a Predator drone, though even at this distance, it was clear the paint job wasn't as professionally administered. Within seconds, they disappeared behind the tree line to Trapp's left, already traveling at speeds that had to be well north of a hundred miles an hour.

"Call it in," Trapp hissed. "We need backup here ASAP."

Pope already had his cell phone in his hand. He looked up with a hint of surprise on his face as Trapp pushed himself up into a crouch. "Where the hell are you going?"

"I don't know what they plan on hitting," Trapp said, gesturing at the point where he'd last seen the two unmanned aerial vehicles. "But those fuckers are moving fast. We don't have time to wait for backup. This thing will all be over by the time it arrives."

39

As Trapp sprinted toward the barn, he cursed himself for being such a fool. He'd been so blind, so myopically focused on the theory that al-Shakiri was intending to bring down a passenger plane that he'd never considered other options.

Drones weren't the weapons of the future; they were already here. Only a couple of years back, the Houthi rebels in Yemen had attacked a major Saudi refinery, increasing global oil prices by tens of dollars a barrel and costing the global economy billions of dollars. There were persistent rumors that the Venezuelan president had almost been assassinated by a cheap store-bought quadcopter jerryrigged with nothing more specialized than a hand grenade.

Hell, the Iraqi prime minister had even posted pictures of the debris left on his roof after his own failed assassination attempt on Twitter.

But all of those attempts—to Trapp's knowledge—had been carried out with technology scarcely more advanced than that used by amateur RF plane enthusiasts. Somehow, al-Shakiri had gotten his hands on miniaturized jet turbines. That changed the game entirely. A propeller-powered UAV was limited to maybe a hundred miles an hour, perhaps fifty percent more at the outside.

The drones they just saw had *lifted off* at that speed. There was no telling how fast they could fly once they reached cruising altitude. At least two hundred miles per hour. Probably a damn sight faster than that. They would be limited only by the fuel they carried on board. Trapp cast his mind back, trying to remember if he'd seen any external fuel tanks, and decided he hadn't. The UAVs had been long, but not bulky. They'd almost looked flat-packed.

Explains how they made it into the country, he thought grimly.

How long could they remain in the air? Twenty minutes? Half an hour? Hell, that was enough time to reach the White House.

"They lifted off a minute ago," Pope said in a low voice as they reached the barn, panting hard from the effort of the fast sprint. "The task force is already aware. They're working up a list of potential targets as we speak."

"Can they see them on radar?"

"I don't know," Pope answered. He glanced at his cell phone. "Damnit, the signal dropped."

"Forget about it," Trapp muttered, sidling up to the barn and creeping toward the far edge. He peered around it and watched as the two men disappeared back into the farmhouse, walking fast, as though in a hurry. There was still no sign that their incursion had been detected. But just before the door closed behind them, he saw a flash of a pistol in Omar's hand.

And then they were gone.

"Shit, Jason, I think I know the target," Pope whispered, his tone suddenly one of abject dread. "The President's holding a rally right here in Baltimore. Today. I saw it on the news. He's kicking off his campaign. Every news outlet in the country will be carrying it live."

Trapp's neck whipped around. "Where?"

"Oriole Park. The baseball stadium. That's what, half an hour's drive from here? Maybe twenty miles as the crow flies."

Both men stared at each other dumbly, knowing Pope was right. It was the only conceivable target. Even Trapp remembered seeing a headline about Nash's campaign launch rally a couple of weeks earlier. Perhaps it had been the plan all along, or maybe just an opportunistic target. Either way, it was the nightmare scenario.

Glancing at his watch, Trapp ran a worst-case calculation in his mind. The drones had been in the air for almost two minutes already. If the UAVs were traveling at, say, 300 mph, they'd be doing five miles a minute. They might already be halfway to the target.

"Call the task force now," he snapped. "They need to get the Secret Service to crash the President. Don't wait, just do it. If they hesitate, he's dead."

"On it," Pope muttered, already bringing the phone to his ear. Trapp stared at his watch, willing the second hand to slow.

If anything, it seemed to speed up. He watched as five full seconds ticked past as the FBI agent waited for the call to connect, picturing the two drones rocketing across the sky as he did so.

There was too much latency in this, he knew, dread building as Pope finally made it through to the switchboard. They needed him to be put through to the right person immediately. That person would hesitate, imagine the consequences for their career of pulling the president out of his campaign launch announcement, only for the supposed threat to turn out to be a false alarm.

Even once they made it past that hurdle, the FBI would have to get in touch with the Secret Service. It would take at least a minute if everything went perfectly, then the same for the message to get out to the president's detail.

"Shit, we can't wait," Trapp swore, adrenaline pulsating through him as Pope finally finished delivering his terse warning.

The terrorists would be watching Nash's rally on live television. Even if the Secret Service managed to crash the president in time and pull him out of trouble, there would be twenty thousand innocent Americans in that stadium. There was no way of pulling Nash out of there quietly. At the first sign of the chaos that would inevitably ensue, al-Shakiri would know the game was up.

But he would still have two drones in the air.

Trapp thought that the political obsessives who took time out of their day to go to campaign rallies were weird, but even they didn't deserve to die for their devotion.

"You're right. What's your plan?"

"They have to be controlling those things from in there," Trapp said, gesturing at the farmhouse. "We need to put a stop to it. Fuck!"

"You think she's still in there?" Pope said in a low, grim tone as he pushed up alongside, pumping a shell into his shotgun.

Trapp didn't answer, but Pope had hit the nail right on its head. This entire tactical situation was FUBAR. They were about to run a two-man building clearance against an unknown number of enemies, with a friendly hostage almost certainly inside. And the goal wasn't—couldn't—be to save Madison.

They had to head off the threat to President Nash.

Even if it cost an innocent life.

"Stay tight to my six," he said tersely, glancing at his watch. If his calculations were even in the right ballpark, they were now running under the hundred-second mark to stop this. "I'll take left, you take right. Copy?"

"Yep."

Trapp quickly brought the scope to bear on the farmhouse,

scanning each of the outward facing windows in turn. He didn't see anyone looking out, but he didn't have time to be sure. "Let's go."

He clutched his rifle as he sprinted. There was a distance of about twenty-five yards between the barn and the main farm building. Powered by adrenaline and weighed down by his ballistic vest, weapons and ammunition, his lungs felt like they would burst by the time he reached halfway. Judging by the ragged, tearing timbre of Pope's breath, he was suffering just the same.

The two men thumped against the outer wall of the farmhouse, Trapp hitting the left-hand side of the doorway that they'd watched the suspects enter just a few moments before and Pope the right. There was no hiding the bangs made by each of the close-spaced impacts. Trapp sucked in a deep breath.

Ninety seconds.

"Go."

He pivoted around his left shoulder and took a step back as he limbered up to kick the door in when Pope squeezed the shotgun trigger. The spot where the door handle had been disappeared in a shower of dust and splinters. Trapp adapted fast and charged toward the door.

Already weakened by the gunshot, it shattered inward as he struck it. He brought his own weapon up quickly, scanning left and right as his eyes adapted to the slight interior gloom.

"Clear!"

They'd entered the kitchen. It smelled faintly of a combination of fast-food grease and recently applied disinfectant. There was a cell phone charger on the kitchen table. Trapp took in a set of cut plastic zip cuffs still lying on the floor. And a circular smudge of something that could only have been dried blood on the flagstones.

"Covering right," Pope said tersely as he entered, holding

his shotgun steady. Two doors led out of the kitchen, each into a different section of the farmhouse.

Trapp rolled the dice. "Let's take yours," he said, barely breaking step.

What mattered now was speed. They had no idea how many terrorists had been left here to guard the launch site, or if al-Shakiri was here himself. If he allowed them even a few seconds to think about their response, he and Pope might pay the ultimate price. And if Madison was still alive, so would she.

"Got it. I'll breach," came the reply.

"Counting on it," Trapp muttered as the two men closed toward the door. The words had barely left his mouth when a second gunshot rang out from Pope's extended weapon. The noise was almost deafening inside the confines of the kitchen.

This time, the broken interior door swung backward of its own accord. The hallway behind was dark. Trapp stepped through the so-called 'kill funnel' and called out, "Clear."

Pope's voice was taut with tension. "Covering behind."

There was an open doorway to the left. It led into a living room that contained a set of 1960s floral-print couches, the designs only barely visible under a thick coating of several years of dust. An old CRT television. There were no signs that the room had seen any recent attention. The windows were still covered by exterior shutters, which only allowed lights to enter where they were already damaged.

"Clear left."

"Following," Pope said, keeping up a running, low commentary. He was good at this.

Trapp pulled open a door a few feet up the wall on the right, heart pounding, relaxing only when he discovered nothing more threatening than an over-stuffed closet. He pulled back as an old vinyl record toppled from a swaying pile on the highest shelf and hit him on the chest.

"Shit," he coughed, a path of disturbed dust tickling the back of his throat. "Clear."

He glanced down at his watch. "Sixty seconds," he called.

"We need to pick up the pace, Jason."

"No shit."

Trapp spun around, knocking the open closet door back, and turned toward the final door remaining in the hallway: the one at the very end. He took a step to his left so that his shoulder grazed the wall as he moved forward.

It likely saved his life.

His foot hovered in midair as he caught a faint strain of muffled voices emanating from whatever room lay behind. A second later, half a dozen holes punctured the wooden door, followed a fraction of a second later by as many gunshot cracks as the sound waves caught up.

Trapp's animal brain begged him to run as far away from this mess as physically possible. But he ignored it. It was only two feet to the door. He closed it in a single stride, hugging the left-hand wall as he moved. Another two gunshots rang out, punching a shower of splinters into the air around him.

"You okay?" he called out in a low voice, not hearing footsteps from behind him.

"I'm fine," Pope hissed, his face turning a shade of purple as he struggled for air. He slumped against the wall to his right for support, lowering his weapon as he probed his ballistic vest where he'd been hit. "Go!"

Trapp swore underneath his breath but snapped his neck back to the doorway. He didn't have time to find out whether his friend was okay. His heartbeat pounded jerkily in his chest as it struggled to provide enough oxygen to a body that was thirstily sucking it down. What a mess.

Fifty seconds.

He sucked in a deep breath to steady himself. It cost him

another whole second. Breaching on his own was suicidal. But what other choice did he have?

Pressing the stock of his M4 hard into his shoulder, Trapp angled the barrel sharply downward, aiming it at the door's lowermost panels. He paused—losing another second—then squeezed the trigger.

The rifle bucked three times against his shoulder. His ears rang from the crack of gunfire in the confined hallway. Almost before the third round had exited his barrel, he drew his right leg back and smashed his heel into a spot half an inch to the right of the door handle. The door swung open, and he threw himself inside.

He emerged into a dining room. The long wooden table that stood pride of place at the center of the room was covered in a thin sheet of transparent plastic. Strangely, Trapp's gaze was briefly attracted to the two chandeliers lying sideways underneath it.

"Get it together," he mumbled under his breath as he swept the room, feeling the familiar sensation of stress tightening the noose around his vision. The edges of his gaze were fuzzy and indistinct and growing more so with every passing second.

Movement.

Trapp spun, his finger tensing on the trigger. He squeezed. The rifle butt thumped against his shoulder. Squeezed again. A throaty cry echoed out as a flash of bright red blood painted the white walls. He fired again. A mixed-race male slumped back, a pistol dropping from his hands and thudding against the floor.

"Shit," Trapp spat, knowing he didn't have time to kick the weapon out of reach. He would have to do this the old-fashioned way, and unfortunately that came with a cost.

For the bad guy.

He squeezed his trigger one last time. Whether his opponent was already dead by this point, Trapp would never know. The man's skull exploded.

There was only one other door leading out of the dining room. It was over to the left, and Trapp figured that meant the room behind angled back around toward the kitchen's other door—the road not taken.

Forty seconds.

"How you doing back there, buddy?" he called out.

"I'm good," Pope choked. "Just winded is all. Took three right to the chest. Wait. Shit...I'm bleeding."

"Stay right where you are. Cover the door behind you," Trapp said as he moved toward the door that the dead man had tried to defend. It was closed. Anticipation tingled within him. This had to be it, surely.

"Roger that," Pope replied.

Trapp scanned the doorway ahead of him. The door looked like it opened inward. It was impossible to say whether or not it was locked. Wishing he had Pope's shotgun, he improvised, drawing his pistol and taking three long strides toward the door, hiding behind the wall to its left-hand side. He moved as silently as possible, aiming his pistol at the door handle.

"Jason—!"

He fired before his brain processed what he'd just heard. He knew that voice. It was Madison.

40

Trapp drove his heel toward the handle, then stepped through the shattered doorway with his weapon raised. His chest was so tight from the adrenaline he could barely breathe. How long did he have left?

Thirty seconds?

Twenty?

The scene on the other side was chaos. The space was a high-ceilinged entrance room, paved with long, polished wooden floorboards. It was easily the largest room Trapp had encountered so far. The farmhouse's front door studded the opposite wall, and to the right of it was a staircase leading up to the second floor.

Almost every inch of the space was covered with electronics. Wires, microchips, even something that resembled a satellite dish was mounted over an open windowsill, from which a tail of cables fed into a bank of computer monitors. They sat on a makeshift desk pushed right up against the staircase, behind which sat a tiny, terrified man dressed in tousled clothing, his hand gripping a videogame joystick.

But that wasn't what attracted Trapp's attention.

Madison was lying on the ground just to his right, her arms raised high over her shoulders and tied with zip cuffs to the staircase's banisters. Practically every inch of her body was covered with ugly purple and black bruises. Her lip was split and seemed to be held together only by an ugly mass of dark scabbing. She looked like she'd been through hell.

And the big man—Omar—was holding a gun to her head. He was sheltering between the man controlling the drones and Madison herself. Trapp didn't have a shot.

She looked up, eyes shining defiantly, and met Trapp's horrified gaze.

"He's the only one left," she said quickly, cut short as her captor jabbed her temple hard with the barrel of his pistol. She let out a guttural groan, her head briefly slumping forward.

Trapp stood, momentarily frozen into inaction as he tried to figure out what the hell to do. He considered emptying the rest of his rifle's magazine into the drone control station but had no idea what would happen if he did. Would the UAVs continue on their present path?

In fact, where the hell were they?

Omar finally spoke as Trapp's eyes began to wander over the computer screens.

"You found us," he said coldly. "But you're already too late."

Trapp said nothing. The brightness on both screens was cranked up all the way, which made it easy to make out what was displayed. Each was split into two, presumably leaving one monitor per drone. On the left-hand side of each screen, a variety of instruments were displayed: altitude, airspeed, altimeter, artificial horizon. On the right was an infrared video feed.

The two aircraft were traveling only a couple of hundred feet over the ground.

He shifted his attention to the right-hand displays, unable to draw anything useful from the instrument readouts. He'd seen similar drone shots before. It was commonly used for night recon, when the visible light spectrum was consumed by darkness.

But why use it now?

An enormous structure loomed ahead of the two drones, growing larger with every passing moment. It took Trapp's brain a couple of seconds to process what he was seeing as he translated the glowing infrared feed into a more familiar picture.

It was Oriole Park, a baseball stadium he'd visited more than once over the years.

The drones hadn't hit their target. But they were close. Hell, he might only have ten or fifteen seconds before they crested the stadium's peak. He didn't even know if they could still be forced to abort the mission, or whether the two aircraft were following a predetermined flight plan.

The guy operating the flight controls trembled. He looked as though he was slipping into shock. No, if he was there, there had to be a chance.

"I don't think so," Trapp said coldly, knowing he had to act fast. "Drop the gun."

"The pilot's innocent, Jason," Madison mumbled, her voice scarcely audible now.

"Silence!" Omar screamed, jabbing her once again with his pistol. This time, the blow appeared hard enough to steal her from consciousness. Her chin slumped against her chest.

"Do that again, you prick," Trapp said, grinding his jaw together.

"Come any closer and I'll kill her," Omar replied. "You know that I have no fear of death."

Trapp's finger tightened on the trigger. He could fire, but not without risking putting a round through the control station behind the terrorist. He took a step to the left, trying to open up a better firing angle, but had no luck.

"Don't take another step," Omar snapped. "Move again and I shoot."

"Please," the guy behind the screens moaned, still clutching the controls but twisting his neck around so that he could meet Trapp's case. "You need to help me. They have my children. I have to do what they say, or..."

"He's correct," Omar said triumphantly. "He knows what will happen if he fails to complete his task. So you see, you are too late."

As Trapp watched, the pilot pulled back on the joystick, and the two drones began to climb as though they were one. They were somehow slaved together, operating from the same controls. It was proof that this attack could still be stopped. On the computer monitors, the all-encompassing view of the baseball park disappeared as the noses lifted upward and was replaced by a fuzzy view of the night sky.

They were climbing. Which meant they were gaining altitude to position themselves for the final descent. To attack.

He had to end this now.

But how? Surely he couldn't talk the pilot into signing a death warrant for his own children. Few men had the moral courage to sacrifice their own flesh and blood, even if the alternative tore the world apart.

Hell, Trapp wasn't even sure he would be able to do such a thing.

Madison stirred underneath Omar, whose attention was now focused entirely on Trapp. She was moving sluggishly, but she was moving. He exhaled a sigh of relief.

The drones stopped climbing. For a second, they levelled out in midair, and then their noses began to drop. Once again, the infrared images glowed with information as it translated the millions of light sources reflecting up from the ground below.

And finally, Trapp understood the purpose of the infrared display.

A bright glow occupied an entire inch of the middle of each infrared image. He'd seen that kind of thing before. A laser was painting the target, guiding the drones in. That was the purpose of the North Korean seeker head. So the drones would hit directly on target.

The president.

Trapp couldn't see the man himself, but he had no doubt what he was watching. The terrorists had someone inside the stadium. That explained the fact that al-Shakiri himself was missing in action. The bastard was there, somehow aiming a laser at Nash without being spotted.

He began to calculate his next—his only—course of action. He couldn't shoot either the pilot or Omar, not without risking destroying the controls. Though he was barely six feet away from seizing the joystick himself, he couldn't move without risking Omar shooting Madison.

But that was his only option if he wanted to stop this. And he guessed he had a matter of seconds remaining.

"You still with me?" he called out.

Madison looked up and met his gaze. She looked woozy, and yet determined. "Uh huh."

Trapp grinned, hoping to all hell she was awake enough to understand what he meant. "Hungry?"

She frowned with confusion, then her expression cleared with what he desperately hoped was understanding. She nodded, the movement jerking Omar's pistol a couple of inches away from her right temple. The terrorist's expression tightened.

"Now."

The moment the words left Trapp's mouth, Madison yanked her head back and to the left, then swung it in the other direction. She bit down hard on Omar's wrist, digging her teeth into his flesh and tendons. Blood spurted, coating her teeth and lips. A gunshot echoed as his trigger finger reflexively squeezed.

Trapp didn't hesitate. He threw himself forward as the terrorist yelled a curse of pain and frustration, clearing the distance that separated them in less than two steps. As he moved, he reversed his rifle in his hands, drew it back, and smashed its stock as hard as he could into Omar's skull.

It was a knockout blow.

He heard the terrorist's pistol drop to the floor with a thump. He didn't have time to kick it away. The drones were diving fast, gaining speed and losing altitude with every passing second. In just moments, it would be too late.

He ignored Omar, grabbing the pilot instead. He squeezed his shoulders and yelled, "Pull up!"

When the man didn't respond, he threw him aside and took over himself. He had no idea what he was doing but pulled the joystick toward himself as hard as he dared, not knowing if the sudden shift in altitude and speed would only cause the UAVs to stall out.

Perhaps it would save the president's life, only to condemn dozens, even hundreds of those who had come out to see him to a sudden and fiery death as the two drones careered toward the bleachers.

He heard a scuffle behind him, then the telltale sound of a pistol skidding along the floor. He dared not take his eyes away from the computer screens in front of him despite every instinct in his body screaming at him to do otherwise.

"Come on," he urged the monitors as though his words might help bend the laws of physics. The airspeed readouts were climbing, not falling. The two drones were plummeting ever faster toward the ground.

Faces glowed like stars in the infrared displays. It was impossible to be sure, but Trapp imagined hundreds, thousands of first curious, then terrified men, women, and children staring up at him. He watched a disturbance in the crowd as the viewscreen narrowed, drawing closer and closer in on a single stand.

The drones were now doing over four hundred miles an hour. Alarms blared through the control station's speakers, and a variety of gauges and dials blinked red as the flight software warned of imminent failure.

Seconds remained to disaster.

"Jason!" Madison yelped from behind him. "He's coming around."

Trapp spared a glance over her shoulder and saw that she was right. Omar blinked groggily, as if his surroundings were a surprise to him, but even in that flash, he watched as consciousness returned to the brute's mind.

"Oh, shit," Trapp whispered. There was nothing he could do to react. He pulled back harder on the joystick.

Wait.

Had he imagined it, or had the viewscreen ticked up a foot?

No, it was real. It happened again. A row of innocent, panicking civilians disappeared from the bottom of both screens. Then another. Then entire sections of the stadium disappeared from view as the drones' noses pulled up.

Trapp clenched his fist around the joystick in triumph. He kept the control pulled as far back as he dared, watching as the airspeed readouts briefly touched 450 miles an hour, hanging there for a long moment before falling back. He was no pilot, but he'd been around enough aircraft to know that you traded SPF for altitude.

And that was what was happening.

The airspeed display began to tumble. First 400 miles an hour, then 350, then 325, 300, before it dropped into the twos. Trapp swallowed hard as the stadium disappeared from the viewscreen entirely. The artificial horizon dial wobbled from side to side as wind and speed battered the two airframes, but both began to climb.

The second the video feeds both showed nothing but sky, Trapp backed off on the controls. He put the two drones into a shallow but stable climb, not confident enough in his piloting abilities to know how hard he could push them. The altitude readout started to climb. A wave of relief flooded through him.

"Talk to me, Madison," he called out.

She groaned, making a retching sound as though she was about to vomit. It sounded as though she was trying to say something but was unable. Ashen-faced and trembling, she finally coughed out his name.

He whipped his gaze in her direction, not sensing the incoming attack until an instant before Omar hurtled into him.

By then it was too late.

41

Trapp released his grip on the joystick as he crashed to the floor, whipping his hand away as though he'd touched a hot stove. He tried to suck in a breath, only to find himself winded by the enormous bulk of the man who had collided with him. Tears formed at the corners of his eyes from the pain, and he retched as acid was forced up his windpipe from his compressed stomach.

If it wasn't for the presence of his ballistic vest, which absorbed some of the force of the blow, he would almost certainly have broken half a dozen ribs on impact.

Omar didn't stop.

He was like a linebacker driving forward through the tackle. Trapp found himself swept forward like debris on a tidal wave, powerless to do anything to resist. The strength of the man he was up against was almost impossible to comprehend. He was lying on his back, looking up at the ceiling through blurred eyes as it moved above him. It felt like being on a supermarket conveyor belt.

Only a heck of a lot more painful.

"Jason!" Madison sobbed, finally able to speak. He dropped

his chin and managed to catch a fragmentary glimpse of her as Omar's drive slowed. She fruitlessly rattled her bound wrists against the banisters, angry tears glinting in her eyes.

And then she was gone. Omar reared up, replacing her in Trapp's vision. He was a fearsome sight, blood streaming freely down his temples and mixing with the sweat that glistened on his forehead as he rested on his shins. His hands formed fists as he prepared to strike the stunned man on the floor below him.

Trapp sat up dumbly, his reactions slowed by the lack of oxygen making it to his brain. He knew he was supposed to do something to stop this, but...

Roll.

The instinctive command came from somewhere deep within. He obeyed without questioning, twisting to his right with his last reserves of energy as darkness swept in on all sides. His chest heaved, muscles still twitching from the earlier impact, and yet somehow, he forced himself to twist through two full, messy rotations along the deck.

Dulled by a combination of anger and frustration, Omar didn't react in time. He brought his fists down in a powerful, pre-planned blow, only pulling away at the last second. Not fast enough. He roared with pain as he beat the empty ground beneath him.

Trapp dug his heels into the floor and pushed himself backward, struggling for every measly inch of space he could put between him and his attacker. Finally he gasped, his lungs no longer rejecting their prime directive. The first few breaths tasted like the sweetest mountain air. He sucked at it greedily, awareness of his sight and senses opening back up like a driver exiting a long tunnel. He searched for his opponent.

Omar's neck snapped left at the exact moment. He held his right fist up in the air as his face contorted in a rictus of agonized fury. Trapp wondered if he'd broken a bone in his hand.

You deserve it, you prick.

For a moment, both men observed a silent truce as they gathered up their strength for the battle to come. Trapp's chest heaved as his lungs fed oxygen back into his bloodstream. He didn't bother getting control of his breath.

Not yet.

He glanced down, searching for the pistol he'd earlier thrust through the elastic loop on the front of his ballistic vest. It was gone, somehow knocked out from the force of the impact. He swiveled his neck left and right in search of it but came up empty. It must have fallen somewhere inaccessible. That wasn't ideal, but at least Omar wasn't armed, either.

He was, unfortunately, a hell of a lot bigger than Trapp. It was hard to believe that such a thing was possible, but Trapp's body still smarted from the fundamental truth of it. He felt like a chimney sweep stepping into a ring with a sumo wrestler.

As one, both men seemed to decide that the truce was over. Omar clenched his injured fist once more, gritting his teeth over the pain that ensued. He climbed to his feet. Trapp was surprised that the ground didn't shake underneath him as he copied the movement.

The two men circled each other in the large space, never breaking eye contact, never giving the other the opportunity to strike. The pilot Trapp had wrenched aside was now cowering somewhere to his left, separated from the drone control station by the two circling predators. Madison was to his right, still manacled to the stairs. He glanced at her for a second, watching as she tried to struggle upright, to somehow break free of her bonds.

"Give it up, asshole," Trapp called out, snapping his attention back to Omar. "You lost. It's over. Surrender now and make it easy for yourself."

He spoke as loudly as possible, wondering as he did where

the hell Pope had gotten to. Had one of those bullets done more damage than he'd initially thought?

Shit, they needed medical attention here. And backup. Where the hell was their backup? He dared not take his eyes off the dangerous terrorist opposite long enough to even check how Madison was doing. She'd sustained a heavy blow to her temple. Her movements were sluggish and erratic. If she had a brain bleed, she might take a turn for the worse in a matter of seconds.

He needed to end this. Fast.

Trapp grinned, showing his opponent that he wasn't scared of him, despite the fact that he resembled a Viking berserker who'd come off his meds. "You deaf, or just stupid?"

"Go to hell," the Syrian fired back.

"That's up in the air," Trapp said, his voice coming more freely now that he was up and moving. He took another step to his side, continuing the eddy around the center of the room. His chest still smarted from the tackle that had kicked off this fight. "But not for you, I don't think."

"What are you talking about?"

"You think your god is going to look kindly on this clusterfuck? If you're going to do something, at least do it right. It was a good plan. You just screwed it up."

Omar's temple pulsated with internalized rage, but he didn't take the bait.

"Adnan," he said instead. "Do you love your wife? Your children? Your beautiful daughter?"

The pilot whimpered. Trapp glanced at him for a fraction of a second, not stopping circling, unwilling to give up any advantage. "Ignore him, Adnan. It's over. The police are on their way."

"They're on their way *here*, Adnan," Omar interrupted forcefully, his accent growing thicker as the stress built inside him. "But my men are already at your home. They will kill your family unless you do exactly as I say. Take the controls and finish this. Or let them die. You choose."

The pilot—who Trapp now knew as Adnan—moaned incoherently. It was immediately clear that he was no hardened terrorist. Just an innocent man acting under coercion. Yet he was no less dangerous for it.

"Don't listen to him," Trapp called out, still pacing to the left, maintaining separation between him and Omar. Every few steps, he scanned the ground, searching for one of the two dropped pistols, but found only the rifle he'd struck Omar with, which was lying tangled in the cables behind the drone control station.

There was no way he could access it in time.

Adnan said nothing in response, just made an incoherent sound that indicated he was succumbing to panic. That suited Trapp just fine. All he needed was the man to stay out of it. He had no doubt that President Nash had now long since been hustled out of Oriole Park by the Secret Service and into the hardened presidential limo known as the Beast, but there were still hundreds of juicy targets that could be struck in downtown Baltimore.

Trapp lifted his foot a few inches higher as he stepped to his left in order to avoid a stack of large cardboard boxes that must have contained parts for either the drones or the control setup. It hadn't been in his way last time he circled round, and he realized that this meant he was inching toward Omar the way a whirlpool narrows as it flows into a drain.

"End this, Adnan," the terrorist hissed, glancing at the cowering Turkish engineer to drive his message home, and taking his eyes off the ground underneath him at precisely the wrong time. His foot caught on a toolbox, and he stumbled forward, arms flailing at his side.

Now!

Trapp struck, finding fresh energy from the depths of his

reserves. He pitched himself forward from the soles of his boots and charged much like Omar had just a few seconds earlier. The Syrian tried to right himself in midair, but without anything to grasp, the leverage only flailed his arms harder.

The two men collided in the center of the room. Trapp dropped his shoulder a second before impact, then bucked it up as he felt contact, tensing his core and driving upward with all his might. He used Omar's own momentum to flip him through the air. He sailed headfirst toward the ground.

A flash of berserker rage washed through Trapp now, the heat of the anger burning away the frustration of failure and disappointment that had been building for the last two weeks. Hell, the last five years—ever since Khaled al-Shakiri had first disappeared without a trace. The mastermind of so much evil and hatred wasn't here to pay for his sins.

But his right-hand man was.

And just now, that would do.

Omar came down to earth heavily, the impact first forcing a grunt of breath from his lungs, then a crack as a bone snapped in his wrist. He howled with pain, the sound at once both impossibly loud and surprisingly high-pitched for such a big man. He rolled onto his back and stared up at his crippled left arm—now useless after the combined blows of a broken hand and a fractured wrist.

"Get up," Trapp said, curling his lip derisively. He wasn't tired any longer. He no longer felt pain. He welcomed this fight. And he didn't want to stop until Omar was beaten to a bloodied pulp for everything he'd done.

It was a stupid, irrational reaction. Even as he stood there, eyeing his enemy on the ground, Trapp knew that he was going against all his training. He should've charged right then and there, kicked Omar hard in the side of his torso, then brought his heel down on the man's face as he writhed in pain.

He should have.

But he didn't.

Trapp wanted a fight, not to inflict a beating. He wanted to suffer, as if the pain he'd take in doing so was some kind of cleansing.

Omar reached up and gripped his left wrist, letting out a gasp of pain as he did so. His face had turned an ashen white. If Trapp wasn't careful, he'd slip into shock.

And that just would not do.

"I said get up," he spat, kicking a loose wrench across the floor. It skidded across the ground and bounced off Omar's side. "Or are you too much of a coward?"

The jibe seemed to bust through his opponent's agony. Omar rolled onto his front, pulling his injured non-dominant hand to his chest as he struggled to his feet. He turned to face Trapp, baring his teeth in defiance.

"Show me what you've got, asshole," Trapp said. He felt bloodlust building inside him. He rarely gave in to his basest instincts, but he would today.

Omar dropped his shoulder and charged. Trapp waited until the moment of impact, then stepped to his left like a trained matador, striking out with a vicious blow with his right elbow as his opponent passed. It was a glancing hit. He grimaced with frustration, knowing he'd squandered a perfect opportunity.

Angry as he was, he knew he wouldn't be presented with too many more. Omar had spent the last decade in warzones and the kind of prisons where life was nasty, brutish, and short.

He'd survived it all. Even with a broken wrist, even in abject failure, he was no quitter.

The big man spun and didn't stop. His chest heaved heavily from the combination of exertion, frustration and pain that had to be coursing through him. He came for Trapp again, and something in his eyes said that he wouldn't fall for the same trick twice.

Trapp pulled his right elbow back and snapped his torso around, putting all his momentum behind a powerful blow. He drove his fist directly into Omar's face, and his opponent didn't even look away. He felt bone and cartilage snap underneath his knuckles, but even the agony of a broken nose didn't appear to have cut through the frenzy now driving him.

Oh, shit.

Omar pushed forward, driving through Trapp and physically forcing him back. It was now Trapp's turn to stumble on something underfoot. He tripped and fell hard to the ground, landing heavily on his ass. As the terrorist passed over him, he brought his right heel down hard, striking the center of Trapp's chest and driving the breath from his lungs for the second time in almost as many minutes.

Madison cried out, "Jason!"

But he had no attention to spare. Not now. Omar was hurt badly, but he had no intention of giving up. It was patently clear that he was in the fight of his life.

Not just yours, you fool.

It was equally certain that he now had at least one broken rib and probably more. Lying still hurt, let alone breathing.

He allowed himself a flash of guilt that he'd thrown Madison's lot in with his own fate, but only one. Now wasn't the time for introspection. Gasping for breath, he flung himself upright, backing away as the world swayed around him. He reached for the rage that had driven him this far, savored it, and pushed on.

Be smarter, he reminded himself.

Omar was bigger than him. That mass could easily tell. It would only take one lucky blow to succeed in stunning him, and this thing would be over. And then, driven to rage by the failure of his plan, the terrorist would doubtless extract the harshest of revenge.

But he had a weakness. He was angling his right shoulder

forward to hide his injured wrist. Trapp knew he had to take advantage of it to bring this fight to a close.

The right way.

Trapp only half-faked doubling over. He placed his left hand on his knee and sucked in air, grimacing from the pain this caused him. Omar began edging toward him. He backed away another step, injecting sluggishness to his movements. His opponent's face lit up as he decided he had his measure, and he came for Trapp yet again, clenching his right fist and driving it through the air.

The blow caught Trapp in the stomach. He twisted to his side at the precise moment of impact, not to dodge the strike, but in the act of extending his own right hand. He cast it out and grabbed Omar's injured wrist, closing his fingers in a vise around it and twisting hard even as he rocked from the impact of the punch.

Omar screamed in agony. Instead of continuing his attack, he jerked instinctively away, the whites of his eyes growing wide and swallowing his beady pupils whole. As spittle flew from his lips, he now resembled a panicked beast more than a man. Trapp gritted his teeth and held on tight, securing his grip, then pulling the man hard toward him.

The powerful terrorist jerked like a puppet on a string as he stumbled forward, whimpering in pain. Trapp swept his clenched left fist down hard, aiming for the trapped, shattered wrist. He felt the joint pop, practically exploding from the force of the impact.

The Syrian sank to his knees, his arm still pulled upward like an anchor line.

Trapp didn't pause. He switched his grip, then drove his right elbow down against Omar's defenseless, gently swaying skull with all the force he could muster. His opponent collapsed as all electrical impulses traveling through his nervous system shorted out.

He lay at Trapp's feet, his chest barely rising and falling. Trapp kicked him in the torso once for good measure, but it was like hitting a sack of meat. There was no reaction. No cry of pain, no flinching, no nothing.

He looked down at the unconscious terrorist and felt a fresh geyser of fury rising within him. This bastard had caused so much harm to so many innocent people, all for what? He'd tried to kill the president, attempted to provoke a fresh wave of violent religious conflict across the entire Islamic world, and attempted to pull the United States into yet another fruitless, draining war.

And he deserved to suffer for it. Trapp drew his leg back, giving in to an ancient, primal anger. He didn't just want to beat his enemies; he wanted to destroy them.

"Jason, stop," a familiar voice called, sounding impossibly distant through his berserker rage. Blood hissed in his ears like a mountain waterfall, deadening all other sound. "It's over."

Trapp wanted to ignore the voice. Wanted to give in to his basest instincts. But he knew it wasn't right. He looked up, chest heaving like a forge's bellows, to see that Pope had stumbled into view. He was clutching his right shoulder and had the shotgun sandwiched in between his right arm and his torso. His fingers were stained with blood.

"I guess he got me after all," he said wryly, his face taut with pain. "I blacked out for a bit. I'm sorry I missed the show."

"Don't be," Trapp replied roughly, his throat raw. "The reviews were shitty anyway."

He looked up sharply, searching for Adnan, and to his horror saw that the man was once again seated behind the flight controls. "The hell do you think you're doing?" he yelled.

Adnan twisted, eyes wide with fear at the clearly unexpected reprimand.

"Jason," Madison said, her voice calm amid the chaos. "He's okay. He's piloting them somewhere safe. He said they're equipped with an explosive payload. We need to get them out of the city."

In the distance, Trapp finally heard the low wail of incoming sirens.

Better late than never, he thought darkly as he looked around for the zip cuffs that had been used to secure Madison. He saw a handful of them lying by her side and cut her free, then used them to truss Omar by the wrists and ankles.

"What about al-Shakiri?" he asked, seeing that Pope had his cell phone clutched in his right hand, along with the shotgun.

The FBI agent shook his head. "It's chaos out there. Secret Service are sealing the stadium down, but we might have lost him. Too early to say."

Trapp began to turn on his heel, then caught himself at the last moment. He stopped, and turned to look at Madison, suddenly lost to indecision. He wanted—needed—to end this. And yet he couldn't bring himself to leave her alone.

There was no such confusion on her face.

"Go!" she yelled, gritting her teeth through the pain.

"You sure?"

She mustered a strained grin. "I'll survive. Just promise me one thing."

"What?"

"That you'll get the bastard."

42

Trapp leapt out of the unmarked FBI Suburban almost before he had braked to a complete stop and jumped out of the vehicle, leaving the engine running. He ducked underneath the police tape, only to run into a pair of local cops, both of whose hands went to their weapons.

He didn't blame them. He already had the makings of a black eye, sustained sometime during his battle with Omar, and there was a rip in the upper sleeve of his T-shirt. He was still wearing the Bureau's ballistic vest and had only delayed long enough before hurrying to the scene of the attempted drone attack to move the pistol that had previously been looped through the elastic on its front to a side holster.

To forestall a confrontation, Trapp reached into his pocket and pulled out Pope's FBI credentials, flicking the leather case closed before either officer had a chance to realize he wasn't who he was claiming to be. "I need to speak to the incident commander. Where can I find them?"

The two cops visibly relaxed. One of them, a woman, gestured toward a large truck-trailer unit that was about fifty yards away. "Secret Service is in overall command of the scene. I don't know anything more than that."

"Thanks, Officer," Trapp said, already hurrying toward the crime scene's nerve center. Hundreds, perhaps thousands of people milled around him, wearing a variety of expressions. Some seemed confused, others were still shaking with fear or had gone numb with shock. Others still were borderline ecstatic, riding high off the adrenaline of the near-death experience.

In the distance, he could see media crews setting up and hoped he was far enough away to avoid being caught on camera. The last thing he needed was for his cover to be blown by a video editor selecting the wrong piece of footage for the nightly news.

And there was no doubt that the day's events would lead the news for weeks. There would have been dozens of cameras focused on Nash as he announced his reelection bid, hundreds, probably thousands more in the audience watching.

"Hold up," an agent in a Secret Service sport coat called out as Trapp approached the command trailer. "I need to see some ID."

Trapp attempted to sidestep the man but pulled up short as the agent artfully blocked his path. He considered flashing Pope's badge a second time but guessed that the agent would know better than to fall for the trick he'd pulled with the two local cops.

"You were here when those drones came in?" he asked instead.

The agent nodded. "Sir, I'm still going to need—"

"I was the one who stopped the attack. They were both carrying a hundred-pound fragmentation warhead. Why don't you ask your boss if he wants to speak to me?"

His mouth gaping, the agent nodded. He reached for a radio handset clipped to his waist and called it in. A few moments later, the door to the command trailer swung open, clattering against the hard-shell wall. A man wearing suit pants and a navy-blue windbreaker emerged. His head was shaved and gleamed in the late-afternoon sun.

He glanced around, searching for the source of the radio call, then beckoned Trapp to join him. The uniformed Secret Service agent stepped aside, and he did as he was bid.

As Trapp approached, the man in the windbreaker growled, "Name?"

"Jason Trapp."

The man frowned. "Agency?"

"Exactly," Trapp said.

"Huh?" the incident commander said, screwing his face up a little tighter. "Right. You're CIA?"

"Yes sir, I am," Trapp replied. "If you need to confirm—"

"Don't worry about it. I can smell it on you," the man replied. "Name's Liam Curry. I was incident commander for this shitshow. Probably going to be my last rodeo, so I might as well enjoy it. I want you to tell me what the hell just happened. I've never seen anything like it before. Looked like a pair of MQ-9 Reapers swooped out of the sky. Our countermeasures didn't do shit. It was a miracle nobody got killed."

"Not a miracle, Agent Curry. Her name is Madison," Trapp replied, knowing that if the tip to the FBI tip line had come in just a few minutes later, if he and Pope hadn't accepted the tasking and gone to check it out, then the unthinkable would most certainly have come to pass.

"Who was behind this, Trapp?" Curry growled. "My people are hunting a damn cripple."

"The president's safe?"

"Of course he is. Answer the question."

Trapp hid a smile. "It was an Islamic State plot."

Curry frowned. "The missile thing? I read the bulletin about it the other day."

"Sorry about that." Trapp grimaced. "That's where the

evidence was pointing. We didn't put everything together until about half an hour ago."

"Just in time, I suppose," Curry said with a frustrated shake of the head. "God, he could've been killed. On my damned watch. This is a brave new world, Trapp. How the hell are we supposed to defend our principals against military-grade drone attacks?"

"Glad that's your job, not mine," Trapp replied.

"Yeah, but for how much longer?" Curry groused before seeming to straighten and forget his own personal troubles. "I'm guessing from that black eye you're sporting that you were the one who sent us the warning about the guy in the wheelchair?"

"Not just me."

"Well, whatever. I guess I owe you my thanks."

"Just tell me you know where he is," Trapp said, an image of Madison's battered face flashing across his mind.

"Who?"

Trapp tapped his holstered pistol. "Khaled al-Shakiri. He masterminded this whole thing."

"First thing we did after crashing the president was lock down the entire area," Curry said, guiding Trapp inside the trailer. "Could be a few dozen people got out, but the moment we ascertained there was no secondary attack, we sealed it up tight."

He got a few stray, curious glances as he entered, but within a moment, the agents operating the computer terminals inside the trailer focused back on their work.

Curry pointed at the topmost right screen, which was focused on the exterior of a large multi-story red brick building with white-painted facings that was surrounded by a ring of dozens, perhaps hundreds of armed cops and federal agents.

He coughed into his elbow, then said, "We think this al-

Shakiri character is holed up somewhere in the old Babe Ruth Museum. Hey, Jake, run that footage back."

"What do you mean old?" Trapp asked as a video file was pulled up onto an adjacent display.

"Lease ran out. It's currently under construction. Not sure who or what took it over. We're just waiting for local SWAT to tool up. My team crashed on the president. Should be another twenty minutes. No longer than that."

"You mind if I go down, see it for myself?"

"You'll get a better view from in here," Curry said with a shrug. "But be my guest. Like I said, I owe you one. I'll never grouse about a CYA Agency briefing entering my in-tray again."

Trapp made his own way down to the scene of the standoff but not before plucking a dark-blue baseball cap from where it lay on the sidewalk, presumably knocked off at some point during the chaos of the last hour.

"Any sign of movement?" he asked one of the cops deployed on the perimeter, crossing his arms over his chest as he looked up at the surrounded building.

The officer was staring down the barrel of an M4 rifle, which was aimed at one of the building's windows. He glanced away from it just long enough to give Trapp a quick once-over.

"No. Sir," he added just in case.

"You guys sure he's in there?"

"No way out. But we've got officers in the sewers, just in case they try and make a break for it."

"You think it's just the two of them?"

"Sir, they don't tell me shit."

Trapp grinned, despite the severity of the situation. "Yeah, I guess sometimes that's how it goes."

He rubbed his chin as he watched the building site. It was surrounded by metal fencing covered with lime green banners printed with a construction firm's logo that blocked the first floor from view. Curry had informed him that the building site was supposed to be empty that day, on account of the rally.

He swept his gaze across the windows on the second floor. Most of them were covered in plastic sheeting to prevent accidental damage during the refurbishment process. As he passed over one of them, he thought he might've seen a shadow wash over it and paused for a long moment to study it. But nothing further presented itself.

"All units, hold your positions," the police officer's radio crackled. "SWAT will stay back until we get a negotiator on site."

"What's there to negotiate?" Trapp muttered under his breath. He tapped the holster at his right hip with frustration.

"You're telling me," the cop replied. "You think the assholes in there had something to do with those drones?"

"Your guess is as good as mine," Trapp lied.

The cop glanced at him curiously. "Yeah, I doubt that. Listen, I didn't vote for that Nash guy. But he's still the president, you know? This is America. You don't like him, go ahead and boot him out of office. You don't get to take matters into your own hands."

"No," Trapp murmured as an image of Eddie Muniz floated into his mind's eye. "You don't."

Eddie still looked in his twenties, the way Trapp remembered him. Young, with so much life ahead of him. Acid gnawed at his stomach from the guilt at sending his friend to an early grave. The decision hardened in his mind before he knew he'd made it.

He took a first step through the crowd of cops that surrounded the building, then another.

"Hey, jackass, where the hell do you think you're going?" A voice cried out from behind him, before being joined by a melee of others as dozens of local cops and agents belonging to a laundry list of federal agencies got onto their radios to report this development.

Trapp ignored it, picking up the pace as he neared the entrance to the worksite at the front of the building. He drew his pistol, then hurdled the security gate, grunting with exertion and a twinge of pain from the right side of his torso, presumably wrenched in his fight with Omar.

He blocked out the growing cacophony behind him as he thought over his tactical position. There was almost no chance that either al-Shakiri or his minder were armed, since they would have by necessity passed through the Secret Service security gauntlet on their way into the baseball stadium. He briefly considered the possibility that one of the two might have been wearing an explosive vest but discounted it for the same reason.

A calm drew over him as he crossed the dusty space between the security barriers around the worksite and the building itself. The main door had been removed and was covered only with a thin layer of transparent plastic sheeting. He pulled it aside and ducked underneath.

The entire bottom floor of the building had been cleared out and was self-evidently empty. Trapp took in the entire space, his gaze only interrupted by a few concrete pillars that supported the floor above.

He paused for a moment and scanned the space around him, just in case.

It was clear.

"Where are you, asshole?" he whispered.

He picked up the pace. The last thing he wanted was to be interrupted by the SWAT team, who were no doubt already hustling to get into place while cursing the moron who had just walked into the building.

He would have to apologize to them. But that could wait until this was over.

Trapp spied a staircase to his left and paced toward it with his pistol held level in front of him, his footsteps barely making a sound on the bare concrete floor. As he closed on it, he heard the muffled sound of voices from upstairs. He couldn't make out what they were saying, or even the language, but it was clear that whoever was speaking was upset.

He crept slowly up the stairs, stopping every thirty seconds or so to cock his ear and listen. They weren't far. He paused just before cresting the second floor and took a deep breath. He lowered his hands onto the topmost step and inched above the flowline so that he could just see what lay beyond.

Like the floor below, all interior drywall had been cleared from the space. A few pieces of construction machinery rested on the floor. But that wasn't what drew Trapp's attention.

Al-Shakiri was slumped against a concrete pillar, clutching his stomach. His wheelchair was compacted for transport and lay at his side. He was breathing heavily, his agony audible in the empty space. His companion had fallen silent and was holding the back of his own head as he stared at the floor.

Time to end this.

Trapp sprung upward, sensing no other threats. The able-bodied man spun around at the sound of his footsteps, fear washing over his face. Figuring that he presented the most immediate threat, Trapp aimed at his center mass.

At least, until he did something unexpected and dropped to the ground. He splayed his arms and legs wide and yelled, "Don't shoot me. Please, just don't shoot me! I did what she said."

Ricky.

"Stay where you are," Trapp yelled firmly. "Place your hands on the back of your head."

He watched as the terrified young man complied. He was now crying freely.

"Are you armed?"

"No. I swear, I didn't know what they were planning. I, I—"

"Just shut the fuck up," Trapp fired back, no longer in the mood to care. He took several steps to his right so that he could keep Ricky in his sight and switched his aim to al-Shakiri.

"What about him?" Trapp asked. "Is he carrying?"

Ricky looked uncertainly up from the ground, hesitating before finally muttering, "I don't think so."

"Get up," Trapp said, looking away and meeting al-Shakiri's gaze. "Search him."

He waited until Ricky was done, the man's movements jerky and uncoordinated from the flood of hormones no doubt coursing through his system. He did a surprisingly professional job, then lay back down on the ground of his own accord, tears marking the dusty concrete floor.

Trapp walked slowly over to al-Shakiri, not looking away once. He crouched down in front of him, leveling the pistol at the man's head and putting an ounce of pressure on the trigger. Another ounce, maybe two, that's all it would take.

"Do it," the man snarled. "Pull the trigger. I know you want to."

"Yeah," Trapp said grimly, leaning forward. He placed his left hand around the terrorist's neck and squeezed. "You deserve it, you piece of shit."

"Then do it!" al-Shakiri wheezed. A sheen of sweat glistened on his skin. He was ashen-faced and looked to be at death's door.

Trapp brought the barrel of his pistol down and pressed it against the terrorist's forehead as hard as he could. He squeezed his eyes shut and pictured Eddie, and Madison, and the Iraqi girl from all those years back. He knew that Khaled al-Shakiri deserved to die a hundred times over. The man encapsulated pure evil, perhaps more than anyone he had ever come across.

He squeezed the trigger another ounce. His hand shook

from the pressure. It was on a hair-trigger now. The slightest movement would be enough.

"What are you waiting for?"

His heartbeat thudded in his chest as he heard engines roaring outside, the sound muffled but audible through the building's walls. SWAT was making their move. He didn't have long.

Trapp's eyes snapped open. He stared down at al-Shakiri, saw the manic gleam in the man's eyes, and realized that he no longer felt anger for the terrorist underneath him.

Just disgust.

"It's going to hurt, you know," he said in an almost conversational tone, leaning backwards and coming down heavily on the ground behind. He safetied his pistol and returned it to its holster.

"What are you talking about?"

"Knowing you came so close. I hope you liked prison, asshole. Because you're going back. And this time, you're not getting out."

EPILOGUE

Madison's private room at Johns Hopkins Hospital was festooned with flowers, boxes of chocolates, and other get-well-soon gifts. Trapp stepped inside quietly as he realized that she was sleeping. He folded his arms across his chest, horrified by what he saw. The CIA analyst had taken a horrific beating. He would be surprised if she climbed out of that bed before a couple of weeks.

You should have moved quicker, he thought grimly.

"You took your time."

Trapp started as he heard Madison's voice. Her eyes flickered open.

"You're awake," he said lamely.

"Nothing gets past you. You know, there might be an open slot in the intel shop. I could put in a good word."

He walked over to her, guilt clenching his chest with every step he took, and stopped. "After what you did, I think if you told the director to jump, he'd ask how high. You saved the president's life, Madison."

"I think you had something to do with that," she replied,

wincing from the pain the effort caused her. "I was a little tied up."

Trapp winced at the reminder.

"It was a joke, Jason." She grinned. "If I can laugh about it, you damn well have to."

"I guess."

"How do I look?" she murmured, her heart rate monitor inching up slightly as she stirred, pushing herself up on the pillows at the head of the bed.

"You want the truth?"

"Always."

"Like shit." Trapp grinned, studying Madison's battered face. Her lip had been closed with a couple of stitches, and bandages covered other contusions on her face. Both her eyes were black. "And it's only going to get worse."

"Yeah," she said, shaking her head slightly. Her eyes cleared. "I figured. What happened at the stadium? Nobody's telling me anything."

"We got him," Trapp said. "They built a laser designator into a Nikon DSLR camera. The thing didn't actually take photos, but it looked like it did. That's how they planned to guide the drones onto target."

"Alive or dead?" Madison asked.

Trapp bit his lip. "I could have pulled the trigger," he admitted. "Nobody would have known. But I let them take him in."

He'd played the decision over a hundred times in his mind. About half those times he went the other way.

"It's better that way," Madison said. "That sonofabitch is going to stare at a wall for the rest of his life knowing he screwed up. And every now and then, I'm going to pay him a visit and remind him of exactly that."

"You mind if I join you?" Trapp said with a smile. He didn't doubt that she would do it.

"Any time. Can you do me a favor, Jason?"

"Sure."

"I need a beer," she said.

"The moment they discharge you, I'm there. You got a bar in mind?"

Her eyes flashed. "I mean now. I refused painkillers, and now I'm starting to regret my decision. I need to take the edge off."

"How do you suggest we get past the nurses?" Trapp said, playing for time. "You're not exactly inconspicuous right now."

Madison rolled her eyes. "Jason, you're supposed to be a freaking spy. I'm pretty sure you'll figure it out."

FOR ALL THE LATEST NEWS

I hope you enjoyed Hand of God. If you did, and don't fancy sifting through thousands of books on Amazon and leaving your next great read to chance, then sign up to my mailing list and be the first to hear when I release a new book.

Visit - www.jack-slater.com/updates

And keep reading if you want to learn more about the real-life inspiration that led me to write *Hand of God...*

Thanks so much for reading!

Jack.

AUTHOR'S NOTE

Jack here,

Thanks so much for reading my latest *Jason Trapp* thriller. As always I had a heckuva time writing it. I hope it showed!

At the end of these books I like to just spend a little time talking about the real-life basis for the stories I used in my fiction. In this case, *Hand of God*, as you might be able to tell, was sparked by couple of ideas coming together in my mind.

First was an ISIS prison break in Syria, just like the one in the start of this novel, and the second was the proliferation of low-cost and yet near-military grade drone technology that we are beginning to see out in the wild. Both have the potential to change the world.

The US-led coalition largely beat ISIS and its so-called caliphate into a pulp by the end of 2017. In the process our Syrian and Iraqi partners have imprisoned tens of thousands of ISIS fighters—and those merely unlucky enough to live in the areas they conquered.

Five years later, thousands of those fighters are still imprisoned in pretty horrific conditions, living dozens to a cell, missing limbs and without proper medical treatment. I believe we should treat our enemies with humanity, at the very least for our own self-interest. Instead we have a situation we find today, where the Syrian Democratic Forces are trying—and failing—to keep a growing cancer in check.

If we don't find a solution to this problem, we will have more situations like the Hasakah prison break. ISIS is wounded, but it's not gone for good.

Worse still is the fact that teenagers and adolescents are imprisoned in these facilities. Many of these kids were twelve or thirteen years old when they were incarcerated, others even younger. Child soldiers are victims of ISIS, just as those who suffered and died under their rule were.

Anyway, let me get down off my soapbox!

As for drones, I mentioned in the book that the Venezuelan president was nearly assassinated by a cheap thousand-dollar quadcopter drone with a grenade strapped to it, most likely controlled using an app on someone's cell phone.

It really happened. There's video on YouTube. It's...crazy. And a little bit frightening.

A few years back, Yemeni rebels really did fly half a dozen low-tech explosive-equipped drones on suicide runs into Saudi oil refineries, crossing through airspace that is supposedly some of the best-defended in the world. And Iranian-backed militias really did attempt to assassinate the Iraqi Prime Minister by attacking his official residence with a drone.

In Mexico, drug cartels are dropping mortar rounds from store-bought drones. In Ukraine, regular army units are doing the same to knock out Russian tanks.

(I'm all for that one.)

In all these instances, we see the same thing. Cheap, often off-the-shelf technology that is exceedingly difficult to counter. A Patriot missile costs $3 million per shot. A drone large enough to carry a reasonable explosive charge and fly couple of hundred miles below radar range might cost a sixtieth of that amount.

To put it mildly, that isn't a comforting equation.

I would not be particularly surprised to see a world leader assassinated in the next couple of years using this method. Defense companies are developing countermeasures as I write this, but there are times in military history where the "offense" get a jump on the "defense", and this appears to be one of those times.

However, I hope dearly that I'm wrong!

If you have come across my *Jason Trapp* series before, thanks for sticking with me all this time. If this is your first time stepping into his shoes, why not go back to where it all started: *Dark State*, the first book in the series.

I have included the first couple of chapters as a sample at the back of this book.

Enjoy, and my thanks as always,

Jack.

DARK STATE

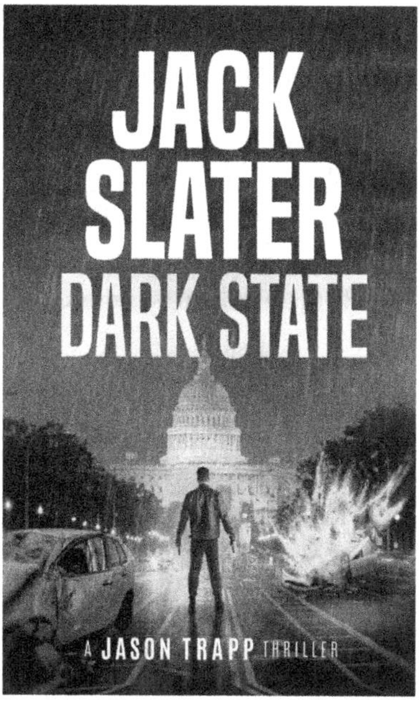

Long ago, men of violence ruled with an iron fist. They owed loyalty only to themselves. Their names were whispered, but never spoken.

In parts of the world, those old traditions still hold strong. Power there spews from the barrel of a gun. Laws are shaped with lead, taxes paid in cold dread.

But not America.

Because we too have those whose names are whispered. Men who know nothing but the gray zone between life and death, whose only calling in life is to do the things the rest of us dare not, the things that keep us safe.

Men like the Hangman, a covert operative whose feats became the stuff of legend. He was the tip of the spear—the man his country unleashed when all hope was lost.

Six months ago, someone sold him out. The Agency listed him as killed in action. He lost everything he held dear.

But legends never die...

The Hangman is back. And he's looking for blood.

Visit Amazon to read Dark State, book one in the *Jason Trapp* thriller series.

1

The California Zephyr Amtrak line is often described as the most beautiful rail journey in all of North America. The route runs from Emeryville, California to Chicago, Illinois, and takes over fifty hours to complete.

The two men boarded the Zephyr in Provo, Utah at 4:35 a.m., using tickets booked under assumed names and paid for using prepaid credit cards. They were of Middle Eastern extraction and carried no form of identification, save fake drivers licenses that would stand up to a moderate amount of scrutiny. The licenses bore the seals of different states – Virginia and Nevada, a detail which investigators would puzzle over for months, but which meant nothing.

They did not acknowledge each other at the station. They could not have if they wanted to, for they had never met, nor seen so much as a photograph of the man with whom they would go down in history. It was basic operational security, and both men knew it was for the best. And besides, what they were to accomplish did not require idle conversation, just steely resolve.

They had arrived in Provo by different means. The taller of

the two men had purchased a used car from Craigslist in Phoenix, Arizona, and paid cash. It was not registered under his name – real or otherwise. The shorter, and younger, man had made his way there by Greyhound bus from Las Vegas, after discarding his worldly possessions in a trashcan outside the station.

Each had rented a motel room for a night, paid for in crumpled, non-sequential bills, and freshened up before heading out. They dressed smartly in case they were stopped for any reason by local cops, and had believable cover stories that were more than skin deep. Both spoke more than passable English, accented of course, but were comfortable with American idioms. Their beards were shaved.

The younger man was booked into an ice climbing "experience" the next day, along with a wife who didn't exist; the elder had lift tickets and equipment reserved for a day on the slopes at Sundance ski resort only fifteen miles away. As it happened, neither was stopped, asked a question, or even spoke a word that night, beyond ordering dinner at nondescript local diners.

One visited Lakeside Storage, the other Provo Central Storage, where each accessed a unit that had been rented months before by more men they had never met. Inside they found hard luggage cases – both used, so as not to stand out, and in different colors. Everything they would need was in those bags. Nothing had been left to chance.

As they stood in line, waiting for their tickets to be checked, surrounded by yawning travellers—vacationers and businessmen look much the same that early in the morning—they understood the righteousness of what they would do that day. The message that they would send to the entire world. Both were nervous. It would be unnatural not to be. After all, they would die that day. Glorious deaths, to be sure, and they would be rewarded with eternal Paradise, but they would die nonetheless – and no man goes into the darkness without feeling at least a hint of trepidation.

"Ticket, sir."

The younger man, his head filled with visions of the future, took a second to respond, and the Amtrak employee thrust out his hand impatiently.

"Sir, I need to see your ticket."

"Of course, of course," the man replied in accented English as he hurriedly reached into his nondescript bomber jacket.

As he did, his eyes passed over a woman, a mother, with her young daughter and several pieces of luggage. The child had blond hair and beautiful blue eyes, but so early in the morning she was struggling to keep them open. She was holding a little white teddy bear.

"Come on, Anna," the mother urged. "Stay awake a little longer, and then you can fall asleep on the train. Just not yet, okay honey?"

"Okay, Mommy," the little girl replied. "I will."

The sight of the mother and child, dressed for a holiday, or to visit grandparents, might have warmed the man's heart, if he had been there for any other reason. But he wasn't, and it did not. If anything, it was a reminder of what he had lost: a wife and a child just like this little girl, stolen from him in the night by an American bomb.

There wasn't enough left of either to fill a burial shroud. With his family gone but unburied, the man's grief fermented into rage. Rage drove him to violence.

And violence had brought him here.

What investigators would not learn until some weeks later was that the man was Iraqi. His real name was Raheem. He was in his early thirties, and this was not his first encounter with bureaucratic American efficiency.

Raheem was first apprehended in 2006 by military police working alongside the 503rd 'First Rock' Infantry Regiment outside of Ramadi, the capital of Iraq's Al Anbar province, after an unseen, unheard Predator drone circling overhead identified him as a suspected insurgent. Lucky for him, military intelligence refused to okay a kinetic strike, and ordered that he be brought in for questioning instead.

As he was discovered in the middle of the night beside an unburied Improvised Explosive Device – a converted M107 high explosive, 155 mm artillery shell – Raheem was lucky not to simply have been shot and buried in an unmarked grave.

An extrajudicial killing would, of course, be illegal. Forbidden by both the Rules of Engagement and the Uniform Code of Military Justice. But in Al Anbar province in 2006, the 503rd was losing good men every day to IED attacks, and the general feeling in the ranks was that the only good militant was a dead one. So, that day, Raheem was very lucky indeed that it was the MPs who apprehended him, and not the fine men of the First Rock.

America would never know it, never learn that history could have been changed by an act most would consider reprehensible – and yet which, more than a decade later, could have saved so many lives.

"That's fine, sir. You've got a Superliner suite, car number seven. Next."

Raheem shook off the unaccustomed wave of memories, and noticed he was holding up the line. He chided himself silently, knowing he had only one job: to remain unnoticed. He had his mission, one that Allah willing he would complete. And Allah no doubt willed it so. He had provided everything so far through his servant, from passports to weapons to instructions to be on this very train at this very time. All so that Raheem could be remembered for generations as the man who struck the first blow in the final crippling of the Great Satan, America.

THE TWO MEN lay in their cabins, at opposite ends of the ten-car train, for over seven hours. Neither could sleep, their brains suffused with adrenaline, cortisol flooding their veins. Their heartrates were elevated, and the younger man was sweating slightly. The rhythmic *clack-clack-clack* of the locomotive's wheels did not disturb either as they silently prayed.

They did not perform the *rak'ah*, the prescribed movements and words typically performed by Muslims, just in case someone entered their cabin. The doors were locked, of course, but they knew it was better to be safe than sorry. After their work today, Allah would forgive any transgressions against his faith.

As the train pulled out of Glenwood Springs, Colorado, Raheem pulled a cell phone out of his jacket pocket. He inserted the sim card and battery and turned it on. He did not know if anyone would call, but he had his instructions. Outside the cabin window, the small town disappeared into the distance and the rugged beauty of the mountains returned.

His instructions were simple: if the train departed on time then he was to conduct their operation as planned, at 30 minutes past the hour. If, for any reason, it did not, then 10 minutes after the train finally left Glenwood Springs, they were to begin. If he received no telephone call, then he was to destroy both the phone and sim card and throw both out of the window.

"*Allahu akbar*," he whispered under his breath, reaching up to the empty top bunk of his cabin. He flicked open the battered hard travel case, revealing its contents: a brand-new Brügger & Thomet MP9 Maschinenpistole with a shoulder sling and folding stock, two G19 handguns, a set of combat webbing complete with holsters for both pistols, more loaded magazines than he could count, and half a dozen green-painted

M67 fragmentation grenades. The weapons – grenades notwithstanding – had been recently test-fired, cleaned and oiled. They were ready.

As was he.

The phone rang. A jolt of adrenaline flooded the Iraqi's brain. Why would his handler phone now? To call off the operation?

Ignore it, he thought, dreaming of the rewards waiting for him in Paradise. *Your duty is to Allah, not to him.*

But Raheem answered the call. Though they had never met he owed this servant of Allah too much, and trusted his judgment implicitly.

The voice on the other end of the line sounded the same as always: flat and tinny from the software being used to disguise his identity. "Raheem?"

The man's reply was short and curt. "Yes."

"You are ready?"

"I am."

"Good. Everything is in place. I wanted to check that you are prepared to do what must be done."

Raheem's response was harsh and angry. "You doubt my faith?"

The flat voice paused for a long second. "I do not. Go with Allah, my brother. The whole world will be watching."

The line clicked dead, and Raheem discarded the phone.

With seventeen minutes left on the timer on his Casio wristwatch, Raheem made his final preparations. He shrugged on the desert-colored Army surplus combat webbing and loaded the pouches around his waist with ammunition.

In total, by the time he was done, Raheem was loaded up with almost 500 rounds, six fragmentation grenades, and filled with a sense of cool, calm determination.

As the General Electric P42 locomotive pulled its ten-car train out of Glenwood Springs, Raheem raised the blinds that covered the windows, and took one last look at the peaceful snow-dusted hillside outside, zipping past so fast it was almost a blur.

The alarm on Raheem's wrist beeped. The one-time Iraqi militant grasped his MP9 to his chest, exhaled deeply, and stepped out of his cabin to face his destiny.

2

Jason Trapp sat in a café in Boston's Chinatown district, watching the world go past the steamed-up windows and wondering if he would ever feel a part of it again. It was eight in the morning, on February first, and he had been there for the best part of an hour, observing the street – watching for anything and anyone that didn't fit. So far, he was all out. As far as he could tell, the street was clear. No one was watching, no one was waiting. Not for him, or anyone else.

Trapp knew there was no reason that he should have picked up a tail. After all, the world, and more importantly his former employers in Langley, thought that he was dead.

He liked being a dead man. There was a freedom to it. He had spent the last twenty years in the service of his country, shuttling from war zone to war zone, solving America's problems with the barrel of a gun. That kind of work does things to a man. Changes him. Makes him jumpy.

The kind of jumpy that had him sitting opposite the street from his objective, pretending not to study every person passing by for a hint of a weapon, or the subtle tell in their walk that hinted at military training. It was an old habit, and it died hard.

It was better that way, Trapp thought, since the alternative was ending six feet under the ground. He'd screwed up six months ago and almost lost everything. It had taken that long to recover, at least from his physical wounds. The mental scars would take longer to heal.

Absently, Trapp fingered the faded scar that ran the circumference of his neck like the mark of a noose. It was the reason for his call sign: Hangman. It was a name fit for a dead man, he thought. The man who'd given him that name was gone, too. And that was why he was here.

The scar was faded now, the line a gentle white against his weathered, tanned skin, not the raw red it had once been. It was marked at intervals with thicker cuts, like beads on a necklace. The scar was far older than the ones he'd acquired in Yemen; the mark of a desperate childhood. Trapp caught what he was doing and grimaced. It was an ugly habit, one he'd quit years ago.

But it was back.

He attracted the waitress' attention and motioned her over. As far as he could tell, the coast was clear, and sitting here wallowing in the past wasn't doing him a damn bit of good. He had a job to do, a man to see, and a conscience to clear. In that order.

"Can I get you something?" she asked. She was Chinese, at least by birth, but spoke unaccented English.

"Just the check."

Trapp left cash and didn't stick around to pick up the change. He didn't tip either enough or too little to give the girl any reason to remember him. Just another anonymous face in the sea of tourists she served every day.

Mostly, Trapp looked like any other man. His face wore a rough, dark stubble that could be shaved off or grown out at will, and often was. He was tall, at least six three, and topped with dark brown hair that was tousled and overgrown, intentionally disguising his rugged good looks. His sizeable, muscular frame was similarly lost in the bulk of a jacket that was two sizes too large.

The only outward clue that he wasn't like other men could be found in his left eye. The right was a cold battleship gray, cold in the gloom and glittering in the light. But the left was different: split in two, black as night on one side, the same icy gray on the other.

It was a benign medical condition that affected one in ten thousand, and Trapp had never bothered to learn its name. In a way, his eye resembled the Rio Negro in Brazil; the black river which meets another without their waters ever mixing.

The locals in that area believe the Rio Negro births shapeshifters. Perhaps Trapp was one, just born in the wrong place at the wrong time. A wraith in the night.

He stood up, shifting the chair back with a heavy, dark boot, and left the café. The Beretta 9 mm felt comforting where it sat in the groove of his lower back. He was wearing a Yankees cap pulled low over his face, dark jeans and a sheepskin lined black leather jacket that he'd picked up in a Goodwill a few blocks over. The leather was soft and supple and wouldn't stick if he needed to draw his weapon.

Trapp's unusual eyes scanned right and left, falling on face after face as he stepped into the streets of Chinatown. Except for the Beretta, he was only carrying a small wad of cash, a safety deposit box card, and an envelope. The last item felt heaviest.

He walked across the street, stopping at a small bodega. It was run by an elderly Chinese man, wrapped up warm enough against the biting cold of the winter morning that Trapp thought he'd survive a climb up Everest. He stepped into the shop, making sure his face was obscured from the security camera above the entrance. It probably wasn't functional, he thought, and even if it was it almost certainly didn't have a high enough resolution to pose him any problems in the future. But Trapp was a careful man who knew that his enemies only had to get lucky once.

He grabbed a nondescript black rucksack off a hook against the wall and turned to the cashier.

"How much?"

The man looked up from his cell phone. Judging by the tinny sounds emanating from the slim black device he was watching some Mandarin talk show. Trapp almost grinned. He didn't carry a cell phone. Didn't have anyone looking to contact him. Especially not these days. But if even this old guy had one, Trapp figured he was about the only person left who didn't.

"Ten dollar," the old man said, in thickly accented English. Then he squinted. "No – that one, fifteen dollar."

Trapp peeled a bill out of his jacket's inner pocket. His fingers grazed against the envelope as he did, and he winced.

"Got change for a Jackson?"

The man nodded, bending his arthritic body to retrieve a five-dollar bill from the register.

"Hey, you need a bag for that?"

"I just bought one."

Trapp stepped out of the bodega with the empty rucksack slung over his shoulder. His eyes flickered right and left once again, fastidious as always with his countersurveillance routine. He knew there were a million ways someone could track him, and there was only so much he could do if someone was observing him through Boston PD's camera network, or had rented an apartment a few floors up, and was even now gazing down at him through the lens of a DSLR.

But he thought it was unlikely. He had a pretty good sense for when he was being watched, and that instinct wasn't telling him anything, not right now.

Trapp walked across the street and entered the building he'd been observing for the last hour. The sign on the door read *Orchid Federal Savings Bank*. The bank only had a few branches up and down the East Coast, and was mainly used by Chinese immigrants. It was old world – they didn't ask very many questions, and that's the way Trapp liked it.

"Hello, sir," a smiling woman called out. "Can I help you?"

He walked up to the counter, as always careful to make sure his face was hidden.

"I'd like to open my safety deposit box," he said. "And I've got a letter of authorization here from my –" He paused, and a trained observer would have picked up a flicker of emotion on his face. "– my friend. I need to pick something up from his as well."

"Of course, sir," the bank teller said. According to the name on her tag, she was called Mei. It was a nice name, Trapp thought. "Can I see your card? I'll need to see the letter as well."

"Sure thing."

As Trapp slid the two documents over the counter, he thought about how the contents of the envelope had come into his possession. A special operator's career could, if they were lucky, be a long one. After all, they were the best of the best. Given millions of dollars of training, flown on well-maintained helicopters by dedicated special forces aviators. Over the course of a long career, the US of A might invest twenty million dollars in training a tier one operator. If the government was good at anything, it was making sure an investment like that didn't go to waste.

On the flipside, in organizations like the three-letter agency that once employed Trapp, operators were treated as deniable. If anything went wrong on a mission, if they were careless enough to allow themselves to be captured, if their existence merely became embarrassing to the US government, a man like Trapp might find himself cut off behind enemy lines.

No exfiltration plan. No pension. Don't pass go. Don't collect a million dollars. Just disappear.

That was the reason that Trapp had rented the safety deposit box in the first place. He'd done it almost ten years ago now. He had others elsewhere, but this was the primary. His backstop. If everything went to shit, the contents of this particular box would buy him enough time to breathe.

At least, that was the theory.

"Thank you, Mr. Flynn," Mei said, tapping something into her computer terminal as she looked at the assumed name on the card. "I'll just be a second."

"Take your time."

Once every six months, Trapp purchased a burner phone with cash. Using its Internet connection he navigated to a specific webpage – its address just a random collection of alphanumeric characters. Once there he entered a code and reset a timer. Somewhere, a letter just like the one Mei was currently reading would sit for another six months, and maybe another six after that.

As long as he reset the timer.

For Trapp to have received the envelope now lying on the counter in front of him meant that someone was dead. But he knew that already. He had been there when it happened. Had been unable to do anything to prevent it.

"Okay, you can follow me, sir. Everything looks good here. Have you got the keys?"

Trapp nodded, pulling his T-shirt collar down a couple of inches to reveal a stainless steel necklace, like a soldier's dog tag chain, hanging around his neck.

"Perfect. Then follow me."

Trapp did as he was told. The bank had certainly seen better days, but Trapp liked the fact that they weren't wasting his money front of house. He trailed the bank teller down a flight of stairs into the basement and turned away as requested while she punched a code into the vault door. It clicked open.

"You know which boxes you're looking for?" Mei asked.

"Yeah."

"Great. I'll wait outside. Just yell if you need something."

Trapp didn't say another word as Mei pulled the heavy vault door open. Behind it lay hundreds of safety deposit boxes, chrome locks accenting polished stainless steel. The air smelled of stale disinfectant, like it always did. He walked confidently over to his own, which he hadn't accessed in a couple of years, lifting the chain from around his neck as he moved. He inserted the key, twisted, and waited for the click to signal the mechanism had unlocked.

The moment it did he opened the door and pulled the box out, setting it on a stainless steel table that stood in the middle of the room. He lifted the lid and was pleased but unsurprised to see the contents exactly as he'd left them. He swung the rucksack off his shoulders, unzipped it, and began filling it with stacks of hundred-dollar bills, each about an inch thick. They were worth ten thousand dollars each, and by the time he was done stacking them, the rucksack held a little over $1.1 million.

And then there was nothing left but brushed steel. Trapp just stood there, dreading what came next. The only memorial service the best man he'd ever known was likely to get. And Trapp was here to zero out his life savings.

"Just get on with it," he said, his voice husky in the deathly quiet of the bank vault. A nuclear bomb could go off overhead, and Trapp doubted if he'd even notice.

"Sir – did you say something? Are you done?" Mei called out.

"Give me a couple of minutes."

The necklace clinked in Trapp's fingers as he pulled the key from his own box, heavier than it had any right to feel. He chewed his lip, then chided himself once more for procrastinating and unlocked the second. He knew that there wouldn't be anything as melodramatic as an 'if you're reading this, then I'm already dead' letter. That wasn't Ryan's style. Besides, a courier had delivered that message with the authorization document a few days before, just not in so many words.

Just as he had done with his own, Trapp set the second safety deposit box on the steel table. It was weightier than his own, but only fractionally so.

The first thing he noticed upon unlocking and opening it was the pistol, along with half a dozen neatly stacked magazines. Despite his somber mood, a slight grin forced itself to the corners of his lips. Trapp shook his head.

Ryan, you paranoid bastard.

He considered pocketing the weapon, but even for a man of Trapp's not inconsiderable bulk the Desert Eagle was a hell of a weapon. A forty-four caliber, the pistol packed a punch that could tear a fist-sized hole out of a man's side. In Trapp's view, it was overkill. But Ryan Price always did have a flair for the dramatic.

Maybe that was what had drawn the two men together; opposites attracting like fire and ice. Trapp the shy, awkward teen, no family left, and broken by the tragedy in his past. Price the exact opposite: a tall, blond kid from the streets of Boston, son of a bartender, mouth as loud as his hair.

Trapp set the weapon aside before continuing. Just as his own had been, Price's box was stacked with cash. Dollars, of course. Euros too, thick folds of five hundred denomination notes. Fewer of them than the stacks of hundred-dollar bills, but more valuable. And all of it taken from black budgets and slush funds, from suitcases of cash delivered in the night to warlords in conflict zones across the globe. A little here. A little there. The CIA knew exactly what its operators were doing and turned a blind eye.

It was part of the bargain, if never stated aloud – 'if we

disavow you, you're toast. So you'd better be prepared. We won't stand in your way if you don't get too greedy'.

Trapp started filling the remaining space in the rucksack with Price's cash. It didn't take long. Combined with his own take he'd have enough to retire on a beach somewhere, drink beer and scuba dive until the end of his days. Maybe take up deep-sea fishing. Buy a charter boat. Take tourists out. The full works.

As he was almost done, something fell out from the jacketed cash. A Polaroid photo, judging by the shape, though it had fallen face down.

"The hell?" he muttered.

Trapp picked up the photo and flipped it around. The memory hit him like a truck. Him and Ryan, taken at a Company barbecue maybe three years before. Sun flickering through the trees at the Farm. They were both younger then. Less worn. He remembered it being taken, and the scent of meat sizzling over the coals. Remembered *who* had taken it.

Mike Mitchell. The deputy director of the CIA's Special Activities Division. A friend, once. And the man that now Trapp suspected of betraying him. His jaw tightened, and his heart beat a little faster as he contemplated once more what had to be done. He would be called a traitor. But that wasn't the truth. They had been sold out, and Ryan had died for it. What lay ahead wasn't murder, it was justice.

"I'm done," Trapp called out after sliding the two safety deposit boxes back into their respective slots. He doubted he would be back. But the leases were paid up for another twenty years, so unless the place got robbed, he didn't have to worry about anyone stumbling across the fake IDs, or the Desert Eagle.

Trapp walked out of the vault, rucksack heavier on his shoulder now. He noticed Mei's eyes on him, on the bulge in the bag. Knew what she was thinking. Maybe a younger version of himself would have taken her with him. Gone to that beach. Whiled away his days drinking and screwing until they were both worn out, or dead, or both.

But this money wasn't Trapp's. Not really. And in his world, the world of shadows, wraiths and shapeshifters, there was no currency more valuable than a man's honor. So it was time to pay a debt.

3

Glenwood Springs has a population of 9,962 residents. Its police department employs just seven full-time officers and several part-time administrative staff. The most common cause for a local citizen to contact the department is due to a misdial, which the previous month had occurred 62 times.

Garfield County, however, does maintain a Special Weapons and Tactics unit. While they frequently send representatives to the US National SWAT Competition, they are not particularly well-trained, and do not perform well when compared with their peers. With a limited budget, in statistically one of the safest counties in the entire continental United States, this is no great surprise.

Sadly for the 422 passengers aboard Amtrak train number Six on the California Zephyr line, no response time could be good enough to save them from the onslaught that lay ahead.

At precisely 12:28 p.m., Mountain Daylight Time, a small explosive charge detonated on a signal box about 10 miles down the track. Within seconds, a warning message blared in the Amtrak Control Center in Chicago. Seconds after that, the driver of Amtrak train number Six was informed that there was a technical issue further up the line, and that until more information could be established, he was to halt the train immediately.

He did so. It was the last thing he ever did.

Raheem's partner shot out the lock on the door that separated the locomotive with the rest of the train, stepped through, and fired three rounds into the driver's chest before spinning around and heading back down into the main body of the train. The man was dead before the locomotive stopped rolling.

Raheem shivered as he heard the sound of gunfire. It reminded him of years spent fighting in the desert. First against the Americans, who had defiled his country. Then against the Iranian-backed *Shiite* militiamen who had attempted to take control of its burning wreckage.

"*Allahu akbar*," he whispered once again.

God is the greatest. It was a statement so obvious, it did not need saying. And yet he said it anyway. Because it was the truth. God was the greatest, and he, Raheem, was his most faithful servant. His reward would come not in this life, but the next.

Shrieks of horror punctuated the carriages. "Oh my God," a high-pitched voice screamed. "Frank, Frank, did you hear that? It sounded like –"

After stepping out into an empty hallway, he proceeded up the train, weapon braced at his shoulder, handguns holstered against his chest. His MP9 barked twice as a man stepped into the corridor. Perhaps his name was Frank. Raheem would never know, as the man's now lifeless body slid to the floor, arterial blood spraying from his neck and painting the walls of the hallway a bright red.

"One," Raheem muttered.

More shrieks now. Animal howls of terror as man became beast. Some would freeze, Raheem knew. They would be the easiest to kill, and he would do so, sending them to Allah himself to judge. And they would be found wanting.

Raheem's MP9 clattered almost continuously as he stepped through the train carriage, the shot selector on the side of the weapon set to fire three-round bursts. The short-barrelled machine pistol was perfect for the cramped environment of the train. Unlike a rifle, it didn't catch against any impediments. Raheem held it close to his body, where no hero could reach out and attempt to take it from him.

"Please," the blond woman from the platform screamed, her beautiful daughter nowhere in sight, "I have a –"

"Two."

The Iraqi suspected she was about to say that she had a child, that he should spare her life, oh please, just spare the child's life, but he never found out, because he put a tightly-aimed burst of lead through her body, at least two of the rounds exiting the ribcage and punching through the seat in front of her and sending up a spray of white cushion stuffing like a flurry of snow.

"Run!"

Raheem shot the man in the head while his lips were still moving, the screamed command not yet dead before he was. He paused for a second after doing so, watching the fine spray of red mist, fragments of skull and brain that briefly filled the air before falling back to earth. It was a damn good shot.

Or it would have been, if he'd been aiming for the man's forehead instead of his chest. Then he shot the man's wife, and she slumped over his body. It was almost poetic. In sickness and in health. To love and to cherish.

"Four."

Till death do us part.

Out of the corner of his eye, he saw that he had missed a young man, maybe nineteen years old, built like a linebacker, wearing a red baseball cap pulled backwards over his head.

The kid must have been cowering behind the seat as he first stepped through the coach, but now he wanted to be a hero. He lunged toward Raheem's weapon, attempting to pull it from the terrorist's hands.

"Fuck," Raheem muttered in flawless Arabic, taking a step back to avoid the kid's outstretched fingers.

He figured he probably didn't need to bother speaking English anymore. Judging by the trail of death he had wreaked through the carriage already, and the sound of gunfire and abject terror coming from the other end of the train, the ruse was most definitely up.

He took a step back, letting the MP9 thud against his chest and hang loose against the strap that was wrapped around his torso. As the kid charged toward him, scrunched up with fear and rage, not knowing he was about to die, Raheem clenched his fist, twisted his body, and smacked him in the temple. The boy was half stunned before he knew what was happening, and Raheem took full advantage of the situation.

He reached down, grasped his black MP9, careful not to touch the barrel, which would now be easily hot enough to blister his skin, and with all his strength he brought the stock of the weapon down on the back of the boy's skull. It connected with a sickening thud, and his victim crumpled.

"Five," Raheem said with undisguised pleasure, as for good measure he took a step back, brought the stock of the MP9 to his shoulder and fired a single round into the kid's now limp body.

He looked up and saw faces of horror staring back at him. It was like the world had stopped for a second to watch the little vignette of terror.

"*Allahu akbar*," he said, conversationally. God is great.

Raheem fired three-round bursts until the magazine was empty. He could taste pennies at the back of his tongue, the air was so thick with blood. Now the infidels began to run, clambering over seats and tables and the bodies that littered the floor like an obstacle course.

It just made it easier for him. Aim and fire. Aim and fire. The empty magazine dropped to the floor, and within a second Raheem had replaced it. The fat, lazy Americans fell one after another, just like the cartridge cases spat relentlessly from the side of the MP9 cradled in his hands.

He had spent months in training camps, from the deserts of Libya to freezing mountain passes in Syria. Back then, mostly, he'd been taught to fire the Kalashnikov AK-47. It was, in his opinion, a superior weapon. It never jammed, could fire whether it was wet or dirty or hadn't been cleaned in months. It was chambered with a heavier round. But this gun would do, too. Any weapon used to kill an American, the pathetic spawn of the Great Satan, was a good one.

Raheem emptied another magazine, and then another as he stepped through into the second of the train's coaches. Behind him, men, women and children lay dead or dying, some gurgling as blood filled their lungs, others crying out for mothers, brothers, fathers, sisters, lovers. To the Iraqi, it was like the sound of an angelic choir.

In front of the terrorist – for that was what he was – the coach was more empty than the last. Those who could had run. The others, the freezers, were no threat. He had time.

He reached down to the webbing around his waist and selected a fragmentation grenade. The M67 grenade, designed as a replacement to the M26 grenades used during the Vietnam War, had been sold as part of an arms deal to supply the Mexican Marine Corps. The batch that this particular grenade came from had found its way into the hands of the cartels some years before.

How it had made its way back across the border, perhaps no one would ever know. Raheem certainly didn't. But if he *had* known its history, he would have found satisfaction in the knowledge that the Great Satan's greed in selling weapons all across the globe had come back to haunt it.

"There is no God but Allah, and Mohammed is his messenger," Raheem murmured as he pulled the grenade's safety lever.

He tossed it as far down into the previous carriage as he could, crouched out of the way, and counted.

Four, five...

Six.

The grenade exploded, filling the carriage behind him with shards of steel from its casing. The fragments ripped through windows, seats, tables, and the bodies of the wounded and the dead. Three survivors, who had pressed themselves against the floor of the train when the gunfire broke out and covered themselves in dark clothing so as not to be noticed, were ripped apart, after the grenade fell just a couple of yards away from where they hid.

As the sound of the explosion faded away, Raheem experienced a sensation of complete calm. Of bliss. As though his entire life had been leading up to this moment, as if this was the task for which he had been born. Of all the battles that the Iraqi had fought, against the infidel soldiers of the Great Satan, against the Iranians, this was the greatest.

And God would reward him.

He gripped his weapon. Ejected another empty magazine. Looked to his waist, noticed with surprise that he was out of magazines, and discarded the weapon entirely.

Raheem drew the first of his Glock pistols and caressed it with a lover's touch. He strode forward once more and murdered every infidel who stood in his path.

4

Trapp was seated in a dive bar on Prince Street in Boston near the waterfront, nursing a beer. It was barely a quarter to one in the afternoon, and it wasn't his first. He was there because he had a debt to pay, owed to a man he'd never met.

Or at least, a man he'd never introduced himself to.

The room was decorated with American flags, and had an M1903 Springfield rifle mounted over the bar, along with a variety of other military memorabilia. Trapp knew the rifle had belonged to the man's grandfather, who had carried it in the trenches at Belleau Wood, near the River Marne in the First World War. Could still see the mark of a bullet that had scarred the wooden stock, saving its owner's life. Or that was how the story went, and Trapp should know: he'd heard it often enough.

The man was called Joshua. Joshua Price. And for almost the first time in his life, Trapp was having trouble working up the courage to introduce himself.

Joshua Price was a friendly man, as far as he could tell from this distance. Like his brother, he stood well over six foot tall, with light blond hair and shocking blue eyes. He wasn't a twin, but it was a close enough resemblance to make Trapp shiver with recognition. It was the eyes, Trapp thought, before he was whisked two decades into the past.

The bunched electrical cord whistles through the air like a whip. It cracks against the little boy's back, leaving red, angry welts in places, deep, bloody scores in others. The boy's body strains against his restraints, rope biting into his wrists. His frame is weak, more like a boy of five than nine. His mother cowers in the corner, her palms pressed against an already swelling eye socket. She is a broken woman. The boy understands that already – she will clutch him to her breast when her husband is finished, wipe away tears and soothe his wounds.

But she will not stop him.

He doesn't blame his mother, not even as his body sags against the stained bed, exhausted from the pain, or as tears leak from his eyes. He knows better than to cry out loud. It will not help, only blast more air into the furnace of his father's rage. This is how his mother was broken. But the boy vows that it will not be the same for him.

The salty tears cut pale gorges through his filthy cheeks and puddle on the bed. The cord cuts through the air once more, and the little boy can't help it this time. He screams with pain, and then the blackness takes him.

~

He wakes, his bedsheet tangled into a rope, and clutched between fingers turned white with pressure. The dream's clutches release him, but adrenaline still surges through his veins. His heart thunders in his chest.

He's not a boy anymore, but not a man either. Just sixteen, a few weeks from his birthday. A figure looms over his bed like a scarecrow in the darkness. The figure's eyes are a piercing shade of blue, even in the murky gloom of the army barracks. He's looking down with an unaccustomed emotion – one the young man doesn't immediately recognize.

Concern.

"What's your name?" the scarecrow asks, speaking in a low whisper.

The teen's sheets are soaked wet with sweat. He steals a look down before answering, checking whether he has soiled them. Not this time. He sags back against the bed with relief. A trickle of sweat dances down his temple, cool against his skin.

Trapp doesn't know whether to answer, or how. He knows he is the odd one out in a place like this. His back is already marked with a lifetime of scars, his frame thin and pale. He's younger than most of the recruits, but he is hard where they are soft.

He is a survivor.

"Who's asking?" he replies. His voice is gruff, but still boyish.

"Price," the man replies, leaning forward with his hand outstretched. A shaft of moonlight briefly passes across his face. "Ryan Price."

Price isn't much older than Trapp himself. Eighteen, perhaps a year older. He's a little taller than Trapp, but with a broad, well-fed frame, where Trapp's own is narrow and starved. He looks like a surfer, like he strolled into basic training straight from Long Beach.

Trapp studies the man for a few seconds, his heart racing. He is wary – not used to kindness. He loosens his grip on the bedsheet and accepts the man's hand. It is warm and dry, where his own is cold and clammy.

"Trapp," he whispers. "Jason Trapp."

Price beckons Trapp to follow him, a grin on his face. They sneak out of the barracks, each knowing if they are caught, they'll be on KP duty for weeks. But Trapp has to be out of the darkness, so he follows Price to the center of the parade ground, where they lie on their backs looking up at the stars. The air is cool, but the sound of crickets chirping in the background reminds them the heat of the day will soon be upon them.

"So what's your story?" Price asks, his accent tinged with a Boston brogue.

Trapp doesn't know how to answer. No one has ever asked him a question like that before.

"Why?"

"You're different," Price replies. "The rest of us, we're just kids. But not you."

Trapp is silent for a long time. He closes his eyes, and sees a police sergeant's concerned face staring back at him, red and blue lights playing across the man's brow. Trapp knows what he looks like to this man.

Beaten.

Broken.

Abused.

His mother is dead, her battered body lying at the bottom of the stairs, a trickle of blood beginning to escape her ear. Her body is shattered, but her face is at peace. Trapp doesn't regret what he had to do, but he knows he's going away for a very long time.

And then the police sergeant tells him a story that will set him free. Says he must never reveal the truth. It would be a heavy burden resting on a grown man's shoulders, let alone a scared, lonely teen.

Trapp opens his eyes. He stares up at the sky and decides to tell Price the truth.

"I killed my dad," Trapp admits. Angry tears sting the corners of his eyes. He's ashamed; he's never shown emotion before. It was always a route to more pain. He's never felt more like a child.

When Price replies, he speaks with no judgment, just a curiosity, tinged with sadness.

"Why?"

Trapp lifts his T-shirt, revealing the cuts that mark his body. His fingers trace the angry red scar that runs the width of his neck. Price reaches out, his face torn wide with horror, his finger grazing a welt on Trapp's side.

"Because of this," Trapp whispers. "And because he killed my mom."

"Hey buddy, you want to order anything?" Joshua Price asked, coming over and startling Trapp back to the present. The shock of the man's sudden presence was almost physical. It was as though Ryan himself was standing right in front of him, and not his brother.

"Kitchen's closing up. I'm short on staff today. You know how it is, Warriors come to town and big surprise, everyone calls in sick."

"I'm good," Trapp replied, his voice thick with pain. Was he imagining it, or was there a hint of sadness in Joshua's eyes? Was he still grieving, as Trapp was, in his own way? It had only been six months. Just a blink of an eye.

Price shrugged. "No problem, man. You want another beer?"

"Sure."

Trapp glanced down, checking that the black duffel bag was still at the bottom of his stool. It contained just over two and a half million dollars, in a variety of currencies. He'd kept a hundred grand for himself, and the passport. Enough to leave the country and start fresh somewhere else. He didn't want the rest. Maybe it could buy him a little peace.

Of course, that would rely on Trapp plucking up the chutzpah to strike up a real conversation. Right now, he was a mute. Introducing himself meant explaining who he was, and why he was there. And that meant reliving that night in Yemen, and the friend he had lost.

So right now, it could wait. Maybe another beer would help.

There was a lot to like about Price's bar. It was anonymous. Loud. A place a man could lose himself, and not have to think about the things he had seen, the things he had done, or the people he had lost.

And, naturally, it sold beer.

Trapp drained the dregs from the bottle he had been clasping for the past twenty minutes – warm, not that he cared, and accepted its replacement gratefully. He sent the empty sliding down the wooden bar.

"Hey Josh," a man from the back of the bar yelled. Trapp couldn't help but listen in; two decades of instincts were hard to ignore, especially when the yeller referenced the man he was here to see. "Change the channel. You – shit man, we *all* gotta see this. Put the news on. Any channel. It'll be on all of 'em."

"What you talking about, Jimmy? I turn the game off, people in here are gonna riot."

All around the bar, cell phones began to chime and buzz and rattle. In spite of himself, Trapp looked around, at the faces of surprise, then confusion, then horror as people stared down at the shining screens of their phones, or else held them to their ears. One woman began to sob, great, heaving, choking cries that tore through the suddenly deathly quiet bar.

"Just do it, Josh," the man said in a tone of horror that rang true. "Trust me."

Josh grumbled, but did as he was told. He reached back to a control panel behind the bar, fiddled with something, and suddenly the massive, widescreen TVs that decorated every wall in the sports bar began to flick through the channels – reality TV, HBO, all the crap that fills five hundred cable channels from dawn to dusk. It settled on ATN News. The two anchors looked ashen.

"Hey dude, what the hell are you doing?" A drunk man yelled from the back of the bar. He was quickly cut off by whoever was with him. By now, the bar was silent. In spite of himself, in spite of the alcohol coursing through his system, Trapp was now alert.

"– And of course, we're still getting reports. As we just said, what you are about to see is live. We don't know where it's coming from. Less than nine minutes ago, an anonymous email hit our tip line, containing only a link to a stream which we are putting up for you now."

The TV screen filled with an aerial shot of an Amtrak train, standing motionless on the tracks. The video danced a little, became blurry, and then resolved.

"This is Amtrak train number six, which travels between Chicago and Emeryville. Right now it's about ten miles out of Glenwood Springs, Colorado, and ATN has received information that there's been some kind of – some kind of terrorist incident on board. What you're seeing on your screen appears to be footage from overhead, a helicopter, maybe, or –"

"– or a drone, Tom –"

"– that's right. Our analysts are telling me that due to the altitude of the shot that it's most likely to be a drone. As we just told you, we don't know where this footage is coming from, and if you are a viewer with a sensitive disposition, or if you have children in the room, then we advise you to look away now."

Trapp was engrossed now. As he watched, the TV went to split screen.

"The video you are about to watch was posted on Twitter just moments ago. It's 19 seconds long, and it's from *inside* the train."

The anchor was clearly vamping. Trapp figured that they didn't know any more than he did. He watched as a fuzzy, blurred image came up on the screen, and then as the video began to play. As the anchor had suggested, it was clearly taken from inside the train. Bodies lay everywhere, and blood painted the windows and walls and floor. Scorch marks and damage from the shrapnel fragments that had ripped through the coach made it look as though there had been a terrible accident. But this butchery had been intentional.

"Jesus fucking Christ –"

Trapp didn't know if he had said the words, whether it was someone in the bar around him, or hell, whether it was the

ATN anchor himself. But they fit. What he was watching was carnage – the kind of thing he had seen dozens, maybe hundreds of times through a long career, in more countries than he could count.

But he'd never seen it in the US before. Certainly not on a train in the middle of the Colorado country, amidst snow-kissed mountaintops and the surging Colorado River.

"Oh my God," someone gasped behind him as the camera panned around, now showing the scene outside of the train. There was no sound, but Trapp watched as two men sprinted away from the tracks. Both were armed. They were hurrying toward a third man, who was cradling a rifle of his own, standing next to what looked like three motorbikes. Dirt bikes, probably. Trapp half-nodded with appreciation. In that terrain, it was as good a move as any.

As Trapp stared in horror, every fiber of his being wishing he could be on-scene, so that he could do something instead of sitting here impotently, clutching a beer, he saw the third shooter raising his rifle to his shoulder, dropping to one knee and firing a burst toward the train – toward the camera. The footage cut out, and the overhead shot returned to fill the screen.

"According to the metadata on the file," the male news anchor said, sounding distracted, as though he was reading the words for the first time, "this video was shot about ten minutes ago. It appears to depict the shooters – the terrorists – fleeing the scene of this terrible attack. We can only hope that the person who shot the footage is still..."

He paused, and didn't finish the sentence.

"Let's bring in ATN's security analyst, Kyle Walters," the other anchor interjected. "Kyle, what can you tell us?"

Trapp didn't care what Kyle, Kyle Walters, had to say. The images told their own story. The attack had been planned and executed brilliantly. It looked like two shooters, at least two shooters, had waited until the train was in an isolated area, and then attacked the defenseless passengers with rifle, handgun fire and maybe even explosives.

And most interestingly of all – because it was merely *interesting*, now that Jason's brain had processed and compartmentalized the sensations of overwhelming horror that he had experienced only a few seconds before – were the clear signs of coordination and planning that had gone into this attack.

Trapp ran through it in his mind. The train was stopped. Either the shooters had killed the driver, forced him to bring the train to a halt, or they had somehow knocked out the track signals.

If he was a betting man, he would have gone with the latter option. It made sense. It was how he would've done things in their shoes. The terrorists had given themselves both time to complete their mission, and space – they had halted the train far enough away from any population center to know they would most likely not be interrupted by the authorities before their murderous rampage was complete.

But the most interesting hallmark of the operation, the one that pointed both to the clear signs of planning that lay behind it, and the inevitable conclusion that the track signals had in fact been knocked out, was that the train had come to a halt in a predictable location – a location at which the shooters had support, getaway vehicles, the whole works. They'd known exactly where this was going to go down. Had planned the whole thing. Had somehow arranged for the act of terror to be *livestreamed* around the globe.

Onscreen, the security analyst was still talking.

"And Tom, it looks like the authorities are starting to arrive on-scene. What I would expect to see, in a situation like this, is a full-spectrum response from federal, state and local authorities."

The sound of the man's inane chattering faded away as

Trapp watched ambulances, police cars, even a couple of small fire trucks driving down the tracks, and converging on the train from either side. The convoy wasn't just made up of rescue vehicles, either, but civilian pickup trucks too; it looked like anything in Glenwood Springs that could drive had headed directly for the scene.

Trapp clenched his fists together, then cracked his knuckles. Without intending to, he ran through a mental checklist of the actions he would take if he was on site. Secure the area, first. Ensure there were no more shooters. Get some aerial support. The attackers were heading away from the scene, and in this kind of terrain, if someone didn't start tracking them fast, it would be too late.

On the TV, tiny figures ran toward the train. By now, survivors were starting to stream away from the tracks. The resolution wasn't good enough for Trapp to see the blood that no doubt coated them, but he could tell by the way they were walking, stumbling, some dragging injured limbs, that they were in shock.

But something wasn't right here. He could feel it at the back of his spine. A sense of danger – not to him, but simply the finely honed instincts of a trained killer screaming out that something was *wrong*.

He watched as it played out on screen, only a second later.

"Oh, Jesus, no..."

Made in the USA
Monee, IL
22 December 2023

50182938R00223